Nicole Helm grew up with her nose in a book and the dream of one day becoming a writer. Luckily, after a few failed career choices, she gets to follow that dream—writing down-to-earth contemporary romance and romantic suspense. From farmers to cowboys, Midwest to *the* West, Nicole writes stories about people finding themselves and finding love in the process. She lives in Missouri with her husband and two sons, and dreams of someday owning a barn.

New York Times and *USA Today* bestselling author **Caridad Piñeiro** is a Jersey girl who just wants to write and is the author of nearly fifty novels and novellas. She loves romance novels, superheroes, TV and cooking. For more information on Caridad and her dark, sexy romantic suspense and paranormal romance novels, please visit caridad.com

Also by Nicole Helm

Hudson Sibling Solutions
Cold Case Kidnapping
Cold Case Identity
Cold Case Investigation

Covert Cowboy Soldiers
The Lost Hart Triplet
Small Town Vanishing
One Night Standoff
Shot in the Dark
Casing the Copycat

Also by Caridad Piñeiro

South Beach Security: K-9 Division
Sabotage Operation

South Beach Security
Lost in Little Havana
Brickell Avenue Ambush
Biscayne Bay Breach

Cold Case Reopened
Trapping a Terrorist
Decoy Training

Discover more at millsandboon.co.uk

COLD CASE SCANDAL

NICOLE HELM

ESCAPE THE EVERGLADES

CARIDAD PIÑEIRO

MILLS & BOON

First Published in Great Britain 2024
by Mills & Boon, an imprint of HarperCollins*Publishers* Ltd
1 London Bridge Street, London, SE1 9GF

www.harpercollins.co.uk

HarperCollins*Publishers*
Macken House, 39/40 Mayor Street Upper,
Dublin 1, D01 C9W8, Ireland

Cold Case Scandal © 2024 Nicole Helm
Escape the Everglades © 2024 Caridad Piñeiro Scordato

ISBN: 978-0-263-32233-0

0624

MIX
Paper | Supporting
responsible forestry
FSC™ C007454

This book contains FSC™ certified paper and other controlled sources to ensure responsible forest management.

For more information visit: www.harpercollins.co.uk/green

Printed and Bound in the UK using 100% Renewable Electricity at
CPI Group (UK) Ltd, Croydon, CR0 4YY

COLD CASE
SCANDAL

NICOLE HELM

For oldest daughters and organized souls.

Chapter One

Mary Hudson was not like her siblings. They seemed to be determined to run toward danger, no matter the costs. Jack, her oldest brother, was the sheriff of tiny Sunrise, Wyoming. Grant had gone to war, though he'd thankfully returned. Cash, well, Cash had a daughter and had sworn off danger as much as he could, so maybe he and Mary were a little more alike than the others. Then there was Palmer, who'd played football and done a few years in the rodeo, and while he had settled down a bit the past year, he still took on dangerous cold case investigations as part of the family business.

And then there was Anna, who had been forced to slow down because of her current pregnancy, but Mary had no doubt her baby sister would be wreaking havoc once again when the baby was born. Though her husband, Hawk, would try to tame her, fool in love that he was.

Mary, on the other hand, had much preferred a life of order. Ever since her parents had disappeared when she was ten years old, she'd stepped in to be the structure sorely lacking in a household of five children being raised by their eighteen-year-old brother.

Oh, Jack was stern and strict and all those things, but he had nothing on Mary. Mary just knew how to wrap it up in a pleasant smile and soft words, and give people the impression she was biddable and sweet all the while she maneuvered them into exactly what she knew they needed.

At the end of the day, people were simple. Life was hard, violence and tragedy inevitable, but people themselves were easy.

So, she knew that instead of going to Jack with her request, she'd need to go to one of the other officers at Sunrise SD. Because Jack was by the book and tired of hearing her talk about this one administrative error.

Her four brothers—all older, hardheaded, obnoxious— seemed to think that it was perfectly acceptable for them to hold on to a client's deposit when the client had disappeared before they'd done any work for them.

Mary did not agree. Though she didn't do any of the cold case investigations with Hudson Sibling Solutions, she did everything else. Accounting, administration and a long list of other tasks it took to run a business, while her siblings did all the dangerous work.

So, Mary was the one who got to call the shots in this case. In her estimation, it was imperative they return the money to the client. If she had to be the one to track Mr. Joe Beck down and return his money to either him or, if he was no longer, one of his kin, then so be it.

It was only right and fair.

She currently sat at the small diner in Sunrise, waiting for Chloe Brink, both her friend *and* an officer with Sunrise SD. Because Chloe was not afraid of bending a few rules.

Mary was pretty sure her brother Jack would spontaneously combust at the mere thought.

Chloe came in wearing her Sunrise SD uniform—more casual than a lot of the police departments as it was just a polo with a badge and then pants of the officer's choosing. Chloe slid into the booth across from Mary, immediately reached across and swiped Mary's mug of coffee and took a big swig.

Mary wasn't sure why, but she tended to make friends with

people who were not like her. She supposed it came from always running herd on her baby sister, who was brash, outspoken and, well, a pill. It took a strong personality to enjoy Anna, and so any person Mary might have enjoyed who was more reserved didn't stick around for long.

At least Mary knew what to do with brash, outspoken women.

"I ordered you one to go," Mary said primly.

Chloe only grinned. "Yeah, but I needed a jolt ASAP." She plopped a folder onto the table between them. "So, I did some digging into your guy. Looks like he's got some aliases."

"Oh." Mary frowned. Aliases seemed bad. "Criminal type aliases?"

"Not exactly—at least nothing concrete on any record I could find. But definitely someone who wants to stay under the radar. This is the last known address I have for Joe Beck," Chloe said, taking out a piece of paper from the folder. "It's over in Hardy."

Mary reached for the paper, but Chloe held her hand over it before Mary could fully pull it toward her.

"You're just going to send him like a check or something, right?" Chloe asked suspiciously.

"Who do you take me for?" Mary replied primly.

"A Hudson," Chloe replied with a laugh. "You might fancy yourself the calm, organized one who lets her siblings do all the wading in and causing trouble, but Mary Hudson, you *always* get your way."

Mary didn't bother arguing with it. It was true. She knew how to get her way, because more often than not, her way was correct.

The waitress appeared with the to-go cup of coffee and handed it to Chloe, who had to relinquish her hold on the paper.

Mary took it. An address in Hardy. She could take a drive out that way this morning and be back at the ranch before anyone really noticed. "Do you have a list of the aliases?"

Chloe passed over the whole file. "He's a bit of a mystery, Mary. You go poking around in it, it's possible you're wading in deeper than you want."

"I never wade in deeper than I want." Mary looked at the list. Joe Beck—the man she was looking for. Steve Mier. Paul Anderson. Well, it didn't matter what he went by, she'd get his money back to him.

"You just jinxed yourself," Chloe said, quite seriously for a cop who had to know *jinxing* had nothing to do with life.

"I don't believe in jinxes or curses or your rabbit's foot or the crystals you evangelize. I have also never once burned sage."

"Oh, no, you're really doing it."

Mary shook her head. "Go ahead, universe. Throw it all at me," she said, because she enjoyed the look of pain and amusement that crossed Chloe's face.

"Don't go trying to find this guy, Mary. That area of Hardy isn't the best, and I hate to break it to you, but I agree with Jack on this one."

Mary scowled. "You should really second-guess your life choices if you're agreeing with Jack."

"Trying to return money someone doesn't seem to want returned is a pointless exercise. Send the guy a letter. Send him a check, but don't go down there. Or if you simply *must*, since it's you and you will, don't go alone. Take one of your brothers, or I'll go with you on my next day off."

"I'm sure that won't be necessary."

"Oh, don't pull out the queen of the ranch voice on me," Chloe said, standing. She was frowning, but Mary knew it was out of concern.

Mary stood, too, and handed Chloe the to-go cup. "Don't forget your coffee."

Chloe's frown didn't change, but she sighed. "Be careful, Mary."

"I always am." And she was. She *was* the careful one. This wasn't reckless. This was seeing something through. It wasn't right to keep the money. She could hardly put *money for services not rendered* on their taxes, so she wouldn't keep it.

Mary left the diner and drove out of Sunrise, the pretty Western town surrounded by ranches—including her family's. Then to the larger town of Hardy that had more jobs to offer. She didn't call one of her brothers. She didn't ask someone to come along.

She could handle this on her own.

She may have had second thoughts as she pulled into a parking spot in the run-down apartment complex, but surely if the man lived *here*, he needed the money returned to him all that much more than she'd thought.

She was doing him a favor, and the right thing. That was all that mattered.

She got out of her car. People sat on porches eyeing her, or her car more likely. Maybe her purse. But she was not the little princess she might appear. She was tough. She had been shot. Actually shot last month. Maybe the bullet had just grazed her arm, but she was officially tough.

Or so she told herself as her insides shook with nerves. She moved forward, chin high and not bothering to make eye contact with anyone. She ignored comments and attempts to get her attention and walked up the stairs to the door listed on the address.

She knocked. She heard something inside, but no one opened the door. She knocked again. "Mr. Beck?" she called, ignoring the creepy feeling she was being watched. "My name is…" Well, maybe she shouldn't be shouting her name around here. "I'm from Hudson Sibling Solutions. I wanted to—"

The door opened. A man stood there. He was dressed all in black, which matched his hair and maybe even his eyes, which were a dark, dark brown. He was tall and broad-shouldered, but rangy. Those dark eyes were direct and angry.

He had an old scar on his chin and a crooked nose, and it *shouldn't* have been appealing, especially when matched with the angry eyes, but she couldn't ignore the fact that he was startlingly handsome. Wild, sure, but handsome.

Not that she went for the wild sort, but—

With no warning, she was jerked inside and all she could think was: *well, darn.*

She had dared the universe, and now she was going to pay.

WALKER DANIELS DIDN'T have the first earthly clue who the pretty, primly dressed woman who came to his door was, but he'd recognized one of his aliases and figured ignoring her wouldn't work.

Especially here. Especially with what was coming.

"Who are you?" he demanded.

Her eyes were wide on the array of guns he had laid out on his table. He'd been packing up, getting ready to go. Someone had figured him out, and he knew it was too dangerous to stick around and find out who.

Though the *who* was the answer to everything, Walker was determined to stay alive first and foremost. If it meant another few years chasing down his mother's killer, he'd do it.

He'd do whatever it took to find answers, and to keep his sister and brother safe.

End of story.

"Are you Joe Beck?" she asked, and he'd give her credit. She might be a willowy thing, looking better suited to walk a runway than slum it here in this crappy apartment building, but she had backbone.

He paused for a second he didn't have. Joe Beck had been an old alias, but he couldn't remember ever dealing with this woman under any of his names.

He'd remember. He remembered faces. Besides, she was pretty. Always a pleasure to remember a pretty woman. But he couldn't place this one, so there was no way he'd met her.

"Come on, we've got to get you out of here." He moved for the guns, began to put them in his bag as she inched her way back toward the door. He'd let her go if she ran, but it'd be safer if he escorted her out.

Safer for *her*. Then again, maybe this strange woman would throw whoever was close off his scent. They'd be looking for one man, not a man and a woman.

Especially a woman who had legs like that and was wearing a billowy skirt that showed them off when she moved.

"Mr. Beck, I only need to refund you your money, and then I will be on my way." She pulled an envelope from her purse and handed it to him.

He stared at it. Was this some kind of trap? "What the hell are you talking about?" But he didn't give her a chance to answer because he got that feeling. The skin prickle at the back of his neck. That gut feeling that always kept him just one step ahead of the people who wanted him as dead as his mother.

He pulled the woman to the ground. He was about 90 percent sure she was an innocent bystander, so he'd protect her. But he'd also keep an eye on her because there was a 10 percent chance his gut was wrong. He covered her body with his.

She let out a little squeak of surprise from underneath him.

"I don't know who you are, lady, but you sure walked into the wrong apartment complex."

"My name is Mary Hudson," she said, as if she was sitting behind a desk, or maybe in the front of a classroom, giving a lecture. "I am with Hudson Sibling Solutions. Now, you're going to need to get off me."

He was barely listening to her, though he was surprised at how still she remained rather than try to fight him off. He didn't know if it was terror or sense that held her still, but right now it didn't matter.

The shots would come. He knew they would.

As if on cue, the window shattered at one side of the apartment. Which gave him enough information to know where they'd storm his apartment from.

Time for the escape route. He rolled off her but pulled her

with him. "Keep low," he muttered, grabbing his bag from the table without standing up. She kept up. Clearly someone shooting his window out had not rendered her into the expected terrified mess.

He didn't have time to wonder why that was. He could only grab what he needed and pull her with him to the back of the apartment. His rear window looked out over an alley, and he'd had this escape route planned for a few days now.

He tossed the bags out onto the little cushion he'd made behind some random-looking boxes and other alley debris the trash truck wouldn't pick up. He unfurled the makeshift ladder he'd worked out how to attach to the windowsill so it could bear weight. They'd have to take it one at a time since he'd only tested it with his weight.

"You first," he said, motioning for the ladder.

She looked out the window, then down the side of the building, then back at him. She opened her mouth to say something—likely an argument, or maybe she'd try to shove some money at him again, as if *that* made sense. But there was no time.

"Better hurry," Walker urged. "They'll figure it out soon enough and come around back."

The woman firmed her mouth but listened, climbing down the rickety ladder. She definitely wasn't dressed for it, and Walker couldn't help but wish he were on the bottom of the ladder to catch the show, but as it was, he kept an eye on his front door.

Just as Mary took the last little jump onto the concrete below, a bullet crashed through the door.

Walker swung out and onto the ladder, going down as fast as he could, then jumping off the minute he was close enough to the ground not to break a leg. He gave the ladder a hard yank and it tumbled to the ground. He tossed it into the dumpster, then grabbed the woman's hand and pulled her down the alley toward his car.

Well, one of his cars. One that fit in in this side of town.

She tugged her hand out from his grasp and stood next to the car. He kept expecting her to break into fear or panic, but she was filled with nothing but a cool kind of skepticism as she looked at his car. "I don't believe I should go with you."

"Maybe you'd like to go with the guys shooting at me instead?"

"Well, no."

"Then get the hell in," Walker said, sliding into the driver's seat. He tossed his bags in the back—except one gun he put in the middle console for easy reach. The way he saw it, they had a minute, tops, before the bullets started again. "This car leaves in three seconds," he told her before closing his door.

He thought she'd hesitate longer than three, but she was in the passenger side—and buckled of all things—in two. She clearly wasn't pleased, but she still didn't look scared. Walker shook his head, reminding himself that he'd have time to figure that out later. "Keep low," he instructed. "They're going to follow. Hold on."

Chapter Two

Mary understood danger better than most, so she'd gone ahead and gotten in the car with the man. She knew how to pick the lesser of two evils.

But she was considering all her escape options as the man—clearly *not* Joe Beck—drove like a lunatic through the, thankfully, rather empty streets of Hardy.

"Do you know where you're going?"

The man did not look at her, which was good since he was currently conducting an illegal U-turn, then screeching into a turn down a one-way street.

The wrong way.

Mary wanted to close her eyes, but instead she kept her gaze steady on the driver. The man was likely to get her killed before he even took her wherever he was taking her. Which was also, likely, her eventual death.

"Yeah, I know." He turned again, this time onto a two-way road that allowed Mary to breathe a little easier. He zoomed onto the highway, headed west. Mary wondered how long he'd go. She tried to get a glimpse at the gas gauge, but the dashboard was so dusty she didn't think even *he* could see it.

He slowed his pace now. Drove more like a normal person who cared at all about safety. Even his posture relaxed, and he flicked a glance her way.

"You're a cool one, aren't you?"

She clutched her hands a little tighter, lifted her chin. Because *cool* was about all the defense she had against fear, and fear had been a rather constant companion since she'd been ten years old.

So, she had her coping mechanisms, and if that was *cool*, so be it. What did she care what this mysterious, dangerous stranger thought anyway?

"Where are you taking me?" Mary asked, keeping her tone prim and *cool*.

"I've got a few places. The one outside Sunrise is probably the best option for this."

"Sunrise," she repeated. Close to home. Close enough she might be able to *get* home.

"Don't worry, I'll get you back to wherever you came from eventually," he continued. "Just got to make sure the coast is clear first."

Mary tried to wrap her mind around what he was saying. That he didn't plan on hurting her. Of course, a criminal didn't tend to announce his intentions to his victims.

"Who *are* you?"

He flashed a grin in her direction. "I've gone by Joe Beck, and a few other names."

"Steve Mier. Paul Anderson." She thought she maybe saw a flash of surprise that she knew his other aliases, but only a flash, if that.

"You can call me any of those," he said with a shrug.

"But what's your *real* name?"

He paused. She wasn't sure she expected the truth out of a man who'd just...whatever they'd just done. Certainly she shouldn't find a man with a bag of guns and planned escape routes from his apartment trustworthy.

"Not important really," he said at long last.

Mary sighed and looked at the world around them. They would pass right by the Hudson Ranch. She eyed his profile. Her gut hadn't told her to jump out of the moving car just yet. Besides, if anyone could handle themselves against one man with guns, it was her family. She pointed to the turnoff up ahead.

"Turn up there."

He eyed her then, suspiciously. "Why?"

"Because that's where I live. We can figure out this money situation, and you'll have a decent place to hide for a bit. The ranch is huge. We may even be able to help you. Depending."

"Depending on what?"

"On whether you're on the right side of the law."

"The right side of the law." He snorted derisively, but he turned at the road. "I don't have much concern about the law."

"Well, that might be a problem as my brother is the sheriff of Sunrise."

The car began to slow, but Mary reached over and put her hand on his arm, pointing ahead.

"Don't stop. Go on up and around the house to the back. Jack won't be here. You helped me, in a way, I guess. If you really need to get out of here before he comes, I'll be sure you do. But we need to sort out this Joe Beck money."

He eyed her. She thought he was coming to the same sort of conclusion she had come to. Certainly they couldn't trust each other, but gut feelings didn't lie. And *she* wasn't bad or a liar. She didn't think he was...bad precisely.

Besides, with everything that had happened in her life— from her parents' disappearance, to the past few months of repeated and constant danger for her siblings—it was easy enough to take this in stride.

She dealt with cold cases as a matter of course. Weird was the name of the game. And learning to trust your gut was just part of the process.

He looked down at her hand on his arm, and though she told herself not to react, she jerked her hand back anyway. A bit like she'd been burned. Embarrassment fought its way up her face.

She didn't even know why she was embarrassed.

Except maybe because she'd noticed his arms were very impressive.

She wanted to close her eyes in shame, but instead she turned her gaze to the house.

He let out a low whistle as his dark eyes surveyed the world around them—all Hudson land, for a good century or so. "Should I be calling you Princess?" he asked, turning his attention to her.

She lifted her chin. "I prefer Queen, thank you."

He grinned at her, and she felt a strange little flutter deep in her chest. And the strange desire to smile right back, when honestly his smile was predatory. At best.

"Park around back, Mr. Beck. And we'll get this all sorted," Mary said, hoping she sounded as contained as she usually did.

He shook his head, though he did keep driving the car around the back. "You know what? I changed my mind." He parked, even got out of the car, and she had to scurry after him.

"Changed your mind about what?" she asked, suddenly wondering if she'd made a terrible mistake trusting her gut.

"I don't like the way you say *Mr. Beck.* Call me Walker. That's my real name." And then he strode toward the back door, like this was *his* house. Like *he* was in charge.

And no, that would not do.

NONE OF THIS made a heap of sense to Walker, but this big old house wouldn't be a hardship to hide away at. He didn't love the whole brother-sheriff thing, and thought maybe she was tricking him into some kind of citizen's arrest.

But a man didn't survive years chasing his mother's killer to get caught quite so easily—whether by shooters or sheriffs.

Mary stalked in front of him, clearly trying to keep a handle on her temper because even though her strides were brisk, her expression was perfectly calm on her very beautiful face.

He wondered if she tried to look a little plain, a little severe on purpose.

But it didn't quite work, because her hair was mussed from everything that had happened back at his apartment, and her color was a little high. Admirable control, but someone didn't have admirable control unless there was a tempest of responses underneath it all.

A tempting thought, that. He knew, even knowing next to nothing about her, she was as far out of his league as this house was, but that didn't mean he didn't enjoy the view.

She opened the door, held it for him with the understanding he'd follow her inside.

"Thanks, Your Highness."

He watched her face get a little pinched and tried not to laugh. "Sorry, what did you say your name was again?"

My name is Mary Hudson. I am with Hudson Sibling Solutions. Now, you're going to need to get off me. She'd said that very calmly back in his apartment, and Walker didn't forget much. But he found it best to pretend like he wasn't paying attention. Let people think he was forgetful or concerned with other things.

Underestimating him always worked in his favor.

"My name is Mary Hudson," she said, and it seemed a bit like she spoke between gritted teeth. But then she smiled blandly at him and gestured him inside.

This back door led into a kind of mudroom, filled with all sorts of coats and boots. It was a big house, so he supposed it made sense it was full of a big family.

But he'd already checked out her hand and she didn't wear any rings. Even if she worked the ranch and kept things more subtle, she was definitely not the kind of woman who didn't wear a ring if she was married.

He followed her deeper into the house, into what appeared to be a dining room, where a woman paced the length of a very long table, muttering darkly into the phone at her ear. "I'm going to skin you alive, I hope you know."

Mary seemed wholly unfazed by this threat. "She must be speaking to her husband," she whispered. "That's my sister. Anna."

Walker winged up an eyebrow at that, but the woman pulled the phone away from her ear and shoved it into her pocket. Behind pretty hazel eyes, she studied him as if filing all the ways he might be a threat.

The sisters didn't look too much alike. This one was a little shorter, a little curvier. Blonde and fairer than Mary. They didn't even hold themselves the same. This woman looked like a brawler, even with the little hint of a baby bump.

"Anna," Mary said in her prim way. "This is Mr. Beck."

The woman's eyes registered surprise, and she studied him once more with this new information. "So, you finally tracked the ghost down. I don't know why I'm surprised."

"The ghost?" Walker looked at Mary.

"It's been almost a year since we received a down payment for a case we never were given the details about. Which left us unable to actually investigate. I've been trying to refund the money ever since, but by then Joe Beck seemingly disappeared."

Yeah, into Paul Anderson when his Joe Beck identity had gotten a little too easy to track. But that didn't explain *this*, because he had certainly never contacted anyone about an investigation or paid anyone. "What do you mean *case* and *investigate*?"

"Hudson Sibling Solutions," Anna supplied, as if those words might mean something to him.

He shrugged. "Never heard of it."

The sisters frowned at each other.

"You bring home the wrong Joe Beck, Mary?"

"No, I most certainly did not," Mary replied, and it was clear the more prim she sounded the more pissed she was. "Perhaps you don't remember because it was so long ago. Hudson Sibling Solutions investigates cold cases. We have a staff of trained private investigators skilled and experienced to get to the bottom of cases law enforcement can't give the necessary effort toward any longer."

She sounded like a brochure, and he had better things to do with his day. Or so he told himself as it was no hardship watching her talk.

But he shrugged, looked from Mary to Anna. "I don't have the first clue what you're talking about."

There was a tiny crack in Mary's calm facade. Her eyebrows lowered, though her mouth was still arranged in that polite little smile.

"Okay, what about this? Do you have any cold cases in your life, Joe?"

He didn't scowl, though he desperately wanted to. Something about these Hudson women and the way they said his fake name really scraped at him, like nails on a chalkboard.

And like hell he was going to bring up his cold case. Because he didn't need help, had never once asked for or hired help. And never would.

"Look, I didn't pay you this money. I didn't hire any Hudson Sibling Solutions. Maybe it was some other Joe Beck, because I can handle my own..."

Anna smirked, because it was enough to confirm that yes, he did have a cold case. This time Walker did scowl. He didn't have to stay here. He didn't have to deal with these two. His car was right out back, and no doubt there'd been just enough time that he'd lost whoever was shooting at him.

The plan had been to go hide out at the shack he had outside Sunrise, but unfortunately that was connected to the fake Joe Beck, and with them bandying about the name, it'd be better if he went back to his Paul Anderson identity.

Which finally made him think about what Mary had said. A year ago. A cold case. Joe Beck.

Damn it. Carlyle. "Hold on. Let me make a phone call." Because if this was true, his sister had some explaining to do.

Chapter Three

Mary could *feel* her sister studying her. So she went about tidying the dining room while Walker stepped outside to make his phone call. She expressly ignored Anna's study.

"Soooo…" Anna said after a few seconds, because that was all her impetuous sister was capable of staying silent for.

"So?" Mary went around the table, straightening all the chairs so they looked the way she preferred.

"He looks…wild."

He did indeed look wild, and Mary was no fan of wild. She liked order. Hence the chairs. "If you say so."

"And *you*, Mary Hudson, came in looking disheveled."

Mary stopped what she was doing, because the insinuation Anna was making was so beyond ludicrous even she couldn't pretend. She glared at her sister. "What are you suggesting?"

"I'm *wishing* you got hot and heavy with the attractive outlaw-looking gentleman who may or may not be our Joe Beck ghost, but I'm *suggesting* it's something much more boring. I want to know what."

"It wasn't boring," Mary said with a sniff. Then regretted it, because she really didn't need any of her siblings knowing she'd thrown herself into all the trouble they'd warned her against. "He's in trouble."

Anna huffed out a breath. "Oh, Mary. Don't go collecting strays."

"I'm not collecting strays. I accidentally stepped into the middle of some of his danger, and since he was…" She couldn't say *kind enough*. She didn't think it had anything to do with kindness. "Since he didn't leave me to get caught in the middle and fend for myself, I offered him a place to hide out while he sorts through what needs sorting."

"Did you bother to check if he was on the right side of all this trouble?"

"When has that mattered to you, Anna?" Mary returned, wondering if she had time to vacuum the rug before Walker came back in.

"Touché," Anna replied with a grin. "But it matters to you, and it'll hardcore matter to Jack."

At their older brother's name, Mary turned her gaze back to Anna. "About that."

Anna's eyebrows winged up. "You're going to keep a secret from Jack?"

"I'm a grown woman. And it's not a secret. We just aren't going to mention it because it's not going to matter."

"Awfully high on our royal *we* horse."

Mary took a careful, calming breath. "I know you'll keep it from Jack because there's no point discussing it with him. I'm going to get Mr. Beck to take the money, and then he'll likely go on his way." She glanced at the door where he'd walked out. She wondered if he was taking off as they spoke.

None of her business, of course, but… She couldn't help but wonder what he was running from.

"Anna, I'd like you to look into this." She looked at Anna. "Without anyone knowing. It's delicate, I think. But he might be in trouble, and we could possibly help. If you need to tell Hawk, I understand, but—"

"That won't be necessary."

At the sound of the deep male voice, both women turned to find Walker standing in the doorway. Mary inwardly cursed herself for speaking so freely knowing he was around, but she'd half expected him to already be gone. She also understood he'd reentered the house silently on purpose.

"I don't need you interfering in what's already a delicate business. I am a grown man, and I've been dealing with this for over a decade. So just…leave it."

Mary felt her heart pinch at how closed off he seemed. Angry. Like something had changed. "Mr. Beck—"

"I told you, it's *Walker*," he snapped.

"And Beck isn't your real last name."

"You're damn right it ain't. And if you think I'm about to tell you what it is, you're out of your mind. Now, I'll be going. But I'll take that money, because apparently, it's my sister's. She used my name with some insane idea to… Well, it doesn't matter. I'll be taking it." He held out his hand, anger pumping off him.

Interesting he'd be angry now, when back at his apartment with people shooting at him he'd seemed…not happy about it, of course, but very comfortable and resigned to whatever danger he was in.

Maybe wanting to stop him from leaving came from her penchant for wanting to help. Anna called it *taking in strays*, but Mary considered it the very human need to want to make someone else comfortable.

"Over a decade is a long time, Walker," Mary returned calmly. She pulled the envelope from her purse once more. "We specialize in cold cases. Whatever it is you're searching for, it's possible we could help."

"I don't want or need help."

"That's too bad." She held the envelope out to him, and he snatched it out of her hands before turning on a heel and leaving out the door again.

Mary watched him go, resisting the urge to follow. He'd made it clear he didn't want her help, and she tried not to be like her family of steamrollers, but… He clearly *did* need help if he was running from gunmen. Which, of course, didn't mean he was a good person or doing the right thing. She knew this.

Logically.

She also tended to trust her judgment of people. She'd always had an inherent ability to understand when someone was in trouble. Okay, so her therapist in college had said it was a trauma response to losing her parents so tragically at ten, and that she'd learned how to read a room and a person from there. Sought to fix other people's problems as a way of not dealing with her own.

Mary preferred to think of it as a useful skill.

"Go on after him," Anna said a few seconds after Walker had disappeared. "You know you want to. You can never resist an injured bird. Even if it's a criminal bird."

Mary knew she was supposed to laugh, but there was something about the man… A familiar kind of desperation she understood all too well. Even without bullets flying. "I don't think he's a criminal."

"No, I don't think so either. But we better make sure about it. I'll do that. You go on after him. Stay where the cameras can see you."

Mary nodded. Due to all the danger over the past few months, they had an extensive video surveillance system, so Anna would be able to keep an eye on her in case Walker did turn out to be more of a criminal than a man on a mission.

And hopefully nothing out of the ordinary happened today so Jack didn't feel the need to look through the footage.

Mary stepped outside, surprised to find Walker had stopped himself. He stood next to his car, though he had his driver's side door open. He was looking out over the mountains. When she came closer, he turned his dark gaze to her.

"You've got a hell of a view," he muttered.

"Yes, we do," she agreed pleasantly, though her heart had begun to drum oddly in her chest when his eyes met hers. She swallowed down that strange, foreign feeling and forced herself to make the offer.

"You've made it clear you don't want Hudson Sibling Solutions' help, and I won't belabor the point except to point out we have almost fifteen years' experience, and while our track record isn't perfect, our success rate is high. We have a lot of different services to offer, and if there's something that's been going on in your life for an entire decade, we would be an asset."

"Yeah, you're really not belaboring the point."

She ignored him, and his focused gaze. "All that being said, this is a big ranch. If you need a place to stay for a while, to hide, I can accommodate you. Even if you don't want our help."

He looked down at her skeptically. "What about this sheriff brother of yours?"

"Like I said, it's a big ranch. He doesn't have to know. If you're careful."

"I'm always careful."

"I highly doubt that," she said with a sniff.

Which seemed to cause his mouth to curve. "What about your sister?"

"She'll keep it on the down-low. Anna lives to keep things on the down-low. Particularly from Jack."

"Why?"

"She's contrary?"

"No, why are you trying to help me?"

Mary sucked in a breath and looked around the ranch, her home. It should be a safe place, but her parents had disappeared out there. Danger had come for her siblings, time and time again. And she'd always had someone to step in and help. Help didn't magically solve every problem, but it sure eased things.

"Sometimes you have to be the help you wished you'd had."

"That's stupid."

She wanted to scowl but didn't let herself. "Only if you're

unarmed and unprepared." She turned her best officious smile on him. "We're always prepared, and *very* armed."

He chuckled at that, then shook his head as if he couldn't believe what he was saying. "I guess if you've got a place I could lay low at for tonight, I wouldn't say no."

WALKER WAS WELL aware of the risks he was taking as he drove Mary to the stables as she instructed. She insisted his car wouldn't make it to the place she had in mind, so she was going to lead him by horse until the car was hidden away, then he'd either have to walk the rest of the way or hop on the horse with her.

Walker waited in his car while she disappeared into the stable. He was sure he was walking himself into more trouble than he could afford, but something about Mary Hudson was compelling enough, he couldn't seem to resist.

It wasn't a strange sensation, exactly. He tended to skirt the line of danger in his quest to get answers, tended to make some rash or spontaneous decisions simply because they *felt* right.

But he'd never had it come in such a pretty package before.

She emerged from the stables with a horse, and she swung up on the huge animal in a mesmerizing move of grace and a flash of leg, since she was still wearing that floaty skirt.

She motioned for him to follow, and he found himself doing so without even questioning it. It was clear she loved horse riding. The land. Walker felt compelled to understand that, follow that.

She led him along a gravel road that got less and less gravel and more mud the farther they got, moving away from all the buildings and closer to mountains and cows.

She came to a stop, motioned for him to do the same and pointed to a little patch of dirt behind some scrubby bushes and scraggly trees.

He pushed the car into Park, turned off the ignition and got out. "This pasture isn't going to be used this year," she said to him, from where she sat high on the horse. "A little bit more of a walk and there's a cabin you can stay in for a spell. You can either walk, or you can climb on." She patted the back of her saddle.

He eyed her, the horse and said saddle and briefly wondered if she was insane. "I'll walk."

She cocked her head, still staring down at him. "Afraid?" she asked, and amusement curved her lips into an alluring smile.

Walker had grown up hopping from city to city, in what as a kid he'd thought was his mom's wanderlust. Once she'd been murdered, he realized she'd been running. All those years, running and making them think it was a grand adventure.

But he was a city boy, even if his investigations had brought him to the wilds of Bonesteel, South Dakota, or Bent County, Wyoming. He didn't trust horses, or any animal that could crush him. It was hardly fear.

But he figured any way he denied the question would only make him sound afraid. So he shrugged. "If you say so."

She didn't belabor the point, just made a noise and the horse started trotting, slower than before when he'd been following by car.

They came around a little cluster of trees eventually and Walker stopped. He'd been expecting some kind of lean-to shack. Like what he had outside Sunrise. Sure, this ranch spread was nice as all get out, but he didn't think that extended to the far reaches of a not-used pasture.

But the cabin looked to be in pristine condition. It was small, sure, but it wasn't anywhere near shabby or falling apart. He forced himself to finish walking and met Mary at the front porch as she swung off her horse.

"One of our ranch hands lived here a while ago. We haven't hired a full-time replacement, so there won't be any reason for anyone to be coming out this way. The electricity's been turned off, but you've got water, a bed. You shouldn't start a fire to cook anything, so I'll bring you some food out in a bit."

She pulled a little key chain out of her pocket and twisted a key off the ring. "This'll get you in. I know you've got quite a few weapons, so you'll want to lock up just in case. You just leave the key behind on the kitchen counter when you go for good, and that's how I'll know to stop bringing you food. How's that?" She looked up at him, dark eyes squinting against the now-high sun.

"You're letting me stay here. For an undetermined amount of time. You're going to feed me. All because…"

"Well, the way I see it, you could have left me back there to get shot at. So, one kindness deserves another."

He hadn't had a whole lot of good in his life. The world had been cruel and unfair, and he'd figured that was fine. He could deal, try to protect his brother and sister from that. In the end, protecting them was all that had ever really mattered to him as an adult.

Mary handed him the key, and he took it. But he didn't go inside. He narrowed his eyes at her, wondering who let her wander around so naive and trusting. "I could be a dangerous criminal. You know that, right?"

"Of course."

"I could kill you. Right here. Tie you up in there and torture you, if I had a mind."

She didn't flinch, didn't back away, just held his gaze with that steady coolness that shouldn't irritate him as much as it did.

"If you had a mind. But you don't. Or you would have already done any of those things." She lifted that chin, all regal and dismissive. "I'm not afraid of you."

"Maybe you should be." He wanted her to be, so she'd keep her distance. Stop making his thoughts drift to strange places he didn't recognize within himself. Like someone who believed she might really be helping him out of the goodness of her heart.

"You have a sister, you said. Is she younger?"

He frowned at the change in conversation but nodded. He probably shouldn't have mentioned Carlyle, but it was what it was. She *had* been the one to hire HSS anyway. Luckily it sounded like Zeke had been as in the dark as Walker, so only one of his siblings was a traitor.

"And you've likely protected her for some portion of her life?" Mary continued with that lady-of-the-manor chin lift.

He frowned deeper and didn't bother to agree even though, yeah, he'd protected her for more than a portion of her life.

"So you should understand I have four older brothers. One's a sheriff, as I mentioned. One is a former marine. If you tried to harm me in any way, I can guarantee, no matter how tough you think you are, they would hurt you right back. And worse, especially when all four of them get together. They can be very unreasonable when provoked."

"That so?"

"And then, worst of all, there's Anna."

"The tiny pregnant woman?"

"She'd flat out kill you, Walker. Without batting an eye. And her husband would help her bury your body, no doubt. With a smile on his face. He's very devoted."

He wanted to laugh—not because he didn't believe her, but because he just couldn't quite peg her, when he usually had everyone down within seconds of meeting them. Like her sister, for example, whom he fully believed would kill him if given the chance.

"What about you? You're not dangerous?" he asked, wondering how she fit into the little tableau she'd painted.

"I'm whatever I need to be. Now, you go on and settle in. I'll be back later with some dinner." And before he could refuse, she was easily mounting the horse and trotting away. A woman on a mission.

He watched her go, enjoying the view and wondering if he was the naive one, believing in a pretty face just because it came in a nicely dressed package that didn't seem to blink at oncoming danger.

And danger was coming, whether he stayed or left.

Chapter Four

Mary went through dinner as if she was not harboring a potential fugitive from the law in their currently unoccupied ranch hand cabin. She made the meal while her brother Cash and his daughter, Izzy, took their turn setting the table. She sat with her family and discussed the ranch and HSS business all the while eating the dinner she'd prepared.

She was quite sure no one suspected anything—she was quite adept at keeping things to herself—but every time she glanced at Anna, she felt guilty. After dinner, Palmer and Cash pretended to argue over whose turn it was to do the dishes, which made Izzy grin and was likely why they did it.

Mary made herself scarce as she often did this time of night. She couldn't keep up with all the chores if she handled them herself, but if she couldn't have them done her way, she could *not* be witness to the incorrect loading of the dishwasher or putting leftovers away.

She might be a control freak, but she could delegate. As long as she didn't have to bear witness.

So, she went to her room for a few hours and caught up on the necessary paperwork for both the ranch and HSS. Anna popped in about halfway through her work. "Couldn't find anything bad on him. Doesn't mean it isn't there. I couldn't find a Walker who connected to any of the aliases, but if he's got aliases, he's hiding something."

Mary agreed, but for some reason that just didn't change what she felt like she needed to do.

"Thank you."

"No problem." Anna settled herself on Mary's bed, clearly wanting to say more, but holding back.

"Did you have something else you wanted to discuss?" Mary asked, in the prim voice that usually irritated Anna.

On cue, Anna scowled at her. "Look, I'm not going to lecture you on being careful. I happen to think you should do at least one un-careful thing in your life. But I don't want to see you hurt." Anna's gaze dropped to Mary's arm, where she'd been shot last month when someone had tried to hurt the family.

But that had been about protecting her family. Not flinging herself into danger. "I know how to look after myself, Anna."

"Yes, I know you think you do. But sometimes…" She swept a hand down her body, her little baby bump. "A handsome man can create unintended consequences."

Mary laughed. "Anna, you can't be serious."

"He's good-looking. A little wounded animal—which is your personal kryptonite. I just want you to be careful-ish. Like, have some great, protected sex with a handsome, charming stranger. Be wild, but not too wild. Like not dodging bullets or getting kidnapped wild."

"So not *your* brand of wild?"

"Mary."

"I have no intention of getting caught up in whatever danger Walker has going on. I just offered him a place to lay low for a brief period of time. No doubt he'll be on his way tomorrow, to do whatever he needs to do."

Anna sighed. "If you say so."

When Mary didn't take the bait and argue, Anna left. Likely to go check on her husband, who was still recovering from his serious gunshot wound he'd gotten the same day Mary had gotten her minor one.

She studied the mark on her arm. Nothing more than a mostly healed scar. She couldn't say she'd handled any of that moment well, but she'd decided to move forward thinking of it as a badge of honor.

It was much better than thinking about how close Hawk had been to dying, or Anna had been to getting killed, or Cash and Izzy...

No. She wouldn't go down that road again. It was over. Done. They'd survived.

When it sounded like the house was still, she crept back down to the kitchen. She packed up some leftovers for Walker, sticking to things that would taste good cold or room temperature. She packed them in a cooler. He'd likely leave in the morning, but if he didn't, she wanted him to have enough food to get by on.

A handsome man can create unintended consequences.

Well, he was indeed a handsome man, but Mary was a controlled, careful woman. There were no unintended consequences in her future. God knew Walker had more pressing things on his mind than an uptight administrator of her family's businesses.

She frowned at her own description of herself. She liked her life. If she didn't, she'd change it. She didn't want excitement or what Anna called being *un-careful*. What happened this morning was the most excitement she needed, thank you very much.

But, in fairness, Anna was right about wounded animals. Mary couldn't resist trying to help. So, she crept out of the kitchen and to the back door. For a moment she paused and listened, just to make sure everyone was still and quiet where they were supposed to be.

Grant cozied up with his girlfriend, Dahlia, in his room. Louisa and Palmer in theirs, an arrangement that wouldn't change until after their wedding when Palmer finished building a place on his stretch of land. Cash and Izzy lived in a cabin across the yard with their menagerie of dogs that Cash trained. Hawk and Anna were still in the house with their ever-growing puppy, but Pita slept in their room with them. They were talking about building, too, but Mary secretly hoped they stayed until after the baby was born.

Mary loved babies. She enjoyed Izzy at eleven just as much as she'd enjoyed the girl as an infant, but there was something about snuggly little babies that just turned Mary into goo. She supposed it helped she was an aunt not a mom, so didn't have to be plagued with pregnancy sickness or sleepless nights.

But tonight she wasn't worried about that, or her paired-up siblings. She was worried about Jack—the only person who didn't have someone claiming most of their evening attention. Well, the only one besides her.

Jack would likely be up. Poring over a case for work or checking up on HSS business. Would he hear the door open and close and come snooping? She frowned a little, because it struck her as sad, and she didn't want to feel pity for Jack when she was trying to commit a little subterfuge against him.

He would most definitely not approve of Walker in any sense. At least not until he had him fully checked out to make sure he wasn't a criminal. And since Anna hadn't been able to figure that out for sure, Jack would not approve.

It was only one night. A little help. And if she was aiding and abetting a criminal? Well, she supposed it'd be a mistake she'd learn from.

Careful, with all the stealth of a criminal, she slid out the back door and walked with calm purpose to the stables. She saddled Pippi, settled the soft cooler in a saddlebag, then set off.

Mary loved riding. It was one of the few things she remembered doing with her parents that didn't bring the pain of grief. There was too much joy here, in the wind whipping through her hair. In the moon glowing high above the mountains.

Or maybe she didn't miss them here because she *felt* them. In the wind, in the moonlight. It was one of the few fanciful thoughts she allowed herself.

As she approached the cabin, it was shrouded in darkness, though if a person really looked they might notice the slight glow coming from the gap in the curtains.

She pulled Pippi to a stop, loosely tied her reins around the porch post, then went up to the door and knocked.

Walker opened the door. The inside was illuminated by a battery-powered lamp the previous tenant must have left behind. She slid inside, though this side of the ranch should be isolated enough not to have people seeing anything.

She held out the cooler. "Here you are, as promised. There's some food. I didn't pack any water since the sink water should be potable."

He unzipped the top, peered in. "This is quite the feast."

"It'll hopefully keep you going through tomorrow."

He opened one of the containers, gave the food a little sniff, then grabbed a bite. He nodded as he chewed. "Good."

He was clearly hungry. He made it through one container without saying anything else. Mary knew she should go, leave him to it. But she just stood there.

"So. What did the fam find out about me?" Walker asked, handing her the empty container so she could take it back with her.

"Nothing."

He raised an eyebrow. "You're telling me they didn't look into anything about me?"

"Oh, Anna looked. Well, she looked for a criminal record associated with any of your names."

"Yeah, don't have one of those."

"Because it was the middle of the night and she was alone in this cabin with a stranger.

A very handsome stranger.

"Either that," he agreed easily, "or I just don't get caught."

WALKER WAS FASCINATED by the way Mary's expressions changed. Or didn't, as the case might be. She wore that coolness like a mask. A cloak of *I am not affected by you.*

Which meant he wondered, when she was looking down her nose at him and firmed her lips like that, if she was in fact *quite* affected.

And you do not have the time to care either way.

A fair reminder.

She didn't immediately leave, though she hovered there by the door. He was too hungry to care if she was watching him eat. He'd been busy with preparations this morning and hadn't had a chance to eat breakfast, then there'd been the shooting and Mary and the Hudson Ranch.

He could have gone foraging earlier—he'd made sure a long time ago he could survive any situation—but he'd trusted her to bring him food. That trust bothered him a little bit, but here she was. Watching him with those serious brown eyes.

"Did you want some?" he asked.

She shook her head. "I was just curious. What did your sister want us to investigate?"

The question surprised him when it shouldn't have. He'd already read Carlyle the riot act for involving other people, for using one of his fake names. But yelling at Carlyle never did anything.

So he wasn't sure why he still engaged. Something about his baby sister brought it out in him, he supposed.

He studied the woman asking the question, not afraid to let the silence stretch out. She didn't seem to be either. She just stood there, with a patient, steady stare, reminding him of the social worker he'd had to deal with when he'd wanted custody of Carlyle.

Not a bad person, not an enemy or a threat, and yet just like then, Walker kind of wanted to make her one.

He didn't like that reaction at all. He didn't mind the truth. The problem was it came with a hell of a lot of danger, and

Mary… Well, she wasn't the kind of woman who was equipped to deal with danger, no matter what her family did.

"You planning on sticking around watching me eat or what?"

"I can go, if you'd rather."

He couldn't help but scowl at that placid nonanswer. "I'll probably be out of here by tomorrow afternoon. Once I'm sure they've stopped sniffing around Bent County."

"All right. Well, if you need to stay longer, know that you're more than welcome. I'll come by tomorrow evening around the same time with more food. If you're still here, it's yours. If not, no harm done." She smiled. Kindly.

And he didn't know what the hell to do with her kindness. He couldn't even muster his usual skepticism. She was just too…something.

She turned to leave and that seemed wrong. "My mother was murdered." What the hell was wrong with him? "Ten years ago."

She turned back to face him, her expression not shocked or pitying like the usual looks he got. She crossed the way and put her hand on his arm. "Oh, Walker. I'm so sorry."

She seemed so genuinely distressed for him. Not the usual pity, which came with either skepticism or a distancing of not knowing what to do with that information. Just a genuine expression of sympathy.

"And your father?" she asked gently, like she knew. When she didn't know a damn thing, in her prissy outfits on this sprawling ranch with her own damn horse.

"Mom ditched him when my baby sister was born. Fine enough to knock us around since we were boys, but once the girl came along it was time to do what she could." He didn't know where that came from, so bitter. So ugly. He knew his mother had tried her best.

Unfortunately, sometimes people's best wasn't good enough.

"You have a brother too?"

"Going to collect all this information, put it in some little database?" he returned, scowling down at her.

"I don't even know your last name, Walker," she said calmly, not at all put off by the snap in his tone. "My family could likely find it if they dug hard and long enough, but we won't poke if you don't want us to. But I hope you understand, we could help you. It's what we do. Because we've been through it."

He snorted. "Yeah? How?"

"My parents disappeared when I was ten years old. No one ever could figure out what happened to them. They were good, loving parents. But they just…" She swallowed. "They were gone. No hints. No evidence. If I believed in aliens, that would make sense, but I don't. So it's just this unsolved mystery."

Walker didn't know what to say, and that was a weird sensation. He'd been a fast talker in all situations as long as he could remember. He'd talked dear old dad around so he didn't start punching, sweet-talked his mom into letting him do something dumb, then the social workers, the teachers, then every person he'd had to work around to try to get to the bottom of what his mother had been running from.

What had caught up with her.

But he did not know what to say to Mary Hudson. The woman looked like she had it all but she'd lost her parents mysteriously at ten. Younger than Carlyle had been when Mom had died.

"We don't take our cold cases lightly, is my point," she said, when he didn't speak. "And you don't have to make the decision now. Anytime you want or need our help, we'll be happy to supply it."

"For a price?"

"Would you rather it be charity?" she returned archly.

He found himself wanting to laugh of all things. Who the hell *was* this woman? "So what happened? After your parents? You live with your grandparents or something?"

She shook her head. "Jack, my oldest sibling, he was eighteen. He fought tooth and nail to keep us and keep us together. And he did. While he was doing that, he also figured we might as well try to help people like us. Because we never got answers, and it'd be nice if someone did."

"I'm close enough to the answers all on my own," he returned, more out of reflex than anything else. How could he bring in outside help when someone wanted him and his siblings dead?

Mary didn't react to that, except to nod. "I guess I should go then."

But he had the bizarre and deep-seated urge to keep her here. "I don't really know what to do with help. I sure as hell don't know how to believe in the goodness of anyone's heart."

"Then *I'm* sorry, Walker. That sounds sad."

Maybe it was. But Mary needed to understand. "It's dangerous. Whoever killed her? They're trying to kill me so I don't find out who they are."

"You must be close then," she returned as if potential murders were just a matter of course. "We know what to do with danger. You know, I was shot last month."

Walker was tempted to laugh. "Shot, huh?"

She moved closer, pulled up her sleeve, and there was indeed a red little mark, clearly healing. He narrowed his eyes at her. "That's a graze."

"Done by a bullet."

"How?"

"Well, someone had set a fire at my brother's cabin. He and his daughter were trapped inside, so I ran outside to get to them, but someone was waiting and shot me. It was this whole thing about getting back at us for not finding a previous client's son before he died."

"Sounds pretty far-fetched."

"If you think *that's* far-fetched, I won't even tell you about my other brother uncovering a human-sacrificing cult a few months before that."

"You sound like bad luck, sweetheart."

She smiled at that when he thought she'd balk at him calling her sweetheart. In fact, he kept expecting her to balk—from that very first moment in his crappy apartment in Hardy to this one.

And she never did.

A moment of silence stretched out, and maybe he was staring a little too intently trying to figure her out. Or maybe it was just that she was a pretty little thing and he was a man with an impressive imagination, but a little pink seemed to creep into her cheeks and she took a step back toward the door.

"Well, I should go back to the house. Just understand, like this cabin, help is an open offer."

"All right."

She slid back out the door as carefully as she'd entered, and Walker knew he shouldn't. But like everything with Mary, knowing better didn't seem to change his actions. He moved over to the window, looked out the gap in the curtains. Watched her gracefully mount her horse.

Her profile looked suitably regal in the silvery moonlight, especially up there on her horse. He felt like a peasant watching a queen, and it didn't even bother him. She looked like she *should* be a queen, and so far she'd been nothing but helpful. Kind.

The terrible part was he couldn't find a way to mistrust her.

Chapter Five

Mary had been raised to believe in integrity, no matter how hard it was to stand for the right thing. First, by her parents. Then by Jack.

Jack always made it look easy, and Mary had never struggled with it. Until now. Walker had given her enough information that she might be able to dig around to find out his last name and the details of his mother's murder.

But he didn't want her to. So she didn't.

Maybe it was common decency, or maybe it was the fact that she'd grown up in a small town where everyone felt entitled to every detail of her parents' disappearance whether she wanted them to or not.

Still, as she went about her day, she found her mind occupied with Walker's story, with what had happened in his apartment complex the morning before and wondering if he'd still be at the cabin when she went down there tonight.

And she wondered at the odd twist inside her that wanted him to be. She tried to convince herself it was the HSS mission, empathy for his situation, and it was. Partly.

But there was a part that had something to do with the way the silence between them had stretched out last night, and how her thoughts had wandered.

It wasn't that she'd never had thoughts about a man before. She had dated. Admittedly mostly in college, because it had been away from Sunrise and anyone who knew the story of her parents so intimately it infected every interaction. But she'd been more of a serial dater, never comfortable getting too deep into it. The two times she'd gotten close enough to sleep with someone, that had seemed to cure any desire to stay with them.

She liked her privacy. She liked her control.

She'd wondered what it would feel like to kiss Walker within twenty-four hours of meeting him, after people had shot at them, and she didn't know what to do with that. It wasn't…*her*.

"Hey."

Mary jumped nearly a foot, and then cursed herself for being so lost in thought. Especially since it was Anna scaring the tar out of her. Because Anna knew about Walker and would no doubt wonder if that's where Mary's thoughts had been.

Mary fixed a smile on her face and turned to Anna. "You scared me."

"Sexy daydreams do tend to distract a person."

Mary scowled. "Hardly." She wasn't going to bite. She was going to change the subject. "I haven't seen much of Hawk lately. Is he feeling all right?"

It was Anna's turn to scowl. "He's busy sneaking out doing things he shouldn't. You'd think a man who'd been shot within an inch of his life would learn to sit still."

"I would not think that of a man who married *you*."

Anna stuck out her tongue at Mary, but then her expression grew serious and Mary turned her attention back to the food she was preparing. Because Anna serious was not anything she wanted to deal with on a good day.

Not that it was a bad day. She was just unsettled.

"Are you sure about this whole Walker thing? Because you don't usually get involved in…well, anything. And your mind never wanders. Maybe I should deal with Walker."

Mary didn't know why something dark and bitter settled within her, or why she allowed the snotty response. "Because I'm so incapable?"

"That is *not* what I said." Anna put her hand over Mary's busy ones until Mary looked up at her sister's serious hazel eyes. "You're probably the most capable out of all of us, but you don't like this stuff. You don't like getting involved. You like—or at least have spent most of your life convincing us that you like—being in the background."

"I prefer the background, yes. And I'm not changing that. This isn't a job. This is providing shelter for someone—which, I might add, *is* what I usually do."

Anna sighed heavily. "I see you're going to be stubborn, so there's no point arguing."

"Wow, pregnancy *has* matured you, Anna."

She snorted out a laugh, then fell into step helping Mary prepare dinner. It wasn't Anna's turn, but Mary wasn't going to refuse the help. Especially when Anna was doing it quietly and competently instead of her usual whirlwind of chatter and purposefully doing things in ways Mary did not do them.

"I'm only going to say one more thing about it," Anna said after a while of working in silence.

Mary fixed her sister with a disbelieving look until Anna grinned.

"Okay, one more thing *today*. If it gets too much, if you feel like you're in over your head, I can take over. Don't try to tackle this yourself just because I'm pregnant." She patted her little bump. "Little Hawklet has still got a while to bake yet."

"If you keep calling her that, we're going to end up using it, I hope you know that."

Anna laughed, but she sobered quickly, pinning Mary with an intense, serious gaze that immediately put Mary on edge.

"I hope you know you're the only reason having a girl doesn't freak me out," Anna said, with all the somber seriousness she almost never used. "That you're here, and I know you'll help. I'd be lost without you, Mary."

Mary kept very still, tried very hard not to be swallowed

up by the emotions that brought out in her. But she had to be strong. The calm one. In control. Always. "Are we saying goodbye?"

"No, pregnancy makes me sappy and truthful," Anna replied with a shrug. "So, I wanted you to know." Then she pulled Mary into a tight hug.

Mary stood there and took it. She was too shocked to reciprocate. Anna was not demonstrative as a rule. Okay, none of them were.

Anna pulled back, and then laughed. Mary couldn't for the life of her figure out why. But Anna laughed all the way out of the kitchen.

WALKER PACED THE small if comfortable cabin, phone to his ear, trying to figure out what the hell he was going to do.

"I lost the tail," Carlyle said, with enough confidence the worry curdled in Walker's gut. She could be too confident. Too sure. It would get her into trouble one of these days out there on her own.

He never should have let her go. He'd known it had been a mistake, but last year she'd begged him. Poked at him and argued with him about the fact that she was an *adult* and blah, blah, blah.

He'd finally caved, and now he regretted it. "Can you get somewhere new without a tail?"

"What do you take me for?"

He didn't respond to that. He had to get her somewhere safe. Somewhere he could keep his damn eye on her. He looked around the cabin. It would be perfect.

But he'd have to clear it with Mary—which rankled. Then he'd have to make sure Carlyle got here without a tail. Then Mary and Carlyle would likely have some kind of interaction and for some reason he balked at that idea.

"Why did you hire these people anyway?" he muttered, before fully thinking the question through.

"Who? The HSS? Oh, I came across their website. They had all this experience, but it wasn't like one of those sketchy private investigator things. It was like…because they'd gone through it, they wanted to help people. And they were a family. It was like the rich, happy version of us. And you were…"

She trailed off. He didn't need her to rehash what he'd been. What he still was. On the trail of a killer. And he'd been getting close.

"It's been ten years, Walker," Carlyle said softly. "You're out there dodging bullets, and one of these days one is going to land. You're not getting any younger. I mean, you'll be forty before you know it."

He scowled into the phone. She really was irritating. "I think the nursing home is a ways off yet, Car."

"My point is, maybe you need help. We've been close for years. Maybe to get over that final hump, you need a little outside input."

He rested his forehead against the rough-hewn board of the cabin's interior wall. They didn't *need* help, but he could hear the note in Carlyle's voice she was usually too busy poking at him to let come through. She was tired. She was lonely. She hadn't had a normal life since she'd been twelve—no, scratch that. Moving around like fugitives as she'd done her entire childhood wasn't normal. She'd never known normal. And that wasn't all his fault.

But some of it was.

"Walker?"

"If I agree to get help, I want you here."

"In Nowhere, Wyoming? With you breathing down my neck?"

"Yeah. You and Zeke. If we're getting help, we need to stick together while we get it. We can't risk it otherwise."

There was a long pause, but he didn't rush her. Just because she wanted a normal life didn't mean she wanted to be with him again. Because, apparently, he was overbearing and unreasonable.

"Okay. If you promise to use the help, I'll convince Zeke. We'll have to make a pretty round-about trip out there to avoid any detection, but we'll get there in a few days."

They discussed details. He wouldn't have her come out to the Hudson Ranch right away. Once she and Zeke arrived in Bent County, he'd meet them somewhere remote. Bring them back, knowing for sure they didn't have a tail.

Mary seemed pretty sure the Hudsons could weather some danger, but Walker didn't feel right about being the one to bring them into the middle of his deal. None of this felt right.

"Don't have second thoughts, Walker," Carlyle said firmly in his ear. "We've done this your way all these years. It's time for a new way."

He didn't disagree exactly. He'd just prefer a new way that was all him and no one else. But he supposed that was the old way, all in all. "I'm going to have second thoughts the whole damn time, Car, but that doesn't mean I'm going to change my mind."

"Good, then I'm taking that as a promise. I'll talk to Zeke. We'll get in contact once we're close."

"All right. Be careful."

"I always am," she said cheerfully, which was a bold-faced lie, but what was he supposed to do about it?

"Yeah." He stood there, his forehead still pressed to the wall. He didn't want this, but it had been almost a year since he'd seen his siblings. So despite the part of him that dreaded what was coming, there was a small part of him just…glad. "It'll be good to see you, squirt."

"Yeah, but I don't want to hear anything about the new tattoo."

He groaned and she laughed as she hung up on him. He shoved the phone into his pocket. He only had a little battery power left. He wasn't about to ask Mary for any help in that department, but he wasn't quite sure what he was going to do about it yet.

He hated not being sure of his next steps, but his siblings joining him here... It was a lot to take in. A lot to accept.

And if he was being fully honest with himself, this was nice. Just him. No distractions, no worry. He'd actually slept last night, hard and long, and he couldn't remember the last time he'd done that.

He blew out a breath. He knew he couldn't get used to it. Mary might not want two more people hiding out here—though if they were using her family's company maybe that changed things.

Walker finally turned away from the wall. He felt nauseous at the thought of bringing in a company. Mary's family. People poking into his business, the case he'd been building for ten years.

Building and failing to find the one answer he still needed.

A sharp knock sounded at the door, and Walker thought about ignoring it. Would she bust in anyway? Or would she go the hell away?

But in the end, he answered it, because he'd told Carlyle he was going to accept help. And he wouldn't go back on his word. He'd promised that to Carlyle a long time ago. He'd broken a lot of promises to her since then, but never that one.

Mary swept in easily, carrying all sorts of things. "I brought some portable batteries if you need them. If you think you might stay for more than a few more days, I can get the electricity turned back on. I handle those kinds of admin processes, and if Jack asks I can always say it was a clerical error."

He stared at her as she set down a new cooler, a bag of batteries and whatever else. Every movement was careful, economical. When she was done and looked up at him, she clasped her hands in front of her, all neat and prim.

And far too beautiful for *his* own good.

He didn't want her family, up in that big house, poking

through everything. Asking him questions it would only irritate him to answer. But he didn't mind *her*.

At all.

"Why'd you track me down to give me the money?" he asked, needing to understand how he'd wound up here. Maybe needing to understand some piece of *her*. "You could have kept it. I know it doesn't matter in the grand scheme of your empire here, but you had every right to keep it when you couldn't find us right away."

She didn't answer at first, though she didn't seem startled by the abrupt question. She stared at him very solemnly, as if deciding what to say. There was something about that stillness, that patience and quiet she had, that he would have assumed would make him uncomfortable or suspicious, but instead felt like peace.

"I have this memory...one of my first, I think, because Anna was a baby so I couldn't have been more than three," she said, and she spoke softly and calmly, with her mouth just barely curved upward. "We were at the county fair, I think. Some kind of thing like that, and my mother found a wallet on the ground. It had some money in it, I think, but no identification. My parents joked about it being their lucky day, but then we spent—well, what felt like to me as a little girl—half the day trying to track down the owner. And I don't know how many people told my dad to just keep it. But every time he'd just say to whoever it was, in this patient, calm drawl of his, 'It isn't the right thing to do.'"

He could hear the longing in her voice, how much she missed the man. What he'd meant to her. Walker didn't understand it. He'd hated his father, loved his mother—but God knew, she was complex, and even knowing he'd loved her didn't make him have a lot of fond memories of the way they'd lived.

"So every time I saw that money sitting in the account," Mary continued, "I'd just hear my father's voice. And my siblings all told me the same thing you did. Anytime I brought up wanting to track you down, everyone would point out if the money was needed or wanted, it'd be easy to return it. But I just kept hearing my father's voice."

"You miss him."

"Yes. I'm sure I always will. Don't you miss your mother?"

"I don't know. Seems these days I curse her half as much as I miss her."

"I think it's all missing."

"Maybe." He was uncomfortable with all this sincerity, so he might as well move the conversation along. "Listen, I talked to my sister about why she tried to hire you guys in the first place. She gave me the whole spiel about your family." He didn't mention the whole *like us, but rich* thing. "We've been stuck at this same place, close to finding out who killed our mother, but not getting there. Just making ourselves more of a target." Damn, that irked. "She wants to try you guys, and I told her… Well, I agreed anyway."

"Walker. That's wonderful. We can't promise results, but with our resources, we just have so much to offer. And a new set of eyes, an unbiased set of eyes, never hurts. It's Grant's turn to take on the next case, so—"

"No, not your siblings. You."

Her happy, earnest expression changed into one he couldn't read. But when she spoke it was calm and to the point. "I don't take on investigations. I don't… It's not my area of expertise." She shook her head, a little too emphatically to his way of thinking. "Grant would be better. He's a former marine and—"

But he didn't want her siblings, didn't trust them. "The only way I'm bringing in your family is if it's you. I don't want to talk to them. I don't trust them, but I trust you, Mary. God knows why."

Chapter Six

Mary couldn't remember the last time she'd been caught so off guard. It felt a little bit like being shot. Surprise and shock and then a little slice of pain.

"I don't investigate, Walker. I file things. I handle the accounts, the phone calls, the accommodations." She'd tried, once upon a time, but the failure of it all ate her up.

And that was the thing about cold cases. No matter how good HSS was, they couldn't always find answers. They hadn't even found answers when it came to their own parents.

She didn't have the heart for it, and if she couldn't find answers for Walker... It shouldn't, but it felt more personal. And she couldn't do it. "I do not investigate."

"So, now you do," he returned, as if he got to decide. As if he could flip a switch.

She wanted to be angry, she really did, but he said he trusted her. So instead of being angry she just felt a bit awed. And a bit trapped.

"If I..." She was not really thinking about agreeing to this, was she? "If I was the lead investigator for HSS, my siblings would still need to know about it. We work as a team, with a lead investigator who deals with the client and the actual investigating, but Palmer and Anna help with any computer research, and we bounce ideas off each other, and Grant and Jack handle law enforcement angles and—"

"That's fine." He shrugged. "Long as I only have to deal with you. And you all understand how dangerous it is."

Yes, I recall being shot at in your apartment just yesterday, she wanted to say. But she didn't allow herself snippy commentary if she could help it. "I'm not a big fan of danger," she said instead.

"We were shot at and you didn't even scream. You climbed out my window like a pro. You hopped in a car with a stranger. You've got that gunshot wound. Seems to me, you and danger are intimately acquainted."

There was something about the way he said *intimately* that made her want to blush, but she didn't. "I didn't say I was unaccustomed to danger. I said I wasn't a fan." She sounded overly prim even to herself.

"You don't have to take the job, Mary."

"And you don't have to make me be the lead investigator, Walker," she snapped in return, then winced a little as she hated when she got snappish.

"I've spent ten years doing this, Mary. Ten years. When the cops stopped, I couldn't. Even when I was trying to get Carlyle through high school, working in the damn school cafeteria to make ends meet and trying not worry about Zeke off in the army, I kept looking. I've been chasing leads for so long, I wouldn't know how to stop if I could. So, if I'm giving up ten years of full control and doing it my way and protecting my siblings, then it's damn well going to be the way I see fit."

His anger didn't poke at her own. Maybe because she understood. So fully. "I know what it's like, Walker. You don't have to prove how hard it is to me."

He blew out a frustrated breath. And she could see how hard he was holding on because…because he was afraid of letting go. He was afraid. Period.

"All right. Then it's settled," he said, looking at her belligerently as if daring her to refuse.

She didn't want it to be settled, but she knew he needed

help. She didn't want to be the one to give it to him, not like this, but… If it was the only way, she *had* to do it. And maybe she'd convince him. Maybe he'd come around to trust her family too. And all the while he'd be here and safe.

She ignored the odd impulse to cross the room and wrap her arms around him in a comforting hug. It wouldn't go over well, clearly. But more, she wasn't sure it was all innocent impulse on her part. "And you'll stay here?"

"As long as I think it's safe to—for your family and mine. My brother and sister are going to meet me here in a few days. Now, I don't want you thinking you have to feed us or—"

"Oh, you won't all fit in here. And with no electricity? If you come stay at the big house, we—"

"No big house. No family. This cabin and you. That's it. And we take care of ourselves. No more dinner packages. You don't need to turn on the electricity. We're resilient."

She frowned at him. "That's stubborn for the sake of being stubborn."

"Well, you and my siblings will get along just fine because I'm sure they'll think so too."

She wanted to laugh at that. How much his family sounded like hers. How she understood that no matter how similar they were, there was a difference. She'd had a support system. Not just because she was younger and she'd had older siblings to see her through. But the fact that she—and her siblings— had inherited this ranch. That her parents had the knowledge and economic standing to have it all in a trust so it passed to them with minimal issue. That no matter the hardship they'd gone through, no matter how her parents' disappearance still haunted them all, they hadn't spent their childhoods or adolescences struggling to make ends meet.

There had been an element of luck to her tragic circumstances, and it didn't seem like Walker and his siblings had run into much luck at all.

He was practically prowling the cabin now. "I mean it. No electricity, no more food. I'll handle it. I take care of my own."

She understood the impulse—to an extent. "Well, that's very nice and all, but I also take care. And I plan on bringing you meals because that's what *I* do. I'm going to have the electricity turned on because it's stupid not to. *I* am going to handle all of this how *I* see fit since you're insisting *I* be the lead investigator."

He glowered at her. "Then we're going to have a problem."

She didn't wilt at his glower. Honestly, did he think it was intimidating? No matter how dark his eyes were, or how impressive the arms crossed over his chest were, she did not feel intimidated. Other things, but not that. She lifted her chin. "Then I guess we are."

His expression turned speculative. "Anything ever rile you up?" he demanded.

"You're hardly the first man to ever ask me that, and I doubt you'll be the last. This is called maturity, Walker. And I have it in spades."

He looked at her, with the kind of belligerence she knew so well. Hurt pride and frustration. She'd seen it on all of her siblings' faces more often than she cared to count.

And she didn't have it in her to be a brick wall to that. Not when she'd spent her entire life being the soft place to land for the people in her life—because nowhere else was soft. Not really.

So she did cross to him then, no matter how many recriminations her mind gave her. *He's a stranger. He's dangerous. He's not your responsibility. At best he's a client who's emotionally manipulated you into taking on tasks you don't want.*

But he was also a man in need of help. In need of that soft place to land, and Mary was never any good at not being that.

"We aren't enemies, Walker," she said, speaking in the same tone she might have used on any of her brothers as she reached out and put a comforting hand on his crossed arms. Except this close to him, looking up at his stormy dark eyes, feeling the powerful, tensed muscle of his arm, she didn't feel particularly sisterly. But that was neither here nor there. She focused on the task at hand. "We don't have to fight. We don't have to rile each other up. We're on the same team."

"In my life, all those things *do* mean being on the same team."

Which made her laugh because she understood that well enough. And for some reason, she didn't think to pull her hand away. She just stood there, a shade too close. And he stood there, looking at her a shade too intensely.

For way longer than could possibly be socially appropriate.

She stepped back, heart beating double time and sure she was being a complete and utter idiot. She retreated to the careful, icy demeanor she'd spent almost a lifetime perfecting.

"I'll come back tomorrow. Let's say ten? I'll get the paperwork started on moving the case forward with HSS."

He didn't say anything, didn't move for the longest time, and she fought off the urge to turn and run.

She wasn't a coward.

But eventually, all he said was "sure." And she turned and walked back to her horse. And if she thought she caught a glimpse of him watching her through the gap in the curtains, she swiped that thought away as foolish.

Whatever strange reactions she had to him were one-sided, obviously. And now he was a client. So there'd be no more thinking about his strong arms and his piercing eyes.

Period.

WALKER HAD WANTED to kiss her last night. A strange, unbidden urge that held him in a grip so strong he'd nearly forgotten himself. Who he was, why he was here. All he could see was her, all he could want was her—this woman he barely knew.

He wasn't a man who spent a lot of time deliberating when

he could act—when action, even mistaken action, often moved the needle forward. And he trusted his gut.

His gut seemed to know her—whether his brain agreed or not.

Then she'd stepped back and plastered on that cool, queen-of-the-manor smile.

Which was for the best. Getting mixed up in Mary Hudson would no doubt be a fatal mistake.

Why was he getting help from her again? It didn't seem to matter if she was talking in that cool, calm voice of hers with her hands clasped, or looking up at him with soft brown eyes, or firming her mouth in a kind of frustrated disapproval.

She did something to him, and he did *not* have time for that. Didn't like the way it distracted him from the complicated tasks at hand.

Bringing people in didn't give him less work, it gave him more. He had to decide what to share, and how. Had to think about the ways he gave Mary information, as she'd no doubt share it with her family.

She'd called it a *case*. It wasn't a *case*. It was murder. Life and death. His.

And now maybe even hers?

He scowled at that damn voice in his head. She'd been the one to push her way in. If meeting him under the rain of bullets didn't clue her in that this was a dangerous thing to get involved in, he didn't know what would.

He glanced at his watch. He'd been useless all morning because she'd said she'd be here at ten, and what the hell was he supposed to do? Right now his next steps involved waiting on his siblings, and waiting on Mary Hudson and her HSS.

He hated waiting. But he knew well that what he hated didn't matter in the grand scheme of the universe. Because the universe did whatever it damn well pleased.

Half resigned, half infuriated, Walker marched over to the

window and glanced out the curtain gap. In the distance, he could see a graceful figure on top of a horse crest the hill.

Why his body tightened, why his heartbeat sped up a little bit was so utterly beyond him he didn't know what to do about it. Nothing about Mary Hudson should get under his skin.

But everything seemed to. He turned away from the window, called it self-preservation over cowardice and waited for her knock at the door.

When it came, he just hollered a "come in" because if he answered the door he was half-afraid he'd be tempted to grab her like some kind of Neanderthal.

She slid in, all quiet, efficient movements. "Good morning," she greeted cheerfully. She had a little satchel tucked under her arm. As usual, she looked neat as a pin. Yesterday she'd been dressed a bit more casually than the day before—jeans and a blouse rather than the flowy skirt. Today was more back to the office. A boxy skirt, sensible shoes, a fussy blouse and pulled-back hair.

He'd never considered prim and proper his type before, but something about Mary made it seem downright mouth-watering.

And so not the point of this little exercise, he reminded himself. She was here to help, when he'd given up on help years ago when the detectives on his mother's case had, more or less, told him to stop wasting their time.

Mary moved into the room, put her satchel on the table and began to unpack its contents. File folders and notebooks and pens and pencils, and just when he'd been about to make a quip about it being the twenty-first century, she pulled out a small tablet.

Walker stood half a room away, leaning against the wall, arms crossed over his chest as a reminder of where his hands should stay. "That's a lot," he said, because he was afraid he'd find himself commenting on how fresh she looked if he didn't say something disdainful.

"An investigation's first and best tool is organization," she returned in that equally bright manner.

He wanted to laugh. He didn't agree for a lot of reasons. The top being neither he nor his siblings had the first clue how to organize anything.

He could fight. He could shoot a gun. He could jump out of buildings and protect his siblings. But he'd never been so happy as the day Carlyle had graduated high school and he hadn't had to worry about permission slips, the right color folders or calls from teachers about missing assignments.

"This feels like school," he said.

She looked up at him, and she did remind him of a teacher. One of the ones who would have given him a kind lecture about understanding the difficult position he was in but needing Carlyle to put forth more effort.

Like he'd ever been able to get that wildling to do anything.

"Well, you're in luck. I excelled at school."

"I just bet you did," he muttered.

"You know, we'd accomplish more if you'd meet me up at the main house," she said, sitting now that all her little pads and notebooks and pens were arranged.

"Too risky yet."

"What exactly are you waiting on?"

"My siblings to get here and to know they weren't followed." He didn't have to divulge the next part. Even if she was agreeing to help, it didn't mean she was a full-on partner in his family's mess. But no matter how he told himself to be circumspect, the truth came out anyway. "And my brother to have a lead on who tried to take me out the other day."

"Do you really believe they were trying to take you out?" she asked, pen poised at the paper like she was about to take notes.

"Huh?"

"Well, it's just…" Mary pursed her lips, looking thoughtful. "I've gone over the events of the day from my perspective many times. It seems to me, someone who really wanted you dead wouldn't go shooting up your apartment in the morning. They'd have someone break in late at night when you might be asleep. They'd have some kind of sniper situation. There would have been men at all the exits of your apartment."

He'd, of course, considered these things, then dismissed them as sloppy work. "I think you messed with their plans."

"Maybe. But you have a murder that you've been trying to solve for ten years. And I'm not saying you aren't good at dodging danger, but…" She tapped her fingers on the table. "I don't know. Something doesn't add up."

Walker didn't have anything to say to that because he didn't disagree. Something *didn't* add up. It never had.

"But that's usually how cold cases go. Though if someone is after you, it's not so cold, is it?"

He didn't bother to answer that, since he didn't get the impression she was talking to him. She was making notes on little preprinted pages in a binder.

"Your father would have been the first person the police looked at back then?"

"Yeah."

She looked up from her little notebook. There was enough pity there to have him bristling.

"No need to be careful about it. Did it bother me that they'd look at the guy who knocked my mom, my brother and me around for years? No, Mary. Weirdly I was right on board."

She stared at him for a full beat, all that coolness wrapped around her like a cloak. It made him feel like a dick when he didn't particularly want to analyze his own behavior at the moment.

"Unfortunately, it was a dead end. In a lot of ways. Dad had ties to a gang called Sons of the Badlands. The cops and I followed that thread for a while, but it never really panned out. If anything, I think it took us farther from whatever the truth is.

The gang doesn't even exist anymore. Wiped out a few years back, so whoever is after me can't be them."

"Unless they were just affiliated but maybe not as involved. But you'd have thought of that, poked into that."

"Yeah."

"Do you have any files? Notes? Lists?"

It was probably perverse of him that he looked forward to showing her. "Sure." He went to the room he'd been sleeping in and grabbed the duffel he shoved things into when he found things he meant to keep. In the old days, he'd handed that sort of thing off to Zeke, but he hadn't seen his brother in so long he'd accumulated quite a bit.

He returned to the table, and then upended the entire contents there in front of her. All crumpled papers and sloppy writing and a slew of things that likely only made sense to him.

He would have felt badly about it—if he'd had some other way of doing it, if he wasn't feeling rubbed raw from sharing all this in the first place, and if she didn't just survey the pile of papers without even a blink.

When she spoke, it was patient scolding. "Walker," she said, as if he'd just presented her with a dead mouse like a house cat.

"Yeah?"

"I don't suppose you have something more…organized? A computer file or…"

He tapped his temple. "The only computer file I need."

"Your siblings then? They have something more tangible?"

Zeke did, but Walker shrugged. "Maybe."

She nodded. "Well, that's something. I guess we should sort through this and make sense of it." She didn't seem irritated by that. She seemed almost…excited. "And once we're done, you'll have a much more organized situation. I'll have to remember a binder tomorrow. Unless you prefer to keep everything here with you?"

"I can't say as I care one way or another. Like I said,

the important information is up here." He tapped his temple once more.

"Yes, of course. But you have help now. The more eyes that can look at the information displayed in an organized, sensible manner, the better chance we have of finding something new to go on."

He supposed that made sense, even if it gave him an itch between his shoulder blades. If he hadn't promised Carlyle, he probably would have put it all back into the bag and told her to go.

As it was, all he could do was shove his hands into his pockets and watch Mary. "I guess I should help or something?"

"Not yet. I'm working up a system. I'll have some questions soon." She smiled up at him over a stack of papers. "I love to put order to things." And she wasn't lying. He could tell by how genuine that smile was.

The thought of trying to make order out of that mess made him want to run in the opposite direction. "You're a strange lady."

"Yes, so I've been told. Usually by people who will benefit from my excellent organization skills. Is your last name really Daniels?" she asked casually, already sorting through things, smoothing out crumpled papers and stacking them in a neat pile.

"Yeah," he muttered.

She didn't react to that information, just kept organizing and even started humming to herself.

She was clearly in her element and while it didn't make a lick of sense to him, he found himself watching her, mesmerized. Not by the efficient movements or even the humming.

It was the smile on her face. It was all that cool control he couldn't seem to get under—and both the admiration and frustration he felt in the face of it. And then there was something underneath all that—something he would have called a gut feeling if it had been bad.

But it wasn't. It was a very simple want.

He wanted it to be simple anyway. Because it wasn't that he *never* took any time for himself. When there were lulls in the case, he went out in the world and blew off some steam and had a good time. He wasn't a joyless robot—as Carlyle had once accused Zeke of being.

The problem was this was no lull, and Mary was no bar pickup. He'd always compartmentalized his life quite well. But Mary felt like soap to all that oil and water. She was mixing everything up.

"You don't have to watch me," she muttered after a while, though she'd never once looked up from her work. She was standing now, almost done turning the mound of papers into neat little piles.

"If it helps, I'm not watching you, per se."

"Oh, really, then what are you doing?"

He knew he should stop. Knew he shouldn't let that prim, cool question allow the lines to blur.

But if knowing something stopped people from doing things, there'd be a lot fewer problems in the world.

"Thinking about kissing you, actually."

He watched her reaction carefully. Wondering if she'd go all cool, or if she'd finally be irritated enough with him to fully snap.

She did still, but her cheeks turned a dark shade of pink. She cleared her throat and rearranged some papers he was pretty sure had already been arranged.

And said nothing. Which made him think that maybe, just maybe, his little ice queen had been thinking a bit about kissing him.

Since that amused him, he didn't let it go. "Just going to let that sit there, huh?"

"What else am I supposed to do?" she said, and there was a snap to her tone as she glared at him. "Kiss a man I barely know over all this paperwork about his mother's murder?"

Well, she could land a blow when she wanted to, couldn't she? He figured it was supposed to knock him back a step, but he'd grown up too rough not to admire a well-placed barb when it was deserved.

"This is like college all over again," she said, and her movements were agitated now, even as she reconcentrated on her little piles.

He could not for the life of him make sense of her comment. "You're going to need to explain that to me."

She blew out a frustrated breath, her hair fluttering with the move. This was definitely getting to her, and it was fascinating. The slow unravel.

"It's just… In Sunrise, everyone knows who I am. What I am. I went off to college and all the rules were different. People didn't know or care that I was Jack Hudson's little sister. Or Anna's boring big sister."

"You don't strike me as boring, Mary. Considering you didn't scream or fall apart when men were shooting at us for reasons you didn't even know."

She opened her mouth as if to make a counterpoint, but then she simply shut it. She looked at him with an expression he couldn't read. Something in his chest twisted and he realized he *wanted* to read it. Wanted to understand what put that odd cast to her eyes.

He knew he should keep his distance. He knew he should extricate himself from this conversation. But he moved toward her. He didn't stop it.

"You just don't understand," she insisted. So seriously, so intensely. Like it was an important truth she had to hang her hat on. "At least here in this little microcosm, I can't just be a random woman you think about…kissing." Her blush deepened, and she practically squeaked out the word. "I'm Jack the sheriff's sister, pretty intimidating. Or Anna's sister, not as pretty, not as interesting. I'm Dean and Laura Hudson's daughter—the *missing* and likely long dead Dean and Laura Hudson, that is. I can't just be—"

"You?" he supplied.

She sucked in a sharp breath, then let it out. Some of her mask was coming back. "I guess. But the thing is, I left. I went to college. And I didn't like it. I didn't like being away from home or my family or even those things I always looked at as negatives. I don't like the order of things upended. I *like* the way people see me here."

"Even if it isn't you?"

"That's the thing. It *is* me. It is all the things that make up me. And I like it better when people know, when they understand, when they..."

He heard a lot of words, a lot of insecurities in all this. He wasn't sure what it had to do with kissing her except that little bit about *the order of things*. She was careful. She was controlled.

And when other people were involved, as he knew all too well, your control got blown to hell. And sometimes it was easier to keep that distance than lose what little control you had on life.

"You like it better that way because that's when people stay at a safe distance?" He supposed, since he understood, he should stay at that safe distance.

But he didn't. He stepped closer. They might still be closer to strangers than anything else, but if he knew anything about Mary Hudson, it was that she didn't back down.

And she didn't. Even when her expression was a little lost as she looked up at him with a kind of sadness in her eyes. "I don't know how to navigate these things. The right course of action or how you're supposed to..."

"I've never heard anyone, not once in my life, use the word *navigate* or the phrase *course of action* to discuss kissing or attraction."

"Because I don't know how to *do* this sort of thing. You

look at me like that, say things like that. What the hell am I supposed to do?"

"How about this?" And then he went ahead and blew it all to hell and put his mouth to hers.

Chapter Seven

Mary had been kissed before. She tried to remind herself of this as Walker's mouth touched hers. As every last thought seemed to drain out of her mind. As his arms slid around her and drew her close and her whole body just relaxed into the great hard wall of him.

She forgot she shouldn't be kissing him. Forgot he was essentially a stranger. Because there was something just right about this moment. Like she'd been waiting for it, long before she'd ever laid eyes on Walker Daniels.

She had kissed men, rebuffed men. She knew how to handle people. She was an expert at getting exactly what she wanted out of a situation.

Which was probably the problem. Kissing him was like exploring some new world and she didn't have the first clue what she wanted out of it.

Except more.

His hands tangled in her hair and she slid her palms against the rough scrape of his unshaven jaw. Something hot, dangerous and wholly out of her control slithered through her. She dimly thought she should hate it, but it was too big, too right. Like she'd finally found something she'd been searching for all along.

He pulled gently away, and her heart was hammering and

her pulse scrambling and every last cell of her body was alive with some kind of impossible buzzing.

Walker was still essentially a stranger, and he'd kissed her. She'd kissed him back. She wanted to keep kissing him. When his mouth was on hers, she didn't feel the need to keep her hands so tightly on the reins of control.

Which was dangerous. So she opened her eyes, tried to find some of her usual command of a situation. Instead, she froze as, over Walker's shoulder, her gaze met the gray-blue eyes of a woman she didn't recognize. Just standing there in the doorway.

They weren't alone.

She cleared her throat. "Walker."

If she was gratified by anything in this very strange day of her life, it was the fact that clearly the kiss had affected him almost as much as it had her. He didn't move, didn't seem to realize they were being watched. His gaze was on her, like she was a puzzle he wanted to solve.

Or undress.

"Yeah?"

"There's a woman staring at us."

He turned slowly, though he didn't let her go.

"So, this is why you finally agreed to help." The woman eyed Mary up and down, but it wasn't malicious exactly. "Nice work, lady."

"Oh, well." Mary couldn't think of anything to say. Her brain was completely and utterly blank.

Walker's hands dropped then as he fully turned toward the woman. "What are you doing here? I told you to—"

A man entered behind the woman—and there was no doubt this was Walker's brother, which likely made the woman his sister. Walker and the man looked so much alike, carbon copies of each other. Dark features and big frames and a sort of grim wildness about them, wrapped up in a very careful, assessing package.

"Yeah, plans had to change," he said to Walker. His gaze flicked over Mary so fast she wasn't even sure it happened. "Things are getting a little hot. What did you stumble onto?"

"Stumble?" Walker scoffed as he walked over to them. "I don't stumble."

She knew sibling devotion. She had it. She was a part of it every day, and maybe that's what made witnessing this scene all the more poignant.

They wrapped their arms around each other. A trio. A unit. Clearly they hadn't seen each other in a while, and no matter the reasons they were seeing each other now, they were glad.

"Where's this new tattoo?" Walker asked the woman roughly.

"Don't worry about it." She nodded over at Mary. "You going to introduce us to your lip-lock partner, or what?"

Mary felt very out of place, and if they weren't huddled in the doorway, she likely would have escaped. But she was going to have to meet them eventually, discuss the case with them eventually.

Tell Jack about them sooner rather than later.

"Mary, this is my brother, Zeke. My sister, Carlyle. Guys, this is Mary Hudson. She's the HSS investigator Carlyle conned me into hiring."

"Not into kissing though."

"Knock it off, Car," Walker said, but it was all affection. There was a softness to him Mary hadn't witnessed—even during that kiss. Which hadn't been soft at all.

She really couldn't think about it. Not with all three Daniels siblings staring at her. So she clasped her hands, fixed a smile to her face. "Well, I'll extend the offer to the both of you that Walker refused. You're welcome to come stay at the main house. You don't need to rough it out here. But, if that's what you prefer, we'll be happy to accommodate."

"I'll stay at the main house," Carlyle said.

"No, you won't," Walker returned, a kind of authoritative growl Mary recognized as an older-brother thing.

Carlyle was clearly not impressed or swayed by it. "I'm not shoving in with you two grunting males. I escaped that, remember? Not going back unless we absolutely have to. And Mary here says we don't."

Walker glared at his sister, but she seemed impervious. She reminded Mary of Anna, though maybe a little more feral, and that made Mary smile.

"Well, then I'll take you up, Carlyle," Mary said, smiling blandly at Walker, even as he narrowed his eyes at her. "Perhaps you'd all consider coming to the big house for dinner so we can discuss the case." She began to arrange her piles together, slide them into the satchel. She'd look through them with Grant later, formulate a list of questions and threads to pull. Organize them into a binder.

She had a plan, and kissing Walker hadn't changed it.

"Dinner? Sounds fun," Carlyle said, grinning at her brothers—who clearly did not look like they thought it would be fun. But they didn't argue with her, so Mary tucked her satchel under her arm and moved over to the trio.

"Carlyle, how do you feel about horses?"

"Intrigued," she returned.

So Mary led her outside to Pippi, and gave Carlyle her first horseback ride. All the while deciding how she was going to explain the Daniels clan to her family.

And putting Walker's kiss as far out of her mind as possible.

WALKER WATCHED THEM GO. A lot of different emotions were twisting deep in his gut.

There was Carlyle, who he hadn't seen in a year, already swanning off to the Hudson residence and agreeing to dinner and more connection than he'd wanted to allow.

And Zeke, standing right next to him. As tall as him now. He'd lived his own life for years, having been seventeen when their mother was murdered. He'd done some work in the military, worked for some secret organization after that and was now fully dedicated, like Walker, to finding answers.

Walker worried about his brother, who he was quite certain never got distracted by pretty women or fun of any kind.

And speaking of women… There was Mary herself—a conundrum, one he couldn't even keep to himself because his siblings had seen evidence. He watched Mary and his sister disappear over the hill.

"I don't like it," he muttered.

"Why? Think Car's going to chew her up and spit her out?" Zeke asked, his thoughts on the matter carefully hidden behind a dry delivery.

"Mary can hold her own," Walker returned irritably. Carlyle was a pill, but she wasn't mean. Usually. Regardless, Mary was a handler. Even if Car proved to be a challenge, Mary would rise to the occasion. He had no doubt.

"Didn't look like it," Zeke said.

The comment shouldn't make him want to defend Mary, but he did. "Yeah, well, she's surprising like that."

"Something I should be concerned about?"

"What would be the concern?"

"That you're getting yourself wrapped up in a romance instead of a murder investigation."

Walker laughed. It was the word *romance*, which was so ludicrous he couldn't do anything but laugh. Still, his brother's harsh tone didn't amuse him. If anything, it worried him.

"I can kiss a woman and investigate all at the same time, and if you can't, you might want to reconsider your life choices."

Zeke scowled. "I know Car's the one who pushed for help, and I can see you're on board, but I've still got some reservations."

"You wouldn't be you if you didn't. I've still got reservations myself." And they'd been made more complicated by kissing

Mary, but Zeke didn't need to know that. "Why did you come right away when I told you to wait? I wanted to make sure—"

"I know, I know. That we weren't followed. That's the problem. I almost didn't see my tail, but I picked him up over in Cody. I called in a friend from my North Star days. Got the tail off me over in Hardy by using him as a body double, but these guys were close and careful. So, Car and I had to act fast before they caught wind again. We've got to hunker down real low until we're sure what we want our next steps to be, and I think those steps should be together. Even if Carlyle hates the idea."

"Agreed there."

"But adding all these people isn't exactly laying low, is it?"

"They're trained investigators, Zeke. Been at this even longer than us and they are far more organized and connected." And why the hell was he defending them when he hadn't wanted to use them in the first place? But he'd promised Carlyle, and… Well, if it had something to do with Mary, so what? "They know how to lay low, and I've explained to Mary how dangerous it is. She stumbled into it quite by accident. She was there when they shot at me."

Zeke's eyebrows rose at that.

"And she held her own. She's not quite as delicate as she appears."

"I'm going to repeat myself. Is this something I should be concerned about?"

The whole warm, loving sensation of actually seeing his siblings in person for the first time in a year was starting to wear off. Real quick.

"Do you not trust me, Zeke?" Walker said in his offhanded way. He didn't let any of the tension winding through him leak out in his voice.

Zeke grunted irritably. "I've seen a few too many people do dumb shit over soft feelings for someone."

Soft feelings. He wasn't sure that's how he'd characterize what he felt for Mary. That kiss had been a little more complicated than soft, but there was enough truth there, and enough worry he *would* end up doing something stupid, he could hardly fault his brother for the concern.

So he changed the subject. "Carlyle pushed for this. She won't say it. Maybe she hasn't even admitted it to herself, but I can hear it. She's tired. She's lonely. She's almost twenty-three years old and hasn't had a second of normal. I'd like to live long enough to give her some normal."

Zeke only grunted in response.

"Maybe this HSS doesn't do anything for us. What's the harm? They get me killed? I've spent years keeping myself from that eventuality. I can keep doing it."

"You trying to convince me or yourself?"

Walker laughed, clapped his brother on the shoulder. "Both of us, obviously."

Zeke almost cracked a smile. But it quickly morphed back into a frown and he sighed. "We're going to have to go for dinner."

"Why the hell would we do that?" Walker replied, shocked his brother would even suggest it. He didn't want to be cozying up to the Hudsons any more than he had to.

Or you want to keep your distance from Mary since you can't seem to keep your mouth to yourself.

Well, maybe some of both.

"We can't leave Carlyle alone with those people for too long," Zeke said. "She's a feral raccoon at best. And those fancy digs up there? Not feral raccoon material."

Zeke wasn't exactly wrong, but as Walker himself also wasn't much better than a feral varmint, the comment stuck under his skin. "You're too hard on her."

"You indulge her."

An old argument, so old, so part of who they'd become that it felt good to have it. Familiar and right. And somehow, together, he figured they'd done okay. Carlyle wasn't perfect, but she was definitely her own woman.

For good or for ill.

Walker heaved out a sigh. "All right then. Let's go."

Chapter Eight

Mary settled Carlyle into one of the guest rooms. The woman
didn't have much, but she seemed comfortable enough. Mary
tried to get a read on the young woman, but it was difficult.
Though she did remind Mary of Anna, there was something
harder about Carlyle. And more… Well, the only word she
could think of was *wild*. Just like Walker himself. Like nothing had quite tamed them into fitting in with the world.

Mary didn't know why that made her feel strangely protective of them. After all, Walker had been the protector when it
came to that shooting in his apartment, and his siblings were
obviously equal to the task of taking care of themselves.

But they just seemed in need of some tending.

"If your brothers decide to come for dinner—"

"Oh, they'll come," Carlyle replied, peering out the window, then back at Mary.

Mary was a little taken aback by Carlyle's certainty. Usually, she wouldn't press on a client. It was her job to smooth
things over and make everyone comfortable. Not dig deeper.
But… "How do you know?"

"Because the thought of me up here, by myself, doing what
I do—which is often saying whatever I want to say, no matter
how inappropriate—will shock and concern them both enough
to do what they don't want to and come up here to play nanny
and chaperone." She took a seat on the bed, gave it a little

bounce. "They'll both sleep out in that cabin to be stubborn, and they won't be able to talk me into joining them, though they'll try. But I'm just as stubborn as they are."

"I told Walker he was stubborn for the sake of being stubborn."

"That's a Daniels specialty," Carlyle said. Proudly. But then she fixed Mary with a certain kind of considering stare that made Mary want to fidget.

She didn't, of course.

"So, should I ask you your intentions with my brother?"

Mary tried very hard not to react. She'd spent a lifetime with Anna so she knew what it was like to deal with people who wanted to shock you. Still, when it came to Walker, her usual impervious mask was hard to hold on to. "Intentions?"

"You're just not really his type." She cocked her head, studying Mary as if she could determine what Walker might see in her. "So I was just wondering what you were getting out of the whole thing."

Mary's chin lifted. She tried to soften her expression, but it was difficult. It shouldn't put her back up—because it was *meant* to—but she didn't really want to hear about Walker's *type*. "I'm sure growing up the way you have, you're all very protective of one another. I can appreciate that. My siblings have a similar relationship."

"That's not an answer."

"No, it isn't," Mary replied. Firmly.

Carlyle laughed. "I just might like you, Mary."

"Yes. Well." What was there to say to that? Or about her intentions? Nothing. But there was plenty to say about the tasks at hand.

"I understand that your brothers are reluctant. And I'm sure there's nothing I can say to either of them to make them feel like involving HSS is a good idea. They're doing it for you."

Carlyle got a strange look on her face at that.

"So, I just wanted to say that I hope *you* feel confident in working with us and understand that my family and I can't possibly promise results, but we do promise to work very hard toward finding answers."

Carlyle didn't move, didn't break eye contact. Just studied Mary, as if is she watched long enough, she'd catch her in a lie. "Do you remember your parents?" she asked after a long stretch of quiet.

Mary was taken off guard but knowing that Carlyle had been through something similar with her parents softened her more than alarmed her. "Yes. I was ten years old when they disappeared. Some days it feels like they're slipping away and I barely remember what their voices sounded like, and some days it's like that was yesterday. I can smell them, hear them, feel them. I didn't go through exactly what you went through, Carlyle, but I understand. And I'll do everything I can to get you the answers you all deserve."

Carlyle breathed out a sigh and looked around the room. "I'm not sure what anyone deserves." She shook her head. "I love my brothers. I'm acutely aware of how much they gave up for me, and how hard they tried to make sure I didn't know that. They're both a pain in my ass, but they're the best men I've ever met. And they've been doing this too long. Walker is getting too close. He's going to get himself killed, and I think… I think in the back of his head, he's okay with that, if it gets us answers."

Mary felt her heart stutter at that. "I would not be okay with that," she said, though God knew why. She'd known the man for no time at all. And yes, he'd kissed her, and yes, she understood his life—and vice versa—in ways it was difficult for others to, but…

But what?

"Yeah, I'm not okay with it either. That's why I first contacted you guys. I want them safe. I want Walker safe." She finally met Mary's gaze again. "And you complicate that."

Mary blinked, taken aback. "How?"

"Well, if he's kissing you, I imagine that means he'll be wanting to keep *you* safe. So, he'll do a bunch of dumb macho stuff to ensure that you are. And no offense, Mary, you don't seem like the type of woman who knows how to keep herself safe."

Mary tried not to be offended, but it didn't work. "You'd be surprised what type of woman I am, Carlyle. Now, I have some work to do and dinner to prepare. You're free to use whatever facilities you see fit. If you're hungry, we'll eat in the dining room at six."

And Mary, far more impolitely than she should have been, turned and left, without even asking if Carlyle had any questions.

MARY PUT ALL her discomfort, worry and anxiety into preparing dinner. The familiar preparations soothed her—and took her mind off what Walker expected her to do.

And telling Jack about…everything.

Until Jack came into the kitchen, as he often did about fifteen minutes before dinner. To catch up on the day.

Jack was almost eight years older than her, but somehow they'd become the de facto parents of the family. Even if she was younger, she was the oldest girl. So they, probably more than anyone else, conferred and worked in tandem.

"Why are there three extra plates set for dinner?" he asked casually.

Mary looked up from her cooking preparations. He was dressed in his sheriff's uniform—utility pants and a perfectly pressed polo shirt with the Sunrise SD logo on it. He looked the same as he always did, but the older he got, the more he looked like their father.

Which made her feel extra guilty. It reminded her of when she'd made all the plans to leave to go to college in secret—because she hadn't wanted to tell Jack she was leaving. Hadn't wanted to face his wanting her to stay.

He'd been wonderful and supportive, of course, but Mary supposed she was always waiting to disappoint him somehow.

Who knew why. It really didn't bear thinking about.

So she fixed a smile on her face. "We have some new HSS clients and I invited them to dinner. One of them is going to stay in the big house with us, and the other two are going to stay out in the foreman's cabin."

Jack frowned. "This is a lot of new information I haven't heard anything about."

"You've been at work. It's been an…evolving situation."

"What's the case?"

"A murder from ten years ago. The kids of the murdered woman have been looking into it on their own and have gotten close, but no clear breaks."

"Grant taking lead?"

Mary looked back at her roast, began to get out the serving plates. "Well…"

"It's his turn."

"Yes, it is, but there's a slight…hiccup there. It's been requested that I be the lead investigator on this case." She counted out forks.

"You don't investigate."

"Not as a rule, no," Mary agreed easily as she shooed him out of the way so she could open the oven and pull the roast out. "But this time I will be."

Jack was quiet, and the silence stretched out, but Mary focused on transferring the roast to the serving platter. On sprinkling some cheese on top of the twice-baked potatoes. On anything but Jack.

"Mary…"

"I can handle an investigation now and again. It's hardly something to get hung up on. They've done a lot of work themselves, so it's more helping to organize, maybe finding a pattern they haven't noticed. I'll be consulting you all. In fact,

I've already got Anna compiling some things for me. Nothing to concern yourself over."

"You may be able to fool the rest of them, but I was there." She hated that his voice was soft, gentle. Hated that she knew exactly what he was referring to.

"I was eighteen," Mary returned. She'd insisted she be given a case back then, before she'd left for college. She'd insisted Jack let her in because she'd wanted to be a part of it. Wanted to help, see if maybe she could swallow the idea of staying in Sunrise. She'd wanted to do more than cook and clean and organize.

At the time.

But she hadn't been able to take it. No matter how she'd dug, how many questions she'd asked, how many hours she'd put in, she'd never been able to find answers on that case he'd given her.

Then Jack had swept in and found them in twenty-four hours. He'd never acted disappointed—but how could he have not been?

"Yes. I believe I even pointed out your age at the time," Jack returned. Still way too gently. "And you vowed to never, ever, no matter what, take on another case. That it wasn't for you. You were very adamant."

Mary turned to face her brother, because facing him down was the only way she got through to him. "Yes. And at the time, I felt all that. But I'm older now. I understand more. I went away to college and learned something about…failing on my own without someone to sweep up my mistakes."

"Name one time you've failed since you came back home." He smiled a little, but Mary didn't find it funny. It made her chest seize. She wanted to turn away and cry.

But Hudsons had never had that luxury. She pointed at her arm, where she'd been shot last month. "Palmer and Anna knew not to run out there. I was the dumb one."

His smile died. "It isn't dumb to want to save your brother and niece."

"It was in the moment. I should have known better. I fail now and again, and I may very well fail this. But they wanted me or they weren't going to accept help and they need help."

"It isn't your job to save everyone."

Mary cocked her head and narrowed her eyes. "Because it's yours?"

Jack sighed. Heavily. "I'll go get washed up if that's all the news."

"It is."

He moved to leave but paused in the doorway, then looked back at her. "Why do they want *you* to do it?"

"Because I'm the one who tracked them down about the money. The Joe Beck money, if you recall. I guess that lends me an air of trustworthiness to them. It's a complicated case, and a dangerous one."

Jack nodded thoughtfully, and it gave Mary too much time to think. To worry. To want to smooth it all over.

"They're three siblings and they're coming to dinner. I just want you to be…"

Jack raised an eyebrow, waiting for her to finish the sentence. But Mary was struggling to find the right word.

"How about nice?" she said finally. She smiled brightly while he continued to stare blankly at her.

"I'm always nice," he finally said flatly.

She was sure he thought that about himself, but poor Jack was hopelessly un-self-aware. It came from too many years of putting others first. Yes, she knew a bit about that. "No. You're always polite. There's a difference."

He scowled at her, so she smiled cheerfully even though she didn't feel cheerful. Or happy. She felt strung tight. Anxious and twisted in a million knots most decidedly not under her control.

But no one would ever know that.

Chapter Nine

Walker stared at the big, cozy-looking house in front of him, hands shoved deep in his pockets. When he glanced over at Zeke, his brother was in the same stance.

"We could just let Carlyle horrify them all," Zeke said after a while.

Walker sighed. It was tempting. Certainly better than trying to run herd on the demon that was his baby sister. But as annoying as it might be, this wasn't so much about Carlyle's feral manners as it was about what Carlyle might say to Mary that could alter Mary's opinion of him.

Not that he had any clue what Mary's actual opinion of him was, or why he was letting that matter.

Before he could say anything or make a decision either way, he heard a dog bark, followed by another and then another. He turned to look and saw two people and three dogs walking toward the house. And toward him and Zeke.

It must be more of Mary's family, and Walker didn't know why that made him tense. He usually didn't worry about handling people—he'd spent a lifetime learning how to maneuver, charm and get what he wanted out of just about anyone.

But everything about the Hudson Ranch made him feel like someone else altogether.

The man approached and stopped in front of them. It didn't take any great detective work to identify him as one of Mary's brothers—and not the cop. He was tall and broad, but scruffy. His gaze was assessing like a cop, but there was something else about him that didn't give off cop or military vibes.

The little girl behind him that he was clearly shielding from Walker and Zeke poked her head around her father's body, and Walker couldn't help but smile.

She looked a hell of a lot like Mary.

"You must be the new client." The man looked him up and down, then Zeke, while three dogs sat at attention as if on some kind of silent command.

Walker had to give himself a little internal shake to find some semblance of who he usually was. He smiled, held out a hand. "Walker Daniels."

"We're doing real names?" Zeke muttered behind him, quiet enough that only Walker heard. When the man turned to Zeke, Zeke did not smile, but he did hold out his hand. "Zeke."

The man shook it and nodded. "Cash Hudson. This is my daughter." He did not offer the daughter's name.

Still, Walker grinned at her. "Hi."

"Hi," she replied with a smile of her own.

This seemed to cause Cash to scowl, but he made a waving motion with his arm. "Come on in then."

Walker shared a look with Zeke, but there was really no other option but to follow the man, and his daughter and dogs, inside.

They were led into the big dining room that was already teeming with people. The huge table was set all fancy like. Some people sat at it, some people stood, all deep in conversation.

That slowly died out as everyone became cognizant of Walker and Zeke standing there. Walker scanned the little crowd for Mary, but she didn't appear to be in the room. Though Carlyle was, and she immediately walked over and crouched in front of the dogs.

They sat obediently while Carlyle petted them and elicited

some face licks. The little girl watched Carlyle closely, while the adults all remained quiet.

Until Carlyle wrapped her arms around one of the dogs, clearly in heaven. "Oh, my God. I love them."

"We have lots more," the girl informed her earnestly.

"You, my friend, are living the dream."

The girl beamed at this.

Walker was quite certain silence would have returned after that, but Mary swept in carrying a huge platter. "So, you did decide to come," she greeted cheerfully. She placed the platter on the table and the delicious scents of food quickly filled the room.

Walker was concerned his stomach might rumble. But he forgot all about his stomach when Mary beamed that smile at him. He didn't have the first earthly clue why she took his breath away, only that she did.

"Everyone, that's Walker on the left and Zeke on the right. Now, you come on in and sit and I'll introduce everyone else," Mary said, waving a hand. "Dinner is ready."

There was nothing else to do but find a seat at the table like everyone else was doing. Carlyle had no problem plopping herself right in the middle of things, but Walker and Zeke held back, waiting for the family to take what he presumed were their usual seats before sitting next to each other on one side.

Mary introduced everyone by name, if not relationship. He knew she had four older brothers, and he'd met Cash. The three other brothers weren't hard to pick out—especially the sheriff and the former military one. Of all of the siblings, the only one he might have struggled with was the sister, but since he'd already met her, it was easy to see how she fit. And how the redhead and the black-haired looker didn't really.

But no matter how they were all related, he didn't miss the suspicious glances he and Zeke received.

But there was also just the very normal activity of a family and some strangers settling down to a meal. Everyone passed around plates, and while conversation didn't exactly resume, there was the easy, normal hum of scraping silverware and requests to pass the salt.

"I've been organizing your research," Mary said, serving herself some salad. She seemed to be the last to be handed every plate, and just took whatever was left over. Except for the rolls. She put the last one on the little girl's plate without saying anything. "Anna's been doing some work from the computer side of things. With her and Palmer's expertise, we might be able to dig into some records that you might not have access to. Carlyle was saying that's one area where you guys have struggled."

"It's more an access issue than an area of struggle," Walker responded pleasantly. "But definitely not something we've been able to utilize effectively."

"Well, we have plenty of access to offer," Mary replied. Her smile was pleasant and polite and Walker understood she was offering it to all of them. But it felt like it was for him, and he was really going to need to get his head screwed on straight.

"It'll take a few days to get fully up to speed on your case," Jack said from his spot at the head of the table. He had such a sheriff way about him and Walker tried very hard not to bristle at the authority in his tone. Of course, both his siblings were scowling, so he knew he wasn't the only one.

"But HSS doesn't have any other cases right now to split our focus. Lots of hands on deck. Mary says you've been investigating yourself for quite a few years."

In a manner of speaking. "Yeah. We worked with the police for the first few." Walker tried to keep the bitterness out of his tone since this guy was the police, but it was hard to maintain the casual smile and relaxed posture. "But there's only so much they can do and for so long."

Jack didn't seem to take offense to that. He nodded. "That's usually where we come in. Mary says this one is dangerous."

Walker nodded. "Someone is definitely out there willing

to hurt anyone who exposes the truth. But that's how I know we're on the right track."

"We've got plenty of security here. It's not foolproof. Nothing ever is, but it's safe here, and you're welcome to use everything we have to offer until we get you some answers."

Welcome. It felt like he was being given the king's approval, and Walker was peasant enough to want to thumb his nose at it. He grinned. "Thanks, Sheriff."

Jack's expression cooled a little at that, but then Mary swept in and changed the topic of conversation so that it turned into just a family dinner. It allowed Walker to get a measure of all the Hudsons, something that came easily to him.

Once dinner was over, there was still dessert and lingering conversation. Walker had expected to want to bolt, that it would be a kind of stiff, stifled, uptight affair for rich people.

But there was something easy about all this. A sort of magnified version of the dinners he used to have with his siblings. There was teasing and sarcasm and an easy camaraderie, albeit one likely born of trauma.

But Walker could tell Zeke was chomping at the bit to leave, so once everyone was done with dessert, Walker got up and excused himself so Zeke could follow suit. He asked Carlyle if she really planned to stay up here in a low voice no one else heard.

But she only laughed at him. Walker sighed and he and Zeke left out the door they'd come in. They'd gotten down the porch and maybe a few feet across the yard when Walker heard the door open.

"Walker?"

Walker stopped, turned to see Mary striding across the little porch and toward them.

"I'll leave you to it," Zeke muttered.

"You don't have to…" But Zeke was already walking away. So Walker was standing in the pretty spring evening, watching Mary walk toward him in the moonlight. Something clutched in his chest, so foreign and confusing all he could do was stare as she approached.

Mary frowned at Zeke's quickly disappearing form. "He didn't have to go."

"No, but he seemed to want to."

Her eyes lifted to his. "I'm sorry if that was overwhelming. I'd hoped it might be reassuring."

"It was. I like your family. Even the cop."

She smiled at that. "So do I."

He saw in her expression everything he felt for his own siblings. It ate at him. "I'm not sure you guys understand what kind of target you might be putting on your backs."

Mary took her time responding. He supposed she was thinking over the perfect words to say. She was careful that way. Careful but somehow not afraid of throwing herself into the midst of danger with a virtual stranger, and it was something about that dichotomy that had him way too interested. Too attached.

"We've been targets before. We'll likely be targets again. That's sort of the price to pay for looking for the truth of ugly things." She smiled up at him, if sadly. "It's worth it to try. We know how hard it is to never have the truth."

That sat there in silence for a while, because he didn't know what to say to her. It was hard to believe what she'd been through after sharing a meal with her family. And yet, he understood. It didn't matter how bad life got, all you could do was march on. Find some new normal. Whether you wanted to or not.

Usually not. So why this felt like a want he didn't know. Just that a few days of Mary in his life made him want a new normal where she could turn that prim smile on him.

"Take a walk with me," he said, without thinking it through. Without weighing all the cons of getting mixed up with the woman who was allegedly going to help him solve this decade-old mystery.

She looked back at the house. He didn't think it was so much a consideration of escape as a woman looking back at all her responsibilities and wondering if she could afford to let them go.

"All right."

MARY NEVER STUCK around for cleanup, but it still felt weird leaving her family behind to meander around the property with Walker. Or maybe it felt weird to want to walk around in the dark with a man she barely knew.

Except there was something about Walker that felt like she *did* know him. He had aliases, had lived life chasing a murderer, so no doubt he was a good actor.

She just never felt like he was acting with her. Carlyle? Yes. Zeke didn't put on an act, just froze everyone out.

And in the middle of that was Walker, who wore a mask most definitely. Who was careful when it came to her family. But she felt like she saw behind those walls.

And you are no doubt fooling yourself.

"Your sister clearly loves animals," she offered because it felt like a safe topic to talk about with a man who made her insides jangle like she was made of bells under her skin.

"Yeah, I tried to get her a dog once, but… We just never had the kind of life that made that feasible. Still, we made it work for a few years before he ran off."

It was that, she supposed, that drew her to him. Those offhanded comments about what he'd done for his siblings. What he'd endured. Like it was just what you did. When she knew that there were plenty of people in the world who wouldn't.

"You sure she's okay there in your big house? She can be…" He trailed off and Mary could practically read his thoughts. He didn't want to bad-talk his sister, but he also had concerns about her behavior, just as Carlyle had said.

"I would have hoped dinner tonight would have eased some of your worries. My siblings are a loud, opinionated, not easily offended lot. However Carlyle decides to act, I'm sure we can take it. And I hope you understand that you and Zeke are welcome to join her."

"I know he won't. And I don't think I'd be able to relax."

"Understandable," she said, clasping her hands in front of her as they walked. And she did understand. It would drive her crazy to go to someone else's house and walk around like a guest.

Because you're a control freak.

Well, yes. But that was neither here nor there.

What *was* here, and why she had agreed to walk with him—aside from the very simple reason that she'd wanted to spend time with him alone—was the hope she could convince him to trust Grant or even Jack with the case.

So she didn't have to have the same obnoxious conversation with every member of her family reminding her she'd sworn never to take on another case.

She'd walked him toward the stables without meaning to, but they, like the house, were two places she felt comfortable. In control.

She stopped walking and turned to face him. If she was one of her more fanciful friends—take Chloe, for example—she might have said he looked like a pirate here in the moonlight. All dark features and dangerous glints.

But he was just a man.

And you are just a woman.

She blew out a breath and forced her shoulders back. She could feign bravery. "I feel like I have to say this one more time. I know you trust me, and you want me to lead this case. I understand, to an extent. But now that you've met my family, surely you can see they're just as trustworthy and capable and far more adept at handling cases."

He seemed to think it over—which she appreciated. No jumping to automatic denial. He was listening, and much like after hearing his story about Carlyle and getting her a dog, her heart softened.

And the rest of her softened when he reached out and stroked a finger down her cheek. "I think you're plenty adept."

Her heart was beating overtime, especially when he didn't remove his finger. Just left it there on her jaw like he couldn't quite part with the contact. She swallowed, hoping her voice would come out sounding remotely firm. "At some aspects, yes. Organization and research. Maybe I'll even find something that helps. But I... I tried to lead a case once. Investigate. I put everything into it and I couldn't find an answer."

"You and your brother made it clear answers aren't a guarantee."

"They aren't. And when I'm not involved, I can deal with that. But when I'm in charge? I can't handle it. It's like softball."

"Well, you've lost me there."

"Failure is part of the game. Sometimes you strike out, no matter how hard you work. I didn't last a season because striking out just *killed* me. I can't... I can't *stand* that kind of routine, accepted failure even when it's just a *game*. When it's a case? It's too important. I want—I need to do everything right."

He studied her, here in the dark. She could hear the faint noises of horses inside the stables, and usually that would offer some comfort, but he was so quiet. His eyebrows drawn together, his expression so serious.

Then he stepped forward and took her hands in his. "One of the lessons I've learned ten years on is that there is no failure. There's only quitting or death. I'm not quitting and I can't control death, so... Nothing is final. Nothing is a failure."

Her heart stuttered over the word *death*, but she supposed he had a point. But it didn't change her point. "I'm not good at it."

"I bet you're not if you gave up after one try."

She couldn't help the little thread of hurt that worked

through her. Who was he to agree with her that she wasn't any good at it? But before she could cool her anger and come up with a suitable, polite rejoinder, he kept talking.

"You guys work on it however you need to, okay? But you shouldn't hold yourself back because you're afraid of failing." His fingers moved across her knuckles. "All that does is hold you back from succeeding."

She could only stare at him. It wasn't scolding so much as advice. Passed-along wisdom maybe.

Since she was the one used to doling out both of those things, she didn't know how to react. He seemed to wade through all her carefully erected walls and foundations and poke them at will. So she was on wobbly ground when she was *never* on wobbly ground.

He stepped closer. "I don't want to talk about the case anymore."

"Oh." This strange spark with Walker was way beyond her experience, but she very much understood the way that heated, intense eye contact made her feel. Decidedly wobbly. "W-what do you want to talk about?"

"The fact that I can't seem to stop thinking about kissing you."

"Oh." She had no idea why she didn't have anything smarter to say. Anything seductive or at least witty.

But apparently she didn't need to say anything, because he pulled her close and pressed his lips to hers. Like it was just a normal thing to do. A normal, *necessary* thing to do. Like breathing.

This kiss wasn't like the one at the cabin—all heat and urgency. This was a slow, drugging savor. His hands touched her face, his fingers rough from whatever work he did, but the touch itself gentle too. Until her knees felt like jelly and she simply had to lean into him or melt into the ground.

His hands slid down her back, everything so tender she

thought she might cry, and she didn't know why. Or what to do with it. Except kiss him back. Hold on to him.

When he finally pulled away, she looked up at him wondering what he'd done to her. Wondering how something like this happened. And there was this strange, stark, retroactive understanding of some of the things Anna had told her about her relationship with Hawk that hadn't made sense in the moment. That you could *feel* things without knowing why or how. That those feelings might eradicate rational thought.

Though Walker had eased his mouth away from hers, he still held her close to him. He was looking at her seriously, like he too was confused. Trying to put together the puzzle of whatever this was.

There was only one thing Mary knew for certain. "This probably isn't very professional of me."

Walker threw his head back and laughed, but he didn't let her go. He held her close and Mary… She didn't know what the hell she was doing, and it was scary, sure, but she was discovering that scary didn't make her want to run away.

At least with Walker.

"Just promise me you'll stay involved, all right?" he said softly. And she knew he didn't mean the kiss, he meant the case. She didn't want to make the promise. But how could she not?

She nodded against his shoulder.

He walked her back to the big house. He didn't kiss her again, but he squeezed her hand, then started out in the dark. She worried about him finding the cabin in a place he barely knew, but he seemed so confident. So in control.

And she had the sinking feeling as she went inside that it wouldn't matter how involved or not she was with the case.

If they didn't find him and his family answers, she was going to bear the weight of it for the rest of her life.

Chapter Ten

For the first time in his life, Walker got used to something. It sneaked up on him, day after day. That he had a routine. That he liked learning about the Hudson Ranch. That letting someone into the investigation he'd been running for ten years felt like relief.

Like all these years he'd only needed to stop. Look around the world. Breathe. And things would have been more tenable. More like life and less like a constant race toward and away from danger all at the same time.

He didn't allow himself to dwell on regrets. Or maybe this new world didn't allow it, because how could he regret anything that had led him to Mary?

He wasn't stupid enough to think too deeply about it. He enjoyed each moment as they came. Late-night walks. Kisses in the dark, in the stables, anywhere he could get her alone for a few seconds. He didn't think about feelings, about the future.

It would complicate things.

So he just took it day by day. Eating with the Hudsons, meeting with Mary and whatever sibling had done something for the case that day. Even horse-riding lessons, because Carlyle had desperately wanted to learn, and Walker just wasn't fully comfortable with the amount of time she was spending with Mary. So he'd pretended like he wanted to learn too.

Of course Carlyle was a natural and he was not, and it irritated the hell out of him. So much he'd tried to convince Zeke to join them.

But Zeke refused. Walker knew Zeke did not share this newfound sense of domesticity. That lying low on the Hudson Ranch while they poked at things from computers and combed through old reports they'd been through a hundred times was Zeke's worst nightmare.

The man wanted to act, and Walker understood that. Even if he'd crossed some bridge where what he really wanted was to rest.

So he didn't say anything to Zeke even though he knew his brother was sneaking off doing his own investigations, not letting anyone into what they were—even Carlyle.

Walker could have pushed, but pushing Zeke never got anyone anywhere.

The Daniels siblings and pushing did not go hand in hand.

"Maybe you should give Walker private lessons. He sucks," Carlyle said from where she sat in the saddle of her favorite horse. A gray animal named Robinson.

"Yeah, maybe you should," Walker said, flashing a grin down at Mary, whose cheeks turned a pretty shade of pink.

Carlyle rolled her eyes. "Gross." She swept off the horse in an easy, fluid motion that made Walker scowl. He still couldn't quite manage that effortless movement.

"Your turn, Walker," Mary said pleasantly from where she stood next to her horse, having also dismounted with ease. "Remember. Relax. It's an easy, instinctual move."

Too bad his instincts with horses sucked, as Carlyle said. But he was not a quitter. He used what Mary had taught him over the past few weeks and managed a decent enough dismount, if decidedly not relaxed or easy.

"That's much improved," Mary said, like a kindergarten teacher might to a kid who'd finally mastered writing his name—with backward letters anyway.

Walker grunted and they began the process of leading the

horses back into the stables. But Mary's phone chimed and she paused as she pulled it out of her shirt pocket and frowned at the screen. "Anna needs me back at the house."

"She okay?" Walker asked, because he could tell Mary was concerned.

"I'm sure she's fine. She didn't say it was an emergency. Just to come back." Mary tried to smile, but Walker could see the worry around her eyes.

"We've got the horses," Carlyle assured Mary, reaching over to take Mary's reins. "You can always come check to make sure after you're done."

Mary nodded. "All right."

Walker would give her credit, she didn't hesitate. She left, which no doubt made Carlyle feel like Mary thought she could handle it.

However, she did look back over her shoulder once. But Walker liked to think that was about him, not the horses. Because she smiled at him, then shook her head a little and turned back to the house.

The sun tinged her dark hair red as it swung behind her. She moved for the house in long, purposeful strides. All that economical movement should *not* be a turn-on, but everything about her got to him.

He could feel Carlyle studying him so he wrenched his gaze from Mary—and boy did it feel like a wrenching—and turned his attention to tending his horse the way Mary had been teaching him.

At first, they did their work quietly, but eventually Carlyle spoke. "You know, I've never thought I could say this to you before."

"What?" Walker asked, grooming the horse carefully.

Carlyle was silent for a long, stretched-out moment. When she spoke, her voice was soft, uncertain. It reminded him of the time before she'd grown into her personality. When she'd had nightmares and worried someone was out to hurt her—just like they'd hurt their mother.

"We could just…let it go. Not find out. Start life over, and just let it go." She didn't look at him. She stared straight ahead at the horse's flank.

Walker was speechless. He could only stare at her, one hand on his horse and one hand hanging limply at his side. "But someone is after us. I don't think that goes away just because we stop. And you know Zeke won't stop. And we can't just let someone get away with it." He thought better of the way he phrased that, but only after he'd said it. She didn't have to be part of that *we*, not if she didn't want to.

Carlyle nodded, but she kept her head uncharacteristically tipped down. "Yeah."

"Car…"

"No, I get it. And you're right. It's just… This is nice." She focused hard on the task at hand. "It's been a while since we had nice."

Walker couldn't focus on his horse. He could only look at his baby sister, who'd never had a second of normal. He'd always wanted to give it to her, but he supposed as she'd gotten older he'd sort of forgotten. Because she was just so different. So herself. He'd thought she'd been just as wrapped up in finding their mother's killer as he had always been.

But clearly she wasn't. "*You* could. You don't have to be involved."

"Yes, I do," she muttered. Then she smiled at him, but it didn't reach her eyes. And something about the whole exchange stuck with him. Ate at him. He couldn't help feeling like there was something else in play. Something he didn't know.

Something he needed to.

MARY WALKED INTO the house, a mixture of worry and concern cooling all the sunny warmth she'd felt in the little horseback riding lesson with Carlyle and Walker. It was her favorite part of the day.

Well, second favorite. Taking walks around the property with Walker after dinner was her favorite. Because inevitably that led to… She didn't know what to call it exactly. *Making out* sounded so high school. All she knew was that she liked it. It was exciting and fun and didn't come weighed down with questions of what came next. With the responsibilities of adulthood and real life they'd have to face at some point.

She wondered if either one of them would ever push for that next step, or if they were both too afraid. She liked this little routine. It felt like if she didn't push for anything, it could always stay just like this.

Which she knew was foolish. Not to mention, it was not the time to think about it. Her sister had asked her to come back to the house and Mary couldn't fathom a reason that would be good.

She opened the door and stepped inside, not letting her worry get the better of her. "Anna?"

"In the living room."

Mary hurried into the room, where Anna and Hawk sat, hip to hip, on the couch. They were leaning over a computer screen and some pieces of paper were spread out on the coffee table.

When she entered, they moved in a kind of unison that reminded Mary of her parents. Oh, Anna and Hawk were nothing like her parents individually, but something about the way they were with each other spoke of a partnership much longer than the time they'd actually been together. Like they'd been made to fit, just like this. Anna's bump getting bigger, and Hawk's overall health improving every day.

"Palmer finally got his hands on those financial records you wanted," Anna said.

Mary tried not to tense. She hadn't been able to write Walker's father completely off. So many times a woman got murdered it was by a partner or a former partner. Add abuse to the equation, and Mary just figured it was a good line to tug. So, she'd had Palmer look into Don Daniels.

Now, irrationally, she wished she hadn't.

"The cops were right, there's nothing off about his financial situation around the period of the murder, but we looked a lot farther than that," Hawk said.

"There's a pretty hefty deposit in his account—for no discernible reason—six years *after* the murder," Anna said. "Palmer's working on figuring out who paid him, but it's the first real hint we've had to go on."

Because if he'd been inexplicably paid a large sum, even if it was a time later, it was off. A strange circumstance that needed looking into.

She'd have to be the one to tell Walker they needed to look deeper into his father. She doubted he'd be *angry* about that, since he'd been clear that Don had abused him and Zeke.

But still, she didn't want to be the one who had to tell him and taint all the *nice* of the past few weeks. Which was pure cowardice.

She had Anna and Hawk show her the financial records. Not only was there a curious lump sum deposited about six years after Walker's mother's murder, but there were a few smaller ones from the same place, a name that didn't exist, after that.

She went and talked to Palmer about what he was finding on the payer.

"It's very hidden," he said, tapping his fingers next to the computer keyboard. "Which means it's a good thread to follow, but also that I've got to be careful. Which takes time."

Mary nodded.

"I'm also looking into the possibility of aliases for Don Daniels. He mostly disappears about four years ago. No record of death or imprisonment or anything, so I've got to wonder if he's out there under a different name."

A different name. Like Walker used. She tried to just absorb the information. Not jump to conclusions. Not worry about how it would make Walker feel, and what she could do to cushion those feelings.

Palmer studied her. "You okay?"

"Of course."

"You know, when you get personally involved in a case—"

"I don't need lectures, Palmer," she said, with too much snap in her tone, because obviously Palmer would read into that. And be right.

Palmer stood, slipped his arm around her shoulders as he led her out of the small room. "Lectures are not my style, Mary. But getting personally involved in a case just so happens to come under the umbrella of experiences I've had and not done so well at."

She knew he was talking about when he'd helped Louisa solve the mystery of her parentage. "You and Louisa handled it."

"Yeah, we did. But I've done it both ways and getting twisted up in clients makes it harder. Scarier. And more important. So, I'm not lecturing, Mary, I'm saying I understand. And you can always talk to me if you need to."

She leaned into her brother a little bit. She didn't want to talk, but the gesture was nice. Even if taking care and soothing was *her* job.

"I really am fine. I'm just preoccupied with how to tell them. They don't have a great relationship with their father, but I think they'd written him off as a possibility a long time ago."

"He's still only a possibility. Who knows what the money is for. We'll keep digging."

Mary nodded, but she knew the Daniels siblings well enough now to know they wouldn't see it that way. They'd immediately see guilt.

And they'd want to act. Not always wisely. She kept using the word *wild* to describe them, because in essence they *were*. There was no structure. The Hudsons had always had the ranch, Jack's—and to an extent her own—belief that they grow up and go out into the world as productive members of it.

Walker, Zeke and Carlyle had existed in a weird fringe space. The only system or routine they'd ever seemed to have was when Carlyle had been in school.

It was a stark contrast to her own life, one Mary didn't always know how to deal with—no matter how charmed she was by them all. Or how infatuated she was with Walker.

But this case was why they were here. This case was why she knew them. So she could hardly ignore it. Still, she allowed herself a little procrastination. She went to her room and the binder she'd been compiling of all pertinent information and carefully added the new findings.

It was an hour later when she couldn't put it off any longer. She walked out to the ranch hand cabin, binder under her arm, dread creeping in her gut. She tried to assure herself she could be professional no matter how unprofessional she felt toward the man.

She was, after all, excellent at cleaning up after bad news. She was just the person to handle this.

She knocked on the door and waited.

He opened the door, already that big grin on his face. She didn't know what to do with him, with what he made her feel. It was how she imagined being swept out to tide might feel or getting stuck in quicksand. Like she had absolutely no choice against the force of the way his eyes seemed to dance when he grinned at her.

When he kissed her. Which he did now, without saying a word.

She wished so much she could enjoy this moment, sink into the kiss and him. Wished they could forget why he'd been here the last few weeks and just keep pretending this was normal.

"Zeke is off doing what Zeke does," he said, pulling her inside. "Carlyle conned Cash into letting her help with dog training, which means you and I are alone." He grinned at her, then kissed her again.

She wanted to cry, and that was so foolish. Whatever was going on between her and Walker was clearly a kind of fling. She didn't know how to navigate that, but she knew he was very careful to keep things light. Casual.

Which was fine. She'd never had light and casual in her life. Why not have it with the man who was just stopping through? A fling. A moment in time. Something to look back fondly on.

But the binder was still under her arm and no matter how good it felt to kiss Walker, to have his hands on her, the corner of the binder dug into her arm like a sharp reminder of why they knew each other in the first place.

She managed to pull her mouth away from his, though she was a little breathless. "Walker…"

Something stopped him then. The tone of her voice, the look on her face, she didn't know. He studied her carefully, that grin slowly morphing into something far more guarded.

"You found something," he said. And shock was clearly etched across his face, though he tried to wipe it off. "You found something," he repeated. Then he nodded, taking a breath. "All right. Lay it on me."

But he didn't let her go, and Mary decided to hold on to that.

Chapter Eleven

Walker figured it was an effective enough cold shower. Mary was clearly in some kind of emotional turmoil over what she'd found.

She hesitated, then moved out of the circle of his arms, pulling a binder he hadn't even noticed from under her arm. "It's just a potential something, not a full-on something, but it involves your father."

"We already looked into my father."

"I know, but sometimes in cold cases you have to go over things that have already been done." She moved over to the little table, setting the binder down and opening to one of the back pages. "It's not that what you've looked into is wrong, just that it might lead to new avenues."

He didn't know why, but the idea of new avenues pissed him off. Still, he tried to keep that reaction out of his tone. "If it's him, that's great. But—"

She looked up, her eyebrows drawing together. "You're already dismissing the idea."

He didn't know what to say to that because, hell yeah he was dismissing it.

"You haven't even listened to what we found."

"I just don't think he did it, Mary. I wish I did. But I know the guy. He's not smart enough for some kind of ten-year conspiracy."

She didn't say anything for a few moments. She was just utterly still. "You hired me to look into this. Insisted I did. Now you won't even to listen to what we found?"

"I'll listen. I'm just saying, we've been down this road. I get why you guys might think it's *the* road, but it's not."

Something flashed in her expression. Not quite anger, but something like it. She closed the binder very carefully. "All right. Well, I'm sorry for bothering you then." She turned, as if to leave, and Walker was dumbfounded.

He stepped in her way before he'd fully thought the move through. Just that her leaving with that blank expression on her face was unbearable. "I don't understand why you're mad. I said I'll listen."

"But you don't *want* to listen."

"So what? Life is just full of what we want? Not my life."

"Not mine, either, Walker."

"I didn't say—" He raked his hands through his hair. What the hell were they doing? He didn't have the vaguest idea why they were arguing, why she was mad. Which was his first clue that this wasn't actually about him. The root cause was hers.

Then he remembered her softball analogy, and the failure comment. The way she said she wasn't any good at it—because getting it wrong messed with her head.

"Honey. This isn't…" He didn't know how to say it. What the right words were. It flirted with something more serious than he could afford. And she and this place all conspired against him to make him believe he could.

"This is why it isn't smart to blur lines," she said coolly.

"I like all the blurred lines just fine." He tried out a grin.

It clearly didn't land. Her eyes narrowed.

"So, you think I'm so incapable, you'd rather talk me into bed, then—"

"Talk you into bed? Are you kidding me?" It poked at his own temper because didn't he wish it was just about talking her into bed. "It's been weeks and we're sneaking around like teenagers. Because I can't stop thinking about you. Because I want to be where you are. Because something about you makes my lungs feel like they've been tied in knots. When I'm with you, I don't think about my damn goal in life. I think about you. About us. So yeah, sorry if I'd pick that over dealing with all the shit and ugliness of my past."

He felt like an idiot, and still he couldn't walk away. He reached out, fitted his palm to her cheek. "I don't want to argue with you, Mary."

She closed her eyes and blew out a breath. "My fault," she said. "I just…" She sucked in a breath that must have been fortifying because she opened her eyes and met his gaze. "I'm really not good at people telling me I'm doing something wrong."

He laughed, couldn't help it. Damn, why did he like her so much?

"Show me what you found. It's not about being wrong. It's about ripping a scab off an old wound. Who wants to do that? But if it has to be done, it has to be done." Because more and more he wanted an end to this.

It wasn't so much about finding answers anymore. It was about building the life that came next.

She swallowed, looked down at the binder, and he could see the tug-of-war playing out all over her face. He supposed that was a kind of progress, that she wasn't trying to hide that from him.

She cleared her throat. "We looked into your father's financial situation."

"Yeah, the cops did that too."

"For a specific period of time. We looked for longer." She took a deep breath. He noticed that her face was very carefully arranged in that neutral expression he didn't care for, but her hand shook a little as she pointed to the page she'd just opened up to. "A lump sum. Six years after the murder, deposited into his bank account."

He frowned, because that *was* new. He knew Zeke kept an eye on their father, but he hadn't mentioned this. And what would have prompted them to look into his finances when he was basically a nomad?

So he looked at the page, the list of deposits. The large one and the date. And his blood went cold. Because it wasn't just six years after the murder.

"That's Carlyle's birthday."

Mary whipped her head to look up at him. "What?"

"July fourteenth. That's her birthday." He didn't even need to do the math to realize it. "And that year? That was her eighteenth birthday."

Mary shook her head and looked up at him with big, sympathetic eyes. "Walker, I don't know how that could be a coincidence."

"I don't either." It was hard to get his breath because this was hardly all. It was just the tip of the iceberg. "Mary, our apartment complex burned down on that day. We got out, and no one ever thought it had anything to do with us." He was seeing little spots. "Carlyle did."

"Come on. Let's sit down." She took his hand and led him over to the lone chair. She nudged him until he kind of collapsed onto it.

The whole thing at the stables kept playing in his mind. That Carlyle wanted to let it go but he couldn't. He thought it was devotion to their mother. She didn't remember the things he did.

But what if it was something else?

"She's acting weird. I keep trying to tell myself it's just she doesn't know how to stick in one place. Or trust people to help. But this…"

"Is it possible she knows something she hasn't told you or Zeke?"

It crushed him. Because he didn't know how it *wasn't* possible now.

MARY COULD ONLY stand next to the chair and watch Walker deal with this new set of facts. She felt like an idiot for over-reacting earlier. For making his tragedy about *her* issues.

This wasn't about her. So she brushed her hand over his hair as he sat there, elbow on his knees, hands curled in his wild, dark hair. She could imagine what he was feeling. Try-ing to wade through all the reasons Carlyle might have kept something from him.

She'd had a hand in creating this problem, so she needed to fix it. "Why don't I go track her down? I'll bring her back here and you two can talk."

Walker laughed. Bitterly. "Talk. And say what? Demand answers? That's not how you get through to Carlyle."

"Why don't you show her what I showed you? See what she has to say."

Walker shook his head. "If she wanted to tell me, she would have by now."

Mary tried not to sigh. Men could be so stubborn. Partic-ularly when it came to their sisters, as she knew firsthand. "Maybe, Walker. But maybe she's afraid. Or protecting you. She *is* the one who contacted HSS originally. There could be an understandable reason behind this."

"Yeah. They'll all piss me off."

She kissed the top of his head because it felt like the right thing to do. "Probably. But they're still answers. And forward movement."

He grunted, clearly stewing over the fact that Carlyle hadn't told him something, rather than focusing on the fact that they now had this new lead to tug on. The information about Car-lyle's birthday and their apartment fire and the hefty deposit didn't tell them anything—except that they had to be con-nected.

They just had to be.

"If you don't want to, why don't I talk with her?" Mary sug-gested. "I'm very good at getting information out of people."

He shifted so he could study her, somewhat skeptically. "Are you?"

"I got your real name out of you in under an hour."

His mouth curved, not quite that grin she'd wanted, but a smile nonetheless. "So you did."

"People see a calm, dowdy demeanor—"

"I have never once thought of you as dowdy." As if to prove his point, he pulled her onto his lap. It should have felt ridiculous, but instead felt kind of nice to have his arms around her, to have him close.

Like they were in this together.

"The point is, people tend to underestimate me. Because I don't have a temper—"

"You don't let your temper loose *angrily*. You just get all frosty. But that's still temper," he interrupted. "It's just not the one people are expecting."

She resisted a groan at his constant interruptions. "I can be very persistent, but I know how to gentle it so people don't know I'm being persistent. So they feel like they want to tell me, rather than get all defensive."

"You're a fluffy steamroller."

"You wouldn't be the first to call me that."

"Danielses are just flat-out steamrollers, Mary."

"Yes, well, fluffy steamrollers are flexible. And they might get flattened, but they pop right back up."

"This is the weirdest analogy." He blew out a long breath, his arms tightening their hold around her. "It'd probably be better coming from you. It'll feel like an unbiased voice. I'll end up yelling."

She could picture him angry. She'd seen him run away from men with guns with an immense amount of calm, but underneath that had been a sharp-edged anger. She'd seen it flash in his eyes a couple of times.

But no matter how she tried, she could not picture him losing his temper with Carlyle. "I don't think you're the stern taskmaster you think you are."

He pulled a face. "Well, now you just sound like Zeke."

Yes, she could picture the stiff, stern younger brother yelling. It was strange, that though a similar thing had happened to the Daniels siblings when they'd lost their parents and then had to take care of one another, the dynamics had settled differently. Walker might be the oldest, but he had a softness to him she hadn't seen out of Zeke.

She wrapped her arms tighter around him, settled easier into his lap, into this little cocoon of warmth. His shoulders were tense, but they relaxed a little when she did.

"I feel like it's all about to crash," he said, shaking his head a little. "After all these years juggling balls, they're all about to fall."

Her heart ached for him. Because she knew what it was like to worry about that kind of thing. The strength it took to keep taking care of everyone even when you felt that way. "Balls bounce."

"Important ones shatter," he returned flatly.

She pressed a kiss to his temple, couldn't resist the urge to soothe him. "Carlyle won't shatter. She has you and Zeke. All three of you have each other. It's what's gotten you this far, and it's what will get you through figuring out what this all means."

He took her hand in his, ran his thumb over her knuckles. "This is usually the part where I throw myself into something dangerous and impulsive."

Her heart ached for the young man he must have been, and all he'd had to deal with. She knew, firsthand, what that kind of weight did to you. The ways coping mechanisms helped you cope but didn't always help you thrive.

Her issues with control might be twisted up in everything she couldn't.

She had to clear her throat to speak. Because control or not, she wanted to help him. Soothe him. Fix this. "Well, let's sidestep that for now. I'll talk to Carlyle, and we'll go from there."

He looked up at her then, those dark eyes meeting hers and searching for something. She didn't know what, but it made her heart beat in triple time.

"I've never wanted to know what comes next," he said, seriously. "Never thought about the future. It's only ever been about answers—and usually for Carlyle and Zeke. Not me. Not my mother. I think if it had just been me, I would have been happy not knowing. Happy to leave it all behind. But I didn't have a clue what I'd do if I did. This is all I've had since I was twenty years old."

The air was clogging her lungs, but she forced herself to speak carefully. Neutrally. "What were you doing? College?"

He snorted, but it wasn't exactly a bitter sound. "I barely survived high school. Sitting still in a classroom for hours on end is not for me. Even if it had been an option, I wouldn't have put myself through that nightmare. I considered the military, but eventually I just went to trade school. Now, don't laugh, but the idea was to become an electrician."

"Why would I laugh at that?"

"I don't know. It seems very uncool when compared with saying I spent ten years tracking my mother's murderer and avoiding certain death. Though, in fairness, cooler than saying I worked in the school cafeteria to keep my little sister in line."

It surprised a little laugh out of her. She supposed that was a big piece of why she couldn't help but like him so much. He surprised her, and it never felt bad. No matter how she didn't know how to deal with it, she wanted more of those surprises.

"I'd like to know what comes next. What happens after. Know that Zeke and Carlyle are good and maybe I can have that life other people get to have."

She wanted to cry for him, wade in and fix it for him, but

she couldn't think of a way to do that. Except to start by talking to Carlyle. "You should have that, Walker. Everyone should."

He studied her hand in his again. She couldn't read his expression. It was as serious, as focused as he'd been in that first moment she'd met him when he'd been clearly preparing for whoever was after him.

And is after him still, or will be. She didn't let that thought take root. She didn't want to be afraid. Not in this little pocket of warmth. She'd been through too many bad times not to believe in enjoying the bits and pieces of good that came along with them.

"And would you be in it?" he asked, his voice quiet but firm. He didn't meet her gaze, but she couldn't call it nerves or hesitation. It was something else, and it had more to do with how weighty this all was.

How important.

This was a turning point for them. Walker didn't fit into her ordered world. Not the reality of it. These last few weeks had been like a bubble, away from reality.

Choosing him, accepting the idea of some sort of "after," would mean change. Losing some of that control she'd had a death grip on since she'd been ten years old.

And in this moment, looking into his dark eyes as he studied her, waiting patiently for an answer, control seemed like the last thing she'd want to hold on to if it meant losing him. So she leaned forward and pressed her mouth to his. "I'd like to be," she murmured against his lips.

His grip tightened, taking the kiss deeper, until it seemed it was all that mattered. All that would ever be.

"Come to bed with me, Mary. Let's put this all away, just for a little while."

And she knew, if she wanted to later, she'd be able to convince herself she was just trying to make him feel better. That it had been about soothing him because she was good at that.

But she went to the bedroom with him because she *wanted*

to. Because something deep and meaningful twined them together, and it didn't matter what was going on around them.

As long as they could enjoy each other.

Chapter Twelve

Walker dozed. He wasn't a man for afternoon naps, but with Mary cuddled next to him, satisfaction warming his blood and his bed, why not catch a few winks? Why not lie here and feel the steady rise and fall of Mary's breathing? It was the first place he'd ever been in his life where things seemed to make sense.

But before he could fully relax into sleep, he heard the telltale sound of the front door creaking open out there in the cabin. He winced. It would no doubt be Zeke, and it'd be hard to hide what he and Mary had been up to.

She shot up into a sitting position, pulling the sheet with her. "Is that Zeke?" she asked in a hissed whisper.

"Probably."

She practically leaped out of bed, frantically searching for her clothes and putting them on so haphazardly and with such panic, he could only watch in amusement.

"I'm not sure I've ever seen you move so fast."

She glared at him, pants and bra on, but one sock missing and no shirt. Her hair was disheveled. She looked more rumpled than she had when they'd been on the run from gunmen.

She really was something. He crossed his arms behind his head and grinned at her.

"How are we going to explain this?" she whispered.

Walker shrugged from his comfortable and enjoyable position on the bed. "Zeke knows I'm not a monk."

She paused, just for a second, then found her shirt and pulled it on—less haphazard, more stiff. "Just how much of a not-monk are you?" she asked primly.

He grinned at her, though she had her back to him as she pulled her shirt into place. "Do I sense jealousy, Mary?"

Her back stiffened and she turned to face him with that cool, regal expression. "No. Of course not."

He got out of bed, didn't bother to grab his boxers just yet. Her cool expression didn't falter, but her cheeks turned pink and her eyes definitely dropped. "Because monk or not, it was all before you."

"Yes, exactly." Her chin went up in the air. "That's why I couldn't care less."

God, she was amazing. He pulled on his boxers, then crossed the room to her. Touched his finger to that silky jaw. "None of them mattered," he whispered into her ear, before pressing a kiss just beneath her earlobe.

Her exhale was shaky, but her words were firm. "Oh, now, I don't need charming words and pretty lies. It hardly matters—"

"Not a lie. Wish it was." Because that would make this simple, but it only seemed to get more complicated with every step. And he didn't just mean her. But she was the reason all the fear and frustration and discomfort seemed infinitely worth it. "You make everyone and everything fade away."

She let out a little shuddery breath. "I don't know how to be when you say things like that."

He knew he'd almost distracted her enough from Zeke's arrival, but the jerk kept making noise out there and she shook her head and pulled herself together.

"Well, Mary, it's probably about time you didn't know how to be. Now come on. You're helping me explain this whole thing with my father to Zeke. He'll have all sorts of questions

I didn't." Because Walker never wanted to ask questions when it came to his father. He'd spent years blaming his mother's murder on Don Daniels—with no proof, and in fact quite a bit of proof to the contrary.

It hadn't mattered. Don was an easy target. Walker had wanted it to be him so all that hate just stayed in one damn place.

But he'd never been able to get anywhere near proving it, and even Zeke had told him they needed to move on years ago. Now Mary was reintroducing the possibility—with not proof exactly, but possibility—and Walker...

Well, he wanted to run away from it. Because those were his two MOs. Impulsively throwing himself into danger or turning away from it altogether.

Mary had introduced some kind of weird middle ground where his instinct was to do both, and yet he knew he couldn't do either.

Most alarming and unsettling of all was that it didn't seem to matter. Because Mary was here, with her implacable steadiness and her hand in his.

"You need to put on clothes, Walker," she said, and her tone was a mix of gentle reminder and stern schoolteacher. Was it any wonder he was halfway in love with her? No one had ever stepped in and talked him down from a ledge. Zeke or Carlyle might have tried, but he'd never listened.

But Mary... She'd sat there with him, talked him through, and suggested he sidestep the whole diving headfirst into danger. She'd comforted him, and it hadn't occurred to him not to let her.

He smoothed a hand over her tangled hair. "You might want to fix this mess."

She reached up and patted her hair. "Oh," she said with some distress. "Do you have a brush?"

"There's a comb in the bathroom."

She frowned. "I'd have to go out there to get to the bathroom."

"That you would."

She fisted her hands on her hips, all scolding censure. "Walker."

"Come on, Mary. I'm guessing Zeke's figured it out. But luckily it's Zeke and not Carlyle, so he won't say anything. In front of you anyway."

MARY HAD NEVER felt more off-kilter in her whole entire life. She'd just had sex—fantastic, mind-blowing sex in fact, which was definitely a first as her college experience had been less than stellar—and then Walker had said all those sweet things in that matter-of-fact way he had that made it hard not to believe them. Harder still to remain ordered and calm.

Now he wanted her to just walk into the living room where his brother was and talk about the case? When her heart was still thundering and her knees felt a little weak? When Zeke would absolutely know what had just gone on in that bedroom? Mary wasn't ashamed. She'd likely go home and tell Anna all about it.

But who wanted to face their partner's brother in the midst of the after-good-sex glow?

Walker was pulling her along, though, and what else was there to do? She wasn't going to cower and hide in the bedroom and find some way to sneak out. That felt wrong.

More wrong than facing this awkwardness.

She lived with siblings who were in committed relationships and quite obviously had sex in the privacy of their own rooms. They never acted awkward.

Well, Grant and Dahlia sometimes did. But they were more introverted. And Mary, well, she supposed she was too. But the point was it certainly hadn't stopped them.

Zeke was standing in the little kitchenette. He was making coffee and the way he was setting things down hard and closing drawers loudly when he usually moved like some kind of feline predator made Mary realize all the noise had been for their benefit. Walker just squeezed her hand.

"Hey, glad you're back. We've got something of a lead," Walker announced.

"Is that what we're calling it these days?" Zeke muttered, with his back to them and so quietly Mary almost didn't catch it.

She in fact wished she hadn't.

But he turned and his expression was unreadable. "All right. Let's hear it."

Walker dropped her hand and went over to her binder. He explained the financial records and handed them over to Zeke, who studied them in broody silence.

"Who's the one paying him?"

"Palmer is digging into that," Mary explained, "but since we know there have been threats against you guys, he has to be careful. Which takes time."

Zeke nodded.

"Did you notice the date?" Walker prompted.

"Yeah, I noticed."

"I think she knows something."

Zeke's expression didn't really change, but Mary sensed a darker mood all the same.

"I'll talk to her," he said. And Mary couldn't hide the wince. She definitely wouldn't want to be Carlyle if Zeke was going to talk to her in this mood.

"I think we need to try an alternative route to answers," Walker said, and she recognized the attempt at peace. She was usually the one accomplishing peace in her family. It was a little surprising to see Walker do it. She'd just supposed they never had peace—went about every family discussion in their wild, lawless way. "Mary could talk to her. Maybe she'd open up to someone else. Someone she didn't feel the need to protect."

Zeke's dark gaze turned to her, hard and cold. Mary smiled

kindly in return, though it was difficult to maintain under that mean stare.

"She's not going to listen to us," Walker continued. "We know this. We've been down this road a hundred times with a hundred things. She'll shut down or worse."

"But she'll listen to a stranger?"

She saw the flash of anger on Walker's face on her behalf so she stepped between the brothers and spoke before Walker could.

"I understand why you'd think that, Zeke. I see this from your point of view, but maybe you should see it from Carlyle's. She doesn't see me as a stranger because she's engaged with me and my family the past few weeks. She hasn't made herself scarce or refused to be drawn into conversation." Maybe scolding wasn't the way to go, but it was only the truth.

Zeke's scowl got deeper and deeper. But he didn't argue with her.

"What's more, sometimes a stranger is better. You're her two older brothers, who've protected her for the majority of her life. Or tried to. She likely feels a responsibility to you— whether not to upset you, or to protect you, or something else. She has none of those things when it comes to me. I'm just part of the family she hired in hopes of some answers. And maybe, if you two hadn't gotten involved, she would have told us these things earlier."

Zeke crossed his arms over his chest. "So it's our fault?"

"There's no fault when it comes to how you deal with tragedy. Everyone's doing their best. I know that's hard to see sometimes in the middle of it, but whatever Carlyle knows, or doesn't, she's doing her best too."

She looked back at Walker, and she couldn't quite read his expression, but she knew the words resonated with him too. Because she knew he blamed himself for things. That's why he tended to choose rash or impulsive methods of dealing with situations. It was better to do that than marinate in guilt. But when it came to tragedy, raising and protecting your siblings, guilt was just a cornerstone of it all. She understood that, and he'd likely never had anyone in his life who did.

She hadn't outside of her family.

It made her feel a wave of warmth and care and other things she couldn't pick apart and analyze in this little cabin with two complicated men and one frustrating mystery.

"I'll go talk to her. If she tells me anything, I'll encourage her to tell you both herself. If she doesn't, I'll let you know and we can look at our options. In the meantime, Palmer will be researching where the money came from, and I'm going to start looking into the apartment fire. And maybe while I do that, you could discuss with Walker whatever it is that you've been doing."

Zeke's expression grew cold again. "Excuse me?"

"It doesn't escape my notice you're not here. So you must be somewhere doing something. Walker is content to let you do it, and maybe I should be too. It's none of my business after all, what with me being a stranger. But if I wanted to solve a mystery, I'd stop being secretive and start working together." She delivered it all with her cool, older-sister voice and a pleasant smile. She ended that little speech with, "I'll see you both at dinner." Not a question.

A command.

Then Mary turned on a heel and walked, head held high, out the door. She didn't know Zeke well enough to know if that little speech would be effective, but she liked to think it would be.

Either way, she knew she was right. And that was all that mattered. She was down the porch stairs before the door opened behind her.

"Wait a sec," Walker called.

She turned and watched him approach. He didn't say anything, though, just pulled her into his arms and pressed his mouth to hers. He kissed her, clearly not caring at all if Zeke was watching, and that helped her not care too. Because this wasn't about the case. It was about them. They'd found each other in the midst of the case and they certainly didn't need anyone's approval.

"You are something else, Mary Hudson." And he grinned down at her, like to him she really was.

It scared her how much she wanted to be.

And how much failure was waiting if she couldn't be.

Still she smiled at him, straightened her shirt that he'd rumpled. "If you're not opposed, you could spend the night in the big house tonight."

"Is that an invitation to your bed?"

She had never in a million years thought she might invite someone, let alone someone like Walker, to share her bed in her family home, but... "Yes, it is."

"Then I'll be there."

Chapter Thirteen

Mary walked back to the ranch focused on Carlyle. She practiced what she'd say to the woman and tried to focus on process over results.

Mary liked to believe that a lifetime with Anna meant she knew how to get through contrary natures. A lifetime with Jack and Grant meant an incredible amount of experience fighting against stubborn hardheadedness. And being herself meant she understood the strange and complex role of being a woman in the midst of men who thought they had to handle everything.

She liked to believe she was especially equipped to get through to Carlyle and get the necessary information, but...

Well, what if she couldn't?

She slowed her pace as she walked to the stables. She didn't know where Carlyle would be, but if she had to guess it'd be with the horses or with Cash's dogs.

The thought of having to face Walker at dinner with no answers, with only failure, twisted her gut into knots. She was flirting with disaster here, and now it wasn't just her own. It was failing Walker, who she...

She...

She couldn't really love him, no matter how her heart seemed to think that was the case. Maybe she'd gotten to know him these past few weeks, but that wasn't enough to love him.

She tried to ignore all the times Anna insisted she'd fallen in love with Hawk at first sight. Mary was too practical to believe in such a thing. Love required a foundation.

And this was not about love. It was about murder.

She reminded her brain of this over and over and once she finally found Carlyle—throwing a rope bone to one of Cash's dogs behind the dog pen—it wasn't so hard to switch focus.

Carlyle threw the rope with a great heave that had Copper the dog yipping with delight as he zoomed after it. Mary came to stand next to Carlyle.

"You know you live in just about the coolest place, right?" Carlyle said by way of greeting. She was tracking the dog's movements as she spoke.

Mary smiled in spite of all her turmoil. Because she did in fact know that, and she was glad Carlyle appreciated it.

"Yes, we do. I hope this isn't jumping any kind of gun, but whenever this is over, I'd certainly be able to find you a place here."

"What do you mean?" Carlyle turned to her for a moment, and the happy enjoyment in her expression had turned wary. Suspicious.

Mary felt instant sympathy for the Daniels clan. Clearly they'd had so few people to trust. "Well, we always need help around the ranch. We're in the process of hiring a ranch hand and we might promote someone, which would open up an entry-level position. I've also been trying to convince Cash to hire an assistant. Then there's Sunrise itself, where I could help you find a job. If you're looking to stay, that is."

"Because you have a thing for my brother and you want *him* to stay?"

Mary didn't sigh at the skepticism, though she wanted to. "I do have a thing for your brother," she replied, because there was no point lying about it. That would only discredit her. "But this offer doesn't have anything to do with him. I'd offer it to all three of you because I know how lucky I am and have been to have this as home base. Everyone deserves a home base."

Carlyle crouched as Copper returned with the bone. She did a little tug-of-war with the dog, before giving him the order to drop, which he did dutifully. She threw it again.

"Well, I guess we have to figure out this stuff first," she finally said, still watching the dog.

"Yes, we do," Mary agreed. "But we're getting somewhere with that."

"Oh, yeah?"

"We did some digging into your father's finances." Mary watched Carlyle's face carefully. There was no change, but Mary thought she sensed a stiffness. "He received a lump-sum payment from a mysterious source about six years after the murder."

"Huh. Well, that's weird, but he's a shady guy so who knows what shady things he was up to."

An interesting take, and as Walker had a much stronger reaction to it, Mary could only find herself even more suspicious of what Carlyle knew. Still, she kept her tone light. Completely benign.

"The deposit happened on July fourteenth." There was no reaction from Carlyle, but she was staring pretty hard at the dog. "Walker said that's your birthday."

Carlyle crouched as Copper returned. She kept her head down as she tugged on the bone. "Yeah."

"Six years after would have been your eighteenth birthday, to be precise."

"Huh."

"Walker also said your apartment complex burned down that day, and you thought it was connected to the murder."

Carlyle stood abruptly, heaved the rope bone. She turned to face Mary and her expression had gone a little belligerent. "Yeah, I was pretty paranoid back then. I'm not following how this has anything to do with the case. Walker and Zeke ruled Don out of the equation a long time ago."

Mary studied the young woman's lifted chin, flashing eyes and wanted to engulf her in a hug. She wanted to soothe that restless, hurting soul. But she knew it wouldn't be welcomed, so she only smiled softly.

"Carlyle," she said. "We can't help if you're keeping secrets. My family can't and your brothers can't. And we all want to help."

Carlyle's expression changed, almost imperceptibly, from all that anger and what Mary thought was probably fear, to something icier. But the woman smiled politely. "I don't know what you're talking about, Mary. You have all the information I do."

But it was a lie. Mary knew it. "Okay. Maybe we're just missing something. What can you tell me about your father?"

"Nothing. Because we got out of there before I remember anything about the guy." She crouched, immediately told the dog to drop it this time.

"You never met him? Never heard your mother talk about him?"

"Why are you interrogating me?" Carlyle demanded, standing with the rope bone still in her hand. "That's not how this is supposed to go."

"You started this. Last year you tried to hire us under Walker's alias."

"Yeah, because I thought maybe you guys could protect him."

An interesting way to phrase it. Not about answers, but about...protecting. Mary filed that information away. "But not you?"

"What do you want from me, Mary?" Carlyle said, frustration and anger clearly bubbling over. "Answers I don't have? Okay, so my dad got paid on my eighteenth birthday. Six years after my mom died. The day our apartment complex burned down. What am I supposed to think about that?"

"I don't know, but I'd like to."

"You're supposed to be the one with answers. Your grand HSS."

"And maybe we could find them if we had the whole picture," Mary continued calmly, never letting any kind of emotion show. Because it seemed to be getting under Carlyle's skin and Mary figured that was the best way to get answers. It was how she always succeeded.

And if you don't...

Carlyle heaved the rope. "Find them your damn self." Then she stalked away from Mary—not toward the big house or even the ranch hand's cabin. Mary wasn't sure where she was going, but she knew that this was a big fat failure.

She tried to remember what Walker had said about failure. That giving up was the failure, but this felt pretty bad. She'd have to tell him Carlyle hadn't given her anything, after all her grand talk about being so persuasive and the right person to talk to Carlyle. All she'd done was make Carlyle mad.

Copper returned, nudged her leg with the rope bone. Mary swallowed back the tears. She wouldn't cry. She would try to take a page out of Walker's book and just not give up.

But how?

ZEKE HADN'T SAID MUCH. He'd spent an inordinate amount of time with his nose buried in Mary's binder. Walker had gotten more and more stir-crazy, but he didn't know what to do with himself.

His impulse was to find a flight to California and track down dear old Dad and demand answers. A month ago, that's exactly what he would have done.

Somehow, everything had changed.

Zeke finally closed the binder, then glanced at the clock on the oven. "Guess we should head up to the big house for dinner."

Walker studied his brother. *"We?"* Zeke had been keeping

scarce, living off whatever leftovers Mary shoved into the refrigerator when he wasn't looking.

Zeke shrugged. "I want to know if Mary got through to Car or not."

Which felt like pressure. And Walker knew how much pressure Mary put on herself. How afraid of failure she was. He couldn't let Zeke make that worse. "Even if she didn't—"

"I thought you were so confident it was the right course of action."

"I am. It is. But Carlyle's tough and if she has a secret she's been keeping for many years, then you can't be hard on Mary. She's doing her best."

"Is she? Or is she sleeping with you?"

Walker had fought with his brother a lot. As kids. As adults. Sometimes, when they'd been younger, they'd even traded punches. Life had been hard, and sometimes when it was, you took it out on the people you knew would be there no matter what.

But Zeke talking about Mary like that made him angrier than he'd been in a long time. Since he hadn't spent any time with Zeke in so long, he worked to keep his temper in check rather than throw the first punch. "You don't have to like it. You don't have to approve of it. But I care about her, so you'll watch what you say."

Zeke's expression didn't change, but he didn't offer any more commentary. Just nodded, once.

"Good," Walker muttered and turned on a heel, feeling like a hundred different kinds of idiot. Care about her. It sounded so stupid. He tried to walk off the irritating, confusing feelings rattling around inside him as they headed over to the big house, but he didn't succeed.

This was such a habit by now, though, that he didn't feel weird about walking right in the house anymore. It just felt like what you did. He'd walk in and everyone would be getting the table set up, and Carlyle would be elbow to elbow with Izzy playing with the dogs, and then Mary would sweep in and maybe something in him would settle.

It usually did.

But the air was different, he could tell that immediately. Anna came out of the kitchen. "Well, she's not there." Anna looked over at him. "And she's not with you, apparently."

"Mary? No, she came back ages ago."

"Dinner's all ready, but I don't know where she went."

Walker couldn't help but glance over at Carlyle. His baby sister currently had her head bent over a dog, clearly hiding her face. It didn't take a genius to put together what had happened.

"She must be up in her room. I'll go get her," Anna said.

"You mind if I do? I've got something I want to talk to her privately about." He kept his gaze on Carlyle, hoping she'd look up so he could glare disapprovingly at her.

She didn't.

"Uh. Okay. I guess," Anna said, clearly not fully okay with that. "Upstairs. The first door to the left."

Walker nodded, then went to the stairs. He'd spent a lot of time in this house over the past few weeks, but never had cause to venture upstairs. So this felt strange, and wrong. But if Mary was deviating from her schedule, Walker just knew it couldn't be good.

The first door on the left was closed so he lifted his hand and knocked.

"Oh. Just…just a minute," Mary's voice came from inside.

But there was something about the tone that didn't sound right. Maybe it was wrong, but he hadn't grown up in a nice, big house learning manners. A Daniels barged in. So, that's what he did.

She was sitting on the edge of her bed, some little box next to her. She wiped her cheeks quickly, clearly trying to hide the evidence that she'd been crying, but she was still crying, so it didn't work.

"What's wrong?"

"Oh, Walker. What are you doing up here?" Her hands fluttered around, which was when he noticed a bandage and realized the box next to her was a . "I'm sorry. I'm late for dinner. I just burnt my hand." She held up her hand.

"That's why you're crying?"

She straightened her shoulders, clearly trying to get a hold of herself. And not quite getting there.

"Of course," she said firmly. So firmly it sounded like a lie. "It hurt."

Walker crossed the space between them, moved the first-aid kit out of the way, then took a seat. He grabbed her hand, studied the bandage. "Should you see a doctor?"

She shook her head vehemently. "It might blister, but it's fine." The word *fine* seemed to get stuck in her throat and more tears began to fall.

This was clearly not about the burn. "What did Carlyle say? She never learned any manners, and that's my fault. So, blame me. Be mad at me. Just don't cry." He brushed tears away with his thumbs as something painful twisted deep in his gut. He couldn't stand it, her being sad.

"It isn't your fault. It's mine. I thought I could get through to her, and I didn't. Which is fine. I mean, it isn't fine, but it... I just... I was fine, and then I didn't have enough onions."

"Okay." He had no idea why they were suddenly talking about onions, but he'd dealt with enough upset people to know you just rolled with it until you found the thread.

"I had the meal all planned out. I should have had enough onions, but then I didn't and I had to do everything on the fly. And then I burnt my hand." She sniffled.

"Well, if it makes you feel better, if I had to cook for a million people I'd be burning my hand every day."

But she didn't laugh like he'd hoped. She just kept frowning at the floor. And the tears kept coming.

"Everyone thinks I'm so with it, but I'm just a mess. I used to be able to hide it better. It's why I don't get involved. It's why..."

"Hey." He lifted her chin until she met his gaze. He wasn't sure where this had all come from, except he knew something about breaking points. Maybe he didn't get why onions might have set her off, but he knew it didn't always have to connect.

And he understood her. He really did. "Nothing that happens with Carlyle or this case is something I'm going to blame you for. You not having immediate success with my wildling of a sister? Not even close to blaming you for."

"Only because you're usually too busy blaming yourself."

"Hey, your fear of failure and my martyr guilt together? We might just be onto something."

She laughed, then sniffled. "I feel like an idiot. I just thought I could get through to her, and I wanted... I just wish you had answers. I wish I didn't fall apart when I don't get it exactly right."

"Don't we all? If you're going around thinking you're the only one who struggles and tries to hide it, or the only one who *should* hide it, you're wrong."

She looked at him, her eyebrows drawn together in a line creasing her forehead. Like she'd never heard such a thing in her whole life.

Maybe she hadn't. "I get it. Parenting your siblings is hard and messed up. It leaves you with stuff that feels untenable, but you just get through it."

"This is about you. Not me. You shouldn't feel the need to like...comfort me, because it isn't about me or what I'm dealing with."

He tilted his head and studied her. Was anything ever about her? He almost asked her, but figured she'd only put on that queen-of-the-manor look and waltz down to dinner. So he took a different approach. "I wish it was that simple. But it's about both of us. Because we're both here. So some days you get to fall apart, and some days it'll be my turn."

Her mouth trembled, then firmed. "What happens when we're both falling apart?"

"I figure we'll survive. What did you say to me earlier? Having a family, caring about each other, it means the balls don't shatter. Hell if that doesn't sound weird, but I think you get my point."

She nodded, looking down at her hands. "I just wanted to make everything okay."

"You can't. No one can. My mother was murdered. Your parents disappeared. Sometimes bad stuff just happens, and it'll never be okay." He lifted her hand to his mouth, kissed the bandage gently.

"No one's ever comforted me before, Mary. Not like you did earlier today. No one's ever taken care of me like you do. Zeke, Carlyle and I, we've always tried to take care of each other, but it's survival when you're moving around. When you're dealing with losing your parents. Even if we never find answers, I'll always be grateful that you've been a part of this these past few weeks, taking care."

Mary sniffled again. "She does know something, Walker. Carlyle. She got so angry. You don't get that angry if you don't know something. But I don't know how to get through to her. She's scared."

Walker nodded, feeling so many different things.

"She said she contacted HSS originally to protect you."

Walker frowned. "Protect me from what?"

"I don't know. But it wasn't about answers for her. It isn't about answers for her, I don't think. Which means…"

"She already has them."

"At least some of them."

"Well, we'll keep trying. See, you got something out of her after all."

Mary blew out a breath. Whatever she thought about that, she hid under that mask of coolness. "I think we should get down to dinner. They won't start without me and it's already late." She stood, but he couldn't quite let go of her hand so he was sitting on her bed and she was standing in front of him, looking down.

He knew he wanted to say something, but he couldn't find the right words. Something about how the past weeks had settled some restless part of him that had spent the last ten years—maybe longer—searching. He'd thought it was for answers, but now he wondered.

"You've lived without answers most of your life," he said softly.

She nodded solemnly.

He didn't have to ask her how. She had her siblings. She loved them, cared for them and had them at the center point of her life. Family and love.

"It's different though," she said. She reached out and brushed her fingers over his temple with her free hand. "Whatever Carlyle is or isn't hiding, she's right about wanting to protect you. And the three of you aren't safe until whoever has been trying to hurt you is brought to justice."

He'd never thought of it like that. He'd thought of it like answers. Like protecting Carlyle. And Zeke. Never about justice. Because there was no justice in murder. Ever.

But Mary was right about one thing. This wasn't over until they figured out who'd been chasing him the past few years. Which made him think of what Mary had said a long time ago. That the people who'd shot at him at the apartment complex hadn't been very subtle. She'd questioned whether they'd really wanted him dead.

The relative quiet of the past few weeks made that theory hold even more weight. It also meant he was going to have to stop hiding out and start meeting some challenges head-on.

Once he figured out what the hell his sister was hiding.

Chapter Fourteen

Mary tried not to dwell on the mortification of Walker seeing one of her little breakdowns. They weren't common exactly, but they happened. Particularly when things were stressful. A little snowball of failures and she sometimes just needed to hide and cry it out.

He hadn't been horrified. She wasn't even sure he'd been surprised. He'd seemed to understand.

It was such a relief, such a wonder.

But she still hated that he'd seen her cry. Still hated that she'd failed him. And that she couldn't fix it. Because that moment existed—always, no matter what she did.

Strangely, that didn't make her want to hide from him. It was an embarrassment that didn't change how she felt around him. If anything it made her want to double down. Somehow be worthy of how easily he dealt with all her weaknesses—and she didn't know what to do with that, except go on as planned.

Walker spent the night in her room, in her bed, just like they'd planned. She woke up beside him the next morning, in the same room she'd been waking up in since she was a little girl, and she watched him sleep.

His dark hair was a wild, tangled mess against her pillowcase, his dark eyelashes fanned against his cheeks. The relaxed expression in sleep made him almost seem younger—but then there were his broad, muscular shoulders, the sheer amount of space he took up without even being stretched out, that made it clear he was every inch a man.

A man who liked *her*. Trusted *her*. Even seeing the parts of her that she kept so ruthlessly hidden. And she understood now how her siblings had settled so quickly into a significant other, into intimacy and love.

She'd always thought romantic love was supposed to be hard or fraught or painful, but all it seemed to be was realizing someone loved you no matter what ugly parts of you they saw.

Not that Walker loved her, necessarily, but he certainly cared. And that was enough.

So, she was determined to talk to Carlyle again. To find some way to get through to the angry young woman. And if she didn't, at least she could tell Walker she'd tried. He seemed to think that was good enough.

She hoped she could convince herself it was good enough.

Eyes still closed, Walker shifted, unerringly moving to pull her closer to him. And even though she needed to get up, she let him. Because it was warm and safe here in this little cocoon before she let the real world invade.

He made a soft, contented noise, then pressed his mouth to her jaw, pulling her closer, holding her tighter. And it was far too tempting to turn in his arms, to press her mouth to his.

"I have to get up and make breakfast," she said against his mouth as his hands slid down her back.

"Sounds lame," he murmured.

"I like it."

"I know you do." He kissed her again but then he released her and yawned. "I should probably round up Carlyle and have a talk with her."

He swung out of bed, pulled on his clothes while Mary watched. He really was ridiculously handsome.

She got out of bed too. She had insisted on wearing pajamas last night. *Honestly, men.* She needed to run through the shower before she headed downstairs to make breakfast, but more than that she had to talk to him.

She crossed to him. "I'd like to try again with Carlyle. I mean, you can talk to her, too, but that might feel like ganging up. I just think I should take another shot at it."

He stopped zipping up his pants and looked at her with a searching gaze she couldn't quite figure.

"Yeah," he said. Then he pressed a hard kiss to her mouth, and she didn't know why that felt like soft, romantic confessions, only that it did. "You go ahead. We'll see how it goes and reevaluate."

Mary nodded. Then they just stood there, staring at each other.

"Mary…" he said.

And for some reason the way he said her name, the way he looked at her, made her heart jitter and she felt the need to hold her breath.

His eyebrows drew together and he looked from her eyes to the wall behind her as he sighed. "Zeke is going to want to do something. Probably something stupid. The kind of stupid I'd usually join him in."

She put her hand over his heart, because hers was tripping over itself as it had when Palmer and then Anna had gone off to the rodeo. Or when Grant had signed up for the military. Chasing that danger, that stupid risk. "I wish you wouldn't."

Walker paused, then put his hand over hers. He lifted it off his chest, pulled her palm to his mouth and pressed a kiss to it. "I'll do my best."

It wasn't a promise exactly, but she supposed it was something. And she held on to that something as she ran through the shower, as she went down to the kitchen and started prepping breakfast about fifteen minutes later than usual.

Being late didn't bother her this morning. She didn't let it. She was going to talk to Carlyle. She was going to get to the bottom of Walker's father.

And if she didn't, she'd just keep trying. Walker would be by her side either way. It put her in a good enough mood as she moved through breakfast. When Carlyle didn't show, she worried a little, but kept going through her routine.

Just about the usual time she went to the stables to give Walker and Carlyle their lessons, she finally decided to go on a search for Carlyle. Had the woman run away? Was she just hiding out because she didn't want to deal with Mary? Or was it something else?

Mary found her sitting on the back porch, two of Cash's dogs on either side of her. She had an apple in one hand and a mug of coffee in the other. She must have sneaked into the kitchen when Mary had been helping Izzy with her hair before school.

She was wearing ratty shorts and an oversize T-shirt definitely not fit for riding. "Aren't you going to get dressed for our riding lesson?"

"I thought…" Carlyle sat there looking very young for someone who was only four years younger than her. "I just figured you wouldn't want to do that today."

"Why not?"

Carlyle's frown deepened. "Because I was a bitch to you?"

Mary waved that off. It hadn't even occurred to her. "You can be mad at me, Carlyle. You can even be mean to me. I may not look it, but I have a thick skin." With some things anyway. "But I promised to teach you how to ride a horse, and I don't go back on my promises. No matter how someone else behaves."

Carlyle clearly had nothing to say to that, so Mary pointed to the spot on the stair next to her. "Can I sit down?"

"Your house," Carlyle replied, scooting over a little to give Mary room. Mary settled herself on the stair, looked out at the Hudson Ranch. Home. Her life, her love. Things were changing, but this didn't, and maybe that was why it didn't scare her to open up to the change—open her life, her heart up to Walker and his family.

Besides, they fit right in.

"I see you got Walker to stay in the big house last night," Carlyle said, and it wasn't bitter exactly, but it definitely wasn't happy.

"Yes," Mary replied, and she tried to think about it from Carlyle's point of view. She tried to think of how she might have felt if Jack had brought some woman home.

It was unfathomable, and she realized in this moment it probably shouldn't be. "I can't even imagine if Jack brought some woman home. I'm sure he dates. Or whatever it is men do on their own time that I'd rather not think about when it comes to my brothers. But he's never in all these years brought anyone home or introduced us to anyone. I never really thought about that, how lonely it must be for him."

"Oh, I'm not under any impression that Walker's been alone," Carlyle replied loftily.

Mary tried not to frown at that, but it was hard. Carlyle said it to upset her, and so she shouldn't let it land. But she couldn't help hating the idea of Walker with other women, even if he'd had every right to be. "No, I'm sure he hasn't been alone. But being lonely and being alone are two different things."

Carlyle's shoulders slumped at that, and Mary couldn't help but think she'd scored a point.

"I care very much about Walker. And how you feel about it doesn't really change anything more than you being rude does. But I understand the impulse and the discomfort, so I don't hold it against you."

They sat in silence for a while, and Mary let it stretch out. She petted Copper, watched some birds fly across the bright blue sky. And she waited, because if Carlyle wasn't trying to get under her skin or leaving, maybe she'd end up saying something worthwhile.

"Mary." Carlyle said her name very gravely, and when Mary looked over Carlyle was staring straight ahead. She had a mulish set to her chin, and her expression was determined. "If you really care about him, then you should be on my side on this."

"You haven't told me your side."

Carlyle nodded at that. "And I won't. Just know that it protects Walker." Finally, she turned so her gray-blue gaze met Mary's. She didn't share her brothers' dark eyes, or thick wavy hair. Of course, Anna favored their mother, while Mary and her brothers all looked more like their father. Such differences certainly happened.

"If we get any closer, everyone is going to get hurt," Carlyle said, very carefully. "If you give me some time, I can make sure that doesn't happen. The HSS was only supposed to buy me some time, but you're getting too close. Leave Don Daniels out of it. Go in another direction. Just for a little bit."

Mary absorbed that information that somehow told her so much and so very little. "If I give you time, if you make sure it doesn't happen, does that mean you're putting yourself in danger?"

Carlyle's expression went blank, but not blank enough for Mary not to read the answer in it.

She reached out, put her hand on the young woman's arm. "I know you want to protect your brothers—"

"You don't understand. You can't. Please, Mary. Let me handle this. I promise I know what I'm doing. They won't believe me because they think I'm perpetually twelve, but I know what the hell I'm doing, and I have to do it. But I can't if you and your family mess it up."

"I can't lie to Walker, Carlyle."

"Even to save him?" Carlyle demanded.

And that was quite the conundrum.

WALKER WAS ABOUT to get worried that he was first to the stables, considering he was always last. And Mary was never late for anything. He was already wound tight. He didn't know where Zeke was, and while that was normal, Zeke usually texted him back. He hadn't yet.

Walker checked his phone again for good measure.

Nothing.

He tried to busy himself by getting all three horses ready for the ride, but with every ticking moment, he felt closer and closer to panic.

Just about the time he was about to say *screw it* and call Mary, he saw her walking across the way, along with Carlyle, and the tight knot of anxiety in his chest eased. At least a little.

He hoped Mary had gotten through to Carlyle. Hoped there were answers to be found and quick. But more, he hoped, wished, prayed that this would be his real life. More than he wanted answers, he wanted Mary and his family to be in one place. Here. Together. Living whatever life had to throw at them.

Unfortunately, no matter how much he wanted that, he needed his baby sister safe. First and foremost. If she was holding back, if she knew something…

"Sorry we're late," Mary said by way of greeting. Her smile was genuine, but something like worry danced in her dark eyes.

Carlyle had gone straight for her horse, so Walker stayed by Mary and lowered his voice. "So, how'd it go? She tell you anything?"

Mary smiled at him, put her hand on his cheek. "A little. Nothing specific, but it was a good step. We'll get there."

Walker wasn't sure what to do with that nonanswer, but it was better than her crying, he supposed.

Then she surprised him and lifted to her toes and pressed her lips to his. The move surprised him because he didn't think she particularly liked being affectionate in front of people, and Carlyle might be distracted by horses, but she *was* right there.

"All right, lovebirds," Car said, mounting her horse in that easy way she had that made Walker feel guilty he hadn't been able to give her a childhood in some place like this. "Let's get this show on the road."

Mary nodded and kept smiling and moved to get on her own horse. She gave him a last few reminders as he mounted his. It was getting easier. More natural. He didn't know if he liked the rides so much for the sake of them or because Mary and Car were right here.

He supposed it didn't matter why. He just enjoyed this strange new part of his life.

They did their normal ride, Mary sometimes offering little lectures about what to do if different things happened while riding. She answered Carlyle's question about the cattle operation. For an hour, Walker put Zeke out of his mind and just relaxed.

But when they returned to the stables, Zeke was standing there, arms crossed over his chest. Clearly waiting for them. Clearly restless—which meant he'd found something and was ready to act.

Walker wanted to turn the horse around and canter in the opposite direction, but that was a luxury he didn't have. He pulled his horse to a stop and swung off. "What is it?"

Zeke jerked his chin at Mary and Carlyle. "Everyone should hear."

So Walker waited impatiently while Carlyle and Mary dismounted and walked over to Zeke.

"This morning I met with one of my contacts who's been digging into our father for me."

"You're involving other people?" Carlyle demanded.

Zeke shrugged. "If I have specific questions or concerns, some of my former North Star friends look into certain things for me. They're not really involved, but under the radar and necessary."

Carlyle clearly didn't like this, but she didn't say anything else and Zeke didn't look at her. He looked at Walker when he delivered the news. "Don's dead. Confirmed."

Shock rocked through him, but that was only part of the story. Walker could tell just by the way Zeke held himself. "When?"

This time Zeke's gaze turned to Mary. "Yesterday. Shot to death in his apartment. The cops think it was drug related, but I think otherwise."

Chapter Fifteen

"You think it's connected to what we found in his bank account?" Mary asked, trying to work through this new information and what it meant for moving forward.

It was possible Don was still their mother's murderer even if he was dead. But if he had died yesterday, it likely meant it was connected to what they were digging into

"I think it's connected to you looking. Not sure it's about what was found or not," Zeke returned. "And I think whoever is doing your computer work needs to stop."

"Palmer was very careful."

"Not careful enough," Zeke replied, clearly angry about it.

Mary could hardly blame him. "Let's all go to the big house. We'll sort this through with Palmer and see what—"

"Walker. Carlyle. We need to have a discussion." Zeke said it firmly, and in fact started walking away from the stables and toward the ranch hand cabin before they'd even responded.

"No," Walker returned just as firmly.

Zeke stopped and took his time turning to face Walker. Mary swallowed. She'd seen brotherly arguments that got out of hand before and could see this one brewing a mile away.

"We hired the Hudsons for a reason. We knew the risks, and we also know how often it's no one's fault when things go sideways. We'll all head back to the big house and sort this through."

"You can go play house with your girlfriend, that's fine. But I won't be a part of it. I'm going to finally get to the bottom of this since apparently you can't."

"And neither could your little group of spies, could they?" Walker retorted.

"Let's just go up to the house and talk to everyone," Carlyle said. Mary thought she was maybe trying to sound bored, but she didn't.

"So now you're on his side?" Zeke demanded.

"No, I'm on *my* side," Carlyle returned, anger poking through. "While you both have your little fringe groups to run off to."

They faced off, three angry, hurting people who Mary knew deserved to have their fight. She had no place wading in and trying to diffuse things.

But she could hardly just stand there. So she moved into the center of them, being careful not to align herself with any single Daniels, and spoke to them all. Calmly.

"Guys. You just found out your father died. I know you all had a complicated relationship with him. I know this throws our current investigation into more flux than it has been. Tempers are high. Rightfully so. But you're all three going to regret turning on each other. And if you keep going, you'll regret what you end up saying."

Even Zeke had nothing to say to that.

Before Mary could say anything else, Walker spoke up. "I'm not turning on you, Zeke. I'm thinking about answers. For all of us. So, I'm going to go with Mary and discuss Palmer's computer work with him. Get HSS' take. You can go get North Star's theories, take some time to cool off or come with." He turned to Carlyle. "Same goes, Car. But I know you know I'm always your side, no matter what. There's no fringe group. There's just the people who care."

Carlyle's gaze went from her brother to Mary. And Mary knew the woman didn't understand it yet, but Mary did care.

Not just about Walker, not just because of Walker. Because she knew what it was like to be an orphan. To be raised by your older brothers. To try to make sense of a world that never really did care.

"I'll handle the horses. Meet you up there," Carlyle said with a little nod.

Zeke made a sound of disgust and continued to stalk away.

Walker took her arm gently. "Come on, Mary." She let him lead her toward the main house, but that didn't mean she was 100 percent comfortable with the move.

"Walker, you don't have to spare my feelings on this. Your brother—"

"Is angry and isn't thinking straight." He looked down at her, and this was serious Walker. The man she'd first met. Clear in his path, certain he was right. "Cutting your family out doesn't make sense for a wide variety of reasons, but mostly, we have to know what Palmer uncovered, how and who might have been able to pick up on that. We can't do that if we march off to our corner. We need to work together, or there was no point bringing you guys in. What's done is done. All we can do is keep trying. Zeke and I rarely agree on what that looks like."

Mary sighed and nodded. Walker would know his brother better than she did, certainly. She texted Palmer and Anna and asked them to meet her in the living room. She sent separate texts to Grant, Jack and Cash to keep them informed. They'd come if they had breaks in their schedules, and she would catch them up if they had to miss it.

"Walker…"

"I can't care that he's dead, Mary."

"I wouldn't expect you to. But caring and grieving aren't the only two responses to a death."

He took her hand, gave it a squeeze. "Maybe. I just… If he's dead, and it's because of this, we have to move. We have to act. Because eventually…"

Eventually whoever had killed Don Daniels would come after the rest of the Daniels clan. Mary wasn't sure she believed that, but she understood why he was reaching that conclusion.

"I know Zeke is blaming Palmer, and he has his doubts about us, but—"

"I don't," Walker returned. "Seriously. I've seen how you guys work. You're meticulous. If something slipped through, it's just the way it goes sometimes. Zeke has kept everything to himself, including working with his North Star group. So, he doesn't know, and that's on him."

"Are you always so good at taking things philosophically?"

Walker laughed, though there was no mirth in it. "I suppose I wasn't for a long while. But life has taught me it doesn't make much sense to be mad all the time. As far as I can tell, that's only ever hurt me. God knows whoever killed my mother doesn't care if I'm mad. So, I could blame Palmer. Or my brother. Or a million things, but at the end of the day, blame doesn't do much."

"Then let's work on finding justice."

"Yeah, let's do that."

THEY GATHERED IN the living room. As they waited for Carlyle, Mary made snacks. It was all very organized and somber. No one panicked. No one got defensive. The Hudsons, HSS, worked like a well-oiled machine.

Walker understood in these moments that Zeke had kept himself purposefully away from this, because it was a stark reminder of all the ways they'd failed Carlyle. The ways they hadn't been able to give her something stable like this.

A few years ago, Walker might have had the same trouble. But something had changed when Carlyle had demanded she go out on her own. Walker had been forced to let go, and in that letting go he'd realized a person could only do what he thought was best any given moment.

Sometimes it was the right thing. Sometimes it wasn't. But you had to live with both.

Carlyle finally came in, and Walker couldn't read the odd expression on her face, but Mary called their little meeting to order and Walker had to focus on the task at hand.

"Don Daniels is confirmed dead. Happened yesterday and was clearly a murder. According to Zeke the police are thinking it's drug related."

"That'd be quite the coincidence," Palmer said darkly.

"Yes," Mary agreed, and it struck Walker as so silly she thought she couldn't do this. She was so good at keeping people on task, leading things to a conclusion.

"But something needs to be done," Mary continued. "Because either Don just happened to walk into something dangerous or us finding that payment started this domino of events."

"Digging into who paid him more like," Palmer said from where he stood by the front window, looking out.

"You think someone knew you were looking into them?" Walker demanded of Palmer.

"Me personally? No. That *someone* might be?" Palmer shrugged. "I can hide it well, but someone with more computer skills than me might have suspected someone gaining access. And I'm not finding anything, so whoever paid Don is good at hiding things."

"I don't know how Don could have gotten mixed up with anything that fancy," Walker muttered irritably. "He was a deadbeat, abusive alcoholic with all of the sense of a rock."

"Well, if someone knocked him off because of this, likely Don was a pawn, not a player. Still, we'll want whatever police reports we can get our hands on. Carefully. I'll see what I can do." Palmer looked at Mary, and when she nodded, Walker realized Palmer had been asking Mary's permission to leave.

Once given, Mary turned to face Anna and her husband, Hawk.

"You had people after you," Anna said to Walker from

where she was sitting on the couch. "A group would likely mean they were either pawns themselves or paid muscle. So, we're not looking for who's been after you. We're looking for who's paying *them*."

"So, likely that's going to be the same person that paid Don off," Walker said, frustrated because poking into that carefully meant taking time he wasn't sure they had anymore. Or worse, Zeke would start poking recklessly just to get the job done. "I need to go talk to Zeke. He's got some connections that he uses, but we need to make sure they weren't the reason Don got figured out either. We need to ensure everyone is safe. The rest is secondary."

Once upon a time he'd wanted justice for his mother, and it wasn't that he didn't still want that. It was just that justice didn't change anything. But if anyone got hurt in this, Mary's family or his own, that was a chance he couldn't bear.

"Walker."

He looked back at his sister, barely recognizing it was her that spoke when her voice was thready and uncertain. She looked pale, and he wasn't sure he'd ever seen quite so much upset in her eyes, at least not since she'd been a little girl. He crossed to her. "What is it, Car?"

"There's something…" She trailed off, looked over his shoulder at Mary. Walker glanced over his shoulder too. Mary had a kind of pleading look on her face, like she knew what Carlyle was going to tell him.

Like they had a secret.

"Don Daniels isn't my father," she said in a rush when he looked back down at her. "Mom told me before she died."

"What?"

"The guy who is?" She inhaled shakily. "He's… I'm willing to bet he's the guy paying people to follow you. And that he killed Don or had him killed. And if he thinks people are trying to find him, he'll want me next."

Chapter Sixteen

Mary didn't gasp, though she wanted to. She'd known Carlyle had a secret, and she'd hoped, in time, Carlyle would let her—and Walker—in on it. Before she'd gotten herself hurt or worse.

But this…

"Carlyle, what the hell?" Walker asked through gritted teeth.

"Mom told me that Don wasn't my dad. Right before she died, because she was afraid. And she said I had to keep it a secret."

Mary watched the hurt and worry and betrayal chase over Walker's face. She wanted to go to him, but she understood this was a brother-and-sister moment.

"Did *your* father kill our mother?" Walker asked in a rough voice.

"I don't know for sure. I know she was scared of him. And the timing… I don't know, Walker. I only know she told me I couldn't tell a soul. She said he'd kill all of us, so I always figured…yeah, it was him."

Walker's jaw set and Mary felt her own heart twist. What a terrible burden to put on a little girl, even if it was true.

Carlyle looked beyond Walker. "And he won't like that anyone is getting close. If he was behind those payments to Don…" Her gaze returned to Walker's, imploring. "He might not have evidence, but he'll know it's us. The fact that you two have been going in the wrong direction all this time is the only reason you're alive, I think, but if he has reason to think you know now… You have to stop Zeke." She grabbed Walker's hands. "It was one thing when he was busy with North Star, but now that that's done, he's going to get himself—maybe all of us—killed because he's going to find the answer."

Before Walker could react to that, Mary interjected. Because they still didn't have the full story. "Why is the secret so important to him?"

Carlyle's expression flickered, as she clearly was deciding how many details she wanted to divulge. But this was it. The breaking point. And Mary knew the only reason Carlyle was giving in was because she thought Zeke would get close enough for it to be dangerous.

"We need all the facts, Carlyle," Mary urged. "That's the only way to protect everyone."

Carlyle nodded, but her eyes were on her brother. "His name is… Connor Dennison."

"The *senator*?" Walker said in disbelief. "The grandson of Desmond Dennison? The husband of *Donna Kay*?"

Carlyle looked over at him and nodded. "Yeah, and that's the problem. He's richer than God. Has all the connections in the world between his and his father's politics and his wife's Hollywood status. He's basically a celebrity. And if I ever tell anyone he's my father, I'm not just dead, but anyone who might know is too." She looked up imploringly at Walker. "That's why I didn't tell," she said, her voice a pained whisper. "I couldn't tell."

"I don't understand. I was nowhere near the truth. Why would he try to stop me?" Walker asked, his voice still rough.

Carlyle hesitated. She chewed on her bottom lip, clearly deciding what to keep a secret. But they could not deal in secrets any longer. Mary didn't want to butt into a family moment, but this was bigger now.

She took Carlyle's hand and led her over to the empty couch. She nudged the woman into a seat and then sat right next to her.

"Carlyle, I understand why you kept that secret and for so long. You wanted to protect your brothers. Of course you did. And you were young and impressionable. Maybe you made some mistakes, but we all do. It's not your fault that the adults in your life put you in a position where those mistakes might be fatal."

Her gray-blue eyes were filling with tears, though Carlyle was clearly fighting them. "But—"

"*But* nothing. It wasn't fair and it wasn't right, but now here we are. We need all the facts. We need them. It's the only way we can keep you and your brothers safe. I know you don't worry about protecting yourself—one of those Daniels family traits—but this isn't just about you anymore. And it hasn't been for a very long time. So, let's start at the beginning." She gave Carlyle's hand a pat. "When did your mother tell you?"

With her free hand, she waved Walker over. He moved like a hundred-year-old man, like he might fall to pieces at any moment, but when he sat down next to Carlyle, he took her other hand.

Because Carlyle needed support. She needed to believe this was the right thing.

And they all needed to hear it.

"It was right before she died. She was wanting to move again, and I…" Carlyle took a minute, Mary assumed fighting more tears. "I threw a fit. I had friends. I liked my teacher. I didn't want to move. And I wouldn't let up. You know how I was," she said to Walker.

He nodded with a rueful kind of smile.

"Mom lost it. Asked if I'd rather have friends or be dead."

Mary closed her eyes. What an awful thing to say to a little girl.

"She started talking about my father—she didn't give me a name, but I knew it wasn't Don. I knew…this was a secret, but she was so messed up over having to move again, so stressed about whoever she was running from, she just let it all out.

She said he didn't know about me, but he'd follow her to the ends of the earth. That she'd never be free. He wanted her to pay for leaving him."

Walker muttered something foul under his breath, but Mary just gave Carlyle's hand a squeeze. "So, it's possible he killed her and didn't know you were his daughter?"

"More than possible, I think. If I'd… If I'd let it go, I don't think he'd have known. Or cared, maybe. But I just… When I turned eighteen, I…" She looked at Walker now. "Mom didn't tell me his name, just talked about him in a way that gave me some information to go on. I was just so mad about everything. Zeke doing that stupid North Star stuff. You struggling to make ends meet for *me*. Trying to convince me to go to college and stuff. So, I did some digging. Into where I was born and the like. Then I figured, why not ask the man she was married to when it happened."

"You went to Don?"

Carlyle shrugged jerkily. "He was in jail at the time, so it felt safe. He knew I wasn't his daughter, that much was clear. And he was more than happy to give up a name. I didn't believe him at first, because how would my dad be Connor Dennison? Even *I* knew who Connor Dennison was. But I dug into it, and it seemed as possible as anything, so I figured…"

She sucked in a breath, and the tears began to fall.

"I thought I could get some money out of him, you know. I didn't… I just thought I was so smart." She quickly used the heel of her palm to wipe away the tears, clearly embarrassed by them.

Mary set a box of tissues in her lap.

"He denied it, threatened me, then had me followed on the way home. Luckily I was smarter than his thugs, but…"

"That's why you ran away that time. Not because you were mad about college. But because—"

"I knew if we stayed, he'd find you, find me. I think he's been trying to the past few years. But he needs me dead first, so I can't blow up his life. And he needs my death not to connect to yours or people will start digging, and come up with Mom. It's complicated, I think. That's why it's been so difficult. Last year… The threats to you kept getting closer, so I went to HSS with one of your aliases. I thought they'd find you and if you were dealing with them, I'd have time to figure out a way to take him down."

Mary's head was spinning. If she'd known Carlyle had been hiding all this… Well, she supposed it wouldn't matter. Carlyle wasn't going to tell anyone until she was ready.

Now they had to deal with the truth.

"I'm sorry," Carlyle continued, really crying now. "He doesn't care about you guys. He cares about making sure the truth doesn't get out—and I think that means he's the one who killed Mom. Because I'm just a secret kid, but she's an unsolved murder. Which means he's dangerous. He has to be careful because if anything connects to him his life is over. But he will kill us all if he thinks you know, if he can figure out how to get away with it, Walker, I have no doubt."

WALKER FELT LIKE he'd been gut punched. Maybe run over by a car. Never in a million years could he have anticipated all this.

Carlyle's hand was still in his, but he barely felt it. Barely felt anything. He glanced at Mary. Had Carlyle confided in her?

No, she seemed as shocked as he did. As everyone did. Because Anna and Hawk clearly were struggling to come to terms with Senator Connor Dennison being involved in this mess. And Zeke…didn't know.

Walker pulled Carlyle into a hug. Because she was crying. Because no matter how complicated this was, no matter how angry he was at her, Mary had been right. It had been wrong that their mother had put that kind of burden on a little girl.

"We'll sort through this mess. It'll be okay."

"I can't lose you and Zeke too," she said into his chest.

"Please. I know how good you guys are at this stuff, but he will win. The only reason we've been able to avoid him this past year is because we've been split up, because of Zeke's North Star connections, and how far off you've been from the truth. But if he was behind that money, he thinks you know. Him being careful won't last with the truth out. Men like him always win."

Walker wished he could argue with her. But money and power had more sway than just about anything in this world, and he might have a lot of skills, but he didn't have either of those two things to go along with it.

He broke the embrace and looked into her eyes intently. "I have to stop Zeke before he does something without the full picture. I'll be back, but I need you to promise me to stay put."

"Walker—"

"I'm serious. You stay put. Promise?"

She stared at him, eyebrows drawn together, some new emotion joining all the fear and misery in her eyes. "Fine," she muttered.

Walker nodded, got up and strode to the door. He was already off the porch and a ways across the yard when he heard Mary call his name.

He stopped and turned to see her standing there on the porch, wringing her hands. "I didn't know," Mary said. "She didn't tell me fully."

Walker nodded. It did make him feel better, though maybe it shouldn't. Still, he stayed where he was with enough distance between them he couldn't get a full read on her expression.

He couldn't focus on Mary. He had to get to Zeke. He had to focus on *this*, not her.

"Do you want me to come with you? I could—"

Walker shook his head. "You're a hell of a peacemaker, Mary, but I think maybe peace isn't what we need right now."

"You shouldn't fight with your brother."

She was clearly worried about that. About him. But she

didn't understand. Couldn't. And he didn't know how to explain any of this. "We'll see."

He heard her sigh, but he didn't let that change his course of action. He walked back to the cabin, hoping he wasn't too late. Hoping he had the words to get through to his brother.

Because just like he'd known Carlyle was hiding things, even if he hadn't known *what*, he knew Zeke had more information than he'd let Walker in on. But not as much as Carlyle.

Walker had always thought his siblings kept him in the loop when they weren't together. Even while he'd not been keeping them in the loop of what he'd been up to.

He really should have known better, but he supposed that's why they'd all gone their separate ways last year. To keep their secrets. To protect one another. At least they'd sort of succeeded considering they were all still breathing.

But Carlyle was right. That couldn't last forever. Not when a man had the kind of power and money Connor Dennison did.

So the time for secrets was officially over.

Walker entered the cabin to find Zeke loading his gun, an array of items on the table as he was clearly packing a bag to leave.

"You should have come, Zeke. Carlyle dropped a hell of a bomb."

"Is it about Senator Dennison?"

Walker stared at his brother for a good minute before he could make his mouth work. "How…"

"I just got the name from my North Star contacts. It was hidden well, but that's the origin of Don's payment, so he's connected somehow. So, no, I didn't need to stay."

"You do because that's only half the picture."

Zeke kept loading guns, clearly not impressed.

"Carlyle says Connor Dennison is her biological father."

Zeke's hands stilled and he raised his gaze to Walker. "What?"

"Mom told her before she died, that it wasn't Don. Apparently Dennison didn't know, but then Carlyle…" Walker didn't want to tell Zeke, because he didn't want him to be too hard on Car, but secrets weren't helping them. They needed to work with all the information. Together.

Well, him and Zeke. Carlyle would stay behind and Mary and her family would protect her. And somehow… Somehow he and his brother would make this right.

So he relayed everything Carlyle had said up at the main house. Zeke's expression betrayed nothing, except a cold kind of fury.

"We've got to do something, Walker. We can't hide anymore. *I* can't hide anymore. He could have killed you, but he didn't. I think he could have had me, too, but he didn't. We can chalk that up to our own skills, or we can look at the more reasonable answer."

"It was too risky for him because we didn't know. But he knows Carlyle knows enough. He knows someone has been poking into those payments. He wants her gone, and us, too, if he can swing it."

"And he won't rest until he gets his way. Some rich powerful guy who hasn't made a move yet? He's being careful nothing comes back to him. We have to make it come back to him. It won't be easy. It might not even be possible. But I've got to try." Zeke went back to his guns.

"When are you leaving?" Walker asked, resigned. Because sometimes there wasn't a good approach to something. Sometimes, you just had to make the wrong decision with someone, *for* someone.

"The minute it's dark."

"I'm coming with."

Zeke paused in his packing. He studied Walker carefully. "You sure about that?"

Walker thought about Carlyle. About how everything had changed after that fire on her eighteenth birthday. About the fact that she'd known all this time what that something was.

She'd kept it to herself thinking she'd somehow protect him and Zeke.

And he had no doubt, because she was a Daniels even if she wasn't Don's daughter, that she'd been content enough in the knowledge that if someone died, it would be her. Not her brothers.

He'd come to the same conclusion about himself the closer someone had been on his tail over the past year. So no doubt Zeke had the same thoughts when he'd been out there doing North Star things and who knew what all else.

Which was why Zeke couldn't go it alone. Neither of them could, much as Walker didn't want to go. Didn't want to throw himself into danger anymore. Because he'd found Mary, found a life here.

But none of that mattered if they didn't find a way to protect Carlyle. None of that mattered if he let Zeke go at it alone. He could hardly let his family's issues put the Hudsons in danger for the foreseeable future either. "I'm sure. I've got to get some stuff from the main house, and I'm going to get a few more details about this guy from Palmer. Don't leave without me, got it?"

"She going to talk you out of it?" Zeke asked skeptically.

"No." Mary might try, but Walker had made up his mind.

Chapter Seventeen

When Walker returned, Mary was making dinner. She could tell from his expression she wasn't going to like whatever he had to say.

"Where's Car?"

"I tried to convince her to lie down for a bit, but that didn't work, so Cash offered her some work over with the dogs."

Walker nodded. "That's probably best. Keep her mind busy anyway."

Mary studied him. She could see a little too much good-bye in his eyes and she desperately wanted to find a way to change it. So she crossed to him, put her hands on his chest. "I told this to Carlyle, but I hope all three of you know it. You have a place here. A life."

He put his hands over hers, and she saw the regret, but also that his decision was already made. "Zeke is going after Dennison, with or without me. I can't…"

Mary had to work very hard to hold on to her composure, because she couldn't argue with this, much as she wanted to. "You can't let him go alone."

His eyes were soft, his words genuine as he curled his fingers around hers. "I'm sorry."

"I know." She had to swallow at the lump clogging her throat. "And I understand. He's your brother. You have to protect him, and I know he'll protect you right back. It's something you both need to do." She hated it, didn't want him to do it, but understood. She'd hardly let any of her siblings go off into something so dangerous without trying to alter the course. Granted, she'd use her *words* to not go along with them, but maybe there were no words to stop Zeke. "Will you tell Carlyle?"

"No. She's in the most danger. I need her to stay here. I need you and your family to protect her at all costs. Dennison might be happy to take us out given the right circumstances, but Carlyle is who he really wants."

Mary didn't want to scold, didn't want to tell him he was wrong. Not in this moment where her heart felt bruised, and she knew his did too. But… "You leaving her out of the equation isn't going to go over well."

"We aren't leaving her out. She's the target, so she has to be protected. I know she won't see it that way, but that's the way it is."

"Did it occur to you she might want to protect herself?"

Walker's expression changed. *Detached* was the only word Mary could think of to describe it. Because she'd seen it on Jack's face too.

"I'm sorry," Mary said. "I don't want to argue with you. But I think you should tell her."

"So *she* can argue with me?"

"Walker."

"I don't have time, Mary. If I'm not back soon, Zeke will just assume you talked me out of it and he'll leave. I can't let that happen."

Mary swallowed. The truly frustrating thing was that she understood *all* their points of view. And none of them were totally wrong.

"I just had to say something before I go."

Mary took a step back, because she knew this was some stupid goodbye, and she refused to say it. Still, she couldn't back fully away because his grip on her hands tightened.

She shook her head. "Don't say goodbye because you'll be right back. And you'll keep in touch. And you'll let us help you. I won't accept anything else. So, there's nothing to say."

He heaved out a sigh, and she knew it was not one of acceptance, so she tried to tug her hands away, but he held firm.

"Mary, I love you."

Her mouth dropped open as shock wound through her. She definitely wasn't trying to pull away any longer. *Love.* He'd said... "Walker—"

"I don't want you to say anything to that," he said firmly. "Whether you feel it or not. I know how you'd smooth anything over, and I don't want that right now. I just want you to say it in a moment you really mean it—if you mean it, okay? When it just sweeps through you, and you can't think of a single other thing to say. Not now. You pick *your* moment. This was mine."

"Walker..." How could she not mean it? But that lump in her throat had grown exponentially, and he was shaking his head.

"You gotta give me that, Mary."

She didn't know how, in this moment, not to give him everything he asked for. So she could only let him pull her into him, lift her mouth to his in what felt way too much like a goodbye, except... If she didn't say it, it meant he *had* to come back.

"I'll be back," he said against her mouth, as if he could read her thoughts. He pulled away, looked her in the eye. "Know that. Believe that. Okay?"

She nodded. She couldn't have spoken if she'd tried. Then he released her, quickly turning and exiting the kitchen. He didn't hesitate. Didn't look back. And she thought she knew him well enough to understand he couldn't, or he'd be tempted to change his mind.

But he couldn't because he had to protect Zeke. Who wanted to protect Carlyle, who wanted to protect both her brothers. A never-ending circle that would only end in sacrifice.

When it wasn't right. None of them should have to sacrifice.

Mary turned off all the burners, leaving dinner half-prepared. She texted Dahlia asking her to finish everything up when she got the chance. She found Anna and Hawk, gave them some instructions on how to run the place without her.

Because like hell were Walker and Zeke doing this on their own. It hadn't gotten them anywhere all this time, so now...

They'd hired HSS. They were going to get the full Hudson treatment. Which meant no one did anything on their own.

Once she had all the plans made, she went in search of Carlyle. Since she wasn't with Cash and Izzy or any of the animals, Mary went up to the guest room and knocked on the closed door.

Carlyle opened it, but only a crack. "I think I'll skip dinner tonight," she said.

"I didn't come up here to tell you about dinner."

Carlyle frowned a little. "You didn't?"

"Your brothers are going to do something stupid."

Carlyle nodded, let the door open farther. Which was when Mary saw that she'd packed up what few belongings she'd brought here. "It's okay, I'm going to go after them. They want to protect me, but this is *my* fight. Maybe it shouldn't have to be, but my mother left it to me. So it's mine now."

"You're not going after them," Mary said firmly. "We both are."

It HAD BEEN a while since Walker and Zeke had done anything together. In fact, come to think of it, they really hadn't since Zeke had become an adult. Because he'd been gone in the military, then he'd been out in the world doing North Star stuff.

Walker couldn't think of his brother as a stranger, but it was a strange moment in time to realize that Zeke had turned into a full-grown man in all the time apart.

"So, do you have a plan?" Walker asked him.

"Mallory is getting me some intel on Dennison from a computer expert she knows. Right now, I know Dennison is in Colorado, so that's where we're headed."

Their cousin Mallory was the one who'd gotten Zeke hooked up with North Star in the first place. One of the few people their mother had kept in touch with over the course of their many moves had been her sister—Mallory's mother. Mallory had actually been the one to find Carlyle when she'd run away at eighteen.

It still floored Walker that she'd run away because of Connor Dennison. The fire had to have been Dennison. Don being dead had to be him too. It was all…too much.

So, he focused on his brother, and his brother's 'connections.'

"I thought the whole North Star thing got disbanded," Walker said to his brother, trying to focus.

Zeke shrugged. "Did, but that doesn't erase our skills. Everyone's all married and popping out babies, doing some search and rescue, so they're not going to be running into danger, but they can still get me intel when I need it. Or get me in touch with the people who can."

"And when we have this intel, what do we do with it?"

Zeke's hands tightened on the wheel as he drove. But he clearly didn't have an answer for that.

"We can't go in half-cocked. We'd end up dead, that only leaves Carlyle alone."

"Or maybe something they can pin on this guy."

Walker winced in the dark of the car. He understood that thought process. He would have had the same exact one if he didn't want to get back to the Hudson Ranch as much as he wanted to protect his sister.

He had something to live for now. He'd always wanted to protect Carlyle, but it had been in a selfish kind of way. The need to be the savior, the one who did it. The one who found the answers.

Now… He didn't care who found those answers, as long as

they had them. He had learned to take off the blinders and see not just his own wants and needs, but Carlyle's.

Which, of course, led him to be haunted by Mary's voice telling him he should talk to Carlyle. Include her in this whole thing. He should have. He knew that.

But he wouldn't have been able to bear it, and neither would Zeke. Maybe he was a hypocrite—but sometimes life was hard, and you had to be one.

"I'm guessing if you asked Car she'd rather have us alive than have this guy in jail."

Zeke didn't say anything to that, though a muscle in his jaw twitched.

"What are you really running from?" Walker asked, even knowing Zeke wouldn't tell him. Even knowing that Zeke might not fully understand himself. Walker had gone through that, too, because sometimes you just had to run and it took something, or someone, to finally ask you why.

Zeke sent him a sideways glance, then looked back at the road. "I'm not running *from* anything. I'm running toward the truth. And ending this, once and for all. If he's behind our mother's murder, that's it."

Walker considered his brother's words. The word *end* most of all, because even if they somehow thwarted a millionaire celebrity politician, it wasn't an end. They still had to pick up the pieces and live.

"So you're heading toward a new beginning, then," Walker surmised. "You know, beginnings can be scary when your future can be anything. Much easier when you see what you want it to be."

"I'm glad shacking up with a woman has clarified your future for you, Walk, but—"

"Call it shacking up. Call it whatever you want, but you know it's more than that. I don't need to sit here and have a heart-to-heart about it, but I love Mary. And if I can figure out what the hell to do with my life, and she'll have me, I plan on making that permanent."

"Jesus, you've known her a month," Zeke muttered.

Walker laughed, was surprised he could under the circumstances. "Who knows how long we've got, so why worry about how long something's been?"

"Awful fatalistic for a guy who's talking about futures."

"Someday you'll be old too."

Zeke snorted—the closest Walker figured he'd get to making his brother laugh, so he'd take it as a win.

They drove the rest of the while in silence. Walker hoped Zeke was considering some real plans, not just doubling down on his impulsive actions. Walker didn't think there was any hope of talking Zeke out of confronting Connor Dennison, but maybe they could do it in a way that didn't spell ruin.

Zeke pulled off the highway, drove down some winding dirt and gravel roads. When he finally pulled to a stop, it was in front of a quaint little cabin in the middle of nowhere, illuminated by both the moon and security lights.

"This is not what I was expecting." Walker had anticipated spending the night in a tent in the woods. A vacant motel in some ghost town. Not a decent-enough-looking house. He studied his brother. "We're not committing a crime, are we? Because I didn't sign on for a little light B&E."

"What can I say? I've got connections," Zeke said with a shrug as he got out of the car.

Walker had always known this, but it was strange seeing how helpful those connections were. A reminder they'd lived much different adulthoods.

Still, he followed his brother onto the porch. Zeke punched in a code on a hidden keypad, then once inside did the same on a visible one. "We'll spend the night here, sleep and eat, then make it to Colorado tomorrow."

"You got fancy digs there too?"

Zeke grinned. "Yeah, I do."

Walker shook his head, then moved into the kitchen. He was starving, as they'd skipped out on Hudson family dinner. He missed Mary's cooking already. Canned soup and slightly stale crackers were hardly a replacement. But he ate, while Zeke filled him in on the information Mallory had gotten on Senator Dennison.

"I'm not sure how we're going to get access to a guy who has personal bodyguards," Walker said. "What about involving the cops? You've got proof he's the guy behind the payment to Don. They can look into it."

"But then they might look into *how* I got information that isn't exactly legal for me to have. Something we could get around when we were North Star, but a little harder to fudge now that we're not. I could get around it eventually, but if Dennison knows we're looking, if he killed Don..."

Walker scowled into his soup. Likely Carlyle was next. "Maybe we shouldn't have left her behind."

Zeke shook his head. "We'll keep the man's attention right here." He stilled, the spoon halfway to his mouth, eyes narrowing.

Walker didn't have to ask him why, he'd seen the flash of headlights against the window. "Get your gun."

Zeke was already moving for his bag while Walker crouched so there would be no shadow in the window.

Then a knock sounded on the door. A loud, brash, insistent knock.

"How the hell did Carlyle find us?" Zeke muttered irritably, striding for the door just behind Walker.

Walker jerked the door open, but then just stood there, mouth hanging open. Carlyle looked pissed, but he expected that. What he didn't expect was Mary to be standing behind her with that kind of smile that seemed to say, *I know more than you do, of course*.

"Looks like you're going to need a bigger boat," Carlyle announced, stepping inside and dropping her bag on the ground.

Chapter Eighteen

Even in the midst of danger and concern, Mary found some enjoyment at the utter shock on Walker's and Zeke's faces. If they were surprised, then at least she'd succeeded at something.

"How the hell did you find us?" Zeke demanded. Anger pumped off him, which Mary had anticipated, as had Carlyle. In fact, on the long drive, Carlyle had laughed over the idea of Zeke blowing a gasket.

Currently, he was holding it together, but barely. Mary didn't think the *hows* were going to make him feel any better.

"Well," Mary said, making sure to be extra calm in the face of Zeke's fury, "I may have had Cash put a tracker in Walker's car before you left."

Both Walker and Zeke stared at her like she'd grown a second head. Carlyle slung her arm over Mary's shoulders.

"She's got a secret sneaky side. I love it."

Mary knew neither Zeke nor Walker loved it. She could also tell they were already scrambling to figure out how to get rid of them, but Mary would not be gotten rid of. She'd made a plan, and she, Carlyle and her siblings were part of that plan. And she was sticking to it, no matter how angry Walker looked.

His expression was hard, and his dark eyes pierced hers as he glared at her. "I want to talk with you. Alone."

"Ooh, you're in trouble," Carlyle said in a singsongy whisper, clearly enjoying some part of all this friction.

Mary wished she could have Carlyle's reckless "don't care about people's opinions" attitude, but it wasn't in her. Even knowing she was right, her heart twisted at Walker's cold voice.

Walker glared at his sister, but he took Mary by the arm and led her outside. It was late, but the stars and moon shone along with some security porch lights that created a little cocoon of light outside.

Walker immediately let go of her arm, and the first little alarm bells went off that he was *really* angry. Not that she was surprised. She just had to brace herself for it.

"I can't believe you'd not just risk yourself, but Carlyle," he said. No, not said. That was too tame. She couldn't call it full-on yelling, but it was definitely an angry scold.

"I'm sorry," she said, and she was. Not for doing what she'd done, but that he couldn't see he was wrong. "But I told you I didn't think you should leave Carlyle behind or out of this. She was going to follow you one way or another. This way was much safer. Not only was I with her, but since Cash dropped the tracker, we knew exactly where you were."

"You should have stayed put. You should have made her stay put," he said, closer to a yell this time.

"How?"

His mouth firmed, because—she knew—he didn't have an answer for that. No one *made* Carlyle do anything.

"You said you understood."

"Understanding and agreeing are two different things, Walker. I also told you keeping Carlyle out of this was not the right choice. She was coming after you, one way or another. I think, deep down, you had to have known that."

"Don't use that schoolteacher voice on me. Don't lecture me. You shouldn't have followed us. You should have stayed put."

"So you two could handle it all yourselves?" she returned. Not with his anger and frustration, but with that schoolteacher voice he hated so much. "Because you're so much better and more important than everyone else?"

He inhaled through flared nostrils, and the anger pumped off him in waves, but Mary also understood while he might be angry at her, most of all he was just angry with the situation. So, she didn't take it personally.

She understood too well all the conflicting emotions of wanting to protect, of being protected.

"Are you done yelling at me?" she asked calmly, hands clasped in front of her.

He glared at her. "I haven't decided."

He stood there, arms crossed over his chest, a mix of anger and worry on his face. And that's when she felt it. Back at the ranch he'd told her to wait for a moment when she felt swept by love. And this was it. She was swamped by the need to protect him, save him, all so she could bring him home and get to the work of building a life with him.

She crossed to him. Placed her palms on his chest. "I love you, Walker."

"Mary, I said—"

"I know what you said. You said say it when you mean it. You said pick your moment. This is my moment. I can't let you do this alone. I can't let you just follow Zeke because you need to be there to watch him fling himself into danger. If we all work together—*all* of us—I think we can fix this. So, I'm here because I love you. I'm letting you vent at me because I love you. And I understand because I love you."

He hadn't moved, hadn't let his arms uncross, and still she felt him soften underneath her hand.

"That's not playing fair," he muttered.

"Then it's a good thing we aren't playing. This is serious and dangerous. And I have a plan. But you have to let us help you. *All* of us."

"Are your siblings going to come pouring out of the clown car?"

"Not yet, though we're working on something. But I want it to be a team effort. Which means Zeke has to be on board."

"Good luck. If I thought I could get him on board, we wouldn't be here." He finally dropped his arms, then he reached out and pulled her close. He framed her face with his big, calloused hands.

"I need you to understand, if you got hurt in this, I won't be able to live with myself. It's not about thinking we're better. It's about knowing what it is to lose." She saw that raw pain in his face and realized, maybe for the first time, the differences in their experiences. Yes, her parents had disappeared, and they were likely dead, but she didn't know. She didn't know how it had happened or if it was true. It was all question marks.

He knew. He'd had to deal with the aftermath of murder. Why wouldn't he be that much more protective of anyone mixed up in this mess? He knew that finality of death too intimately. There was no finality in all her life.

Still… The thought of him getting hurt or worse was too much to let her mind dwell on.

"You don't think I feel the same way?" She covered his hands with her own. "But I know you have to do whatever it takes to end this. So know that I have to be here." She sucked in a deep breath. "I know you won't like our plan, but it's better than two hardheaded men wading in without any sense of *why*."

"I've got a damn good sense of *why*."

"No, you have a good sense of who. Of what. But not why. We need to find that why, Walker. Which is why…" Oh, he was really going to hate this. Argue with her. Explode, maybe. But it was best they did this with the little slice of privacy they had now. Best to try to get him on her side without Zeke and Carlyle interfering.

"That's why I'm going to meet with Senator Dennison. As an ambassador for HSS who has some questions to ask him about an investigation we're handling."

WALKER STILL HAD his hands on Mary's face, but he was pretty sure he'd had some kind of stroke. "I must have heard you wrong, Mary."

She held his gaze with that calm, certain one of hers. "You didn't."

He dropped his hands, stepped away from her. She clasped her hands in front of her again, that schoolteacher look firmly in place.

He tried to mimic it so he could be the calm one. "I think the hell not." Okay, maybe not calm.

"I understand your knee-jerk reaction."

"It's far from knee-jerk. Mary, it is more than likely that this man killed my mother *and* father. He wants my sister dead. And the only thing stopping him is that he hasn't been able to figure out a way to get away with it yet. You think anyone is going to be okay with you walking into the lion's den like this?"

"Carlyle is okay with it. Anna is okay with it."

"You're missing a hell of a lot of names on that very short list."

"My brothers aren't opposed. They just want one of them to go with me. I didn't think that was the smartest idea. I think you should come with me."

Walker scrubbed his hands over his face. Maybe he was having that stroke. "Mary—"

"Hear me out. You're the client, right? Joe Beck. He likely knows that alias. If you come with me, and all our questions are about the money Don was paid—nothing about his murder or Carlyle's parentage—it's possible we convince him this is all we know, all we suspect. We act like we don't know he might know who you are, who your aliases are and so on. We make ourselves look out of the loop and barking up the wrong tree so he backs off."

Walker blew out a breath. His insides were tied tight at the thought of Mary putting herself in any kind of danger, but she was being so rational and so reasonable. She'd looked at him with that calm, earnest gaze and said *I love you*.

He wanted to believe it was manipulation, but it wasn't. It was just...whatever existed between them. They understood each other, they fit.

So he didn't let himself fly off the handle—like he might have with Carlyle. Like he had in the past. He tried to find some maturity. Some sense.

He tried to understand, tried to be on her side. He tried to get over the terrifying fear he was putting her in his mother's shoes.

But no matter how hard he worked to understand, he knew his brother wouldn't. "Zeke won't go for this."

"We have to try. Listen to me. Jack is looking into what can be done from a legal standpoint. Anna and Hawk are looking at the less legal avenues we can go down. Palmer is working on some surveillance or something that would allow us to get Connor Dennison saying something incriminating on video or audio. We're going down all these avenues, but we all have the same goal."

Walker didn't know what to say to that. For so long, his inclination had been to handle things on his own. He knew his siblings shared that MO of withdraw and figure it out yourself. It was their protective mechanism.

But maybe a limiting one, too, he realized now.

Could he get that through to Zeke? "Zeke has some connections of his own from when he worked with a secret group. Maybe we can have him, Anna and Hawk work with them to handle the less than strictly legal avenues. If he's occupied with that, maybe he won't totally fight me on this."

"Or I could go alone. He wouldn't have to know and—"

Walker shook his head. "You know that's a no-go. From me. From your family. From common sense."

"I think common sense says that if Dennison has been

this careful for this long he's not going to off me the minute I meet with him."

"But he could, Mary. That's the thing. If he killed two people, he's capable. And capable of getting away with it."

"Then we have to get Zeke on board. Then we have to work as a team. So we can *all* be safe. Now and forever."

It sounded too good to be true, just as it had when she'd said she loved him. That was too good to be true, but it was real. He reached out, pulled her to him. She leaned her cheek against his chest, relaxed into him. Here in the middle of nowhere with the night and danger creeping around them.

So, he pressed his mouth to hers. Because she was here, and they were going to face this together. Complicated. Terrifying. But somehow… Right.

"Say it again."

"Say what again?" she returned, a little primly, clearly knowing exactly what he wanted.

He smiled against her mouth. "You know what."

Her lips curved and she met his gaze. "I love you, Walker."

That was a miracle, so why not believe they could make a few more happen? "I love you too."

Chapter Nineteen

Mary knew how to lead a meeting. She also knew how to deal with surly members of that meeting. She was terrified, but it was easy enough to keep that below the surface. Because the important thing wasn't if she was scared or not. It was what needed to be done.

"I'll try to set up the meeting as soon as possible," she told Walker's siblings as they sat in the cabin, listening to her plan, "but in my experience setting up meetings with people who don't want to meet, his people will try to put me off. There's also the issue of how many people I'll have to go through to get to Dennison himself. But Jack has had some conversations with the local police, and we can use some names there to put some pressure behind it."

"If I went, he'd see me," Carlyle said somewhat belligerently from her spot curled up on an armchair.

"Yes," Mary agreed. "And potentially do whatever it took to have you killed, then and there. Not to mention, turn his attention on everyone involved. If it's just Walker and me, we have the chance to convince him no one knows anything but you."

"That still leaves her a target," Zeke pointed out, all sharp edges and barely restrained anger. But he *was* restraining it, so that was something.

"That's why this is only step one, Zeke. Now, are your friends going to help or not?"

"I gave them Hawk's information. Anyone who wants to will get in touch with him. A lot of people, our cousin included, are pretty involved in their family life and can't really put boots on the ground. But they'll do what they can from the background."

"I think that's good. We don't want to raise suspicion with lots of people getting involved."

"Okay, let's say this sad little plan works," Zeke said, clearly dismissive not just to be a jerk, but because he was worried. "Dennison believes only Carlyle knows something. He hides his connection to Don or whatever. Then what?"

"While we're dealing with Dennison, HSS will continue the investigation, collect any evidence and data we can. If he's occupied with what we're questioning him about, he might not notice that. We get the police involved, carefully. See if we can get a search warrant for his house or office or anywhere he might have evidence. We put together a case against Dennison. One that can take him down, no matter what kind of fancy lawyers he hires. And while all that's going on, we try to get something incriminating on tape."

"And if none of that works?"

"Then we move on to plan B, Zeke," Walker said, or growled, before Mary could. "You know as well as I do there's no foolproof plan. There's only going forward."

"He'll want to meet on his turf, but not anywhere that might be incriminating," Mary continued, not bothered by the complaints or the growling. In her mind, it wouldn't be a meeting with siblings if people didn't argue.

"You can't meet anywhere that's his. Not his house or office," Carlyle said. "It's too dangerous. A guy with that much money can make people disappear in his own space. Especially if it's an appointment and he knows you're coming. I'm pretty sure the only way I escaped back then was because he didn't know I was coming and kind of broke in."

"It's HSS policy to meet in a neutral spot. So, we'll leave

finding one to you and Zeke," Mary said. "Once we get to town, you'll scout out a few good spots we can suggest to meet him at."

"Based on the quiet of the past month, we can reasonably assume Dennison didn't know where you were, so following us would be tough. We'll get to town and lay low for a day first, just to make certain."

Mary didn't balk at Walker making those kinds of decisions. It was a solid plan, so she nodded.

"I've got a car switch planned for the morning," Zeke said, though Mary could tell it was with some reluctance he was handing over information. "It's possible he's got someone on the lookout for Walker's junker, or any of the cars in his little fleet."

"You have a fleet?" Mary asked, raising an eyebrow at him.

Walker grinned at her. "I have an array of a lot of things."

She couldn't help but smile back. But she didn't let it fully distract her. "All right, that's the plan then. Get some rest. What time do we need to leave?"

"Meeting my contact at a place about three hours away." Zeke checked his watch. "So, maybe a two-hour nap. Security is set so no one needs to stay up for watch duty. Car, you're going to have to take the couch as long as Mary and Walker are doubling up."

"How am I still getting stuck on the couch?"

"Because you're still the smallest," Walker replied, giving her a brotherly nudge.

He got to his feet and took Mary's hand.

"You know, everyone should *sleep*," Zeke said, staring at Walker pointedly.

Mary worked hard not to blush, but Walker said nothing as he led her away from the kitchen and toward a door. He opened it and pulled her inside the cozy little bedroom.

"I imagine you packed some kind of bag full of essentials,"

he said, and he waited for her to step inside before he closed the door behind her.

"I did, but I don't really need anything for a nap."

He nodded and didn't say anything else. He didn't even look at her really. He just settled onto the bed and motioned for her to do the same.

Mary didn't have the first clue how anyone would sleep— let alone for two short hours. It'd likely take her that long just to calm her brain down enough to close her eyes. Still, she crawled into bed next to him. He was lying on his back, staring at the ceiling. Likely he was thinking, but still...

"You're uncharacteristically quiet."

His mouth curved slightly, then he turned onto his side to face her. "I guess you throwing yourself headlong into danger will do that to a guy."

"You'll be with me."

He nodded, but there wasn't any levity in his expression. Just a grim kind of acceptance, she supposed. She reached out, touched her palm to his cheek, needing to find some kind of comfort for him. "We're going to do everything carefully, safely. You've made it this far, Walker. Now you have all this help. It's a positive."

He nodded, and she knew he didn't agree—or at least, couldn't find it in himself to have that kind of hope. She could hardly blame him.

His gaze met hers, dark and assessing. "You're not nervous about failing?"

"You told me there is no failure except giving up." She forced a smile. "I'm working very hard on believing that."

His mouth curved, a little glimmer of mischief in his eyes popping up. *There* was Walker. He pulled her close and pressed his mouth to hers, his hands sliding under her shirt.

"I'm pretty sure Zeke told us no funny business," she said primly against his eager mouth.

Walker grinned. "I don't recall ever listening to my brother."

THEY SLEPT—WELL, some people did—then got on the road.
Zeke drove since he wouldn't give them details on where they
were making the car swap.

Walker tried to relax. Trust his brother, trust the Hudsons.
Go with the flow. Not worry about bridges they hadn't crossed
yet.

But Carlyle was quiet, her expression opaque.

She was damn well making him nervous.

After three hours, Zeke started making turns onto gravel
and dirt roads. Mountains were in the distance, but all around
was nothing more than fields.

But after a bit more driving, an old, dilapidated barn came
into view. Zeke said nothing, just drove straight for it, and
then onto the grass and into the wide opening on the side of
the barn.

Inside there was a car, and a woman dressed all in black
throwing darts at a crooked dartboard. She waited until they
came to a stop, then dropped the darts and walked over to
Zeke as they all got out of the car.

"Thought it was going to be Gabriel," Zeke said, shaking
the woman's outstretched hand. There were no introductions
offered.

"Ah, well, Mallory went into labor. Gabriel asked me to
step in." She eyed Walker, Carlyle and Mary in quick succes-
sion, and Walker had no doubt she'd made assumptions about
all of them from that quick perusal.

"I'll take the, well, it's not a car, is it? More a tin can on
wheels." The woman shrugged. "I'll pass it off a couple times.
It'll end up in a barn in Nebraska if you ever want it back." She
wrinkled her nose. "Can't imagine why you would."

"Thanks," Zeke said.

"Anytime." Then she fished something out of her pocket.
A phone. She handed it to Zeke. "Courtesy of Wyatt. Calls
you make on this can't be traced. Shay said she's poking at
some Fed leads. She'll call you on this if she's got anything."

"Appreciate it." Then Zeke handed her a piece of paper. "Names and numbers for some people who've been helping. If Shay finds something and can get the FBI involved, have them give Jack Hudson a call."

She took the piece of paper and shoved it into her pocket. "Got it."

"Hell of a retirement, huh?" Zeke muttered.

The woman shrugged. "I don't mind a little downtime, but it's always nice to dip the toes in the water again. Stay safe, Daniels." She tossed Zeke the keys, gave them all a little salute, then got into Walker's car with a look of utter disgust.

She drove out of the barn door first. Zeke gestured them to get into the small SUV. Gray and bland, it looked more likely to belong to a soccer mom than a group of people trying to take down a rich, powerful senator.

In other words, perfect.

They drove out of the barn, and all the way to the town of Clearview in mostly silence. Much like last night, Zeke drove on back roads and through country fields before pulling to a stop in front of another nice cabin.

"Are y'all sure you're retired?" Walker muttered to Zeke. He didn't know what to do with his brother's other life, or all the evidence of it that Walker had never known any details about.

Zeke shrugged. "You can take the spy group away from the operative but you can't quite take the operative out of the people."

They moved inside, Zeke inputting all kinds of codes.

Then, for the next two days, they focused on the task at hand. They had phone meetings with Mary's family, Zeke had secret calls with his North Star people. They plotted, they planned.

It was strange to watch Mary work with that moment in her bedroom all those days ago in the back of his mind. When she'd been crying, falling apart. Because during this whole thing, she never seemed ruffled. Never broke down or even flinched at Zeke's hard-edged defiance when it popped up, or Carlyle's snarky commentary.

She just carefully maneuvered them forward. Together. Because it had to be done together.

Which was why it was a major concern that Carlyle was *very* quiet as they planned. In the past, Walker would have ignored that. He would have let it go, because he would have had his own secrets he was keeping.

In the present, he couldn't let that slide. It was too dangerous. Too many people were at risk, and he'd been disabused of the notion he was the grand protector who knew everything.

Carlyle had been keeping a secret since she was twelve years old. Then an even bigger one since she'd been eighteen. Walker now realized he didn't know a damn thing.

So he waited to corner her until Mary and Zeke were both occupied with the various phone calls that took up their time in the planning stages. He found Carlyle outside on the porch, sitting on the stairs.

"Missing the dogs?"

She looked back at him and smiled a little. "Yeah. You know… Maybe when this is all over I could con Cash into giving me a job. Mary says he needs help."

Walker settled himself on the stair next to her. "Glad to hear you talking about the future."

She shrugged, but she got that look. How many times had he seen that look over the years and just assumed it was bravery covering up fear? He supposed it was, but it was deeper than that.

It was fear and bravery covering up secrets and lies.

"You're going to stick around Sunrise, aren't you?" she asked. "All that love junk."

"Yeah, all that love junk will probably keep me there."

Carlyle nodded firmly. "Good."

Walker let the quiet settle over them for a few minutes. He could feel Carlyle grow more and more uncomfortable, even as she didn't move, didn't change where she was looking out at the trees.

When Walker spoke, he kept his voice calm, even. Like Mary would. "I know we went our separate ways this last year. Tried to protect each other by staying apart, by keeping secrets and doing our own thing. It was wrong, Car."

She shrugged, somewhat jerkily. "Okay."

He didn't know how to get through to her, so maybe that was also part of why he wouldn't have tried in the past. He'd been stuck with trying to parent her and he hadn't even known how to parent himself. Older, wiser now, he could see all the places he'd failed out of simply not knowing what else to do.

Hard to beat himself up for that.

"If you're planning to self-sacrifice, you're only putting us all in danger. What we don't know *could* kill us. And I just don't mean me and Zeke. Or even Mary. There's a lot of hands in this pie now."

She looked over at him then, frowning. She was quiet for so long he started to think maybe he'd never be able to get through to her.

"It's not your fight. He's not your father."

"But you're my sister, so it is my fight. You always will be."

She looked away, down at her hands, and he thought he saw the glimmer of tears in her eyes, but it was hard to tell with her head bowed. She swallowed audibly. "I'm going to break into his house while you and Mary meet with him."

"Carlyle—"

She looked up, eyes fierce, any trace of tears gone. "You can't change my mind. It's what I'm going to do. I'm going to find something. I have to. I wasn't going to tell you because I knew you'd try to stop me, but you can't, Walker. You won't."

He hated it, but he knew his baby sister well enough to know she was right. There was no talking her out of it, and even if he and Zeke locked her up, she'd just find a way out. A way to do exactly what she wanted. Didn't her confronting Dennison years ago prove that?

"I won't try to stop you," he said, which clearly shocked her enough not to have anything to say. "But you're going to need help."

"I… What?"

It was just what Mary had done—let Carlyle have her way, but give her the foundations and company to do it in a safer manner. "I think you should take Zeke. We can't do anything alone, and God knows Zeke has the skills. While Mary and I confront Dennison, you guys break in and see what you can find."

"You're… Did you hit your head?"

Walker laughed. "If I had my way, you wouldn't do it. But you're going to, so we might as well do it in the safest way possible."

"Zeke won't go for it."

"He will. Because if he doesn't, I'll tell him I'm calling in someone from HSS to go with you."

Carlyle's mouth slowly curved. "Well, that'd do it."

Walker nodded. Then he looked at his sister and told her what he probably should have said a long time ago—instead of high-handed declarations of protection and being the older brother.

"I love you, Car. I'd do anything to protect you, but this is dangerous enough we have to rely on each other. Trust each other. Going it alone hasn't worked in all these years, so now we're going it together. No matter what."

She hesitated. He could see it on her face, that knee-jerk recoil from relying on each other. From truly working as a team. Because it felt like teamwork meant risking the people you loved the most.

But he was coming to realize, thanks to Mary and HSS, that the benefits of it all outweighed the risks. No one could do everything on their own. He held out his hand to his sister. "Deal?"

Her mouth firmed, pushing away that hesitation in her expression. She took his outstretched hand and shook it. "It's a deal," she said.

And he had to believe she meant it.

Chapter Twenty

"I don't like it."

Mary had lost count of how many times she'd heard that over the past forty-eight hours. It was usually from Zeke, but Walker and Carlyle threw one in every once in a while.

Now it was her brother's voice over the phone. "I didn't ask for your feelings on the matter," Mary replied.

She'd told him they'd gotten an appointment set up with Senator Dennison through his secretary. And Zeke and Carlyle had prepared a plan to break into his fancy, well-secured mansion.

"I've talked to Zeke's North Star contact, this Shay woman," Jack said. "The likelihood of any federal or local law enforcement help is slim. Everyone is too afraid of Dennison."

"We're not."

Jack sighed audibly. "Mary—"

"I have to go to the meeting, Jack. We'll regroup this evening and go over what we've found. It's just an initial step," she said, though she wasn't sure she believed that.

"What Zeke and Carlyle are going to find is the inside of a jail cell if they're lucky. And you and Walker could be right there with them."

"We'll cross that bridge when we come to it."

He groaned, which was very un-Jack-like, so she knew he was at the end of his rope. But she couldn't change their plans.

"I'll talk to you soon." She hesitated, because it was not something they said casually, but... Well, she was very well aware she was walking into danger no matter how many precautions they took. "I love you."

"Jeez, Mary, I—"

But she hung up on him, because she knew she'd worried him with those words and she couldn't focus on Jack and his feelings when she had a scary meeting to go to.

She returned to the living room and handed Zeke the untraceable phone. He put it in his pocket.

"You guys should get going."

Walker nodded but pulled Zeke and Carlyle into a three-way hug like he had back at the cabin when Zeke and Carlyle had shown up. But this time, Walker pulled Mary into the little huddle, as well. Their heads were together, their arms were around each other.

A team. A family.

"No unnecessary risks," Walker said firmly. "No self-sacrifice. We get what we can get, and we leave the rest. There's always tomorrow if we don't get what we need today. We have to agree on that, trust that. We have to."

Zeke nodded, then Carlyle. When Walker looked at Mary, she nodded too. Then they pulled apart and collected everything they needed.

Mary got the messenger bag with all the things she would usually carry if she was questioning someone. A tablet, a notebook, a list of typed-up questions about the situation at hand. She was prepared and ready just as if this was an average HSS questioning.

Too bad she didn't usually conduct those. And too bad it wasn't. This was far from usual, because Carlyle and Zeke would be attempting to break into a well-secured house while she and Walker faced down a potential murderer. A rich, powerful murderer.

She walked outside with the Daniels siblings. First, Walker

dropped Zeke and Carlyle off at a bus stop—where they'd take a bus to a meet up with one of Zeke's North Star people and pick up a new car. While they did that, Mary and Walker drove deeper into town, toward the library, the neutral meeting point that had been arranged with Dennison's secretary.

They drove in silence, both too lost in their own thoughts and worries to come up with conversation. All those worries doubled when they pulled into the library parking lot. The library was supposed to be a public meeting place, with people and witnesses.

But the parking lot was empty.

Walker's frown got progressively deeper as he pulled into a parking space.

"I don't like this," Walker said, staring up at what appeared to be the empty building.

And though she'd heard that a lot over the past few days, this was the first time she fully agreed. "Me either."

Walker studied the surroundings. She could see him filing things away. She also knew he was armed. In her bag, she had a recording device, and a little panic button that would send a text to everyone saying they needed help.

They had so much help, there was really no need to be this afraid. Or so she tried to tell herself.

"We still have to go in," Walker said grimly. "We have to make sure he's here, or Carlyle and Zeke are in trouble."

Mary nodded. They got out of the car and met at the hood. Walker took her hand. They weren't supposed to look like people who had anything more than a working relationship, but Mary knew he needed the connection.

And so did she.

They moved carefully up to the library front doors. Mary tried not to hesitate when she saw that the doors were open and there were people waiting in the lobby. Not a public kind of people, but Senator Connor Dennison himself. He was flanked by two large men in black, no doubt his security detail.

Walker squeezed her hand, then released it as they stepped through the open doors, which closed behind them with what sounded like a very menacing *click*.

"Dennison. This isn't quite what we anticipated," Walker said. His voice was strong. Unafraid. "We did say somewhere *public*."

"Yes, you did. But you want to talk about things that are… let's say, private. So I rented out this place so we could have some of the required privacy." He smiled brightly, as if this was the most reasonable course of action in the world.

"You rented out the public library?"

Dennison didn't so much as flinch or blink. He turned a dark gaze to Mary. "You must be Ms. Hudson. You're the one who has questions for me?"

"We both have questions, Senator. I'm just helping facilitate Mr. Beck's quest for the truth." Mary was proud of how businesslike she sounded.

"Quest for truth." Dennison threw his head back and laughed. "That's an interesting way of putting it. And since we're talking about truth, let's stop dancing around it." All that cold mirth left his expression and he stopped laughing and smiling.

"Your sister has been a thorn in my side long enough," he said, glaring at Walker. "You were kind enough to deliver the one thing she cares about right to my lap." The man smiled, but it was a chilling, soulless kind of smile. "I knew if I waited long enough you three would mess up your own lives."

One of the guards stepped forward and roughly grabbed Mary. She could see the other guard had done the same to Walker, and he was definitely not going without a fight.

So Mary fought. She kicked, she scratched, she punched.

But then a gun was pressed to her temple and she stilled completely.

WALKER FELT HIS entire body seize up in utter terror. There was nothing stopping Dennison from pulling the trigger. He'd rented out this damn library, and it didn't matter that it was broad daylight outside, he could kill her.

And there was nothing Walker could do.

Had they really been this stupid?

"Take him," Dennison said, jerking his chin toward the back. "If he causes a problem, make sure to let me know." Dennison used the hand not pressing a gun to Mary's head to cup her chin. "For every fight," he told Walker, "your friend here gets punished."

Walker was still frozen, and when the guard jerked him forward, he had no choice but to go. He couldn't call Dennison's bluff when the man had a gun to Mary's head, because there was a very real possibility there was no bluff.

Walker was led deeper into the library, then down some stairs and into a back room full of boxes. He didn't fight—he would, when the moment was right, but right now he knew Mary would pay the price for that fight.

So, when they shoved him into the room, he went. When they took his gun, he let them. One held him against the wall and the other landed a hard punch right to his gut, and he bent over but he didn't fight back. They landed blows, one after the other, and Walker simply took them.

Blood trickled down his face from various places, and still he let them.

After a few particularly vicious punches to the kidneys, one of the guards gave him a little shake. "Fight back, you idiot."

Since it seemed to be what they wanted, Walker only shook his head. "No." He tensed, waiting for more blows to rain down.

Instead, they dropped him and he fell to his knees. He struggled to breathe through the pain. Had to fight to focus on what was next. How to survive this—because that psychopath had Mary.

Inexplicably the two guards just left. Oh, Walker was sure he was locked in the room, but this didn't make any damn sense. Still he managed to get to his feet and cross over to the door, just to make sure.

Yeah, locked.

He wiped the blood dripping off his chin with the back of his hand and studied the room. He ignored the pain and kept his brain engaged, moving boxes, looking for any way out or any weapon. Time stretched out until he lost any sense of it. He had no idea how long it had been when the door opened again.

Walker got in a fighting stance though his body throbbed. He'd fight his way out if given the chance.

But it wasn't the guards, it was Dennison himself. Walker's body went cold. Too many terrible possibilities worked through him at seeing Dennison enter alone. Still, he didn't speak. Couldn't.

The senator's eyes were cold staring at Walker, maybe cataloging the damage the guards had done to him.

Walker didn't ask about Mary. He felt like that's what Dennison wanted, and worse, Walker couldn't think about what might have happened to her. Not until he had a chance to get to her.

He eyed the distance between him and the senator, gauging his ability to ram into Dennison and escape. But no doubt the guards were waiting right outside the door.

"My guards said you refused to fight back."

"What's the point?"

Dennison clearly didn't like this, though Walker couldn't begin to understand why.

"Once your sister and brother come to save you, as they no doubt will, I'll wipe the three of you out," Dennison said after a while. "It'll look like a tragic accident. Your brother saw combat, didn't he? Traumatic brain injuries do such a terrible number on people. He got a little drunk, went a little crazy and shot his siblings. Then in a fit of despair he killed himself."

"Bummer," Walker replied sarcastically. No reason to play

into Dennison's little game, even if it left him feeling sick to his stomach.

"Don't you want to know what's going to become of the woman you brought into the fray?"

"No."

"Ah, well, don't worry. I have more long-range plans for her before death."

Walker had to work very hard not to react. It was clear that's what Dennison wanted. Him to be on the attack. Him to give something away.

But it was the senator who'd given something away. The fact that everyone Walker loved was still alive.

Maybe they were in danger, but they were alive, and as long as they were, he'd do everything to stay alive too.

Chapter Twenty-One

Mary stood in the middle of a strangely opulent bedroom. She had expected a lot of things when Dennison had forced her into his car at gunpoint. Being driven to his mansion was not one of them. Being taken to a very nice bedroom even less of one. Especially since no one had hurt her or said anything to her. Just led her here like she was a guest.

Of course, they'd taken her bag, searched her and locked her in. Was Walker as lucky?

She couldn't think about that. She had to think about how to get away. Were Zeke and Carlyle, even now, somewhere in this house looking for evidence? Could she get to them?

And if she could, could they all get out and get to Walker?

He hadn't been in the car with her, and if she let her mind go to where he was being held, it went to too many terrible places to name. There was nothing to be done except get herself out of this mess. Because while she might be safe enough right now, at the end of the day, there was no plan for her that could be positive. Connor Dennison had shown his hand. He'd been the one to hold a gun to her head and essentially kidnap her.

There was no way he just let her go when he'd have to face the consequences.

She decided not to think about any of the reasons he might want to keep her alive for the time being. None of them were good, but all of them gave her the opportunity to escape.

So she searched the room. Carefully, quietly. Pausing every so often to listen for footsteps outside the door. She looked out the window, but all she saw were thick leaves—a tree or very tall bush, she supposed, hiding whatever went on in this bedroom. She'd been walked up at least one flight of stairs, so she definitely wasn't on the ground floor.

She was about to test the window to see if it would open when she heard the doorknob turn. She whirled around to face it, took a few steps away from the window and clasped her hands together in front of her.

She didn't know what she'd be up against, so all she knew to lead with was her usual contained demeanor.

Dennison himself stepped into the room. He closed the door behind him. Fear twined through her, but he didn't have a gun. At least in his hands. Who knew what the suit jacket he wore hid.

He didn't say anything at first, just studied her, the kind of perusal that had her tightening the grip of her hands and fighting the urge to shrink in on herself.

"You seem like the kind of woman who might be reasonable, Mary Hudson. And I could use a reasonable woman."

Mary worked as hard as she ever had to keep her polite smile in place. "It's hard to be reasonable when you've had a gun pointed at your head and been kidnapped."

Connor smiled. She supposed if she took away all the fear, she might understand why someone could find that smile charming, but she only saw the cruelty behind it.

He stepped forward and held out a phone—*her* phone that had been in her bag. "Let's give reason a try. First, I want you to call your family. Tell them you had an informative meeting with me and you'll be in touch in a few days. Can you do that?"

Mary's mind raced for the right answer. Fight? Go along with him? She really had no idea. She knew Walker and his siblings would fight, but that wasn't her strong suit. Why not lean into her strengths?

So she forced herself to smile. As if he was a client. As if it was her job to help him. "Of course."

He touched the screen of her phone and held it out to her—not so she could take it, but so she could type in her passcode. He watched her enter in the numbers, which was probably a bad thing, but in the moment Mary didn't know how to avoid it.

"Now call home, Mary. Tell them you'll be a few days and not to worry."

She tried to take the phone, but he clucked his tongue and held firm. "On speaker, of course."

Mary didn't let that make her falter. She just followed instructions and hoped to God whoever answered didn't give anything away. Or believe her, for that matter. She called the home landline, hoping no one picked up and she could maybe just leave a message.

But Anna answered on the second ring.

"Anna. Hi."

"Hey. Everything okay?"

"Yes, everything is fine," Mary said, keeping her voice devoid of any inflection. She didn't look at Dennison. She just stared hard at the phone. "I've met with Senator Dennison. Everything went as expected. We should be back home in a few days."

"That's it?" Anna replied, somewhat incredulously.

Mary looked up at Connor. He gave her a little nod, so she swallowed. "Yes. We're going to be pretty busy, so I may not call in a day or two and I didn't want you to worry."

"I can barely hear you. Are you on speaker or something?"

"Yes. Yes, I'm driving. I'll call again in a few days, all right?"

"Okay. Be safe. Call if you need anything."

"I will. Goodbye."

Connor hit the end button and tucked the phone away in his inside suit pocket. Mary didn't know if Anna had picked up on anything being wrong as it was highly irregular for her not to want to check in. There was no reason for her to be driving on speakerphone.

Even if Anna had thought something was wrong, what would they do with something so innocuous? Come to Colorado?

Be too late?

No, she wouldn't think like that.

"Excellent work," Connor said. If she'd been in just about any other situation she might have been warmed by such an enthusiastic compliment. But his smile had her fighting the urge to step back. To protect herself.

He moved closer. "We might just make an excellent team, Ms. Hudson." He reached out and touched her cheek. She couldn't resist the urge this time—she jerked away from his touch.

He sighed heavily, like she'd disappointed him greatly. Then without warning his hand shot out, backhanding her cheek hard enough that she stumbled, catching herself on a dresser so she didn't fall.

He leaned in close, eyes blazing with an incongruous fury to the words he spoke. "You need a few lessons in how to deal with your superior, Ms. Hudson."

He moved forward this time, no creepy, gentle touches. His hand was on her throat, and Mary frantically searched her brain for any of the self-defense maneuvers she'd been taught.

He leaned in close. "Say, 'Yes, sir, Senator Dennison.'"

Mary swallowed at the terror and bile threatening to choke her. "Yes, sir, Senator Dennison," she managed, though it was weak and scratchy.

He gave her a hard shove and this time she did fall to the floor. But at least his hands weren't on her any longer. And he was striding out of the room, slamming the door behind him.

Mary gave herself a minute to regroup, there on the floor. To slow her breathing, to wipe away the tears that had filled her eyes. That was scary, but she was still in one piece. She was still alive, and maybe—just maybe—Anna had picked up on the fact that she wasn't herself.

Granted, Mary didn't know what her siblings could do, but it was a hope to hold on to, something she could use to get through this.

Gingerly, she picked herself up. She looked around, her eyes landing on the window.

All those weeks ago, when she'd first laid eyes on Walker Daniels, they'd escaped out a window.

Now she'd have to figure out a way to do the same.

It took hours. Careful, tedious hours. She pulled the bed apart, took anything that wouldn't be necessarily missed, then remade it with the coverlet and pillows. She moved it all into the little en suite bathroom. Since there was no door to the hall in here, she locked herself inside just in case someone came in.

It was like something out of a ridiculous movie, but she didn't let that stop her. She tied together the sheets, the little hand towels, the liner of the shower curtain. Whatever worked that wouldn't be immediately noticed.

If she fell to her death because her makeshift rope didn't work, she figured it was better than the alternative.

She heard something—likely someone coming into her room. She shoved everything behind the shower curtain, flushed the toilet. She looked around for a mirror, but there was none. She washed her hands and swallowed down her nerves before wiping her hands on her pants.

She stepped out of the bathroom to find Dennison again. There was a tray of food and candles on the little desk in the corner. He'd dimmed the lights, and the candles flickered like terrifying spirits of doom.

In another setting, with another man, it might have been seen as romantic, but there was only an ever-worsening fear that there was no way to escape this. And *this* was worse than she'd feared.

"I'm sure you're starving. Sit. Eat."

She wasn't sure she'd be able to stomach a bite, but she also knew his words were not a request. Stiffly, she moved over to the desk and sat. He moved, too, standing right next to her as she surveyed the food.

He watched her every move, and it worried her. Had he tampered with the food? Still, she picked up a fork, not sure what else to do. Claim food allergies? Stubbornly refuse? She eyed the tray itself. Could she upend it in his face and run away?

"No need to worry about the food." He reached down, picked a little potato off the plate and popped it into his mouth. He washed it down with whatever was in the glass—maybe some kind of wine. "I'm not going to poison you, Mary. I want you to work for me."

She blinked up at him. "Why would you want me to do that?"

"Many reasons. I have a need for good staff who can be trusted or blackmailed. I even thought about using those Daniels brothers. They have the skills to be excellent…muscle," he said, as if thinking over the appropriate descriptor. "But unfortunately for them, they just don't suit. And it seems I might finally have a chance to eradicate them both."

Mary couldn't even come up with a response. But she didn't have to. Dennison droned on and on about opportunities.

"You see, I like the people who work for me to owe me." Then he smiled down at her, and she had to pretend like it didn't make her skin crawl. She swallowed a small bite of food even though she couldn't taste anything.

She smiled at him, though she wasn't sure she was a good enough actor to make it come off as polite. Maybe he was delusional enough to assume it was. "And what do I owe you?"

"Your life, of course. And now that I've done my research, your family's lives, as well." He pulled out her phone, angled the screen so she could see, then brought up her pictures. He swiped through until he found one of Izzy cuddling a puppy.

Mary couldn't hold her smile in place, but she said nothing. She didn't move. Maybe she didn't breathe.

"Cute," he said. "I wouldn't kill her, I don't think. It's best to teach them young, you know."

Mary refused to ask him what he meant by that. It seemed exactly what he wanted, and while she was desperately trying to play along, there were some lines she didn't know how to cross, even in pretend.

"But the rest of them would be easily wiped out. That fire investigator your sister's married to got a little too fast and loose with his pyromania and *whoosh*. It'll take some time, just like the Daniels brothers did, but it would be done. You can either work for me in the interim or be tortured by me." His smile widened. "I'm happy with either eventuality, of course. I'm flexible like that. So, it's your choice."

Mary carefully set her fork down. She folded her hands in her lap. "I can't say it feels like much of a choice."

Connor laughed, then took her by the arm and pulled her to her feet. "You sound like my wife, Mary. Unfortunate. *She* has her uses—deep pockets and deep roots. You? You're a toy. At best." His hand came to her face again and he ran his fingers through her hair. "I don't always break my toys, Mary, but I will if you don't cooperate."

His hands slid down her neck, then over her arms, his fingers curling around them in a tight, painful grip. "The people who work for me do whatever I say, whenever I say." His fingers dug into her arms so hard it would no doubt leave bruises.

She was shaking now. She didn't know how to get out of this. He was bigger than her, stronger than her. She had no weapons. No exits. She could fight and maybe do some damage, but she wouldn't be able to get away.

Still, she'd hardly just stand here and take it. She was about to knee his groin when a chime sounded. Connor paused for a moment, though his cold gaze never left hers. After a moment, another chime, then he stepped back. He took his phone out of his pocket, looked at the screen, then scowled.

He said nothing. Just collected his tray of food and candles and left.

Mary nearly collapsed with relief. Tears began to fall, but she didn't acknowledge them. There was no time. There was only trying to get out. And if she fell and broke her neck, it was better than the alternative.

Once he was gone, she ran to the bathroom and got her makeshift rope. She tied one end to the bedpost and brought the rest to the window. She ripped the coverlet off the bed and wrapped it around her arm over and over until it created enough padding against breaking glass.

He'd left in a hurry, so she assumed he wouldn't hear, but if he did, she didn't care. If he came in here, she'd fight him with shards of glass. She'd jump out the window. She'd do *whatever*. But she wasn't standing here taking anything anymore.

She grabbed the lamp off the desk, ripped it from the outlet. She wrapped the base in some coverlet fabric, too, to hopefully muffle the noise.

Then she rammed it into the window. The glass shattered, but the coverlet softened some of the noise. She didn't wait to see if anyone came running. She just kept hitting the lamp against the glass, making a bigger and bigger hole until she knew she could get through it. Her hand throbbed, she could barely breathe, but the gauzy haze of fear made everything kind of surreal and she thought of little else than the next step.

Throw the makeshift rope over the sill. It wouldn't get her all the way down, but it didn't matter.

Nothing mattered except getting out of here.

She didn't look down, just held on to the rope and climbed out. She didn't question whether the knots were slipping. She just worked on shimmying her way down, holding on to whatever branches or pieces of the outside wall that might help distribute her weight.

It was dark, and the rustling of the leaves as she moved through them made her nervous. Everything made her nervous. She had no idea how far she'd gone when she realized things were slipping. The makeshift rope wasn't going to hold.

Oh, God. She was going to fall. She wracked her brain for anything she'd ever learned about how to fall without breaking a bone. Surely Palmer and Anna had discussed how to be thrown from a bull before.

"Just drop," she heard someone say—but it was in a hissed whisper, not a sharp demand. "I'll catch you. I've got you. You're not far."

It was Zeke's voice. She couldn't seem to manage to look down to verify it. Her limbs were shaking, and she was hanging there, slowly going down.

"Damn it, Mary, drop."

She had no choice. She let go and fell. It was a short fall, on that he hadn't been lying. And he did catch her—somehow. It was a little painful. A lot jarring.

But she didn't crash to the ground and she supposed that was something.

"There. I've got you." He put her down on her feet, but she couldn't quite let go.

She held on tight, the relief making her weak. "You're okay. Thank God." She pulled back, looked wildly around. Carlyle was there.

"They know we're here," Zeke said disgustedly. "Not where yet, but they know."

"Where's Walker?" Carlyle demanded.

"I don't know," Mary said. "They separated us. He didn't come to this house, I don't think. But I put that tracker on him this morning. Dennison has my phone, but if we can get a hold of my family, they should be able to get into the tracker and tell us where he is."

"Let's go." Zeke kept her hand in his, and she realized he held Carlyle's with his other one. They stepped forward into the grass, but then Zeke pulled them both to a stop, and that's when Mary noticed that lights were flashing on. Big, bright security lights. One by one.

"We've got to get out of here without them finding us first," Zeke muttered, jerking them all into one of the large shrubs.

Chapter Twenty-Two

Walker had gone through every possible escape avenue. He was dizzy with hunger, shaking with rage and fear, and there was no way out of this basement room. If he thought there was any chance of it doing anything, he might have beat his hands bloody to get out.

Instead, he had to stand around and wait. Wait for Connor Dennison to kill him.

No. No. There had to be a way to fight. Had to be. So he went through everything in the room, and began setting up some kind of trap. Something that would catch Dennison off guard.

If Dennison had guards with him... Well, Walker had fought off more than one man before. Better than just accepting death anyway. So he did what he could to stack boxes in such a way they could come down on an unsuspecting person who might enter thinking they were the only one with a weapon.

Walker worked on finding a good position on the other side that might take Dennison or his guards by surprise. But before he could decide exactly how to position himself, he heard footsteps. After not more than a few seconds, he heard someone shout.

"Stand back."

Walker stared at the door, more than a little confused. But

he stood back. "Okay," he shouted, though his voice was raw from disuse and lack of water.

A loud *boom* echoed through the building, and then the door fell open. On the other side of the dust and debris were three men, with guns drawn. They studied the room, growing expressions of confusion on their faces.

"Just you?" one asked pointedly.

They weren't the senator's guards. They looked like law enforcement, with bulletproof vests and tactical gear. "Yeah. Just me. Who are you?"

The man in front pulled out a badge. "FBI. We got an anonymous tip that there was a human trafficking ring going on in the basement of this library. Who are you?"

An anonymous tip. That had to be the Hudsons or maybe Zeke's North Star Group. It obviously wasn't *true*, so he considered offering an alias. Then he decided against it. Finding Mary was more important than any lie or complication. "My name is Walker Daniels. I was tossed in here by Senator Connor Dennison. He kidnapped Mary Hudson, or his men did. I didn't see. We were separated."

"We have two of his guards in custody. Follow me, Mr. Daniels."

He was led out of the library basement, up the stairs and outside into the dark night where a small contingent of law enforcement officers huddled around cars.

"It was Senator Dennison," Walker told the agent again. "He's who locked me down there. We've got to get to the woman he kidnapped. Mary Hudson."

"I heard you," the agent said. "First, do you need medical attention, Mr. Daniels?"

"No, I need to find Mary."

The FBI agent didn't seem to pay him any mind, just waved over a man in a suit. "I'm sorry, Mr. Daniels, but we'll need to take you into the station to ask you some questions. We'll get to the bottom of this whole thing."

The man who'd been waved over said something in low tones, and the two men began to converse. Then they walked over to a third agent, clearly trying to keep Walker from hearing what they were saying.

They were help—they had to be help—but there was no sense of urgency. Of *movement*. Didn't they understand that Mary was in danger? Walker looked around at the dark night. He couldn't go to some station and answer questions. He had to get to Mary.

"Daniels."

Walker looked around, saw a man standing in the shadows. Walker didn't recognize him, but he took a few steps toward the man while the suits discussed something important, or what they deemed important.

The man held out a hand as Walker approached.

"Granger Macmillan. North Star. Former North Star anyway. If you don't want to go with the Feds, you can come with me."

"Where are you going?"

"To help your brother."

"Then I'm going with you." And Walker didn't bother to look back.

THOUGH IT WAS the middle of the night, the entire yard was flooded with light. Mary stood with Carlyle and Zeke, huddled behind thick shrubbery. It might be hiding them now, but Mary knew their safe harbor wouldn't last. They'd be found. And then what?

"What's the plan?" Carlyle whispered.

Zeke said nothing. Mary didn't know if he was still formulating a plan or was really that concerned about being quiet, but she squeezed Carlyle's hand in hers as a kind of reassurance.

This wasn't ideal, but at least they weren't locked up anywhere. There was still a chance they'd get out of this. "We should move along the shrubs, for as long as they go," she proposed.

Zeke shook his head. "We'll make too much noise."

"Dogs," Carlyle whispered. "Listen! They're sending dogs to sniff us out."

Mary listened to the rustle of shrubs, the muffled sound of men giving orders far off in the distance. And yes, the telltale sound of dogs and dog commands.

"They'd be trained dogs," Mary said. "Carlyle, has Cash taught you any of his whistles?"

"I don't know that I remember them, but I can try."

"You whistle to get them to bark. When they start barking, we run. It'll cover the noise at least for a little bit, and it might create confusion," Mary said.

"And if they don't start barking?" Zeke asked.

"We run anyway. Better to run than be surrounded here." She thought of Connor's hands on her and fought off a shudder.

Zeke sighed. The kind of sigh that was reluctant agreement because there were no other options.

"All right. But you better be ready to run your asses off and—" He reached out, gripping them both hard. "Did you hear that?"

"What?"

Mary strained to hear something, anything. A faint kind of whistle, maybe?

"That's backup," Zeke whispered, and he was clearly happy with this turn of events. "All right. Carlyle, you make the dogs bark and you two run through the shrubs for the woods. You hear a whistle that's not your own, you run toward it. It's help."

"We're not leaving you here, Zeke," Carlyle said, clutching her brother's arms.

"Mary, take her and—"

Mary shook her head. "No. We don't leave anyone behind. We run, you run. That's the only deal."

Zeke swore under his breath. "Fine. But if they start shooting, I'm shooting back. You two keep running. I'm the only one with a gun."

"Zeke—"

"I promise I won't stay behind, Car. I promise."

Carlyle's exhale was shaky, but she agreed.

"Ready?" Zeke asked her.

Carlyle nodded, then whistled. Nothing happened at first, and Mary's heart sank. Fear began to clog her lungs, but then…

One dog yipped. Then another. Carlyle whistled again and the dogs began to howl.

"All right. Go!" Zeke commanded.

Mary grasped Carlyle's hand and they ran. Zeke was right behind them. Mary heard more howling, getting closer, but they kept running through the shrubs. There was no time to feel any sense of victory. No victory to enjoy until they were out of this mess.

A shot sounded as they reached the trees. "Just keep running," Zeke instructed, before shooting back.

Mary tried not to flinch at every shot, but as they cleared the shrubs and got into the trees, away from all those bright lights and detection, it got harder and harder to run. They had to slow so as not to fall over the exposed roots and rocks.

Carlyle stumbled, and Mary somehow managed to hold on to her arm tight enough to keep them from going down.

But then a gunshot exploded in front of them, and she heard the telltale sounds of something falling with a thud. Mary turned to see Zeke hit his knees. She jerked Carlyle back to Zeke and they huddled around him.

"Just my shoulder," he said through gritted teeth. He tried to get to his feet, but they all froze as a figure stepped out of the shadows, the dark that she'd thought had been their safety.

Senator Dennison held a gun in one hand, a flashlight in the other. Carlyle and Mary moved in front of Zeke as if to protect him, though it would take nothing for Connor to shoot them all.

"Thought you'd get the FBI involved? Thought you'd thwart *me*?" Dennison laughed. "You'll never beat me. No one will *ever* beat me."

Mary reached behind her, keeping her gaze on Connor. Zeke had a gun around here somewhere. She only had to get it while Dennison went on and on about how much smarter than them he was.

Then a twig snapped behind Dennison and he whirled around, giving her the opportunity to search for the gun with her eyes. She spotted it on the ground and moved to grab it when she saw Zeke pick it up and hand it to Carlyle. She raised her arm, ready to shoot, but two men stepped into view behind Dennison.

Walker. He stood there in front of her. Alive and well, along with a man she didn't recognize. Each held a gun pointed straight at the senator.

"Drop it," the stranger said to Dennison.

Carlyle had Zeke's gun pointed at Dennison's back, Walker and this man at his front.

"Now," Walker said flatly.

Dennison began a slow crouch, as if to put the gun down on the ground. "You think you're all so clever? I didn't kill your mother. I didn't kill anyone. All I had to do was pay Don to do my dirty work. And when he couldn't keep his mouth shut about that, I had him killed too. You won't be able to pin murder on me. You won't be able to pin *anything* on me. There's no evidence. I made sure of that."

Zeke reached into his pocket, grunting in pain, pulled out a little device and played Connor's words back for him. "I don't know about that."

Connor whirled, but by turning his back on Walker and the stranger, he gave them the opportunity to grab him from behind, wrestle the gun out of his hand.

"There's no getting out of this now." Carlyle smirked at him while Walker and the man held him still. "I knew if I gave you enough time and rope, you'd hang yourself." She cocked the trigger.

Mary held her breath, expecting Walker or even the stranger

to intervene. But they stood there and let her do what she needed to do.

Carlyle held the gun pointed at her father's head. Mary herself almost stepped forward. Maybe her brothers thought it was justice but she didn't. She couldn't let this happen.

"I can't wait to watch this trial play out. To watch all your dreams go up in smoke," Carlyle said, though she kept the gun trained on him. "I'll be first in line to testify."

"I'll die first."

"If you do, it'll be by your own hand. Not mine."

She didn't lower the gun, but she stood there, glaring into his cold eyes. Then law enforcement ran up the hill with their own weapons drawn.

It was chaotic, at best. Walker and his new friend were yelling about getting Zeke medical treatment. Mary had to help Carlyle talk her way out of having been one of the people holding a gun at someone.

Mary tried to reach Walker in the crowd, but she'd only caught glimpses of him. There were questions. Being moved from the woods to the front of the property where Dennison's staff were lined up, talking to different law enforcement officers.

She was led by an FBI agent toward this lineup, while Carlyle was led toward an ambulance with flashing lights. Inside, Walker crouched beside Zeke, who lay on a stretcher.

"Wait," Carlyle said to the guy leading her in the opposite direction. "She needs to come with me to the hospital."

"Family only."

"She's family," Carlyle said stubbornly, jerking away from the agent and striding over to where Mary stood with a different agent.

"You can't all go in the ambulance," the agent told her.

"Then someone needs to drive Mary and me to the hospital while Walker and Zeke ride in the ambulance."

Mary forced herself to smile, to reach out and give Carlyle a little squeeze. "Car, it's okay."

"No, it isn't. She's coming with me. And one of you is taking me to the hospital. Because if you'd done your jobs about five minutes faster, my brother wouldn't have been shot."

Mary watched as the agents exchanged tired, irritated looks. But they didn't argue with Carlyle any longer.

"Come on," the agent said, and Mary and Carlyle were led to a cop car, where an officer was tasked with driving them to the hospital.

Mary was moving purely on fumes. By the time they got to the hospital, nothing fully felt real. She got the impression Carlyle was having the same reaction, so they kind of clutched and leaned on each other as they were led to a waiting room.

And then Mary saw Walker, practically prowling the small room. He stopped short when they entered. Then he moved over so quickly she wasn't sure how it had happened and pulled her close. He didn't say anything, just held on. Mary pressed her forehead to his shoulder and inhaled.

He was okay. Whole and in one piece. Zeke wasn't, but he would be okay. He had to be.

"How's Zeke?" Carlyle asked, a lot of her bravery having faded into a quavering voice.

"Good enough. They'll give me an update soon, but there wasn't any life-or-death concern." His voice was rough, and she could feel a kind of tremor inside him. Likely not just because of emotion, but because he, too, had been hurt.

"Walker, has a doctor looked at you?"

"I'm good," he said, which did not answer the question. She looked up at him, ready to argue because he was bruised and bloody, but something cold and furious passed over his expression as his gaze landed on her throat.

No doubt Connor had left bruises.

"I'm good too," she said, using his same tone and raising

an eyebrow at him, as if daring him to argue with her when *she* had not argued with him.

"Mary…"

She shook her head. Even though she didn't know exactly what he wanted to say, she knew it didn't matter. "We're all okay."

He let out a shaky breath, then led them both over to some chairs. They kind of collapsed in a heap—Mary on one side of Walker, Carlyle on the other. He kept his arms around both of them as they sat.

No one said anything. What was there to say? It was over. *Over.*

There was only one thing to mention.

"When Zeke gets out, we'll all go home. He can recuperate on the ranch. We'll take good care of him," Mary said firmly. "The Hudsons have had lots of practice in that department. You'll come home and we'll take care of everything."

Walker looked over at her. She couldn't quite read his expression, but his mouth curved ever so slightly, then he leaned forward and kissed her temple. "Yeah, we'll all go home."

She didn't miss the way his voice got rougher at that word. That thing he hadn't had in so long. Tears stung her eyes, but she didn't let them fall.

Because she was going to give them all the best home there ever was. Forever.

Carlyle nodded, and they sat there, holding on to each other, ready to go home.

Together.

Epilogue

It took a few days to get back to the ranch. Zeke needed an overnight stay in the hospital and the questions from the FBI were endless. Walker tried not to mind. Whatever could be done to keep Connor Dennison behind bars he would do.

Luckily, Dennison was even shadier than they'd anticipated, and they weren't the only ones trying to take him down. The Feds had just needed a needle that broke the camel's back—and the help Zeke's former North Star group had given made all the difference.

There was always the chance Dennison's fancy lawyers would get him off for some things, but the sheer amount of wrongdoing he'd been involved in would likely keep him locked up for a long time.

Even his wife had come forward with charges of decades of abuse. No, even his money and influence wouldn't get him out of the mess he'd made for himself.

Walker had insisted Mary go home, and he was sure he only got her to go before him by asking her to get a room ready for Zeke. His brother would be fine, but he'd need some help and care while his gunshot wound healed.

There was no arguing that Mary would be the one overseeing that process.

Mary. He still wasn't over the details of what Dennison had

done to her. That would take...time. It would take a hell of a lot of time to get over all of this.

But they'd do it together, so he couldn't wait to get home and get started.

He'd had his SUV delivered to him so he could drive Zeke from Colorado to the Hudson Ranch with some room. Zeke was currently stretched out in the back while Carlyle practically bounced in the passenger seat the closer they got to Sunrise.

And home.

Walker wasn't sure when he'd started to see it that way— but it was sometime before Mary had said it in the hospital the other day. Maybe in those first moments he'd come to the ranch. It had always felt right.

Or maybe that was just Mary herself.

"How much longer?" Carlyle whined, like the thirteen-year-old she never fully got to be.

"Not long," Walker replied, feeling the same frustrating anticipation coiled inside him.

He glanced at his sister. She hadn't said she would yet, but he knew she'd take the dog training assistant job Cash offered. As for Walker himself, he figured he had the skills to be a decent HSS team member, and he could learn how to be a ranch hand if needed.

Zeke would have to make his own choices, but Walker hoped his brother would join HSS too. Do a little good in the world for other people.

But none of what would come mattered when he pulled into the Hudson Ranch, and Mary was waiting for them on the porch.

He nearly leaped from the car, but there were a swarm of Hudsons—to help Zeke, to get their bags. Mary gave out orders, and everyone jumped to follow them. Zeke grumbled a little, but Walker figured he'd earned a grumble or two.

Then finally everyone was inside, except him.

And Mary.

They stood on the porch, facing each other. He wanted to pull her into his arms and just hold on for a hundred years.

And that was just it.

He wanted years. And years and years. That's all he could seem to think about in this moment. He didn't know what else to say to her but "Marry me."

She didn't look shocked, or appalled, thank God. He didn't have a ring or a plan, just a feeling. And she stood there, one of those polite smiles on her face, but her eyes shone.

"I always thought I'd have to know someone at least a year before I agreed to marry them," she said carefully. Oh, so carefully.

"I can wait." And he could. Marriage was just a piece of paper anyway. As long as Mary loved him and was by his side, being married didn't matter. He smiled at her because he was home and that's what mattered.

He reached out for her, wound his arm around her waist and felt a tension inside of him ease. It was really all over, and she was here. Within reach. When he went to bed tonight, she'd be right next to him. Loving him.

"You got any coffee?" he asked, because he was dead on his feet and to get to that point, he'd need some caffeine.

But before he could move for the door to open it, she moved into his way. "That's just it, Walker." She looked up at him, put her hand on his cheek. "With you, I don't want to wait. I want to marry you."

It took a minute—he blamed it on exhaustion. *I want to marry you.* He grinned down at her.

"Soon," she added, emphatically.

Soon. He laughed and went ahead and gave in to impulse and lifted her up.

"Soon sounds good." Then he pressed his mouth to hers. Because she *was* home. His. And he was finally, fully and permanently right where he wanted to be.

"Oh, my God, you guys, get a room!" Carlyle shouted through the window at them. But there was humor in her tone and it made Mary laugh, so Walker laughed too.

Because he hadn't had a home for a very long time, but Mary had given him one. And that was worth everything it had taken to get here.

* * * * *

ESCAPE THE EVERGLADES

CARIDAD PIÑEIRO

To all my friends at Liberty States Fiction Writers for their support and encouragement over the years.

Chapter One

The barrage of gunfire stopped him dead in his tracks.

Carlos Ruiz approached his son's door slowly and peered inside. Lucas slouched in his gaming chair, attention fixed on the video game playing on the monitor.

"*Chico*, it's time to go. I've got a hit on Schrodinger," he said but Lucas didn't budge in his seat. "Lucas, *vamanos*. It's too nice a day to spend it in front of the television," he chided, and his son finally glanced over his shoulder at him.

"But *Papi*, I just leveled up," his ten-year-old complained.

In the nearly two years since his mother had died, Lucas had buried his grief by losing himself in the virtual worlds in his video games. Getting his son to do anything else, even play with his old friends, had become a battle, but Carlos wouldn't give up.

He walked over and stood in front of the TV, blocking his son's view of the game. "*Por favor*, Lucas," he said, hands held out in pleading. For good measure, he used the one guilt-trip he was sure would work. "Schrodinger was your mom's favorite panther. She'd like to know she's doing well."

His son narrowed his gaze and said, "Isn't that the whole idea with Schrodinger? That the cat is both alive *and* dead?"

"Sometimes you can be too smart, *sabes*? Let's go. We're expecting rain later this afternoon." He reached behind him and shut off the television, ending the game, and any further argument, from his son.

With a twist of his lips and roll of his eyes, Lucas dropped the controller and then shot to his feet. "No more tours today, *Papi*?" he said, a note of worry in his tone.

Carlos shook his head. "Rain's keeping the tourists away, but all the boats were full this morning. We're doing fine," he said to alleviate his son's concerns. That was another thing that had changed since his wife's death: Lucas worried about almost everything. The grief counselor he'd taken Lucas to had said that was normal and would pass in time, but so far it hadn't, which bothered him. No ten-year-old should have such worries.

He laid a comforting hand on his son's shoulder and matched his stride to Lucas's shorter one as they walked to the airboat parked at the dock. It was his personal boat that he'd rigged to hold a tablet he could watch as he piloted the boat through the Everglades. The tablet fed him the position of the female panther that had been tagged with a collar equipped with a GPS tracker.

The software had let him know earlier that morning that Schrodinger was in the area and with no afternoon tours, it was as good a time as any to try to see how the panther was doing.

He helped Lucas onto the boat and handed him his life vest and the headset that provided hearing protection as well as a two-way radio and microphone so they could communicate. After Lucas had belted himself into the seat, Carlos unhitched the ropes tethering the airboat to the dock, tossed them onboard and hopped up onto the operator's platform.

He slipped on his own headset and life vest and secured himself in the driver's seat, then positioned the tablet for viewing and connected the lanyard to the cutoff switch in case he got ejected. He powered up the engine and took a quick look at the assorted gauges to make sure all was in order. Satisfied, he stepped on the accelerator pedal and slowly navigated the airboat away from the dock. Keeping the boat in the higher water of the canal behind his property, he gradually increased the speed, staying alert for wildlife, hidden dangers like rogue cypress logs or alligators and the position of the panther.

It would take about thirty minutes to reach the panther's position, but that was only if Schrodinger didn't move farther back into the upland forests that the panthers favored. Those areas had the dry ground that held more prey for them to hunt and places to breed.

As he drove, he pointed out some of the sights to Lucas. He gestured to a flock of ibises wading in some shallower water. "Check it out, *chico*. There are even some pink ones." The birds had resulted from crossbreeding between American white ibises and the South American scarlet ibises introduced into the area.

A sullen grunt was his only response but that didn't stop Carlos from continuing as they moved toward the panther's GPS signal. He identified a roseate spoonbill, with its bright pink plumage, protecting a nest of ugly duckling gray babies. Farther along their trip were wood storks, assorted gray and white herons as well as varying kinds of egrets.

He slowed as an alligator swam in front of them. Formerly endangered, alligators had made a big comeback thanks to conservation efforts and the proliferation of private alligator farms that satisfied the needs for gator meat and the hides prized by fashion giants for luggage, belts and other accessories. But the private farms in Florida and nearby Louisiana had created another kind of problem: illegal poaching of alligator eggs. As his gaze scanned the horizon, motion in the distance had him reaching for a pair of binoculars.

Training the binoculars on the activity, he saw another airboat as well as two men rummaging through the wetlands. His gut tightened with fear as he thought about what they might be doing.

"Tighten your belt, Lucas," he said and pushed the speedboat in the direction of the men. As he neared, he confirmed why they had been traipsing through the sawgrasses. Three large circles of disturbed soil dotted the area. Alligator nests. A fourth nest had been dug up, exposing the fragile eggs that the men were stealing.

He set a pin on the tablet to mark the location of the nests and was about to radio the local Florida Fish and Wildlife Conservation Commission wardens when one of the men whipped a rifle out from the hull of their airboat.

"Hang on, Lucas," he shouted and, heart pounding, he slowed the airboat and sharply pulled the rudder stick to the rear as the first gunshot pinged the safety cage protecting the propellers behind him. As the stern of the boat whipped around, he boosted the engine power, executing the one hundred and eighty degree turn to make their escape as more bullets slammed into the metal of the hull and engine.

"I'm scared, *Papi*," Lucas cried over the headset speaker.

"It's okay, Lucas. We're going to be okay," he said, even as his gut tightened with worry about engine damage as he pushed the boat to its top speed. If the engine failed and the poachers attacked again, he had nothing to protect them. Glancing back at the location of the alligator nests, he realized that the poachers were giving chase in their airboat. The alligator eggs were just too valuable. If Carlos warned the FWC about the location of the nests, the poachers wouldn't have time to dig up that many eggs.

He engaged the radio via his headset and made a distress call, supplying his airboat's registration number and location and advising on the nature of the emergency.

An FWC warden for the area immediately came on the line. "Carlos, what's the situation?" Warden Garcia asked.

He peered back at the poachers still speeding in their direction. "Armed poachers are chasing us, and I have no protection. I have Lucas with me, Gemma."

"We're on our way, Carlos," Gemma said and ended the call.

Leaning forward, as if by doing so he could force the airboat to go faster, he glanced back and to his surprise, the poachers' airboat suddenly peeled away and raced toward deeper water.

He didn't slow his speed, not wanting to take any chances with his young son in the airboat. Minutes that seemed like hours passed until he reached their dock and killed the engine. He quickly tied up the boat and when he turned, Lucas launched himself at him.

He fought for balance as the airboat rocked and wrapped his arms around his son. "We're okay, *mi'jo*. We're okay," he urged over and over, trying to calm Lucas.

The FWC's airboat pulled up to the dock a few minutes later. It was tied up, and the armed wardens hopped off the airboat and rushed over.

"Is Lucas okay?" Warden Garcia asked.

Carlos nodded, let Lucas slip to his feet and placed a reassuring hand on his son's shoulder. "He's okay. Scared, but so am I," he said to calm his son and not make him feel awkward.

Gemma held out a hand and helped Lucas onto the dock. She ruffled the thick waves of his chestnut brown hair and said, "We're here now. You'll be fine."

Lucas smiled uneasily. "*Gracias*, Warden Gemma."

"Do you think you can tell us what you saw?" she said and squatted down, so she was eye to eye with his son.

Lucas shrugged. "Two guys were walking around the wetlands. Then they started shooting at us."

"Can you describe the men? Were they white? Latino? Black?"

Lucas peered up at him and Carlos dipped his head to urge his son to answer. "White. Kind of dirty looking."

"Dirty looking?" asked Dale Adams, the male FWC warden.

Lucas glanced at him and nodded. Gesturing to his face and motioning as if he was stroking it, he said, "Like beards. Bad ones like my dad had and my mom begged him to shave it off."

That prompted laughter from both the wardens and lightened the mood, especially since they were safely at home. "That's exactly how they looked. My wife would have said scruffy," Carlos explained which made Lucas frown and tense beneath his hand.

"Can I go now, *Papi*?" his son asked.

Carlos looked toward the two wardens who nodded. "Sure thing, *mi'jo*. I'll be at the house in a few minutes."

Lucas instantly ran off, leaving him alone with the wardens.

"What else can you tell us?" Gemma asked, gaze narrowed as she rose and looked at him.

"They were poaching four large alligator nests. I can give the location so you can check on them. Like Lucas said—white, possibly Latino. About six feet tall. Nice airboat. Pretty new. Poaching must pay well," he said with a disgusted shake of his head.

"A typical nest would get them over fifteen hundred dollars," Warden Adams confirmed.

"Four nests would be a nice day's pay," Carlos said and blew out a rough sigh.

"And enough to kill for," Gemma said and laid a warning hand on his arm. "You need to stay clear of that area. Let us handle this."

He nodded and raised his hands in surrender. "Got it. I'm not about to take any chances. Lucas needs me now that..." His voice trailed off because the wardens were aware of his wife's untimely passing.

"Like Gemma said, we'll take care of this. Just send us the location of the nests so we can make sure everything's in order," Adams said.

"I appreciate that," Carlos replied. He shook Adams's hand and then Gemma's. She held on to his for longer than necessary and said, "If you need anything, just call."

Any red-blooded man would likely take up the beautiful warden's invitation, but they'd made the mistake of going on a date a few months earlier and it hadn't gone well. It had been too soon after his wife's death and he clearly wasn't ready for any kind of relationship.

"*Gracias*, Gemma. If you don't mind, I'd like to see to Lucas. He's probably still scared about what happened," he said, excusing himself to go check on his son.

But as he entered the house, the familiar sounds of the video game escaped from Lucas's room. It was like Lucas was escaping into the fantasy world of the program.

Carlos sometimes wished he could escape as well. Escape the pain of his wife's loss. Escape the burdens of running the business and parenting Lucas alone. And now, escape the fear that had that spot between his shoulders tingling.

He'd always trusted that instinct when he'd been in the Marines, and he wasn't about to ignore it now. There was something off about what had just happened. The poachers had given up too easily, but he suspected that they weren't done with the alligator nests or possibly him. He intended to find out what was up and more importantly, he intended to be ready for them if they decided to attack again.

Chapter Two

The flashes came in angry rapid-fire bursts of light.

Natalie Rodriguez muttered a curse and grabbed hold of the handle on her Lab's tactical vest as the dog launched herself at the photographer who stumbled and fell onto his ass, shocked by the attack.

"No, Missy. Sit. Sit!" she shouted at the dog as it fought hard to be free of her hold, snarling and barking. A powerful lunge from the dog nearly yanked her arm from her shoulder. She dug her feet into the soft ground as another pull almost made her lose her footing, but with another tug on the harness and both verbal and hand commands, Missy finally settled down at Natalie's side.

The photographer scrambled to his feet and pointed at the Lab. "That animal should be muzzled."

Missy bared her teeth, growled and rose slightly on her haunches as if ready to attack.

"Easy, girl. Sit," Natalie said and rubbed the dog's head to try to calm her.

"She's dangerous," the photographer said and slowly raised his camera to take more photos, but Natalie shoved her open hand in front of his lens.

"Please stop. I asked you not to use a flash. Missy's PTSD makes her sensitive to bright lights," Natalie said, reminding the photographer and nearby reporter about her earlier request when she'd agreed to do the interview. Behind her own eyes, an all too familiar throb and black circles dancing in her vision warned that the tension threatened to bring on a migraine.

"We're sorry," said the news reporter conducting the interview and stepped in front of her photographer to block his view. "I think we have enough photos."

"Thank you, Ms. Ramos," Natalie said, grateful for the reporter's understanding.

"Sara, *por favor*," she said and laid a hand over her heart. "Again, I'm sorry about our photographer's actions."

Missy had calmed down and was sitting close to Natalie's leg, her body trembling from the episode triggered by the camera flashes. Natalie kept a tight hold on the Lab as the news crew walked away and no one else approached them, clearly wary after what had happened barely minutes earlier.

Natalie closed her eyes and did some slow breathing to curb the migraine coming on. Luckily, those short moments of peace abated the headache. For now. With a soft click of her tongue to urge Missy to her feet, she relaxed her grip on the Lab's harness handle while keeping a strong hold of the leash in her other hand.

Together they walked to the big black Suburban with the South Beach Security emblem. The SUV was parked in a grassy area that had been set aside for volunteers searching for the seven-year-old who had disappeared from a neighborhood street festival the night before. She'd asked her boss for time off to take part in the search, but he had said to consider it part of her job as a K-9 agent for SBS. She'd never expected that many hours later, after night had fallen, she'd find the boy fast asleep in some underbrush. Somehow, he'd managed to walk nearly four miles away from his neighborhood to an area bordering the Everglades.

She had just gotten Missy harnessed in the backseat of the SUV and given the Lab a treat when her phone chirped to warn of a message.

Trey Gonzalez. Her boss and the man who had taken a chance on her three months earlier when he'd started the SBS K-9 division.

Fearful that he'd already heard about Missy's meltdown, her hand shook as she read the message.

Good job. Can you meet me in the office in the morning?

She texted: What time do you want me there?

Nine is good. I'll have coffee and breakfast ready, Trey texted back.

Gracias, she replied to end the exchange.

The conversation had seemed friendly enough but depending on the reporter's article, it could negatively affect SBS's new K-9 unit and that's the last thing she wanted. Especially since Trey had been so supportive and understanding of both her and Missy's PTSD issues.

It's going to be okay, she told herself as she slipped into the driver's seat and pulled onto a side street that connected to the Dolphin Expressway. In no time she was flying through the assorted neighborhoods, industrial areas and waterways in Miami-Dade until she reached the one-bedroom apartment that straddled the line between Little Havana and Little Gables. The apartment was reasonably priced, not far from the SBS offices on Brickell Avenue and, more importantly, pet friendly. Even better, the apartment was in the back of the building and quiet because it was away from any street noise.

Quiet being something that both Missy and she coveted after their years of military service and the issues that lingered long beyond their discharge from the army.

She parked in the side lot and walked around to the front of the apartment building. Painted a cheery yellow with a bright teal awning above the front door, the building had welcomed her from the first time that she'd seen it. Entering, she walked down the long hall to her apartment where her smart outlets had turned on lights to make her return home not so lonely.

"How about a nice warm bath?" she said as she unleashed Missy, and the Lab immediately raced to her bowls and sat there, peering at Natalie impatiently.

Natalie chuckled and shook her head. "Food first. Of course, my bad," she said with another laugh and hurried to give Missy cool water and fresh food from the fridge.

The dog bent her head over the bowl and ate greedily, hungry after the long day at work.

Natalie's stomach also growled, reminding her that she had to fuel up as well. Too tired to cook, and since she didn't like strangers coming to her door at night with deliveries, she yanked out a frozen dinner and zapped it in the microwave.

She made the effort to lay out a place mat, poured herself a glass of wine and flipped on the television. Turning to a channel with a game show, she answered the questions along with the contestants while she ate. It made for a quick dinner, and she tossed the last little bit of the fried chicken to Missy and cleaned up.

"Bath time," she said and did a hand command for Missy to follow her. For a small apartment, the bathroom had plenty of room for her to bathe Missy and then dry her down.

She filled the bath with warm water and a lavender scented bubble bath. The fragrance and warmth calmed Missy and after tonight's incident, her pup needed to relieve her anxiety. Missy almost smiled as Natalie lathered up her thick golden fur and then scooped up handfuls of water to rinse away the soap.

"That's a good girl," she said. She gently washed away the last of the soap with the handheld showerhead, helped Missy from the bath and toweled her down.

"All work and no play make Missy a grumpy dog. Go get a toy," she said with a wave of her hand and Missy hurried from the room to find one of the many playthings Natalie kept in the living room.

She turned up the heat in the shower and rinsed away any stray dog hairs, then stripped and slipped beneath the comforting warmth of the spray. Much like what she'd used for Missy, she washed with an assortment of lavender scented products and then lingered in the shower, enjoying the quiet time and slide of the water down her body.

With her hands starting to wrinkle, she reluctantly shut off the water, grabbed a towel and dried off. When she stepped out of the shower, she found Missy peacefully chewing on one of her hard, rubber toys by the entrance to the bathroom.

With a hand command to the Lab, she hurried to her bedroom, Missy following, and slipped into the oversize T-shirt she wore as pajamas. Easing into bed, she grabbed a romance novel from the nightstand instead of flipping on the television. She suspected local news would be plastered with coverage of the rescue and she had no desire to see herself on television, especially if they had caught Missy's loss of control.

Which brought a reminder of Trey's seemingly friendly request for a morning breakfast meeting. *Would he be bringing in coffee and goodies if he intended to fire me?* she wondered.

She tried not to think about that and instead focused on the story in the book, a not-so-sweet contemporary romance set on the Jersey Shore. It made for a nice escape as she pictured the quaint seaside town described in the book which was remarkably like where her mother lived. By the time her eyes started to droop, she had relaxed enough to shut off her light and try to sleep.

It was a quiet night, with the loudest sound being Missy chomping on her hard rubber toy.

Natalie smiled and pictured herself in that Jersey Shore town, away from the heat and humidity of a Miami summer. She drifted away into a dream filled with those images, peaceful until the loud chiming of her alarm warned it was time to rise.

She stared hard at the alarm in disbelief since she couldn't remember the last time she'd slept so deeply through the night. It wasn't unusual for her sleep to be interrupted by nightmares, but luckily not that night.

Maybe a good omen that it would be a pleasant day, especially as she peered over the edge of the bed and Missy bathed her face with dog kisses. "*Dios*, Missy. I love you too," she said and hurried to do her morning prep and dress.

She made coffee and fed Missy her morning bowl of food. While she sipped her coffee and checked emails, Missy gobbled down the kibble and drank some water. When her Lab was finished, Natalie clipped on the leash and took her for a quick walk around the block so Missy could relieve herself. After, she grabbed the Lab's service vest, tossed it into the backseat and harnessed her dog there for the short drive to the SBS offices.

Battling early morning traffic, she fought her way to downtown and arrived early for her meeting with Trey. On the SBS floor, the receptionist greeted her warmly.

"Congratulations, Natalie. We're so proud of you finding that boy," Julia said and swept around the receptionist desk to give her a friendly hug.

"*Gracias*, Julia. Just doing my job," she said, always awkward with praise.

"I'll let Trey know you're here," Julia said, but before the receptionist was even back at her desk, Trey was walking down the hall.

He moved with the confidence of a man used to being in command. Powerfully built, he had mahogany brown, almost black hair cut in a fade. Intelligence radiated from his piercing aqua-colored gaze. The light blue guayabera shirt he wore emphasized the intense color of his eyes.

"*Buenos dias*, Natalie. Please come to my office," he said and motioned to the open door down the hall.

She walked there with Missy, Trey following her. He closed

the door after they entered, and she didn't wait for him to deliver the bad news.

"I know you must be upset with how Missy behaved yesterday. I should have controlled her better—"

He raised a hand to ask her to pause. "*Por favor*, Natalie. There is absolutely no need for an apology. You and Missy did an excellent job," he said, then grabbed a newspaper from his desk and handed it to her.

"The reporter spoke very highly about your efforts and did a nice job detailing your military service," Trey said as she skimmed through the article and realized that the reporter had not mentioned Missy's meltdown. But the reporter had included some information about their time in the army and graciously added a reference to the PTSD support group Natalie had mentioned during the interview.

"I'm…pleasantly surprised," she admitted and handed the paper back to Trey.

"The reporter—Sara Ramos—is one of Mia's friends, but even if she wasn't, you did nothing wrong last night. If anything, her photographer was the one who should be in trouble," Trey said and walked over to a credenza where there were two carafes and some Cuban toast and other pastries.

"Please help yourself. I wasn't sure if you drank coffee or tea," he said with the wave of a hand in the direction of the credenza.

"I love Cuban coffee," she admitted, then rose, prepped herself a *café con leche*, and grabbed a piece of Cuban *tostada*.

Trey gestured her to the small leather sofa to one side of his office. She sat and placed her cup and dish on the coffee table in front of the sofa. Missy tagged along beside her and lay down at her feet, her large head resting on her paws.

Trey sat across from her and was silent for long minutes as he sipped his coffee and took a few bites of his toast before leaning back in the wing chair.

"Are you doing okay?" he asked, gaze direct but full of concern.

She nodded and sipped her coffee before setting the cup on the tabletop once again. "I am. I have to admit I was worried about Missy."

"But not about yourself?" Trey pressed with the arch of a dark brow.

Natalie shrugged. "I've been...fine," she said hesitantly. It had been hard to control Missy last night and the incident had started to trip one of the migraines sometimes caused by the traumatic brain injury she suffered during her last tour of duty.

Trey was silent for a too long moment before he said, "I know that the noise and lights can be tough for Missy." *And you*, he didn't say, although he was aware it could affect her as well.

"They are, but she's been getting better," she said, still worried that Trey was leading up to firing them despite all the seeming pleasantries during their meeting.

"I assume she'd get even better faster if her environment wasn't as challenging. It's why I was thinking the two of you might be an excellent choice to help my friend," Trey said and leaned forward and picked up his coffee cup.

She blew out a breath and every muscle in her body relaxed as she realized he had no intention of getting rid of her.

"You want me to help out your friend?" she said, just to be sure she'd heard him right.

Trey nodded. "Carlos Ruiz. He has a business taking tourists for tours of the Everglades. Not those schlock ones. He's a true environmentalist which is why he needs our help."

"What kind of help?" she asked and munched on the toast, slipping a piece to Missy as a treat, as she waited for Trey to explain.

"A few days ago, Carlos ran into some alligator egg poachers and called in the FWC. The wardens said they'd take care of it but when Carlos went back to check, he found that the alligator nests had been emptied."

Holding her hands out in question, she said, "Is that big business for the poachers?"

"Apparently big enough for them to threaten Carlos if he keeps on interfering," Trey said, then reached into his pants pocket and took out his smartphone. After a few swipes, he handed her the phone.

She tensed at the photos on the smartphone. Someone had driven a knife through an extremely small alligator hatchling and envelope, nailing both into a wooden door. Remnants of what looked like eggshell and blood dirtied the off-white of the envelope. Hand trembling, she passed the phone back to Trey.

"I assume there was a note in there."

Trey nodded. "There was. It warned Carlos to stay out of their business."

She suspected Carlos was much like Trey and wouldn't just sit back when someone was breaking the law. "What do you need me to do?"

"Before you agree to do it, I want you to be totally onboard with what this job entails," Trey said and finished the last of his coffee.

With a nod, she urged him to explain, and he continued.

"It may involve several days out in the Everglades. You can take the company RV for housing. Carlos needs help finding the poachers' camp and protecting his home and business. He also has a young son, Lucas, who needs his attention now that Carlos is a single parent. He was widowed two years ago when his wife was killed in a car crash."

"Will it be just the two of us working this?" she wondered, worried about what it might take to find poachers in an area the size of the Everglades.

Trey shook his head. "You'll have the full resources of SBS, and I suspect you'll need them."

"I will. That's a lot of difficult ground to cover on foot or via airboat," she said.

"Great minds," he teased and continued, "I've already got

our tech experts, Sophie and Robbie, working on how to secure the area and help you and Missy with any searches. Plus, my wife Roni is coordinating with her fellow officers to see what information they can get from the knife and note. Hopefully there will be some DNA on there that they can match in CODIS."

Natalie smiled with relief. "Sounds like you've got things under control. When do you need me to go meet Mr. Ruiz?"

"Is today too soon?"

Chapter Three

Carlos Ruiz stood, arms akimbo, as the RV pulled into the driveway for his home. The nice-looking blonde who was behind the wheel had probably mistaken the turn for that of the tour business about fifty feet farther up the road. But as she expertly turned the RV around to back into the large driveway next to his home, he caught sight of the South Beach Security emblem on the side of the vehicle. The SBS logo combining an American eagle shield with the red, white and blue of the Cuban flag had become well-known in the Miami area.

The woman stopped the RV and slipped to the ground. She was all of five feet six with shoulder length blond hair and lots of lush curves...

He stopped himself there as she walked to the passenger side, opened the door and let a large Labrador Retriever wearing a vest with the SBS logo jump from the RV.

The blonde had the leash in hand and was heading straight for him, alone except for the massive dog. The Lab's head nearly reached the woman's waist.

Carlos was finding it hard to believe that this was the K-9 agent his old friend, Trey, had sent to help him. But as she lifted her chin a defiant inch and met his gaze directly, he had no doubt that's who she was.

She stopped in front of him and stuck out her hand, almost daring him to refuse it as she said, "SBS K-9 Agent Natalie Rodriguez."

THE BEARDED MOUNTAIN of a man before her hesitated, his gaze narrowed, but then he took hold of her hand and said, "Carlos Ruiz."

His hand swallowed hers up, it was so large, and while she had no doubt he could easily crush her hand, his touch was gentle.

"I'm sorry I got here so late but I had to get some things. This is my partner, Missy," she said and gestured to her dog.

"It's not a problem. I just finished up my last tour of the day. I'd love to get started, but I don't have much time before I have to pick up my son at the bus stop," he said, apology filling his tone.

Natalie glanced around the grounds at the modest one-story home, which sat on short stilts close to a dock where an airboat was moored. Neatly coiled lines and cables hung on the posts of the dock. A bright red pickup sat in front of the home.

Turning, she glanced at a narrow path that led away from the home and she flipped her hand in its direction. "Does that go to your business?"

Carlos nodded. "It does. Do you want to take a quick look before I go?"

"I'd like that. This way I can report back to SBS on what I might need to secure the two locations and help you with your search."

With a reluctant dip of his head, as if he still didn't quite believe she could handle the job, he held a hand in the direction of the path and followed her as she walked toward his business.

Natalie kept her gaze fixed on the path, watching for any gators who might have decided to climb out of the wetlands to sun. Missy had her nose in the grasses around them as they walked, investigating the underbrush. Luckily the path was clear, although Natalie did spot some motion about twenty feet away in the waters of a nearby canal.

"Was that—"

"A gator? Yes. There are several that live in this stretch of water," he explained and pointed to the wide canal that ran by his business and house. "This waterway provides access into the wetlands and farther out, the Gulf."

They popped out of the taller grasses around the path and onto the crushed and compacted shells in the parking lot of his business. Two airboats that easily held half a dozen passengers each were tied up at a long dock not far from a large catamaran with a bright blue shade stretched over rows of bench seats.

A two-story hexagonal building covered in cedar shakes silvered by age sat close to the dock. A gaily colored sign proclaimed that this was the site of "Captain Carlos's Cruises— the best Everglades tours with trained conservationists."

She pointed to the sign and said, "Is that true or just tourist hype?"

Even with his beard, his clenched jaw and the flush of anger that darkened his features were visible. "True. All my guides have degrees in either biology, marine biology, environmental science or ecology."

Holding her hands up in apology, she said, "I'm sorry. I'm just trying to get a sense of the business."

"Easy enough," he said and quickly rattled off, "The building has two floors. Top floor has my office and lockers and rest areas for the guides. Bottom floor has a small snack area as well as a shop where we sell T-shirts and the usual trinkets tourists love to buy."

"I saw online that you offer a number of different tours?" she said and walked toward the dock to inspect for places where they might place security cameras that wouldn't be too visible. She let Missy wander along the wooden planks and posts, learning the scents and familiarizing herself with the area.

"We do four tours a day on the airboats and two a day with the catamaran, Monday through Saturday. All the tours take about two hours. We're closed on Sundays so my employees can spend time with their families," he explained and followed her as she quickly walked around, examining the grounds and the building before returning to stand on the dock and peer at the wetlands.

"Did you find the poachers on one of your regular tour routes?" she asked, concerned that innocent bystanders might be in the line of danger.

He shook his head and dragged his fingers through the longer strands of his dark hair. "No. If they were, I wouldn't be taking anyone out."

She nodded, turned back toward his house and gave Missy a hand command to heel. "Did you get the threat here or at your home?"

"Here," he said and gestured to the building. "Luckily I found it before any of my people had come to work."

"Do you think they're in danger? Or your customers?" she asked and looked back over her shoulder at him as they hurried along the path and back to his home.

He shrugged and shook his head. "I don't know. I was tempted to listen to the poachers and ignore what they're doing. Only…we've made too much progress in saving the gators and if we don't stop them, what will they go after next? The panthers? They're almost extinct as it is."

She admired his passion, but worried about how it could endanger his customers and his son. "It might be good to consider shutting down for a few days while we investigate."

CARLOS PURSED HIS lips and sucked in a deep inhale, but then nodded, knowing she was right.

"I'll make calls tonight and let my people know we'll be closed for a few days. I'll offer our customers a full refund and free future ride which will hopefully keep them happy," he said and shot a quick look at his watch.

"I should go. Lucas will be at the bus stop soon," he said, then pulled a key fob from his pocket and opened the pickup doors.

"Can I go with you?" she asked, and at his puzzled look, she said, "I'd like to get the lay of the land and your routines."

When he'd first caught sight of her, he'd been tempted to tell her to go right back to Miami. But he trusted his friend Trey and his instincts. If Trey had thought she could handle the job, who was Carlos to doubt him? So far, she seemed quite competent as she inspected the various areas and led her dog around the grounds. But doing that was a far cry from handling armed poachers.

Despite his indecision, he said, "Sure," and hoped he wouldn't regret it.

Chapter Four

Natalie sat in the backseat with Missy, carefully taking mental notes of the various locations along the short ten-minute trip to the school bus stop located in one of the last developments before the suburbs gave way to the first edges of the Everglades.

"Do you do this drive every day?" she asked, trying to get a sense of Carlos's daily schedule so she could gauge the kind of protection that would be necessary for him, his son and his business.

"Every morning and afternoon. His mom used to do it," he said and paused. A heavy sigh escaped him as he shifted his broad shoulders up and down, almost wearily. "I changed the tour schedules so I can be there for Lucas. He's had too much change already."

"I understand," she said, even though she couldn't even begin to understand what it must be like to lose a spouse, especially at such a young age and with a child to consider.

His gaze met hers in the rearview mirror and a short grunt escaped him. "Do you?" he challenged.

Natalie clenched her jaw and shook her head. "Not really. All I know is it must be tough."

"It is, but it's what I have to do. It's what I *want* to do for my son," he said. He turned the wheel to execute a U-turn and pulled into a parking lot where several other cars sat, occupied by an army of moms.

She suspected Carlos was the kind of man who didn't waver from his responsibilities. A man whose sense of honor would make him do whatever was best for his son. For his friends. For strangers even.

Barely a minute passed before a bright yellow school bus lumbered up to a spot in front of the parking lot. With a loud groan, it jerked to a stop and opened its doors that squeaked loudly. Children spewed from the bus and onto the sidewalk before racing to the cars in the lot, their happy cries loud in the afternoon air.

No one approached Carlos's pickup until one lone child slowly trudged down the stairs.

He had Carlos's chestnut brown hair and chocolate-colored eyes made bigger by the glasses he wore. The young child pushed his glasses up with a finger, walked toward the pickup but paused by the door as he noticed her and Missy in the backseat.

Carlos leaned over and popped the door open. "Come on up, Lucas."

The boy hesitantly glanced in her direction but finally hopped into the pickup.

"Lucas, say hello to Agent Natalie Rodriguez and her partner, Missy. *Tio* Trey sent her to help us with the poachers," he explained.

Tio Trey? Natalie wondered. Her boss had said they were friends, but *Tio* implied that the two men were way more like family.

Lucas's gaze narrowed before he finally stuck a hand over the edge of the seat. "Nice to meet you, Agent Natalie. Are you the lady who found that kid yesterday?"

She shook his hand and nodded. "Nice to meet you and yes, I'm that lady. Actually, it was Missy who found the boy."

"That's so cool," he said in wide-eyed awe.

"Buckle up, *mi'jo*," Carlos said and affectionately ruffled the boy's hair.

Lucas did as he was told and yet somehow managed to twist in the seat to watch them as Carlos pulled out of the parking lot and drove home.

"You're heroes, you and Missy. I read all about you on the internet," Lucas said.

The heat of a blush crept up her face as Carlos met her gaze again in the rearview mirror. "Not really heroes, Lucas. We were just doing our job," she said and awkwardly smiled at the excited boy.

"The article said you served in the army. My mom was a marine just like my dad," he said and glanced at his father in obvious adoration. A second later, he blurted out, "What's PTSD?"

"Lucas," Carlos warned and looked over his shoulder at her. "I'm sorry, Natalie. He didn't mean anything by it."

"It's okay," she said and met Lucas's inquisitive gaze. "PTSD stands for post-traumatic stress disorder. Missy was wounded during an attack and some things make her feel... bad," she said, afraid of scaring Lucas with the reality of how Missy could react when her symptoms kicked in.

Clearly sensing that she was uneasy, Lucas said, "I'm sorry," and twisted around to face forward for the remainder of the ride.

She turned her attention back to the road and the passing surroundings, but as soon as they pulled up in front of the house, she realized something was wrong.

Carlos muttered a curse beneath his breath and shot her a worried look. "Hand me that rifle from the back window. Stay in the car with Lucas and both of you stay down."

She didn't normally take her gun for routine duty but would have to consider carrying in the future. She also didn't normally like being told how to do her job, but it was important to make sure Lucas stayed safe. Because of that she would stay behind and guard Lucas with Missy and her life if need be.

He grabbed the rifle after she handed it to him and slipped

out of the pickup, crouching slightly to keep behind the protective shield of the vehicle's body.

CARLOS HELD HIS breath and, body tense, he raised the rifle, ready to fire as he searched for the poachers. Creeping beyond the protection provided by the pickup, he moved toward the porch on the house. Inching along the front of his home, he worked his way to the side closest to the water. Carefully peering around the corner, he realized it was all clear.

Well, all clear except for the airboats and catamaran that were drifting away from the docks since someone had undone all the lines tying them down.

He lowered the rifle and hurried back to the pickup. Opening the passenger-side door, he said, "You can come out now."

Lucas, Natalie and Missy hopped out and walked with him to the dock as the boats continued to drift farther and farther away in the canal.

"I have to get those boats back to the dock," he said.

Natalie placed her hands on her hips and her gaze drifted back and forth across the waters before shifting to look at him. "How do you plan on doing that?"

Carlos pointed to a bright green kayak tucked against some high grasses along the edge of the waters. "Tourists left that about a week ago. Said they didn't need it anymore."

She glanced at the canal where a few alligators swam in and around the boats floating loose. "What if one of those gators attacks?"

He held the rifle out to her. "An army grunt like you should know how to use this."

Her hazel and gold eyes widened in surprise even as she took the rifle from him. "You want me to shoot it?"

Gesturing to the back of his skull, he said, "You've got to shoot in the soft triangle right behind the gator's head."

"What if I miss?" she asked.

Carlos tossed his head back and laughed. "If you miss, we'll have one very pissed off alligator."

He didn't wait for her acceptance of the task to hurry over to the kayak, grab the paddle and slip it halfway into the waters of the canal. It rocked, almost violently, as he settled into the seat and grabbed the paddle. With a powerful push, the kayak slipped into the dangerous waters.

NATALIE SHOULDERED THE rifle and trained it in the direction of the kayak, vigilant for signs of any alligator that was getting too close. Her hands were wet against the barrel and stock of the rifle, making it slippery as she followed the path of the kayak. Missy whined nervously at her side and rose on her haunches, sensing Natalie's upset.

"Sssh, Missy. It's okay," she urged, hoping Missy wouldn't lose control at such a dangerous moment.

"*Papi*, watch out," Lucas called out and gestured to one gator bearing down swiftly toward the kayak.

Natalie swung the rifle in that direction, heart pounding as she realized the gator was as long, possibly longer, than the kayak and that she had the wrong angle to hit that spot Carlos had identified. But a second later, Carlos did a hard paddle that turned the kayak's nose and with another powerful stroke, he tucked the kayak against one of the airboats.

With a strong surge of his arms, hard muscles bunching and straining, he lifted himself into the airboat and then grabbed the rope on the nose of the kayak to haul it into the hull of the boat.

Releasing a pent-up breath, she lowered the rifle muzzle and pointed it at the ground.

Lucas let out a whoop and pumped his fist in the air. "Way to go, *Papi*!"

Carlos grinned and her heart did a little stutter. He really was very handsome when he smiled.

He slipped into the operator's seat and barely a second later, the engine of the airboat roared to life. The blast of air rippled across the waters and sent the alligators racing away, tails splashing.

He maneuvered the airboat toward the other boats, bringing them in one-by-one so Lucas and Natalie could tie them up, running to the business's dock and then back to the house. Missy chased after them, gratefully losing her earlier nervousness. As Carlos brought the last boat in, Lucas grabbed the line and tied it to the cleat on the dock.

Carlos hopped off and tousled Lucas's hair. "Good job, *mi'jo*," he said as he examined the knot his son had tied.

"Gracias, Papi," Lucas said and was about to dash off into the house, but Carlos laid a restraining hand on his arm.

"Let us check out the house first, *mi'jo*," he said, and his gaze settled on Natalie.

"That's right, Lucas. Just in case," Natalie said and handed Carlos the rifle. With a hand command to Missy, she walked to the door of the house with the Lab and tried the knob, but the door was locked.

Carlos reached past her and tried to turn the knob too. "I guess there's no need for you to go in. I didn't see any open windows when I checked the perimeter before."

Natalie shook her head. "I'd feel better if I inspected the house."

Chapter Five

Carlos didn't want to tell her how to do her job, but...

"Maybe you should work on getting some other security around here so no one can mess with us again," he said.

She tightened her lips into a grim line, but then dipped her head in agreement. "I'll get some cameras mounted and report to SBS on what else we'll need once I do another reconnoiter of the property. I'll be in the RV if you need me."

"That sounds good. If you need any help—"

"I'm good, *gracias*. No need for you to do anything," she said, words clipped and shot through with anger.

She turned on her heel and hurried down the steps, passing Lucas who was standing at the base of the stairs, watching them intently. His gaze tracked Natalie as she hurried by with Missy, and then skipped back to him.

Carlos waved a hand to urge his son up the stairs. "Come on, *mi' jo*. You must have homework to do before dinner."

Lucas pushed his glasses into place with a finger and nodded, then slowly trudged up the stairs, but that tingle between Carlos's shoulders made him stop his son at the door.

"Let me check the house first," he said. He opened the door and did a quick inspection inside, moving quickly from room to room. Nothing seemed out of the ordinary and so he returned to the door and said, "It's okay. Everything is okay."

But despite everything being seemingly fine, that itch between his shoulder blades refused to go away as he went about their normal routine.

He started making dinner while Lucas sat at the kitchen table, doing his homework. He had originally taken out a steak for them to share, but with the upset that had just happened, he put it back in the fridge to make Lucas's favorite comfort food: macaroni and cheese.

He was just finishing the cheese sauce when he caught sight of Natalie leaving the RV and guilt slammed through him. Her job couldn't be an easy one, especially if she was suffering from the PTSD that had been mentioned in the news article about the lost child.

His wife had volunteered at a veterans' home and worked with many PTSD patients. He'd helped her on occasion and seen how hard it could be and because of that, he didn't want to place any unnecessary pressure on Natalie.

Turning down the heat on the sauce, he called out to Lucas, "Do you mind if I invite Natalie to dinner?"

Lucas looked up, eyes wide behind the lenses of his glasses. He poked them upward with an index finger and said, "Missy too?"

His son had always wanted a dog, only there had never been enough time to adopt one and then Daniela had been killed and there was less time than ever to deal with everyday things.

"Sure, Missy too," he said and when Lucas nodded, he hurried out of the house and over to the RV, but as he neared it, he realized Natalie still hadn't returned. Clasping his hands in front of him, he waited by the RV for her and barely minutes later, she came down the path from his business.

CARLOS STOOD BY her RV, his face set in stone, the beard darkening his features. His large size made him look intimidating, but also, weirdly, created a feeling of security. Maybe it was because he was Trey's friend, and that meant he was a good guy. Maybe it was because she'd seen how he cared for his son.

But that didn't mean that she still wasn't a little stung by the way he'd stopped her from doing her job and making sure the house was secure.

As she approached, he said, "I didn't know if you had dinner plans."

Dinner? An unexpected growl and twist of her stomach betrayed her.

"I didn't think about making dinner. I still have some things to do before I eat."

"We can wait for you. It's nothing fancy. Just mac and cheese," he said and rocked back and forth on his heels, clearly as uneasy with this simple discussion as she was.

She hesitated, but if she was going to continue to work with this man, they had to find some common ground. "Sure. That would be nice."

His lips slipped into the barest hint of a smile, and he nodded. "Great. Just come over whenever you can. Missy too."

"I won't be long. I just have to check in with SBS," she said and jerked a thumb in the direction of the RV.

As he walked away, she hurried into the vehicle with Missy and over to the large monitor mounted on one wall, then flipped it on. The monitor jumped to life and within a few seconds, the feeds from the cameras she had placed around the property filled the screen.

All was quiet from what she could see.

"Looks good, Missy. How about I get you some dinner before I call the office?" she said and walked the few feet to the galley kitchen outfitted with a small cooktop, microwave and fridge. She'd packed several days' worth of fresh food for Missy along with some hard kibble.

She removed a packet of the fresh food and scooped it out into a bowl. As Missy ate, she stepped away to call SBS.

Trey immediately answered. "Good evening, Natalie. How's it going?"

"We had a small incident," she replied and relayed the story about the undone lines on the boats.

"How did they know you were both gone from the property...?"

"Unless someone is watching the grounds," Natalie finished for him.

"Then it's a good thing you've got those cameras in place so we can see who's coming and going. Do you think you need more?" Trey asked.

She'd placed at least six cameras on and around the property and yet it still didn't feel like enough. "It would be good to have another camera or two at the house."

"Good. I'll have Sophie and Robbie get them ready and they'll be out in the morning to get a feel for the property and what else we may need to do," Trey said. A second later, a long sigh filtered across the line. "How are you doing? Is the RV comfortable enough?"

She hadn't really spent much time in the vehicle, but like most things connected to SBS, she suspected the RV had the best of everything inside. "I'm good. Missy too. She's getting used to our new space," she said and glanced at her Lab, who had finished eating and was sniffing around the interior of the motor home.

"Great. If you need anything, just call. Sophie and Robbie or another team member can monitor the feeds whenever you need a break. Just let them know and say hello to Carlos for me."

"I will," she said and ended the call, thinking that she'd need someone to watch while she was at dinner with Carlos and Lucas, and later, so she could get some sleep. She texted them and they instantly replied, allowing her to schedule them for dinner and later that night so she could get some rest.

Satisfied that everything was in order, she did a low whistle to call Missy and clipped on her leash to take her for a short walk before joining Carlos and Lucas for dinner.

Once Missy had relieved herself, she headed to the house, but hesitated at the door. She normally didn't get involved with her clients, but her clients didn't normally include a ten-year-old boy who seemed to need a friend. Maybe more.

The decision was jerked away from her as the door flew open and Carlos stood there, his broad shoulders nearly filling the width of the entrance. His head was only a few inches below the top edge of the doorframe, his presence so imposing that Missy rose on her haunches beside her, going on alert.

With a hand command, she urged Missy down, and the action didn't go unnoticed by Carlos.

"She's a good protector," he said, and his deep voice reverberated inside her.

"She is. May I come in?" she said and nervously ran her hand back and forth across Missy's leather leash.

"Yes, of course. My bad," he said with an awkward laugh and a boyish grin that lifted worry from his features. He stepped aside to let her enter.

CARLOS CLOSED THE door behind her and hung back as she walked in and did a quick look around the open-concept great room of his home.

What does she see? he wondered.

The house was tidy and neat. As marines, both he and his wife had insisted on order.

There were a few feminine touches here and there. The boldly colored canvas on one wall and sofa cushions in bright coral and teal in a room of mostly neutrals. The family photos on the mantel above the fireplace that his wife, a former New Englander, had insisted they build into their home even though they rarely used it.

"This is very nice," she said as she finished the slow swivel to check out the space.

"*Gracias*. I can't really take credit for it. My wife did most of the decorating for the house while I focused on the business," he admitted with a shrug.

"It sounds like you had a real partnership," she said and walked toward the table just off the kitchen area.

He hadn't thought about it like that, but it was a good way to describe the relationship he'd had with Daniela. "We were partners. In the business. In life. As parents. But we were also friends." Lovers, he thought.

Natalie gave a hand command to Missy, who lay down beside the table. "You were very lucky to have that kind of relationship."

Carlos nodded and shook his head in regret. "I was. Funny thing is, you don't realize just how lucky you are until it's gone."

An awkward silence followed his words and he understood. How did you respond to something like what he'd just said? To break the silence, he said, "The mac and cheese will be ready in a few minutes. Can I get you something to drink in the meantime?"

"Some soda, please. Anything diet, if you have it," she said and laid her hands on the top rung of one of the oak Windsor chairs.

Carlos took a soda from the fridge, added some ice to a glass, and brought both over to her. As he handed her the soda, she said, "Trey says hi, by the way. Have you known him long?"

"We were ROTC in college and served together in Iraq. Came home and Trey went into the police force. Dani and I decided to take over this airboat business and turn it around," Carlos said, a smile drifting onto his face as he recalled those happy days when they'd all come back from war and banded together to form new lives.

"We're almost like brothers," he admitted.

"I guess that's why Lucas calls him *Tio* Trey?" she asked, gaze narrowing as she examined him.

"It is. We haven't spent a lot of time together lately, but when we do, it's like being with family."

"You're very lucky to have that," she said, and it made him wonder if she had that kind of support in her life.

"What about you? Any family in the area?" he asked and hated the guarded look that drifted over her face.

The ding of the oven timer warned him not to push her for an answer. He grabbed pot holders, opened the oven, took out the dish with the mac and cheese and brought it over to the kitchen table. Placing the dish on a trivet, he said, "Let me go get Lucas. He gets so involved in his video games—he doesn't realize what time it is."

But before he could call out for him, Lucas's pounding footsteps sounded on the wooden floor. He stopped short in front of Natalie and Missy, a broad smile on his face.

It had been a long time since he'd seen that kind of joy on his son's features. While he was grateful for it, he also worried that Natalie and Missy were not going to be in their world for long.

He didn't want his son to suffer with that kind of loss again.

Chapter Six

Carlos marched away, leaving Natalie and Missy waiting with the buttery and irresistible aroma of the mac and cheese cooling on the table.

Barely a minute later, father and son returned to the table. Lucas's attention was immediately drawn to Missy who had sat up with their approach. "Can I pet her?"

She normally didn't allow anyone to treat Missy like a pet, but there was something about Lucas, something so needy, that stopped her from saying no. Besides, it would probably be good for Missy to familiarize herself with him and Carlos since they were going to be here for a few days.

"Sure, but first, let her sniff your hand," she said, and with a verbal command, she instructed Missy to stay as Lucas approached, hand outstretched until he brought it to within an inch of Missy's nose.

Missy smelled Lucas's hand and then gave it a lick. A bright laugh escaped Lucas and when he looked at her, a wide smile had lifted that neediness from his features. Hazel eyes, so much like his father's, gleamed with happiness.

"She licked me," he said with another laugh.

Natalie joined in his laughter and said, "She gave you a doggy kiss."

Carlos grinned and affectionately smoothed an errant lock

of Lucas's hair. "And that means you need to go wash your hands before dinner."

As Lucas rushed to the kitchen sink, Carlos turned that dangerous grin in her direction and mouthed, *"Gracias."*

She dipped her head in acknowledgment and once Lucas returned to the table, they all sat to eat. Carlos scooped out healthy portions of the mac and cheese into bowls and passed them around, but as she accepted the dish, Missy grew uneasy beside her.

Puzzled, she said, "What is it, Missy? What's wrong?"

Missy whined, clearly upset. At Natalie's hand command to go find it, Missy went to a closed door on the opposite side of the room.

"What's wrong with her?" Carlos asked, dark brows pulled tightly together.

"What room is that?" Natalie asked with a toss of her hand in the direction of where Missy lay low by the crack between the floor and the door. "She must smell something." She rose to open the door, but Carlos laid a gentle hand on her arm.

"It's my bedroom and it's probably nothing," he said.

"Just *Papi's* smelly socks," Lucas said with a laugh and easy smile.

Her radar was saying it was more than that, but she also understood that Carlos would rather not have her rooting around his personal things. With them being in new surroundings with lots of different smells that Missy would have to process, maybe that was the reason for the Lab's behavior.

"Missy, come here, girl," she said, but Missy didn't budge at first, her nose still almost glued to that crack between door and floor. "Come here, Missy," she said more sharply, and Missy's head and ears popped up to confirm she'd heard. With a little click of her tongue to call her, Missy finally returned to the table. "Good girl," she said and offered Missy a treat that she took out of a bag in her pants pocket.

Lucas paused with a forkful of mac and cheese in midair. "Do you always carry treats around?"

Natalie nodded. "I do. It reinforces good behavior but so does rewarding her with praise or rubbing her head or her favorite bath."

Lucas narrowed his gaze and it skipped between her and Missy. "She likes to take baths?"

Natalie smiled and forked up some of her meal. "She does. With lavender."

Lucas's nose wrinkled and his glasses slipped down slightly. He pushed them back up and said, "Lavender. Girls like lavender."

"Boys do too," Carlos said with a chuckle and shake of his head.

Lucas crinkled his nose. "I don't think I do."

"Maybe you can help me bathe her next time and decide for yourself," Natalie said.

Lucas's eyes popped open wide, making him look slightly owl-like behind the lenses of his glasses. He looked at his dad and said, "Can I help?"

"If Natalie says you can, of course," Carlos said, and it was impossible for her to miss the grateful tone in his voice but also the worry. It made her wonder what was happening in the Ruiz household and how her being there would impact it. Despite that, she kept silent, especially as Lucas pumped a fist in the air, clearly happy.

She forked up more of the delicious mac and cheese. Pointing the fork at her bowl, she said, "You made this from scratch?"

Carlos nodded and she said, "It's the best mac and cheese I've ever had. I'd love your recipe if you don't mind sharing."

A flush of bright color swept across his face and around a mouthful of food, he said, "Sure."

The rest of the meal passed in comfortable chatter—mostly Lucas asking about Missy.

Natalie answered as best she could until the meal was finished, and Lucas excused himself to go to his room.

As Lucas rose from the table, Carlos said, "No more video games. Why don't you read that new book I got you?"

Lucas rolled his eyes and his lips twisted with disgust but at Carlos's stern look, Lucas nodded and said, "Okay, *Papi.*"

After Lucas had left, Carlos started to clear off the table and said, almost apologetically, "He just spends too much time playing video games."

Natalie nodded and picked up plates and cutlery from the table. "I think I read somewhere that boys spend as much as three hours a day playing games."

Carlos's lips thinned into a harsh line. "He didn't before…"

His voice trailed off and Natalie didn't need him to finish. She laid her hand on his arm and squeezed reassuringly. "He's still hurting."

Looking away from her, he softly said, "He's not the only one."

With a heavy sigh that lifted those broad shoulders that she suspected were carrying way too much weight, he said, "I don't want to keep you if there are things you should do."

Understanding he needed time alone, she laid the dishes on the kitchen counter and said, "I should do a patrol of the grounds. I assume you know Sophie and Robbie."

Carlos nodded. "I do."

"They'll be monitoring the cameras when I'm not. I'll do another patrol around midnight," she said and didn't wait for him before she headed out the door.

CARLOS WATCHED HER GO, grateful that she seemed to understand when not to push.

He'd already had too many people pushing lately. The therapist he took Lucas to see. Assorted friends and family, urging him to get out more. That it would be good for both him and Lucas not to be so isolated, both physically and emotionally.

Which made him wonder if that was part of the reason why Trey had sent Natalie on this case. She was beautiful. Smart. Caring. That was obvious from the patient and kind way she'd answered every one of Lucas's questions during dinner.

His son hadn't been that animated, that interested in anything besides his games, in months.

That worried him again. Lucas was too vulnerable. His emotions still too raw. It would only hurt him yet again if he got too close to Natalie and Missy because they were only in their lives temporarily.

Something else worried him too: Missy's weird reaction at his bedroom door.

Granted, his socks could be smelly at times, much as Lucas had said, but his gut warned him not to ignore the reaction.

He placed what was left of the mac and cheese on the counter to cool and slipped the dishes into a sink filled with soapy water.

Drying his hands with a towel, he walked to his bedroom, opened the door and peered inside.

The room wasn't as tidy as the rest of the house but not what anyone would call a mess. The bed was unmade, and the barest hint of dust covered the oak furniture. Briefs hung off the edge of a hamper where socks that had missed their mark sat on the hardwood floor.

He rushed over to get the socks and briefs in the hamper and did a quick look around the room. Nothing out of the ordinary as far as he could see. With that, he returned to the kitchen to finish cleaning.

Even though Daniela had insisted on a dishwasher, it hadn't been unusual for them to do the dishes by hand while they chatted about the day's events and their future plans. A future cut short by the car crash that had taken her life.

He needed that time tonight to think about all that was happening to them—from the danger created by the poachers to Natalie's presence and finally to Lucas and his issues.

With each swipe of the plates with the sponge, he considered what he had to do. How to protect his business and his son. How to deal with Natalie and Missy and whether they were the right agents for the job.

He was so lost in his thoughts, that he ignored the first brush of something across his foot. But as the touch came again, more insistent against the leg of his jeans, he looked down.

His blood ran cold, and his breath trapped in his chest at the sight of the nearly ten-foot Burmese python that had already coiled itself around his ankles.

With another slither, the snake moved upward.

He shook off shock and reacted.

Grabbing the python's head, he fought to unwrap it from his legs, but the snake just coiled tighter around his calves and continued to move up his body. If it got to his midsection, it would squeeze him so tight, he'd asphyxiate.

"Lucas! Come here, Lucas!" he called out and prayed his son hadn't slipped on his headphones to game.

But as the snake moved upward, Lucas didn't respond.

With another twist, the snake was up to his thighs. He fell to the ground, grabbed hold of the snake's head, and rolled to pound its head into the floor, hoping to knock it out. As he did so, he continued to call out to Lucas, praying he'd hear.

The python squeezed around his legs as he dug his fingers into the snake's eyes and smacked its head on the floor again, trying to break free.

"Lucas! Lucas!" he screamed as the snake moved ever upward, winning the battle.

The front door flew open.

Natalie and Missy stood there for a heartbeat and then she rushed forward, reaching behind her back to pull out a pistol.

He held his hand up and said, "We want it alive."

ALIVE? NATALIE THOUGHT, eyes wide at the sight of over ten feet of muscular snake wrapping its way around Carlos's big body. She'd heard stories of alligators, deer and even a man being found inside a python's stomach.

But as her gaze locked with Carlos's, she realized he was serious and that she had to act.

Missy was barking and lunging at the snake, confused by what it was.

Natalie couldn't afford to be confused.

Carlos still had a grip on the snake, just below its head.

"Put its head on the floor," she said and when he did, she quickly brought the butt of the handgun down hard on the top of its head.

The thick keratin of its skin softened the blow, but she hit it again and again until the snake stopped moving.

Together, they were able to pull the snake off him and lug its limp length outside. Missy tagged along beside Natalie, sniffing the long tail of the snake as it draped over her arm.

"There's a locker by the waterside," he said, and they trudged there and placed the snake down on the ground.

Carlos opened the locker and together they dumped the body of the snake into it. The python almost filled the space and as it moved again, Carlos slammed the lid closed and slipped the lock back on to secure the snake.

Missy sniffed at the locker, barking and pawing at it, prompting a hand command and a sharp, "Heel, Missy." The dog quieted and returned to her side to sit and look up at her, waiting for another instruction.

With a relieved sigh as Missy quieted, Carlos placed his hands on his hips and shot her a grateful look. "*Gracias*. I'd be dead if it wasn't for you."

A whirlwind of emotions twisted through her. Relief. Fear. Anger.

It was anger that took over as she jabbed her index finger into his chest and said, "Don't ever stop me and Missy from doing our job again."

He winced with each poke and shook his head. "I didn't stop you."

"You did, Carlos," she said and dragged her fingers through her hair in frustration. "When we were having dinner, Missy went to your door. She must have smelled something was off, but you said it was probably nothing."

Body tight with irritation, she pointed at the locker. "That is not nothing and I won't hesitate to push next time even if you are Trey's friend. I can't let that relationship interfere with what I think is best even if it upsets you."

He sucked in his lips, clearly digesting what she'd just said. With a nod, he finally said, "You're right. I'm sorry."

"Why didn't Lucas hear you? I came running when I heard you scream," she said and looked back at the house where there was still no sign of Lucas anywhere.

Carlos tracked her gaze and blew out a tired sigh. "He wears his headphones when he games at night."

With that maelstrom of emotions still whirling around inside her, she curbed her frustration as his shoulders dipped down with either defeat or weariness. Both called to her because it was obvious he was a man who cared deeply for his son and wasn't happy about the current state of things.

She trailed her fingers down his arm, hoping to offer comfort. "It takes time to get over something like this."

His lips tightened into a thin slash, and he pinned her with his gaze. "How would you know how much time it takes?"

Like the pages of a book flipping open, the memories rushed back, rousing pain she thought she had dealt with long ago. She dragged in a shaky breath and said, "Because I lost my dad when I was eight."

Chapter Seven

Her words hit Carlos's gut with the force of a side kick to his solar plexus. He reached out to cradle her cheek, but then pulled it back and stuffed his hands into his pockets.

"I'm so sorry."

She gave him a half smile and released a sharp breath. "People say that a lot. I'm sure you've heard those words over and over."

He nodded. "If I had a dime for every time—"

"You'd be a rich man," she said with a rueful shake of her head. "Give him time—but without the headphones."

Missy whined by her side and tugged at her leash, wanting to go explore the locker again.

"No, Missy. Sit. Quiet," she said, and Carlos sensed it was time they get moving.

"I guess you want to finish your patrol," he said and gestured to the restless Lab.

Natalie nodded and tilted her chin up in challenge. "I do, but first I'd like us to check out your house."

He was about to argue, but her earlier words about refusing her flayed him as did the fear that the python might have attacked Lucas instead of him. With a sweep of his hand, he said, "Lead the way."

NATALIE APPRECIATED THAT he was being reasonable. This time.

With a soft click of her tongue, she and Missy hurried to the house.

At the door, she released her tight hold on Missy's leash, letting her take the lead as the dog sniffed all around the room.

She must have immediately picked up on the snake's scent since she went straight to Carlos's bedroom.

Contrary to Lucas's comments about smelly socks, the room had a clean masculine scent, like eucalyptus and mint mixed together. As Missy explored the room, Natalie did as well, taking note of the slight hints of dust on the furniture and the rumpled bedsheets.

Her mind unexpectedly went to an image of him tangled up in those sheets. *Danger, danger, danger*, her brain warned, and she heeded that caution.

Carlos and his son were a job. A job that had started badly in multiple ways as far as she was concerned.

Focusing her attention strictly on the job and not the man standing at the door—arms laid across his broad chest—she followed Missy around the room but paused to check the windows.

There were marks at one windowsill. "Some dirt here and the window is unlocked. They may have come in this way."

Carlos came over, inspected the sill and then locked the window tight. Glancing at her, he said, "I'll check all the other windows and make sure they're secure."

She followed him as they went next door to a guest bedroom, crossed the open-concept living room and kitchen area and finally to Lucas's room. A closed door greeted them.

Carlos knocked, but there was no reaction.

With a harder knock, the door swung open, and Lucas stood there, headphones around his neck, sound blaring from them.

His gaze swung from his dad to her, and then opened wide as he obviously sensed something was up.

"What's wrong, *Papi*?" he asked, his gaze continuing to dart between them.

"We had a little incident, but you didn't hear it," Carlos said and gestured to the dangling headphones.

"I'm sorry, but you asked me to wear them at night because the game's too loud," he said in apology.

Carlos gritted his teeth and nodded. "I did, but maybe while things are going on, you need to not use them and turn down the volume."

Lucas nodded, but glanced at her uneasily, as if seeking her approval. "Your *papi* is right. We really need your help to keep everyone safe."

"I can help. Maybe I can even patrol with you and Missy," he said, voice rising in question. When he finished, he peered up at his father anxiously.

Natalie looked his way too, worried about taking Lucas around for a number of reasons. The safety factor first and foremost. But she also suspected the young boy wanted a connection to both her and Missy and that could be emotionally dangerous for him as well.

Carlos sucked in a deep inhale and rocked back and forth on his heels as he considered the request. With a sideways glance at her, he said, "Only if I go with you and only if it's okay with Natalie—"

"Yes!" Lucas shouted and pumped his fist.

She didn't want to break his heart, but she now had the added worry of Carlos tagging along. His presence was calling to her in all kinds of ways, one of which could be emotionally dangerous to her. But she didn't want to disappoint the young boy.

"You can come with me tomorrow after you're done with your homework," she said and trailed her hand down the boy's arm in encouragement.

He pumped his fist again, a broad smile on his face, and whipped around to return to his room, but then stopped short and whirled to face them again. "Good night, Natalie. Missy. *Papi.*"

"Good night," she and Carlos said in unison.

Lucas grinned, so brightly it made his hazel eyes almost golden, and half closed his door in deference to their earlier request that he be more alert.

Carlos gestured toward the front door. "I'll walk you to the RV."

"There's no need for you to do that."

Despite her words, he walked with her to the door and out and down the steps of his house to the RV entrance. She faced him to keep him from going inside. That would be something more than what she could handle at that moment. As she met his gaze, it was dark with worry and some indefinable emotion.

He clasped his hands before him. "I appreciate you being okay with Lucas being a part of this—"

"But you're worried about that," she finished for him.

"Since Dani died…he hasn't been himself. He's been hiding in those video games. You and Missy… You seem to draw him out."

"And we won't be here for long. I get it," she said, totally recognizing the harm that could do to the young boy. She also held back how being around the two of them was awakening hopes and desires she'd locked away because of the issues both she and Missy had been having with their PTSD. She hadn't thought about a family of her own in too long.

Carlos nodded and narrowed his gaze, scrutinizing her in a way that had her heart knocking against her ribs. "Are you okay with us taking it slow?"

"I am," she said with a certainty she wasn't feeling, especially since the "taking it slow" wasn't just about getting close to Lucas. There was something happening between them that she hadn't expected.

He hesitated, but then finally dipped his head. "I'll see you in the morning. We have breakfast at eight if you want to join us."

"Sure. That sounds great. Good night," she said, opened the RV door and issued a hand command for Missy to enter.

She rushed in after the Lab and quickly closed the door, not wanting to look back at Carlos. Not wanting to see what was in his gaze. Whether it was more than she could handle right now or ever.

Against her leg, Missy whined and looked up at her, sensing her emotions.

"It's all okay, girl. Let's get you a treat," she said, wanting to establish their nightly routine in this new space, routine being important to keep any PTSD issues at bay.

But as she went to grab Missy's dog biscuits from a lower shelf, her gaze drifted out the window to where Carlos was walking back to his house. He paused for a moment and looked back and there was no denying the want in his gaze. A want that awakened a similar feeling in her gut.

Muttering a curse, she forced herself to focus on Missy and *her* needs. She owed that to the K-9 partner who had kept her alive on more than one occasion.

CARLOS THOUGHT HE glimpsed Natalie inside the RV. Just a glimpse and his gut tightened and made him want to go back and explore what it was about her that was drawing him in.

She was beautiful. There was no denying that. But he'd never been a man who only cared about beauty. It had been Daniela's smarts, caring and courage that had drawn him in, not her looks.

Maybe that was it. In some ways, Natalie was a lot like Daniela, but in other ways... The two women couldn't be more different.

Daniela had been physically darker, with her nearly black hair and cocoa brown eyes.

Natalie was lighter with her dirty blond hair and eyes the color of caramel.

Emotionally, that light and dark had been flipped on its head.

Daniela had been an open book of emotions and filled with positivity and joy.

Natalie... She was filled with darkness and emotions hidden by pain.

That pain mirrored what had been in his heart since Daniela had died.

He told himself that's why Natalie called to him. He warned himself that wasn't a good thing. His pain mixed with her pain couldn't possibly result in anything positive.

In his head he heard Daniela's voice chastising him. *Liar.*

"You're wrong, Dani. So, so wrong," he said so softly it was barely audible.

It's time to start living again, Daniela whispered in his brain.

Carlos ignored her, walked into his house and went to his room. Since his bedroom windows faced the RV, he decided to draw the blinds to create much needed distance. The less time Natalie was in his brain, the harder it would be for her to work her way into the cracks in his heart that were still healing.

But as he did so, he caught sight of her at the window, looking his way.

For a long moment they stood there, staring at each other until they both closed the blinds, shutting themselves in. Protecting themselves against unwanted emotions which could threaten their hearts or worse—complicate what they needed to do to protect his family and business.

Chapter Eight

Natalie tried to create a routine for them as soon as she closed the blinds to shut off the sight of Carlos at the window.

She set out a fresh bowl of water and placed Missy's dog bed in the larger living area while keeping an eye on the monitors. No activity on any of the camera feeds, luckily. Removing Missy's tactical harness, she massaged the Lab's body, earning doggy kisses.

"I love you too, Missy," she said and with a quick flip of her hand, let Missy go and relax on her bed.

Shooting a quick look at her cell phone to check the time, she tried to make herself at home by unpacking and laying out her cosmetics and toiletries in the small bathroom area. It would be too small for bathing Missy, but maybe she could rig something up outside.

She returned to the living area and shot a quick look at the monitors. All was quiet thankfully.

Missy had made herself comfortable in her doggy bed. She walked over, kneeled and rubbed behind her ears like her Lab liked. "You're a good girl, Missy."

What looked like a smile slipped on Missy's face. She was so happy at the attention and massage.

Her phone chimed to warn of an incoming message.

Probably Sophie or Robbie, she thought and a quick look

at her phone confirmed it was Sophie, saying her team would take over at midnight so she could get some rest.

To brace herself for the remainder of the night, Natalie prepped the coffee maker and made a big batch of Cuban coffee. The boost of sugar and caffeine would do well to keep her alert as she sat to watch the monitors again and also did a final patrol for the evening. She also whipped out her laptop to do some quick research about Carlos and his business.

She started with reading the reviews people had left on the various travel services. Over and over, people raved about the quality of the tours and the guides.

Much like his sign had proclaimed and he'd defended earlier, the customer comments backed up his claims about the environmental expertise of his employees.

But as she left the reviews, there were multiple articles about his wife's accident, and she couldn't control her curiosity.

She read through all the articles, and they left her…unsatisfied.

An empty stretch of road meant no witnesses. No skid marks. No discernible reason for plowing off the road and into a ditch. A broken neck and head trauma from the impact.

Motion on one of the monitors drew her attention.

A large black-and-white cat loped across the driveway, up the steps of the house and to some bowls at the far end of the front porch.

She hadn't noticed them before. She'd been too busy helping Carlos fight off the python.

The cat finished eating and sprawled lazily on the porch, obviously feeling safe in that locale.

Was it Carlos or Lucas who set out the food for the stray? she wondered. But the answer came immediately.

Carlos. He was the kind of man who would protect those around him—even a stray cat.

Which made her wonder how his wife had ended up dead and alone on an empty Everglades road.

The details of the accident weren't adding up to her, but maybe the crash report would set her mind at ease. Texting Sophie and Robbie, she asked them to get a copy of the crash report from the online database of records and notified them that she was going on another patrol of the grounds so another of their team members could watch the monitors as she did so.

Rising from the banquette, she called to Missy who instantly hopped to her feet and came over. She slipped the tactical vest and leash back on and walked out of the RV and into an Everglades night.

The loud sounds of frogs grunting erupted from the nearby grasses. An almost musical sound from the grasshoppers joined in to create a nighttime symphony.

A heavy dew had erupted since earlier, making the air feel thick and dampening the fragrances of the swamp lilies tangled with the grasses along the edges of the canal. Their squiggly white flowers were almost ghostly in the dark of night.

She started with a quick circle of Carlos's home and stopped by the locker with the python to make sure it was still secure. Thankfully, it was.

She worked her way along the edges of the canal, Missy darting in and around the grasses. Both of them were vigilant for alligators and other nighttime animals and more dangerous humans. All was clear along the path and in and around the business location. Before returning to Carlos's home, she did a quick trip up the driveway to the road and paused there, gazing along the empty stretch of highway. Missy was tucked close to her leg.

Is this what it had been like on the road when Daniela Ruiz had been killed?

Dew glistened on the asphalt, sparkling like diamonds beneath the moonlight. Way down the road, a long, dark body slipped from the edges of the grasses lining the area. A large alligator from the looks of it. Missy must have spotted the motion also since she rose from her heeling position and glanced at the shape.

"It's okay, girl. Nothing to worry about," she said and rubbed Missy's head. Missy settled down at her side again.

Daniela had been an environmentalist like her husband. *Had she swerved to avoid an animal in the roadway and lost control?*

Maybe it was as simple as that, Natalie thought as she turned around and guided Missy along the property close to the road, but all was quiet. Satisfied, she hastened her pace to return to the RV since the damp of the dew was creating a chill in her body.

Back inside the comfortable space of the RV, she removed Missy's leash and vest and grabbed a towel to rub away any damp from Missy. She earned a doggy smile and affectionate lick, and with a soft click of her tongue, she set Missy free to relax.

Texting Sophie and Robbie, she let them know she was back and arranged for their team to take over at midnight so she could get some rest.

A shiver worked through her body from the chill, and she changed into a dry T-shirt and sweats, made herself some coffee and settled in to keep an eye on the monitors. But as she sat there, Daniela's story called to her again.

She powered up her laptop and pulled as much information as she could off the internet, taking notes as she read. Focusing on Daniela's life instead of her death. Daniela had been a superwoman from what she gathered from the various articles that had run in the local newspapers after her death.

Purple Heart and medals for bravery in the Marines. Involvement in an environmental alliance and PTSD support group. Her work with Carlos, of course. Based on the comments in various reviews, Daniela had been a popular tour guide and a great asset to the business.

Everyone had spoken highly of her and yet the sense that

something wasn't right lingered with Natalie. Hopefully the crash report would help to rid her of that feeling.

A movement in one of the monitors pulled her complete attention to the action.

Another gator lumbering from the waters of the canal onto a bank by the nearby dock.

Finishing the last of her coffee, she shot a quick look at her cell phone to confirm the time. Too late to make another batch if she wanted to get any sleep at all. Her SBS team would take over the monitoring in a little less than an hour.

Returning to the notes she had taken, she jotted down ideas about the things in Daniela's life that could have led to someone wanting to kill her. Even as she did the exercise, many of the scenarios were far-fetched, but you could never rule anything out during an investigation. Although she was leaning toward it being related to Ruiz's environmental activities rather than her involvement with local veterans.

Her phone chimed with an incoming text. Sophie confirmed that they were monitoring.

Satisfied that all was in order, she slipped into bed, tired from the long day. Sleep pulled at her, but like the dew that had crept into the night, so did the frightening images of Carlos battling the python.

In that fuzzy state of sleep, the weight of the light blanket on her legs became a snake, wrapping around her ankles. Shifting upward, tightening. Trapping her as she tossed and turned, struggling to be free as Carlos had fought earlier that night.

She cried out and wrenched away the sheet and blanket suffocating her, imagining it was the python, squeezing her breath from her. Hard hands suddenly grabbed her and stopped her thrashing, jerking her awake.

"NATALIE. NATALIE! WAKE UP!" Carlos said while keeping an eye on Missy, who stood nearby, barking and snarling at him since she must have thought he was hurting Natalie.

Natalie's eyes snapped open, but confusion reigned there for a scary moment before she sat up and did a hand command in Missy's direction.

The immense Lab immediately quieted and sat but kept an eye on him as if not sure she could really trust him.

"Are you okay?" he asked and ran his hands down Natalie's arms before pulling them away awkwardly. Her skin had been sleep warm and so smooth.

"What happened?" Natalie asked, clearly confused about his presence in the RV.

He jerked a thumb in the direction of the open door. "I was on my way to check on things before breakfast when I heard you scream." And his heart had stopped beating from fear for a hot second.

Raising his hands as if in apology, he said, "I didn't mean to intrude, and you really should lock your door."

The ring of Natalie's phone surprised them both.

She grabbed it, drawing back the loose strands of her hair with one hand as she answered the phone and said, "I'm okay, Sophie. We're all okay. I know you saw the activity on the monitors, but there's nothing to worry about."

Except for an obviously scary nightmare, he thought, but he kept silent as a dull flush of color worked across her cheeks, down her neck and to the delicate ridge of her collarbones visible beneath the scoop neck of her T-shirt.

"I'm sorry, Carlos. I didn't mean to scare you," she said and looked down at her hands.

He did as well. Her fine-boned fingers were wringing the sheets nervously and he laid his hands on hers and offered a calming squeeze.

"It's okay, Natalie. We've all had a nightmare or two in our lives," he said, even though he suspected that with her PTSD issues, she suffered them more than others. Daniela had often had nightly scares before she'd worked with her support group to relieve her fears.

Her head snapped up and her hazel gaze locked with his. "It was the snake. I'm not a fan of snakes," she admitted and did a rueful laugh.

"On that we can agree. I'll leave you to get some rest, but you're welcome to join us for breakfast in an hour if you want."

She quickly nodded. "*Gracias*. I appreciate it. I'm not much of a cook."

"Great. See you then," he said and hurried from the RV, the small space making everything too intimate, especially with Natalie tangled in the bedclothes.

Get a grip, he warned himself. She was there to do a job and nothing more. Whatever attraction he was feeling had to be contained.

After finishing his quick walk around the house to make sure everything was in order, he rushed back into the house to wake Lucas and make breakfast. It was a routine they'd had since even before Daniela's death. Much like Natalie, his wife hadn't been much of a cook—just extraordinary in every other way.

There wasn't a day that went by that he didn't think of her. Miss her. But he didn't need a therapist to tell him not to let memories hold him back from living.

There were too many things going on right now that were clouding his judgment, though. Natalie's as well. It was best to give her some space and keep everything businesslike.

But as he worked, it was hard to drive images of Natalie from his mind and when the knock came at the door, he rushed to it and eagerly pulled it open.

Chapter Nine

Natalie hadn't done normal in way too long.

Sharing a simple breakfast of eggs, bacon and toast with Carlos and Lucas had brought memories of sitting with her dad before he'd walked out the door one day in his uniform without coming back.

Her dad had been loving and caring, much like Carlos.

Lucas was lucky to have him, she thought as they got into the pickup for the short drive to the bus stop.

Just as Carlos was leaving, a duo of SBS vans pulled into the driveway and parked in front of Carlos's home. In a flurry of activity, Sophie and Robbie Whitaker hurried out of the vans along with a few other SBS techs.

"*Buenos dias*, Natalie," Sophie said and hugged her.

A second later, her older brother, Robbie, added his hug and greetings.

There was no doubting the cousins' relation to the Gonzalez family. They both had the same light eyes, dark hair, Roman noses and dimpled chins that stamped them as family.

The other SBS techs hung back and dipped their heads in greeting, waiting for her report and instructions from Sophie and Robbie.

Robbie rested his hands on his hips and did a slow turn to examine the property. "It's a little wild."

Tracking his gaze, Natalie couldn't deny it. The home and

business sat on the edges of civilization but there was something that called to her about the area.

"That's what worries me about how to add protection," she said and gestured to the various cameras she had already laid out to secure the perimeter.

"You've done a good job so far, but we'll take a walk around and see what else we can do," Sophie said and faced Robbie. "Can you and the techs check it out?"

Robbie smiled tightly and nodded. "Will do. Don't forget we need those coordinates for the alligator nests to send up the drone."

"I've got the coordinates. Carlos texted them and I'll send them to you," Natalie said and whipped out her cell phone to text the information.

"Great," Robbie said, and with a wave of his hand, he herded the two techs away for an inspection of the property.

Once they were out of earshot, Sophie said, "We got that crash report late last night. The autopsy findings also. I'll email them to you."

Sophie gestured toward the dock, as if thinking they needed even more privacy. Once they stood there, she leaned close and said, "Something's not right."

It was how Natalie had felt after reading the various articles detailing the crash. "That's what my radar said."

"We showed the information to Trey last night and he agrees. He had spoken to Carlos at the time of the crash to push for more investigations, but there was too much going on and afterward…"

Sophie didn't need to finish since Natalie understood. "Carlos was too busy trying to make things right for Lucas."

"Maybe he was even in denial. I mean, who would want to kill Dani? Everyone loved her," Sophie said, clearly familiar with Carlos's wife thanks to the friendship between the two families.

"Do you think he's ready to think about that now?" Natalie said and shot a quick glance at the other woman as she stood beside her.

Sophie was of a similar height, with mahogany brown, shoulder-length hair that just skimmed the strong line of her jaw. As she shook her head, the hair brushed against her face.

"I'm not sure," she said and shrugged. "Honestly, we need to focus on this immediate threat first."

Natalie pursed her lips, biting back a response, but Sophie clearly sensed her reluctance.

"Spit it out, Natalie," Sophie urged.

"What if the two things are connected?" she tossed out.

Sophie did a slow turn to face her. "You think the poachers are somehow responsible for the crash?"

"From what I read, Daniela was heavily involved in local environmental causes which could create issues for people like the poachers."

Sophie sucked in a deep inhalation and nodded. "Maybe. And maybe we're just seeing something that isn't there."

"Do you really believe that?" Natalie said just as the sound of a car engine drew their attention to the driveway.

Carlos had returned.

Sophie did another little shrug and said, "No, but if we're going to consider every option, one of them is that it was just a tragic accident."

CARLOS WHEELED THE pickup next to the RV since a duo of SBS vans were parked in front of his home.

As he did so, he noticed Sophie and Natalie by the dock, obviously in deep discussion. A troubled discussion judging from the glower on Sophie's face and the tension in Natalie's body.

He slipped from the vehicle and marched to where they stood.

"*Buenos dias*, Sophie. I can't thank you all enough for helping out with this," he said and hugged her.

"Trey is sorry he couldn't come this morning, but Roni wasn't feeling well," Sophie said.

"I hope she's okay," he said, worried that his friend's newlywed and pregnant wife was ill.

Sophie smiled and laid a hand on his arm to calm his fears. "Just some major morning sickness. He hopes to come by soon."

"Good to hear. I see the two of you were talking," he said and slipped his gaze from one woman to the other.

Their discomfort was obvious as Natalie stammered out, "Just chatting about what to do."

It was more than that, but he decided not to push, especially as Robbie and two other techs strolled over from the other property.

After greeting Robbie and his crew, Carlos said, "What's the plan for today?"

"We're going to get some more cameras and security systems in place here and at your business and send up the drone and do some imaging of the area where you spotted the poachers," Sophie explained.

"What will that do?" Carlos asked.

"Once we get the drone's images, we can process them to see if we can identify possible locations for any poacher camps," Sophie explained.

Carlos peered over his shoulder toward the canal and the grasslands and slough beyond that before facing the SBS crew again. "That's a lot of area to cover."

"It'll take a couple of hours to do the imaging and then about a couple of hours to process the data," Robbie said.

Carlos had heard about drones equipped with lidar locating Mayan temples and other ancient structures covered by vegetation or years of sediment. "Doesn't it take more than a few hours to process that much data from a drone?"

Sophie and Robbie shared a look and then with a grin, Robbie said, "We have an in—Mia's husband and his supercomputer."

Carlos laughed and shook his head. "Right. The billionaire tech guy."

Natalie jumped in with, "Not quite a billionaire yet but on his way. He's been really helpful with a number of SBS cases."

"Whatever it takes," Sophie said with a dip of her head.

Carlos sucked in a long inhalation and jammed his hands on his hips. "What do I do in the meantime?"

Natalie patted Missy's head and said, "You take us to where you spotted the poachers. I'm hoping Missy can pick up a scent, maybe even a trail that can lead us to the poachers or their camp."

With a nod, Carlos said, "We can do that but we're not going out unarmed. I won't be surprised again."

"Agreed," Natalie said and jerked a thumb in the direction of the RV. "I'm going to get my protection and meet you at the dock."

"I'll go get my weapons," Carlos responded as Natalie walked with Missy to the RV.

Once she was gone, he hung back with Sophie and Robbie and said, "I appreciate all that you're doing."

"We will put an end to this," Sophie said and, once again, laid a hand on his arm.

Sophie was a toucher, which he'd learned over the many years that he'd come to know these members of the Gonzalez family. Because of that, he took hold of her hand and gave it an affectionate squeeze.

"I know that and again, I appreciate it. Whatever you need me to do, just say the word," Carlos said and the sound of the RV door opening and closing propelled him to action. "I should go so you can get to work."

With that, he hurried to his pickup to get his rifle and then into the house where he unlocked his gun safe. He removed his Glock, loaded a magazine into the pistol and tucked it into a holster that he slipped onto his belt.

Armed, he hurried out of the house and bounded down the steps to meet Natalie and Missy as they waited at the dock.

"Ready?" he asked, even though the determined look on her face should have been his answer.

"READY," NATALIE SAID, and with a hand command, she instructed Missy to hop onto the boat.

The Lab hesitated for a second but then jumped into the hull. Natalie followed with an assist from Carlos, who held out a hand to steady her as the airboat rocked while she stepped from the dock.

She sat on the bench seat and laid her Sig Sauer AR at her feet where she could reach it easily. With a soft click of her tongue, she urged Missy up beside her. Once they were both settled, Carlos handed her a headset that she secured and gestured with a second pair to Missy. "Not sure how well they'll fit."

"*Gracias.* They should work for her," she said, grateful for his thoughtfulness. Neither she nor Missy were fans of loud noises, and she worried the airboat ride would be a trigger, but they had no choice if they were going to solve this case.

Carlos untied the airboat and climbed up into the operator's platform. He tucked his rifle into a tactical gun case attached to his seat. He slipped on his headset and after a communications check, they were on their way along the canal.

She had worried about the noise from the airboat engines but in truth it was more of a low hum that vibrated through her body. Slipping an arm around Missy, she couldn't detect any worrisome signs. If anything, Missy seemed to be enjoying the ride, her mouth open and tongue hanging out as the air ruffled the long waves of her golden hair.

Relieved, she let herself enjoy the ride, savoring the scenery as they traveled through the low waters, occasionally traversing sections of grass that had earned the area its name: River of Grass.

Here and there—amongst the muddy browns of the soil and water and emerald green and straw colors of the grasses—came bursts of white, pink and gray from a menagerie of birds.

"It's beautiful," she murmured, awed by the majesty of the area and its vastness. It seemed to go on uninterrupted except for the verdant explosions of islands of trees.

"It is. It's why it's so important to safeguard it," Carlos said, his voice mirroring the wonder in hers.

Traveling along that fragile ecosystem, she could well understand why Carlos and his late wife were so involved in local environmental groups. To lose this special place would be a crime.

But she couldn't let the beauty of this place make her forget that crimes also happened here—and not just the poaching. Over the years the area had been a dumping ground for the bodies of murder victims.

They had been traveling for about twenty minutes when Carlos said, "The alligator nests were just up ahead."

She looked at him and he was pointing straight at a slightly higher bit of ground. Tracking the direction of his arm, she peered ahead and spotted the disturbed areas of soil and grass.

As they neared, she realized the higher ground wasn't all that large, only about fifteen feet wide and twice that in length. The area of unsettled dirt took up most of the space.

"There were four alligator nests here," Carlos said and gestured to the dug-up ground.

"Is it safe to step on there?" she asked and at Carlos's nod, she commanded Missy onto the ground and then climbed onto land while Carlos killed the airboat engine and tethered the boat to a small bush along the edge of the canal.

He followed her as she let Missy inspect the area, trying to pick up a scent.

When the Lab started pawing the ground and then sat, Natalie said, "Good girl, Missy. Find it."

Missy excitedly shot to her feet and moved along the tossed-up mounds of dirt, taking them to the farthest end of the strip of land before doubling back to where they'd just come from. She pawed the ground there again and sat, but it was clear to Natalie that the scent wasn't going to lead them off this little strip of land.

Glancing around the area, she said, "They must have taken an airboat or some other kind of transportation off this ground."

Carlos nodded. "They were chasing us in an airboat. A nice new one. By my guess, the alligator eggs they stole easily netted them several thousand dollars."

Natalie let out a low whistle and shook her head. "That's wild."

A series of sharp beeps from the tablet yanked their attention to the airboat.

"What was that?" she asked.

Carlos smiled. "The program on the tablet is telling me Schrodinger is in range."

"Schrodinger?" Natalie asked, confused.

"One of the female panthers we were tracking. She's the reason Lucas and I were out here the other day. Our tracking program warned that she was in the area, and we wanted to see how she's doing," he explained. He hopped up on the airboat, snagged the tablet and returned it to show Natalie the series of pings indicating the panther's position.

Natalie glanced at the tablet and then at a faraway stand of trees in the distance. Pointing a finger in that direction, she said, "Is Schrodinger over there?"

Carlos leaned over her shoulder to peer at the tablet. His action pressed his hard chest against her back, reminding her of his physicality. His body was warm from the heat of the day, rousing his very masculine scent.

Her body responded to all that masculinity, and she had to take a step away as he said, "She is over there. Do you mind if we check on her?"

Chapter Ten

"Sure," Natalie said with a nod and took another step away from him.

He was grateful for that. Sucking in a breath, he quelled the desire that had erupted at the innocent touch of her soft body against his when she'd read the tablet.

"Let's go then," he said and hopped back into the airboat. He turned and held out a hand to help her onto the boat but as he did so, it was impossible to miss the deep blush painting her skin.

That she had felt that sharp blast of desire from the barest touch of their bodies warned him that they had to keep their distance from each other.

Luckily the height of the operator's platform and communications equipment created that distance instantly, giving him the time needed to control the unwanted attraction he was experiencing. There was too much going on in his life for any kind of involvement, especially with a woman like Natalie who also had a lot going on.

Those thoughts chased him from the poachers' area to the island of trees that signaled the start of the pinelands and hardwood hammocks that were home to many of the remaining Florida panthers.

He slowed as they neared and shut the engine, allowing the airboat to drift to where they could tie up the boat. As a few more beeps emitted from the tablet, he silenced it so that the noise would not scare off Schrodinger who couldn't be more than a hundred yards away.

As Natalie looked over her shoulder at him, he put an index finger to his lips to urge quiet and pointed toward one edge of the trees. Grabbing a pair of digital camera binoculars, he slipped them over his neck, unsure of how close they would be able to get.

With a nod, Natalie removed her ear protection and went to the edge of the airboat. He met her there and tied the boat to a small sapling. After climbing onto the ground, his feet sank into the moist softness, making him slightly unsteady. Turning, he gave Natalie a hand up from the airboat and once she and Missy were on the ground beside him, he whispered, "Will Missy be able to keep calm if she sees the panther?"

Natalie shook her head and with a hand command, she directed Missy back onto the airboat and said, "Stay, Missy. Stay."

The Lab's ears rose slightly, as if questioning the command, but as Natalie repeated it, Missy sat on the spectator level of the boat.

With a hand motion, he guided her toward Schrodinger's location, carefully stepping along the grasses and brush leading up to the harder ground of the pinelands.

As they entered the denser tree line, it filtered out the sunlight, creating a cool breeze on their sun-warmed skin.

He glanced at the tablet. Schrodinger couldn't be more than fifty yards straight ahead.

Pausing, he took hold of Natalie's hand and urged her to stand beside him as he lifted the binoculars and searched the trees and underbrush in front of them for any sign of the panther.

Suddenly he spotted the pale brown coat and whitish underside of a panther sprawled against emerald, green underbrush.

He snapped off a photo using the camera in the binoculars before movement in front of the cat had him stand stock-still.

"Amazing," he said as he caught the darker spotted fur of three kittens that were playing in front of Schrodinger before nuzzling up to her to nurse.

He took more photos and then handed the binoculars to Natalie. Leaning close, he whispered, "She's had babies."

HIS VOICE HELD a wealth of awe and joy, making her excited to see what had put that emotion there.

She took the binoculars from him and brought them up to scan the area.

Suddenly right there, right smack in front of her, was a large panther and three precious little kittens. The mama cat was large with a long tail and ears tipped with a darker brown. Although the panther was at rest, her tail whipped up and down as the kittens nursed, as if ready to propel her into action if necessary.

The kitten's fur wasn't as sleek as that of their mother. It seemed almost fluffier and had spots unlike the smooth gold of their mama's coat.

Much like Carlos had done, she snapped a few photos, wanting to capture the moment of the mother nursing her babies.

She handed the binoculars back to Carlos. With a hand gesture and jerk of his head in the direction of the airboat, he led her back. Once they were there, he wrapped his arms around her waist and hugged her hard.

"You don't know how amazing that is," he said, laughter evident in his voice and the broad smile on his handsome face.

"I don't," she admitted and couldn't help but return his embrace and grin at the unrestrained joy that seemed to have lifted years off his shoulders.

He finally released her, but the smile didn't leave his face.

"There are rarely sightings of the mamas with their kittens. Plus, Mama and babies all look healthy. That's a big thing."

She didn't know that much about the Florida panther, but she wanted to—especially since it was so important to Carlos. "Care to explain?"

"Sure. How about on our way back?" he said and motioned to the airboat.

They boarded and got settled, and as promised, he started his explanation as they returned to his house.

"By the 1950s, panthers were nearly extinct thanks to a bounty that had been put on them because some thought they were a threat to humans and livestock—but they rarely attack humans."

"And the farmers with livestock were encroaching on the panther's home," Natalie said, sympathetic to the panther's plight.

"Right. When the bounties didn't finish them off, there were so few left that inbreeding created health issues. Texas pumas were introduced in the 1990s in the hopes the two species would interbreed and that's worked as you can see," he said, obvious pride and relief in his voice.

"They were beautiful. I see why you and your wife want to protect them," she said, better understanding the importance of what they were trying to achieve in the Everglades.

Carlos started to speak, but then paused and slowed the airboat.

She looked over her shoulder to see him standing on the operator's platform and using the binoculars to scan the horizon in front of them. She tracked his gaze.

Dark, violent clouds, heavy with rain, filled the afternoon sky. Angry bursts of lightning brightened that darkness, revealing the torrents of water headed their way quickly.

An almost painful knot formed in her center and a cascade of fears swept through her.

"We have to find shelter," she said.

THERE WAS NO mistaking the dread ringing in her tone, and she was right.

It could be deadly to be on open water with such a powerful storm.

"Hold on," he said, and with a push of the rudder and burst of power, he turned the boat around and rushed back toward the pinelands.

The air bathed his body. It already had the chill and damp of the impending storm.

With another burst of speed, he beached the airboat onto an open space just before the tree line.

"We can shelter in those trees," he said as he tore off his headset and hopped down to the spectator platform.

Natalie's pale face was almost ghostly, her lips tight as she said, "Do you have a blanket or towel or something? I need something to keep Missy calm."

He nodded and headed to a small footlocker beneath the operator's platform. "I think I have some beach towels."

Jerking it open, he pulled out a few towels and a small blue tarp they could use as protection against the rain.

Natalie had climbed out onto the short grasses and moss with Missy at her side. The dog's eyes seemed worried, and her ears were pricked upward, likely sensing the changes in barometric pressure and static electricity that signaled bad weather was on the way.

He joined them on land and placed a hand at the small of her back to urge her into the nearby woods. When they neared the trees, he took the lead, clearing the way for them until they were yards deep beneath a dense copse of pines and underbrush. Urging Natalie and Missy beneath the greenery, he handed her the towels.

Unfolding the tarp, he swept it around his body like a cape and then sat behind her, cradling his front to her back. He spread the tarp up and over them as the first fat drops sounded against the thick plastic.

Natalie had wrapped the towels around Missy, who was already starting to whine and shift nervously beneath them.

"Easy, girl. Easy, Missy," she said as a flash of lightning brightened the sky and Missy fretted—barking and tossing her head. Long seconds passed before the clap of thunder followed, warning that the worst of the storm had yet to reach their location.

But it wasn't just Missy responding to the thunder and lightning. With Natalie cradled next to him, it was impossible to miss the trembling of her body and occasional jump at a loud clap of thunder.

"It'll be okay," he whispered against her ear, but she only grunted, clearly lost in her own kind of nightmare.

He wrapped the tarp more securely around them as a blast of wind threatened to yank it away. With the wind, which whipped the tarp open despite his best efforts, came a fast and furious barrage of thunder and lightning. Cold rain drenched his arms and legs as well as Missy and Natalie who had her arms wrapped around the Lab, trying to quiet its anxious fussing.

"Sing something," Natalie said and between the patter of rain and loud thunder, he wasn't sure he'd heard her right.

"Sing?" he asked, gaze narrowed as he peered at her.

Her lips trembled and her teeth chattered so badly, all she could utter was "Sing."

He couldn't remember the last time he'd sung. Not in the two years since Daniela had died. Maybe even longer—when Lucas had been a baby. That was the first thing that came to mind: one of the lullabies he'd sung to his baby son. A lullaby his mother used to sing to him when he was a child.

"Aruru mi niño, arrurú mi amor, duérmete pedazo de mi corazón," he crooned against her ear and rocked slightly, like he had when Lucas had been fussy. The soft rolling r's, a calming sound, urged the baby who was a piece of his heart to go to sleep.

"*Mami* used to sing that to me," she said and joined in.

Little by little, the storm around them abated, and so did the storm within apparently, since Missy's whines and restlessness slowly relaxed. Beside him, Natalie's body lost some of the tension although not entirely.

When the last patter of rain on the tarp ended, he whispered, "We should head back."

A hesitant murmur came in response and as they untangled from under the tarp and towels, there was no missing the paleness and strain on her features.

"You okay?" he asked, worried by her appearance and her stilted, almost mechanical actions as she grabbed the towels and used a drier one to rub down Missy's fur.

She glanced at him, brow wrinkled with pain. "Migraine. The lights and noise…"

She didn't finish but he didn't need her to. He'd helped Daniela with some of the members in her PTSD support group and had seen the kinds of issues they suffered due to their traumatic brain injuries.

"I've got some sunglasses back at the airboat. They might help," he said.

"*Gracias,*" she said and took a stumbling step toward the airboat when Missy jerked against Natalie's hold on her tactical vest.

He slipped an arm around her waist, steadying her as they slogged over the wet and uneven ground.

At the airboat, he quickly got them settled and offered Natalie the dark sunglasses to protect against the first tendrils of sun breaking through the quickly dissipating storm clouds.

She accepted them with a forced smile and once she had them and the headset on, he hopped up onto the operator platform for the drive to his home.

While he steered the airboat across the storm-flooded canal and grasses, he kept a close eye on Natalie and Missy, worried about their condition. The dog continued to fret and whine, but

Natalie was stock-still except for the hand that stroked Missy's head, trying to placate her.

He pushed the airboat as fast as he could without risking their safety and when they neared his dock, the SBS vans were still in front of the house. At their approach, Sophie and Robbie exited one of the vans and hurried over, clearly worried.

Pulling up to the dock, he killed the engine and left the operator's platform to toss a rope to Robbie so he could tie up the boat.

Even before they were finished, Sophie was helping Natalie and Missy onto the dock.

"We were worried. That was some storm," Sophie said.

Natalie woodenly nodded. "It was bad. I need to calm Missy."

Sophie peered in his direction and at his nod, she said, "Let us help you, Natalie."

Sophie took Missy's leash and grabbed hold of her tactical vest. As he had before, Carlos slipped an arm around Natalie's waist and offered support as they walked toward the RV.

Sophie opened the door and Missy immediately rushed inside as if sensing the RV was a safe place.

Natalie lumbered up the steps and he followed her inside, but it was cramped with all of them in there.

Sophie said, "Why don't you wait outside while I get Natalie settled?"

Like the storm that had swept over them, an eruption of emotions raced over Carlos.

He wanted to protect Natalie but knew she might not appreciate that hovering.

Dani had been much the same way.

Guilt came that he was once again comparing Natalie to his dead wife.

But Natalie intrigued him more than she should. Because of that he stepped back but didn't retreat. Worried. Caring way too much for a woman he'd only barely gotten to know.

Chapter Eleven

Carlos hesitated as Natalie sat at the narrow dining table, removed his sunglasses and laid them on some file folders on the tabletop.

Natalie met his gaze and offered him a tight smile. "I'll be okay," she said, even though her head felt as if it might split open at any moment.

He nodded. "I'll be back to check on you later," he said and finally hurried out the door.

Even with the pounding in her head that normally overwhelmed everything, she immediately sensed his absence.

"You're a good girl," Sophie said as she rubbed Missy's ears and then removed the tactical vest.

"*Gracias* for taking care of her. I feel so useless." Because the migraine had taken hold, weakening her to the point that all she wanted to do was crawl into bed and close out the lights and noise of the world.

"You're not useless, Natalie," Sophie said and hugged her hard. "Let's get you out of these wet clothes and somewhere quiet."

She didn't argue. She couldn't. Dark circles danced in her vision, almost blinding her, and the pain... The pain was worse than it had been for so long thanks to the prolonged battery of light and noise from the storm. Nausea was setting in, and she sucked in a deep breath to control it.

With Sophie's help she staggered to the bedroom, undressed and slipped into bed.

Sophie drew all the blinds closed, plunging the room into semidarkness. "Can I get you anything? Any medicine?"

She fumbled in the nightstand and drew out a small bottle of painkillers. "Just some water please."

Seconds later, Sophie returned with a glass of water and Natalie sucked down two tablets. The cool water slipped down easily.

"Gracias," she said.

"Get some rest. Robbie and I have a few things left to do and we'll take care of filling in Carlos," Sophie said. She walked out and closed the door behind her.

Blissful quiet and darkness filled the space and she let herself drift off into that welcoming cocoon to try to find some relief from the pain.

IT HAD BEEN a few hours since Sophie and Robbie had finished their service of all the security systems and features they'd installed and driven away.

Carlos had picked up Lucas and explained the new alarm system. Once he was comfortable that his son knew how to arm and disarm it, he'd given Lucas a snack and got him doing his homework before starting dinner.

The whole time after he'd arrived at home, he'd kept an eye on the RV, looking for any signs of activity, but there'd been none.

With everything that had been going on, he hadn't had time to prep anything involved for dinner—just some canned tomato soup, that he doctored with salsa for some extra flavor, and grilled cheese on slabs of sourdough bread with a mix of cheddar and Gruyère.

He served the soup and sandwich to his son along with a tall glass of milk, but as he did so, Lucas glanced toward the front door.

"Isn't Natalie coming tonight? Missy too?" Lucas asked, his dark eyes alight with an eagerness Carlos hadn't seen in far too long.

"Natalie had a bad headache. I'll take some dinner to her later," Carlos said and sat kitty-corner to his son.

The life in Lucas's eyes dimmed and his shoulders sank with disappointment.

That disappointment dampened conversation during the rest of the meal. No matter how hard he tried to get his son to talk, every question was met with simple yeses or nos.

When his son's spoon clinked into an empty bowl and nothing but crumbs were left on his plate, Lucas said, "May I be excused?"

Carlos was tempted to insist that his son stay behind to help clean up but knew it would do little to generate conversation.

"*Sí*, but make sure you put your homework away so you don't forget it," Carlos said to his son's retreating back as Lucas raced to his room to play his games.

Disheartened, Carlos made quick work of packing up some soup and a sandwich for Natalie and cleaning. He hurried outside to the RV to check on Natalie and give her dinner in case she hadn't eaten yet. As he approached, he noticed the gleam of lights from behind the drawn blinds and a shadow passed by them for a hot second, confirming that Natalie was up and about.

He knocked on the door and the Lab started barking until Natalie instructed her to quiet.

She opened the door and stood there, the light limning the curves of her body from behind.

Carlos held up the bag so she could see it. "I brought you some dinner in case you hadn't eaten."

"I haven't. I just got up," she said and stepped aside to let him enter.

"It's just soup and a sandwich," Carlos said. He went over to the table and took out the container with the soup and the foil-wrapped sandwich. He set them on the table, careful not to place them on the files sitting there.

She grabbed a spoon from a drawer and then went to the small fridge. Turning, she said, "Can I get you anything to drink?"

"I'm good," he said with a wave of his hand and, taking her offer of a drink as an invitation, he sat at the table.

NATALIE SAT ACROSS from him, pulled the lid off the glass container, and unwrapped the sandwich. "*Gracias*. You didn't have to."

With a shrug of those broad shoulders, he said, "I didn't know if you'd be up to making dinner."

In truth, she hadn't planned on making anything. Although the nausea and pain of the migraine had gone away, they'd left her feeling fatigued. Drained even.

"I hate feeling like this," she said and dipped her spoon into the soup.

Carlos leaned forward slightly, and his presence filled the space, but it wasn't threatening. It was…calming.

"Weak," she admitted and ate the first spoonful of soup. "Delicious," she murmured and picked up one of the halves of the sandwich, hunger awakening.

"We all feel weak sometimes," he said and skimmed his hand across her hair to brush back a lock that had spilled forward.

A scoffing laugh escaped her, and she shook her head as she said, "I can't imagine you'd ever feel that way." He exuded such power and confidence that she couldn't picture him as anything but that.

"But I did. I do actually. Ever since Dani died. It hasn't been easy."

She paused with the spoon halfway to her mouth and narrowed her gaze to look at him. His shoulders had a bit of a slouch, but it was his eyes, those eyes like melted chocolate, that told the story.

It made her heart ache, and she laid down the spoon and sandwich and reached across to hold his hands. "I'm sorry. I imagine it can't be easy."

"It isn't," he immediately said, but quickly tacked on, "But you push on and in time you realize you're not alone. You have people who care and are there for you."

She'd had people who cared after her discharge from the army. Her mom and various friends. Trey and the Gonzalez family when she'd moved to Miami to take the job three months earlier. And as her gaze locked with his, she realized he cared. Maybe more than he should.

Maybe more than made sense, she thought as he leaned forward, and she did the same until their lips met over the narrow width of the table.

It was a kiss filled with gentleness and care. Promise, she thought. His beard teased the edges of her lips. She smiled, liking the feel of it before he hesitantly drifted back into his seat.

"I won't say I'm sorry for that," he said, a lopsided grin on his face.

His grin dragged one from her lips. "Good. There's nothing to apologize for."

Missy came over and sat by the table, her head drifting back and forth between them as if to gauge what was happening. Seemingly satisfied, she did a short, sharp bark that Natalie knew all too well.

"We'll go out soon, Missy," she said as she spooned up more of the soup and took another bite of the sandwich.

"Do you want me to walk her?" Carlos asked.

Natalie shook her head, finished up her soup and tossed Missy the last quarter of her sandwich as a treat. "No, thanks.

It's important we get back to our routine. Although I'm not sure how I'll be able to bathe her in that bathroom."

"You're welcome to use our tub. I'm sure Lucas would like to help."

She considered it for only a second since after today, a bath with lavender would do Missy—and maybe her and Lucas— a world of good.

"*Gracias*. That's very generous of you," she said, then rose and cleared the table. But as she did so, it revealed Sophie's note on one of the folders.

Here's the info from Dani's crash.

Her hand froze and before she could jerk off the note, Carlos took hold of the folder. With shaky hands, he opened it, pulled out the papers and spread them on the tabletop.

"Why?"

He said it quietly, but anger made the word cut through the otherwise quiet night.

"Something doesn't seem right to me," she admitted.

"You have no right to bring this pain back up," he said, his words a controlled whisper.

She sat down again, reached out and covered Carlos's hands with hers. His muscles were tight beneath hers. "I don't want you or Lucas to hurt again, Carlos. But if there was something wrong, wouldn't you want to know?"

After a tortured inhalation, he pulled his hands away before expelling a rough breath and hissing out, *"Sí."*

Like air escaping a balloon, the tension between them collapsed.

"Do you want to take a walk with me and Missy?"

"Sure. I'd like that," he said.

"Let me just get Missy's shampoo out so I remember to take it later," she said and hurried from the room.

CARLOS GATHERED UP the reports and tucked them back into the folder, having every intention to review them along with

Natalie at some point. He wanted to hear what had made her ask for them because he'd had his own doubts about what had happened that night.

But every official involved with the investigation had insisted that there was nothing to say it wasn't an accident and he'd had to focus on Lucas and trying to make life as normal as possible for his then eight-year-old son.

When Natalie exited the bathroom, she had a large purple bottle of shampoo in her hand and as Missy noticed it, the dog pranced up and down happily.

Natalie laughed, a bright, tinkling laugh that reached her hazel eyes, turning them golden. "That's right, you're getting a bath. Right after your walk," she said and at the sound of that final word, Missy raced to the door of the RV.

"She's a good girl," he said, and she wrapped Missy's leash around both her hands.

At his questioning look, she said, "With everything that happened today, she might be a little rowdy."

He followed her out and she led Missy to the house where they started their patrol. As they walked, he said, "Was she always this way?"

Natalie shook her head. "No. The behavior problems started after we were hurt."

"What happened?" he said as they did a loop around the house and over to the dock where Missy sniffed around the edges of the locker, which still held the python since the wardens hadn't been able to make it that day.

Along the dock, Missy pawed the ground at the farthest edge.

Natalie squatted close to the ground, searching for anything, but other than some matted grasses that Carlos could see, there was nothing.

"Did she pick up a scent?" he asked.

Natalie nodded. "It could be she recognizes the scent from

where the alligator nests were poached. Maybe this is where they came to untie the boats and leave the snake."

She rose and as they proceeded along the path, Carlos resumed their earlier discussion. "How were the two of you hurt?"

Chapter Twelve

Natalie didn't like remembering that day. An ordinary day like so many others. Blazing hot, the way Afghanistan had often been during the summer months. Dusty and dry. She'd regularly come home covered in grit that turned the water brown when she could sneak a shower in between patrols.

But Carlos had served with Trey in Iraq and had been wounded so he might understand. She'd read that in the personal history file that SBS had provided so she could familiarize herself with their client.

Not that Carlos was just any client. He was Trey's friend, almost like family.

And he was a man she was developing feelings for and maybe it was right that he knew just how damaged she might be.

"Missy and I had been dispatched with some NATO personnel and Afghan security forces to a village not far from Bagram to investigate a rocket attack. As we were chatting with some of the villagers, a car sped toward us," she said and paused as the memories of that day became vividly alive.

"It was a suicide bomber?" Carlos asked and wrapped an arm around her waist to offer support as her knees grew shaky.

She nodded. "We opened fire to stop him, but it was too late. The car was about ten yards away when it blew up."

She stopped walking, needing a moment to gather herself.

As he tightened his hold on her waist, she offered him a weak smile. "Missy and I were lucky. We survived."

"But not unscathed," he said while they continued their patrol, walking along the docks for his business, where Missy once again pawed at the ground to confirm she recognized a scent.

"The most serious were brain injuries from the concussions after being thrown by the blast. I don't remember much past hitting the ground and then waking up in a hospital a week later."

"What about Missy?" he asked when they turned and headed back toward his home.

"She had brain damage as well and it manifests in several ways, including aggression. It's why they wanted to put her down," Natalie admitted and ran her hand across Missy's back.

"But you wouldn't let them," he said as they reached the RV so they could pick up the bottle of shampoo.

She nodded. "I wouldn't. It took a lot for them not to destroy her and then let me keep her in civilian life, but she was my partner, and I couldn't abandon her."

SOMETHING FILLED HIS heart with those words because he could imagine her giving that loyalty and love to a human partner. To someone like him with all his baggage.

But are you ready for someone like her? the little voice in his head challenged.

He shook off those thoughts and said, "I understand. We never left anyone behind."

"She's a handful at times, but things like the lavender bath really help calm her," she said and knelt to rub Missy's body.

"Then I guess we should get going," he said.

They quickly entered the RV, picked up the shampoo and then rushed to his home.

As he entered, the alarm beeped. Lucas had set it just as Carlos had instructed.

He disarmed the system but once Natalie and Missy were inside, he armed it again.

No sense taking any chances, he thought.

At the sound of their entry, Lucas came barreling out of his room and slid across the wooden floor in his stocking feet.

"Natalie! Missy!" he shouted, excitement animating his features in a way Carlos hadn't seen in a long time. As it had before, a combination of hope and fear swept through him.

"*Hola*, Lucas. I was hoping you could help give Missy a bath," she said.

Lucas replied with an enthusiastic fist bump and huge smile.

"I guess that's a yes," she teased and offered her hand to his son.

Lucas tucked his hand into hers and led her to the main bathroom just off the living room.

Carlos followed and handed Natalie the lavender shampoo bottle as she filled the tub, adjusting the heat while Missy sat near her with what looked like a grin on her face.

"Missy's happy," Lucas said, picking up on the dog's vibes.

Natalie smiled and nodded. "She is. She loves her baths. Do you think you can get her leash off?"

Lucas pushed his glasses up with one finger and then un-clipped the leash while Natalie squirted a healthy amount of shampoo into the water rushing out of the faucet and into the bath. The floral scent of lavender filled the air, even reaching as far as where he stood at the door.

When the bath was just over half full, Natalie did a hand command and Missy hopped into it, splashing water up over the edge and onto Lucas's legs and feet as he stood nearby.

His son let out an excited hoot before anxiously looking over his shoulder at him.

"It's okay, *mi'jo*. We'll get you some dry pajamas later," Carlos said, wanting his son to enjoy this moment since it had been so long since he'd seen him that animated.

Because of that, he stood back, letting Natalie and Lucas engage while they bathed Missy.

MISSY BATHED LUCAS'S face with doggy kisses and the young boy laughed heartily, rousing joy in Natalie's heart. It had been too long since she'd enjoyed such an easygoing time.

Ironic, given that it came in the midst of an investigation and with virtual strangers.

But as she looked back toward the door at Carlos and her gaze locked with his, she realized that in some ways the three of them were kindred souls.

They'd all suffered loss and were still recovering.

Maybe that explained the connection she was feeling, so she didn't give it another thought as she worked with Lucas to wash Missy and give her a relaxing massage once she was covered in shampoo suds.

"The massage helps her," Natalie explained and laid her hands over Lucas's to show him how to rub the Lab's body.

"My mom used to rub my belly when I was sick and it made me feel better," he said.

Lucas was a quick student and enthusiastically worked the suds into Missy's fur. In no time they were rinsing off and drying Missy with some beach towels that Carlos handed them.

With a click of her tongue, Natalie called Missy out of the tub and the Lab instantly obliged. She shook her body, sending droplets of water that bathed her and Lucas, prompting laughter.

Natalie handed Lucas the leash and he clipped it back on, a broad smile on his face.

"I appreciate you helping. *Gracias*," she said and ruffled the young boy's hair which earned her an unexpected hug.

She wrapped her arms around him tightly, moved by his embrace. Maybe too much as tears came to her eyes.

Carlos must have sensed it since he said, "*Vamos*, Lucas. Let's get you dry and in bed."

After another tight hug, Lucas raced out of the bathroom.

Carlos stood at the door, watching her as he said, "I just need to get him ready."

"And I need to get back to the RV to review those reports and coordinate with SBS," Natalie said.

He nodded. "I'll join you as soon as I can."

She was tempted to tell him he didn't need to come over, but he deserved to know what she and her SBS colleagues thought about his wife's death. Truth be told, she also wanted time with him to work through the unwanted attraction and the memories of that short but powerful kiss they'd shared earlier.

"I'll see you soon," she said, then hurried out of the house and took Missy for a final walk so she could relieve herself before they turned in for a few hours before another patrol.

In the RV, she unleashed Missy and called Sophie to find out if there had been any developments from the drone footage they had taken and to check in on the monitoring her SBS colleagues had taken over.

"Everything is going well with the monitoring and luckily, no activity besides you, Carlos and Lucas," Sophie explained. As the timbre of the call changed, she said, "Putting you on speaker since I have Robbie here with me."

"Great. I hope you have news," she said as she sat at the table and laid out the folders Sophie had left her earlier that day.

"We do. John had his supercomputer run our drone images and we think we've identified some kind of camp. We'll send the location and photos to you via email," Robbie advised.

Good thing Mia Gonzalez had married the tech multimillionaire who had so much technology at his fingertips. "That's great that he processed that data for us."

"He's a good guy and we're lucky to have him in the family," Sophie said with a laugh.

As grateful as Natalie was for the new information about

a possible camp, there was still the more complicated issue of Daniela's death.

"You agree with me that Dani's death wasn't an accident," she tossed out, wanting their confirmation of her opinion before she sat down with Carlos to review the reports.

"We agree and so does Trey. Too many things don't add up," Sophie said just as a knock came at the door of the RV.

"I have to run. Carlos is here. Thanks for everything."

"I hope it goes easy," Sophie said before she and Robbie said their good-byes and hung up.

Missy had popped up from her doggy bed at the knock and came to her side, ready to protect her as she opened the door.

Carlos stood there, handsome as ever, but his eyes were dark and guarded. He clearly was preparing himself for what she was about to show him.

"Are you ready?" she asked.

Chapter Thirteen

Ready to find out his wife had been murdered? he thought and even though the answer was a big "No," he nodded and stepped into the RV.

The files sat on the tabletop, almost screaming for him to open them up much like the box had called to Pandora. But much like Pandora, opening those folders could bring a world of hurt and pain.

Despite his reticence, he followed Natalie and sat at the banquette, scooting across so she could sit beside him. Missy settled in at their feet.

She slipped in and they were thigh to thigh, shoulders brushing in the tight space. It awakened all kinds of unwanted feelings that he forced back at such an inappropriate time.

Because of the tightness of the space, he had to lay his arm across the top of the banquette as Natalie tucked into his side to share the reports with him. As he did so, Missy sat up and seemed to shoot him an accusatory look before settling back down at their feet.

"It makes sense to start with the autopsy," she said and shuffled the folders to open the first one.

He examined the report as she pointed out the pertinent facts. "The examination shows that there was an injury to the left side of Daniela's head, as if she struck the side window."

He nodded and she continued and pulled out an X-ray. Gesturing to the image, she said, "The vertebrae also shifted in a way that says side impact."

Looking at the X-ray, it seemed clear since the bones had shifted from right to left rather than from back to front.

As Natalie laid the X-ray down and placed the medical examiner's report above it, he noticed what the bottom line read.

Probable Manner of Death: Undetermined.

Before he could even process that thought, Natalie was moving on to the photos of the crash scene. As she flipped from one photo to another, she said, "There were no skid marks. Damage to the vehicle was minimal compared to the injuries Daniela suffered. No blood on the side window, only on the steering wheel. Those should have been clear signs that there was something off with the accident scene."

Carlos sat back, shocked because everything that she was saying seemed logical unlike what he had been told at the time of the crash.

"I don't get why the cops told me it was an accident. I should have listened when Trey told me to push them for a better explanation only…" There had been so much to deal with. Daniela's funeral. Lucas. The business.

So much but he should have listened to his friend. Taken him up on his offer to help when it had happened.

"Why would the cops lie?" he wondered out loud.

Natalie laid a hand on his as he pulled out the ME's report to review it more thoroughly.

"Chances are that it was just a case of them being overworked and understaffed, and this wasn't a clear-cut case of murder."

Murder. His sweet and beautiful Daniela might have been murdered.

Rage filled him along with confusion. "Why? Why would anyone want to kill Dani?"

Natalie shrugged. "If I had to guess. You guys are involved in a lot of environmental groups and then there's the poachers."

Sadly, it made sense. "Our group members have caught several poachers. Some of them faced felony charges and others lost their hunting and fishing licenses. One of them could have wanted revenge."

"Can you make a list of those people?"

He nodded. "I can."

"Once you do, we'll get SBS to investigate," she said, then took another look at the police report from the night of the crash and continued, "Dani went out with friends that night. Do you think we could talk to them? See if they noticed something off?"

"They went to celebrate a friend's birthday and I'm sure they'd all want to help," he said. Seemingly satisfied with that answer, she gathered up the papers and closed the files.

A heartbeat later, her phone chirped, and she took a quick look and said, "Sophie and Robbie emailed the results of the drone footage."

She scooted off the banquette, stepped over Missy and walked to the small living area to get her laptop.

Laying the computer on the files, she opened the email and the attachments in it.

Carlos scrutinized the maps and images. With a dip of his head, he said, "This camp is on the edges of the pinelands and a slough that leads to some coastal marsh areas and small keys near the Gulf."

Running his index finger across the map, he said, "This is where we were today. If this mapping is right, the poachers' camp is maybe fifteen or so miles from that location."

"Could we go there tomorrow?"

"The FWC wardens are coming in the morning for the python, but we can go after that," he replied and met her gaze.

It started off as a quick glance, but then she held his gaze, hers filled with sympathy and more. It was the more that had him reaching up and cupping her cheek.

Her skin was smooth. Warm. So warm and full of life. Life that he hadn't experienced in so long.

He ran this thumb across the ridge of her cheek and then moved his hand back to slip his fingers through the thick strands of her silky smooth, dark blond hair.

"Natalie." It was the only word he could manage but it said so much.

HER NAME ON his lips was part invitation and part question.

Her heart was pounding so loudly it echoed in her ears and her throat was tight with emotion. So tight that there was only one way she could answer.

She shifted closer and wrapped her arm around his neck. Tenderly, she urged him closer until she could nuzzle his face with hers, exploring the contours of it. The hard line of his aquiline nose. The rise of his smooth cheekbone and then down to the soft brush of his short beard.

"*Por favor*, Natalie," he said, his voice rough with need.

Smiling, she brushed her lips against his in a butterfly-light caress, earning a tortured groan from him until she finally put him out of his misery.

She kissed him, her mouth mobile on his, and he responded, meeting her mouth over and over. He parted his lips as she hesitantly slipped her tongue across the edges of them, and he groaned again.

He reached up and took hold of her hand. Urged it down to rest against his chest, directly above his heart, which pounded loudly beneath her palm. Laying his hand over hers, he trapped it there, as if to let her know that she held his heart in her hands.

That tempered the need surging through her. He needed more than just passion.

He needed a woman who would be there for him and for Lucas.

She wasn't sure she could be that woman.

With a last fleeting kiss, she eased back and met his gaze. "I'm not sure where this can go," she admitted.

"I'm not sure either. What I'm feeling happened so fast. Too fast," he confessed.

"We need a little time. Time away from all that's happening," she said and slid out of the banquette.

With a sad smile, he moved away from the table and said, "I guess that's my cue to leave."

She nodded and met him at the door. "I'll see you in the morning," she said, the tone of her voice rising in question.

"In the morning. As soon as we're done with the wardens, we'll check out the camp," he said, but hesitated, rocking back and forth on his heels before he swooped in and dropped a quick kiss on her lips.

Before she could reply, he hurried out the door and swaggered to his house, but at the front door, he paused and looked her way. Smiled. And it put her a little more at ease about what was happening between them.

She returned the smile, closed the door and went back to the table, her computer and the reports.

Carlos's night might be over, but she still had work and another patrol to do before turning in.

THE BEEP-BEEP-BEEP of the alarm chased him into the house, and he quickly disarmed it, hoping it wouldn't wake Lucas if he was asleep.

He armed it again and hurried to Lucas's room. The door was ajar, and he peeked inside.

The night-light cast dim illumination over his son's body in bed. The sheets had gotten tangled and his calves and feet were exposed, so Carlos slipped inside to straighten them and tuck him in.

The action roused Lucas who rolled over, a smile on his face.

"I had fun today. Natalie and Missy are really nice," he said, voice soft.

"They are," he said and smoothed the sheets around his body.

"Can they stay?" he said, expectant hope in his tone.

"Stay? They're going to stay to help keep us safe," Carlos said, wishing his son wouldn't be expecting more.

"No, like for longer," Lucas said, his voice sharper and more awake.

"Lucas, *mi'jo*. It takes time for people to…you know—"

"Kiss and stuff?" his son said excitedly and jumped up in bed.

"Stuff, huh?" he teased and smoothed out his son's bed-tousled hair. "Time for sleep, *mi'jo*. You have to be up early tomorrow."

With a grin, as if Lucas thought he was right about the "kiss and stuff," his son plopped back against the pillow and said, *"Buenas noches, Papi."*

"Buenas noches, chiquitico," he said and hurried from the room before Lucas could ask any more questions.

He closed the door and swung by the kitchen table to grab his laptop before heading to his bedroom.

Natalie wasn't the only one who still had work to do tonight, he thought and peered out his bedroom window to the RV where lights blazed inside.

He changed into lounge pants and lay on the bed after propping up pillows so he could sit comfortably while he worked.

His first chore was to send emails to the friends Daniela had shared dinner with the night she'd died. Easy enough to do and he hoped they'd be able to chat and maybe remember something that would give them a clue about what had really happened to Daniela.

The second chore wasn't quite as simple.

Over the years, their environmental group and allies had stopped an assortment of poachers. Some had been small-fries, guilty of taking a few groupers or out-of-season snooks. Anything of significant commercial value, like the nests their current poachers had emptied, was a felony and meant jail time.

Since their group regularly issued press releases on their activities, including when they had helped apprehend criminals, he logged into the group's account and began making a list of names. Beside each name he wrote down the activity and whether that person could be out of jail.

Pride built in him at their success, but it also brought worries about which of those people would be pissed off enough to kill Daniela.

After making the list there were a few names that stuck out. He hoped Natalie and the SBS crew would be able to identify if they were possible suspects in Daniela's death.

But for right now, he needed some rest. He needed to be ready for the visit from the wardens as well as the trip to locate the poachers' camp.

Sleep claimed him as soon as his head hit the pillow, but then memories of kissing Natalie wove their way into his brain and body, rousing desire that felt almost traitorous to Daniela.

But as soon as that dream started becoming a nightmare, Daniela's soothing voice said, "It's time, *mi amor*. You and Lucas weren't meant to be alone."

Despite her words, those feelings of love and betrayal continued to weave through his brain, keeping away restful sleep.

When his phone alarm chirped to warn it was time to rise, he hoped the day wouldn't have as much conflict as his night.

Chapter Fourteen

Natalie had just finished her morning patrol with Missy, and all seemed peaceful around the property and Carlos's home, when a Florida Fish and Wildlife Conservation Commission, or FWC, four-by-four turned into the driveway and parked in front of her RV.

Two wardens slipped out of the SUV: a thirty-something woman with cover model curves and a midfiftyish man whose middle was spreading as fast as his hair was thinning.

As they walked in her direction, Carlos bounded down the steps of his home and hurried to her side to make the introductions.

The FWC wardens walked over, and Missy grew a little agitated, tugging at her leash.

"Sit, Missy. Sit," she commanded and tightened her hold on Missy's leash.

Carlos shot a quick glance at the Lab and, with a puzzled look on his face, said, "Natalie. I want you to meet Warden Gemma Garcia and Warden Dale Adams."

Natalie shook the female warden's hand but as she reached out to do the same to the man, Missy acted up again, pawing the ground and emitting a warning growl that forced her to step back.

"Sit, Missy. Sit," she repeated sharply. She shortened the leash, forcing Missy tight to her side.

"I'm so sorry, Warden Adams. She's just a little anxious around strangers," she said, even though it was a gigantic lie.

Adams took a step back from them, clearly worried that the massive Lab still sitting slightly up on her haunches and growling lowly might launch herself at him.

"Why don't we do the transfer of the python," Carlos said and clapped his hands together, drawing the attention of the two wardens away from Missy and her behavior.

"That sounds like a plan," Warden Garcia said and jerked a thumb in the direction of the SUV. "I'll get the crate for the snake."

Not that she was a chauvinist, but it made her wonder about the dynamics between the two wardens as well as Adams's work ethic as Garcia hauled a heavy crate from the back of the SUV. Adams made no effort to help, and Carlos hurried over to grab one side of the crate and walk it to the locker holding the python.

They laid the crate on the ground and Adams finally ambled over, hands on his hips as Carlos opened the locker.

Garcia leaned over to peer in. "If that's a female, it's a small one."

Small one? Natalie wondered in awe. The snake had been at least ten feet long and packed with thick muscle.

"The experts will know for sure," Adams said and scratched his head.

"If it's a male, we may be able to use him to track down a female," Carlos said, and Garcia nodded.

"Definitely, and if not, we've eliminated one more breeder," Garcia replied.

Not understanding, Natalie said, "Is that important?"

With a decided dip of his head, Carlos said, "A female python can have as many as one hundred eggs. It's part of the reason they're decimating the smaller mammals in the Everglades and that threatens the panthers and other predators who can't find food."

His words made Natalie think of Schrodinger and her three little kittens. "I guess there's a silver lining to the poachers leaving this gift."

Garcia chuckled and with a glance at Adams, she said, "Time to crate her up."

Adams hesitated, but then worked with Carlos and Garcia to wrestle the python into the crate. Once it was secured, Adams and Carlos carted it off, and Natalie and Garcia followed them, walking a few steps behind.

Leaning closer, Garcia said in a low whisper that only Natalie could hear, "Your dog didn't seem to like Adams very much."

Natalie wasn't sure it made sense to give the warden the reason why that had happened, namely that Missy had scented something on Adams.

"Missy is a big dog and maybe Adams is a little uneasy about that. Dogs can sense that unease, Warden Garcia," Natalie lied, but the keen-eyed woman didn't buy it.

"Gemma, please, and you can be honest with me, especially about Adams," Gemma said, and her lips twisted in disgust.

"Not a fan?" Natalie said and peered at the other woman just to make sure she had read her right.

"Let's just say he rubs me the wrong way," Gemma said, but as they neared the four-by-four, Missy inched closer to Gemma and, as she had before, pawed the ground—but didn't growl.

Gemma's eyes popped wide at the dog's behavior, her perfectly manicured brows shooting upward.

Natalie was also surprised. If both agents bore the poachers' scents, could either of them be trusted?

"Sit, Missy," she said and with a light tug on the leash, quieted the Lab.

"Everything okay?" Carlos asked as Adams slammed the back hatch of the SUV.

Gemma and Natalie shared a look, but then Natalie nodded. "Everything is cool."

CARLOS DIDN'T QUITE believe it but didn't press. If he needed to know what was happening, he was sure Natalie would tell him.

"You'll keep us posted on the python?" he asked Gemma.

"As soon as we know more, you will too," she said, and with a wave, she hopped into the four-by-four where Adams had already slipped into the driver's seat.

Once the SUV had pulled away, Carlos jammed his hands on his hips and glanced at Natalie, who was standing beside him with Missy.

He was about to ask what was up, but Natalie beat him to the punch.

"Whatever scent Missy picked up on at the alligator nests was on both Adams and Gemma. Particularly on Adams."

He'd been worried about the two wardens since the incident with the alligator nests, but he'd been hoping he was wrong. Especially about Gemma and not just because of the one uncomfortable date and the fact that Lucas and Gemma's son were friends.

Luckily, Natalie said, "The scent on Gemma could be from being near Adams."

She clearly picked up on his relief since she said, "I said 'could be,' Carlos. I can't be a hundred percent sure."

"I get it," he said, but any additional discussion was foreclosed as two SBS vans pulled onto the property and parked. Sophie, Robbie and two techs slipped out of one van while Trey hopped out of the second.

Carlos rushed over and bro-hugged Trey. "*Mano*, I didn't expect to see you here."

"We've always had each other's six. I couldn't let you go to that camp alone," Trey said and held his hand out wide to his team. "Sophie, Robbie and their team will be monitoring us from overhead."

"They'll be watching with their drone?" Natalie asked for confirmation.

Trey nodded. "Definitely. We'll let them get the drone in

the air and then head to the area they found in their earlier investigation."

"Sounds like a plan," Natalie said, and Carlos dipped his head in agreement. With that, the SBS tech crew headed to their van.

"Good. Meanwhile, the three of us need to get ready since we don't know what we'll face," Trey said. He turned and walked toward the second vehicle.

When he reached the back of the van, he threw open the door to reveal shelves with an assortment of equipment and a small armory secured in a locked metal cage. He hopped into the van and handed military-style bulletproof vests to them.

Carlos secured the vest and Natalie did the same. The vests would be uncomfortable with the heat and humidity but necessary once they reached the poachers' camp.

Trey handed him a box filled with communications gear and said, "Commo so Sophie and Robbie can reach us."

As he and Natalie plucked out gear and wired up, Trey finally pulled out the big guns. Literally. He laid out three M16s and several magazines.

Carlos glanced at them uneasily and then up at his friend who said, "No sense taking any chances, *mano*."

His gut twisted with worry, and he shot an uneasy look at Natalie who said, "He's right. They've already shown they're ready to be violent."

"You're right, not that I have to like it," he admitted, then took hold of one of the assault rifles and jammed in a magazine. He grabbed a spare magazine and tucked it into his vest and Natalie and Trey did the same.

"Let's check the commos with the rest of the team and if they're good, we can head out," Trey instructed. He hopped down from the van and secured the vehicle.

They hurried over to the van where the SBS team was already at work.

"That looks good," Sophie said and clapped one technician on the back.

"Drone is up and on the way to the target location. It should be there in about twenty minutes or so," Robbie explained.

Recalling the maps that Natalie had shown him the night before, Carlos said, "That's good because it'll take us at least thirty minutes to get there."

"Let's check the commos," Trey said, and they all did a sound check.

Seemingly satisfied that the gear would allow them to stay in touch, Trey, Natalie, Missy and he rushed to his airboat where they slipped on hearing protection and buckled in for the ride.

Carlos started up the engine and slowly steered away from the dock, charting a course for the location that the SBS team had identified. He had sent the information to his tablet the night before and in no time, they were traveling down the canal and then navigating through the river of grass in the Shark River Slough toward a dense island of palms and pines.

Normally he would have loved the sights along the marshes, mentally cataloging the birds and other fauna and keeping a close eye for the elusive panthers or pythons that were adept at hiding. Instead, he kept his eyes and ears focused for signs of the poachers or the FWC wardens, unsure of whether they were trustworthy.

They were about ten minutes out from their target when Sophie came across their earpieces.

"We have sight of you with the drone. All seems clear at the target."

"*Gracias*, Soph. Keep us posted on any developments," Trey replied.

"Got it, *jefe*," she said, teasing her cousin with the "chief" nickname he hated.

They did a final approach to an area suitable for tying up the airboat and going on foot to their final location. Once the boat was secured, Natalie signaled Missy onto land. The dog hopped off and waited, and Natalie soon joined her there.

"Land is boggy, but it should hold your weight," she said.

Trey went next and his feet sank into the soft ground, but Carlos had no doubt the area would be navigable on foot.

He joined Natalie, Missy and Trey on the island and like a well-oiled machine, the three of them advanced, rifles at the ready. They had about thirty feet of grassy wetlands to cover before the target camp which was about twenty yards in from the start of a thick stand of pines, palms and underbrush.

As they entered, Carlos hacked his way through the dense tangle of vines and bushes that reached his midthigh with a machete. He swung out again and again, clearing the way, but suddenly a trail appeared. Well-traveled by the looks of it.

Natalie joined him, bent and examined the boot prints. A second later, Missy began to paw and whine at the start of the trail.

"Looks like we're in the right spot," Trey said.

Robbie's voice jumped across their earpieces. "You're not far now. All is still clear."

Carlos looked at Natalie and then Trey. "It's a go."

He rushed ahead, crouched low, rifle at the ready, years of military training taking over. His footsteps were catlike against the ground, silent as he advanced. Natalie and Trey were as quiet. The loudest sound was Missy sniffing along the ground and her low growl confirming she was on the trail of the scent she had picked up in the other locations and by the wardens.

NATALIE KEPT A tight rein on Missy as they rushed through the trees and underbrush, not wanting the Lab to get too far ahead until they knew the area was safe.

Carlos raised his hand in a stop command, and they all paused, breaths held until he signaled for them to proceed.

He advanced into a large clearing, and Missy and she followed.

Standing beside Carlos and flanked by Trey on the other

side, she examined the nearly fifteen-foot circle cleared of underbrush but protected overhead by the canopy of trees and camo netting strung above the entire camp.

Two tents were at one side of the camp and opposite them were long wooden tables whose surfaces were dark with what she suspected was blood. At the base of the tables on one side were dozens of coconut shells, a large burlap bag and bright yellow life vests.

She walked to that area first, but as she did, the stench of something rotting made her rear back. "What is that?" she said, trying not to breathe in the foul smell.

Carlos walked farther ahead, past the tables, and gestured with the rifle muzzle to a spot a few feet ahead. "Alligator carcasses. They chopped off the tails for the meat."

Trey approached the burlap bag and opened it. He reached in and pulled out a coconut.

Natalie joined him and said, "I don't get it."

Trey rapped the coconut shell hard against the edge of the wooden table and it split perfectly down the middle, revealing a ball of white powder encased in plastic wrap.

"Cocaine," he said and met Carlos's gaze as he joined them. "Seems like poaching is not the only crime they're committing."

Carlos nodded. "The Slough can lead to either the Gulf or Florida Bay. They must drop these bags from planes or boats and the poachers swoop in to retrieve them."

"We need to get these to the authorities," Natalie said and calmed Missy who was growing agitated as they stood there, probably from a combination of the smells she was picking up. Death, drugs and the poachers.

"We'll take it with us, but before we go, let's see what else is happening here," Carlos said and led the way as they walked to the first of the tents, but not before Trey took several photos with his phone to document the crime scene.

Parting the canvas with the rifle muzzle, Carlos confirmed it was clear.

Inside the tent was another table, but this one was clean and featured assorted scales, small, zippered poly bags and bulk baking soda boxes.

"They're cutting the cocaine here to improve their profit," Trey said and snapped off some photos.

The second tent held cots and lanterns and smelled of stale sweat and the skunky aroma of weed.

"I guess coke isn't the only thing they're trafficking," Natalie said, and when she exited the tent, she caught sight of several large turtle shells.

Carlos muttered a curse beneath his breath. "Hawksbill sea turtle shells. They're an endangered species but prized for their shells. People call it tortoiseshell by mistake."

"How much would these shells be worth on the black market?" Trey asked as he knelt to inspect them.

"Shells like these could be worth several thousand dollars," Carlos explained.

"Heads up, Trey. We've been tracking an airboat coming in hot from the west. You've got maybe ten minutes before it's at your location," Sophie warned.

"I guess we've got our marching orders," Natalie said and glanced from the turtle shells to the burlap bag with the cocaine coconuts. "We're taking those with us, right?"

"We are. I'll get in touch with the local PD about the cocaine," Trey said and peered at Carlos. "What about the turtle shells?"

Carlos hesitated and shook his head. "I don't know which of the wardens we can trust."

"And now that we found out about the drug dealing, there's even more motive for someone to kill Daniela if she somehow stumbled upon it," Natalie said.

Carlos's features hardened into stone and grew dark. "That makes sense," he grudgingly said.

"I know you're working on it, Natalie, but I'm going to see if the police will reopen the case," Trey said and shot a quick glance at his watch. "We need to get moving."

He peeled off in the direction of the burlap bag while she and Carlos picked up the first turtle shell and took it back to the boat.

Trey dumped the burlap bag in the hull next to the shell and then joined them in loading the remaining two shells.

"You've got to move. That airboat is only a few minutes out and moving fast," Robbie said.

The three of them exchanged a quick look. Natalie spoke first, "If we're on the water and they're armed, we'll be too exposed."

Trey nodded. "I agree. If this is the poachers returning to their camp, we need to find shelter."

Carlos peered all around and pointed to the farthest point of the island of trees. "We could swing over there and beach the airboat behind the line of trees."

Trey nodded. "We'll take up positions until we know their plan. Did you copy that, Sophie? Robbie?"

"Copy that. We'll keep eyes on them," Sophie confirmed.

They all boarded the airboat and Natalie had barely buckled in when Carlos executed a 180 degree turn and raced toward their hiding place. With another sharp turn, Carlos pointed the airboat toward a narrow ledge of marsh and surged onto land with a rough bump.

Natalie urged Missy off the boat and toward the protection of the trees while Trey and Carlos used machetes to cut down some underbrush and drape it over the airboat to try to hide it from prying eyes.

"They've landed on the far side of the island and are headed for the camp. It must be the poachers," Robbie said.

Sophie added, "There are four of them and they're armed. AK-47s from what we can see."

"I like those odds," Trey said.

"Me too, although I'd rather avoid a confrontation," Carlos said and peered at her.

Natalie didn't like feeling as if she was the weakest link, but she wasn't going to be foolish either. "I'd rather avoid it also, but I'm ready if need be. Just worried about Missy. She doesn't handle the loud sounds very well," she admitted.

"I'll go get her ear protection," Carlos said and hurried to the airboat to retrieve it.

Once Natalie had secured it on the Lab, she said, "This will help."

"Let's hope she won't need it," he said. The three of them took up positions in the underbrush, vigilant for any signs of the poachers who were sure to start looking for whoever had taken their merchandise.

"They're moving inland, but it's tough to see them beneath the canopy. Going to infrared to track them," Sophie said.

Natalie hunkered down, hidden beneath the thick scrub, holding her breath. Anxious. Expectant. All they could do now was wait and hope they didn't end up in a deadly gunfight.

Chapter Fifteen

Natalie lay beneath the underbrush directly behind and to the left of the airboat, Missy beside her. Peering around, she could see where Carlos and Trey had taken cover nearby, flanking her on either side.

Her hands were slick on the stock of the M16 and the feel of the weapon brought back unwelcome memories of her service in Afghanistan even though the two locations couldn't be more different. But that cold sweat of fear drenching her body and the pounding of her heart were painfully familiar.

She forced back the fear, hoping the poachers wouldn't engage. Her hopes were short-lived as Robbie said, "They're back on the airboat and slowly moving in your direction."

Trey muttered a curse beneath his breath, but then silence reigned again as they waited.

"They're about fifty yards from your airboat. No sign that they've spotted it or you," Sophie said.

In her brain, Natalie counted down, guesstimating how long it took to move through the grassland. She had barely counted to ten when she heard the boat's droning engine, almost like that of a low-flying prop plane.

The sound grew louder by the second and Robbie's warning confirmed her worst fear.

"They've spotted the airboat and are headed in your direction."

The drone stopped, replaced by the pop of gunfire and ping of bullets against the metal of their airboat.

"Hold your fire," Trey instructed.

Another barrage of gunfire erupted and was followed by the sound of the poachers' airboat engine again.

"They're moving in," Sophie said.

Natalie braced herself to shoot, waiting for Trey's command.

"Hold. Wait until we have a clear line of sight," he said.

She held her breath, waiting, and the tip of the hull appeared in her scope. Soon the entire airboat and its occupants were visible, but she held her fire, still hoping they wouldn't come their way.

Suddenly one of the men stood up and peppered the trees above them with a fusillade of gunfire. Bits of bark and leaves drifted down on them.

Beside her, Missy whined, discomfited by the sound.

That drew the attention of another man since he rose and aimed in her direction.

"I've got him," Trey said and with one shot, he took down the man about to shoot.

The man grabbed his wounded leg with a loud shout. "Get down," he warned just as his companions opened fire, spraying the trees and ground all along the tree line with a fusillade of bullets.

Dirt kicked up directly in front of her. She inched back from the gunfire and hugged Missy tight as she fidgeted, as if about to run.

Carlos and Trey shot at the men in the airboat, drawing their attention and gunfire.

With a break in the bullets in her direction, she aimed and fired at the airboat, trying to protect herself and Missy. Shooting defensively rather than for center mass as she'd been taught.

"Do you want us to call the wardens for backup?" Robbie asked, obviously hearing the battle over the earpieces.

"No," they all shouted, almost in unison.

A muttered curse exploded from another of the men in the airboat.

"I'm hit," he said to his companions and a second later, another man said, "Let's get out of here."

The roar of the engine driving away replaced that of the earlier gunfire.

"They're backing off," Sophie said, and her relieved breath cut across the line and was mirrored by Natalie's own grateful sigh.

"Let us know when you think we're in the clear," Trey said and long, expectant minutes passed before Robbie came back on the line.

"They're headed toward the Gulf coastal area. They'll be out of our drone range in about five minutes, so I think it's safe for you to return to base."

"Roger that. Do me a favor and call Roni. See if she can't coordinate with the PD to meet us at Carlos's. We've got some evidence and contraband for them," Trey said.

"Got it. See you soon," Sophie said.

Natalie slowly came to her feet, vigilant despite the SBS team's advice. Once she determined it was clear, she shouldered her weapon and issued a command for Missy to follow her. But the dog remained hunkered down and peered up at Natalie with anxious eyes.

"It's okay, girl," she said and massaged the dog's body which trembled beneath her hands. "You're a good girl," she crooned and continued her massage until Missy finally rose to a sitting position and grew more animated.

"Everything okay here?" Trey said as he walked over.

She hated that her boss was catching her K-9 partner in another vulnerable moment, but she wasn't going to lie either. "She's still a little sensitive to gunfire," she admitted.

Trey scrutinized the Lab and surprised her by saying, "I get it. I'm not a fan either." He jerked a thumb in the direction of the airboat. "Come down when Missy's ready."

Carlos was already clearing away the underbrush they'd used to try to conceal the airboat and Trey joined him there, pulling away the debris to free the boat.

"Heel, Missy," she said and clicked her tongue in the command for her to follow. Satisfaction filled her as the Lab finally obeyed.

They quickly boarded the boat for the trip back to Carlos's home. They were still yards away when she spotted Trey's wife, Roni, and the police car.

As they approached the dock, Roni and her colleagues met them there. Sophie and Robbie slipped out of the van and also came to peer at the hull of the boat filled with the turtle shells and burlap bag with the coconuts.

Robbie let out a low whistle. "Would I be wrong to guess those aren't just regular coconuts?"

"You wouldn't be wrong," Carlos said and the worry in his voice and tension in his body was obvious.

She stood next to him and stroked a hand across his broad shoulders. The motion didn't go unnoticed by Trey, although he remained silent as his wife said, "These officers are going to take your statements. Are you ready for that?"

BECAUSE OF HIS need to pick up Lucas at the bus stop, Roni and the police officers had taken his statement first. He'd laid out what had happened with the alligator nests and his worries and that day's encounter. He'd thought he was done when Roni had laid a hand on his arm and said, "The officers have advised that they're reopening Daniela's case."

Carlos had thought that he'd be relieved by that, but ever since Natalie had first floated her concerns, he'd grown increasingly worried about how that investigation might affect Lucas.

Would his son grow even more withdrawn if he knew his mother had been murdered? But then again, his son already knew there was trouble and seemed to be handling it well.

If anything, his son seemed more easygoing, Carlos thought as Lucas bounded down the stairs of the bus just behind Gemma's son. The two boys were laughing and jostling each other playfully.

Which brought guilt, especially as Gemma met the two boys and hugged Lucas affectionately.

He exited his pickup and rushed over.

Gemma greeted him with a welcoming smile. "Good to see you, Carlos."

"Likewise. Did you have the day off?" he asked since Gemma wasn't wearing her warden's uniform like she usually did when she came for her son.

"I had some errands to run. See you soon," she said, but he detected a note of hesitancy in her voice. *Maybe even deception?* he wondered as Gemma and her son walked to her car—a new BMW, he realized.

Pricey car on a warden's salary, he thought, but drove those thoughts away to focus on Lucas.

"How was your day?" he asked.

His son surprised him by launching into an enthusiastic recounting of an escaped rabbit in his classroom. "You wouldn't believe how fast he was, *Papi*," Lucas said with a laugh.

"I bet," he said and smiled, grateful for a glimpse of the old carefree Lucas.

They got into the pickup and Lucas kept up his excited storytelling throughout the short drive home.

When he pulled up in front of his home, the SBS vans were gone, but Trey's personal vehicle and a luxurious red McLaren Spider sat beside it.

"Wow, look at that car," Lucas said, voice filled with awe.

"Nice," he said with a low whistle and wondered who was visiting although he could guess. John Wilson, Mia's newlywed husband, had once had a pricey Lamborghini before it had been blown up months earlier.

He had barely stopped the pickup when Lucas flew out and over to inspect the fancy supercar.

Lucas leaned into the McLaren convertible with its top and windows open. "Look at that dashboard, *Papi*," Lucas said and then did a slow walk around the vehicle. When he had finished, Carlos said, "Come on, Lucas. Time to do homework and make dinner."

With a gentle hand on his son's shoulder, he guided him to the house even as Lucas kept on looking over his shoulder at the McLaren.

As they reached the porch, the door flew open, and Trey's little sister, Mia, stood there.

"Carlos," she said and launched herself at him.

He wrapped his arms around her and swung her around, laughing. In the many years he'd served with Trey, Mia had become like his little sister as well.

Only this Mia was dressed more casually and looked far happier than the elegant Mia who had made her fortune being a top influencer and socialite on the South Beach scene.

"You look good," he said as he set her back on her feet.

"Gracias," she said and immediately turned her attention to Lucas. "How's my favorite guy doing?"

"Good, *Tia* Mia," he said with a light laugh.

"Glad to hear that," she said, then slipped her arm through Lucas's and led him into the house.

Inside there was a whirlwind of activity as Natalie and the Gonzalez clan were at work in the great room.

At his questioning look, Mia said, "We thought it made sense to share dinner and some information with you."

Information that he might not want Lucas to hear. "Why don't you go do your homework, Lucas? I'll call you when it's time for dinner."

His son hesitated, clearly wanting to be amid all the activity, but then he nodded and raced to his room with his knapsack.

Mia tracked Lucas's departure and as soon as the door to

his room closed, she said, "Why don't you come over to the table so we can discuss what we have so far."

Roni, Trey and Natalie were gathered around the table while John, Sophie and Robbie were at work in the kitchen. The smells of garlic, basil and tomatoes spiced the air, making his stomach growl.

Mia patted him on the back and said, "You'll love John's sauce and meatballs."

As if he'd even be able to eat after what they were about to reveal, he thought as Mia left to join the others preparing dinner in the kitchen.

He walked over and gripped the top rail of the chair as Roni spread out several witness statements in front of him. As she did so, it was impossible to miss her growing baby bump, reminding him that she was close to four months pregnant by now.

"How have you been feeling?" he asked, recalling how sick Daniela had been during her early months of pregnancy.

"A lot better, *gracias*. A little tired at times," she admitted.

"You'd better take care of her, Trey," he teased, although he suspected his friend was treating his newlywed wife with kid gloves.

As if to prove it, Trey walked over and wrapped a protective arm around her waist. "Definitely, *mano*. We have to take care of Ramon number four," he said, which earned him a playful elbow in the ribs.

"No number four. It's going to be a girl," Roni joked but quickly tacked on, "Let's get to work. These are some of the statements from the friends Dani was with that night."

Roni pulled out one. "Most are pretty similar but this one from Sandy Cruz is slightly different."

He picked up the statement and read through it, scrutinizing every word, and one line popped out at him. Running his index finger across it, he said, "Sandy thought something upset Dani. Maybe something she saw."

"Sandy also says they all left soon after that since Dani seemed so upset," Natalie said and walked over to stand beside him and point out that comment in the witness statement.

He laid the document on the table. "If she saw something—"

"Or someone—like one of the wardens," Natalie said.

Carlos couldn't argue with that. "Is there any CCTV footage we could watch? Maybe I can spot someone there."

"There was. The police department is trying to find it in the evidence room since it somehow got misplaced," Roni explained and gathered up the statements.

"I guess the first step is to talk to Sandy again. See what she remembers," Carlos said.

"Do you want to do that or should Roni or I go see Sandy?" Trey asked from across the table.

Carlos shot a quick glance at them. "Natalie and I can do that. Maybe we should also talk to the wardens as well about the alligator nests. Get a feel for how they react to that and the news that Dani's case is being reopened."

Trey looked in Natalie's direction and then to where Missy was stretched out on the floor. "Are you both up for that?"

Natalie nodded. "We'll be ready."

"Great. We'll keep on pushing for any evidence that the PD has and work on it at our end as well," Roni said and slipped all of the papers into a folder that she handed to Natalie. "In case you want to take another look."

"*Gracias*, I will," Natalie said and tucked the folders with the papers under her arm.

Mia walked over while drying her hands on a kitchen towel. "If you're done, why don't you set the table? Pasta should be ready in a few minutes."

Trey did a playful salute. "Whatever you say, *hermanita*," he teased his little sister.

"Except Roni and Natalie. They should get some rest after a hard day," Mia said and eyeballed the two women.

It made Carlos take a closer look. It was obvious Roni was

tired, much as she had said earlier, but he had missed the slight lines of tension across Natalie's forehead—a possible sign that another migraine was brewing.

Knowing Natalie well enough that she wouldn't want undue attention, he leaned in close and whispered, "Can I get you anything?"

She shook her head. "I've got my medicine with me."

"I'll get you some water," he said and hurried off to do as promised.

He returned quickly and she took the pill, Carlos hovering nearby.

"I'm good, *gracias*," she said.

"Why don't you take it easy while we finish getting ready for dinner," he said and didn't wait for her reply to join the others in the kitchen.

Chapter Sixteen

Natalie didn't like being singled out but since Roni had also been included, she didn't fight it to not make the other woman feel bad.

Taking a seat next to her, she was surprised when Roni said, "It's okay not to be strong all the time."

She eyeballed Roni who was the kind of detective who didn't let much stop her. "Interesting comment coming from you."

Roni did a carefree kind of shrug and then looked down and ran a hand across her growing baby belly. "When I almost lost Trey, it brought new perspective to a lot of things."

Natalie was aware of the investigation into the murder of Trey's partner that had nearly cost Trey and Roni their lives. But she suspected that Roni, despite being a Miami Beach detective, didn't have the kind of baggage she had in her life.

"It's different for me," she said, the tone of her voice filled with a surprising amount of pain. Yet, beneath that, there was hope as well.

Roni reached out and laid a hand on hers. "I know you have things—"

"Trey told you?" she said, shocked he would reveal private details to his wife.

Roni shook her head and patted Natalie's hand in a gesture meant to reassure. "Trey would never betray a confidence, but… Detective, remember? I can see that you're not feeling well. Migraine?"

She could deny it but clearly the keen-eyed woman had noticed. Nodding, she said, "I have issues from a concussion I suffered during my military service. Also, some PTSD issues I've mostly worked through, but on occasion, I have nightmares."

"Mia told me that Trey had some as well when he first came back from Iraq," Roni said and glanced lovingly toward her husband as he and Carlos approached to set the table.

Trey had mentioned his issues when Natalie had told him during her job interview about her PTSD and lingering issues from the TBI she had suffered.

As the men reached the table, Roni peeled her hand away, but not before Carlos took note of the action. His gaze pierced hers, filled with worry, but she relieved his concerns with an easy smile.

Roni and she rose and helped the men prep for dinner and as soon as they were done, the rest of the Gonzalez crew brought over individual bowls filled with pasta swimming in tomato sauce and meatballs, a basket with garlic bread and a large salad.

"Let me get Lucas," Carlos said, but Lucas must have smelled the goodness emanating from the food since he came running into the room, an almost radiant smile on his face. He was clearly happy about either the dinner, the company or maybe both.

In deference to Lucas, the conversation around the table was limited to pleasant things, like what Lucas was doing in school and how he would soon have a break for the Labor Day holiday. As plates were emptied, it was clearly time to take care of other things.

The Gonzalez crew cleaned up and they all exited Carlos's

house, although Lucas tagged after John Wilson in the hopes of being able to sit in the supercar.

As he did that, she took Missy to the RV and fed her. The Lab ate well, relieving her worries that today's shooting incident might still be bothering her.

Come to think of it, the medicine and good company had done the trick and driven away the migraine that had been threatening.

Since Sophie and Robbie's team was monitoring the location, she exited the RV to do a quick patrol around the grounds, although with as many people as had been around that night, she doubted the poachers would be bold enough to do anything. But she wasn't taking any chances.

She did a slow and careful reconnoiter around the grounds, inspecting every nook and cranny. Satisfied all was in order, she walked back toward the RV but stopped when she noticed Carlos coming down the steps of the house.

Detouring, she met him where he stood, hands jammed into his pockets. Rocking back and forth on his heels, uneasy.

"Are you doing okay?" he asked, his sharp gaze traveling over her for any worrisome signs.

With a dip of her head, she offered him a reassuring smile. "Surprisingly, I'm fine. Missy too," she said and rubbed the Lab's head.

An easy grin erupted across Carlos's face, lifting the weight of worry from it. "Mind if I go over those reports with you?"

She normally didn't turn down an extra set of eyes, but Carlos's hot, chocolatey gaze did all kinds of things to her insides, and she worried he'd be a distraction.

"If you don't mind, I'd like a first look at them by myself."

The light in that tempting gaze faded like the dying embers of a fire and his grin flattened into a frown.

"Sure. I get it. I guess I'll see you in the morning," he said and with a stilted wave, he returned to his house.

Fool, the little voice in her head said, but she ignored it.

It was time to get to work and put an end to the threat to Carlos and Lucas as well as the drug smuggling that hurt so many lives.

FOOL, HE SCOLDED HIMSELF.

Natalie was here to do a job and he had to remember and respect that.

Securing the house with the alarm, he checked on Lucas who was actually reading a book instead of playing one of his video games.

Before Daniela's death, he and his wife would regularly take turns reading with Lucas and as his son saw him, he scooted over in the bed to make room for him.

He didn't refuse, pleased that things seemed to be getting back to normal.

He took the book from Lucas's hands, and only stopped reading when his son's body softened beside him and his breath had become soft and measured, signaling that he had fallen asleep.

Feeling the weight of the day dragging on him, he took a quick look around the house before going to his bedroom. But as he reached his door, he heard what sounded like a scream from the RV.

Racing to the door, he disarmed the alarm and took the steps two at a time. When he got to the RV, he tried to open the door, but it was locked. Taking out a spare key that Natalie had given him, he opened the door and Missy was immediately there, growling until she seemed to recognize him.

Another shout, softer than before, drew him to the bedroom where Natalie was tossing and turning amidst a pile of papers and her computers.

Satisfied it was only a nightmare, he rushed back to his house to reset the alarm, but then returned to the RV. He wanted to make sure she was okay and as another soft, almost pained groan escaped her, he sat on the edge of the bed and gently brushed back a lock of hair that had fallen on her face.

She roused slightly with that tender touch, her hazel gaze fearful for a heartbeat before they warmed with relief.

"What are you doing here?" she asked, resting against the pillows. She gathered the papers and laptop scattered on the bed's surface into a bundle.

"I heard a scream. You must have been having a nightmare again." He took the bundle from her hands and set them on the ground a few feet away from the bed.

Her lips tightened and she nodded. "Sometimes the memory of the day I was wounded comes back."

Cupping her face, he ran a finger along the ridge of her cheekbone. "Are you okay now?"

With a controlled little dip of her head, she said, "I'll be fine."

Despite her words, likely meant to convince him that he should go, he remained, stroking her face. He dipped his thumb down to trace the edges of her lips. They trembled beneath his touch and opened with a shaky breath.

"This isn't a good time, Carlos," she said, but despite her words, she cradled his jaw and shifted closer.

"It isn't but if there's one thing I've learned in life, it's not to waste a moment," he said and closed the final distance to kiss her.

HIS LIPS WERE so warm and full of life. The kind of life she hadn't experienced in so long.

She opened her mouth on his, taking in his breath as if it was her own. Feeling it fill all the empty spaces in her heart. Making her feel whole.

He dipped his hand down and cupped her breast and she moaned with need.

She needed him. She needed this, she thought, but Carlos hesitated, as if worried he was hurting her.

Covering his hand with hers, she urged him on with a soft, "*Por favor*, Carlos."

Shifting away slightly, he met her gaze. "Are you sure?"

She nodded and licked her lips, tasting him on them. "I'm sure."

With her words, he urged her to lie down on the bed and half covered her body with his, the weight of it comforting. Calming even as her heart raced, pounding a staccato beat against her ribs.

He kissed her again, but this time the kiss was demanding, urging her to join him on this journey.

She did, letting go of any fears or worries. She could trust this man. Worse, she could love him.

Carlos slipped his hand beneath the hem of her T-shirt and slowly inched his hand up to cup her breast. Tenderly, almost reverently, he caressed her. Each little tug and pull reverberated through her body, building need so intense it couldn't wait to be satisfied.

"Carlos, *por favor*. I need you," she said and jerked at his shirt, wanting to feel him against her.

He yanked off his shirt and she did the same, exposing herself to his gaze.

As he swept it over her, it was like a caress. "*Eres tan linda.* So beautiful," he said.

His body was hot, so hot as she ran her hands across the broad muscles of his shoulders and down to cup the hard swell of his pecs.

It was a warrior's body with the history of his life as a marine. She ran her fingers along one long scar, silvery with age. Beside it was a small circle from a bullet wound.

She examined him, wanting to know every inch of his body, and he did the same. But her scars were buried deep since the shrapnel from the explosion had only left a few faint lines across one shoulder.

Lines he found and kissed, as if with that caress he could take away their pain.

For a fleeting moment, he did, and she let herself feel the joy of his love. Of the tender way he treasured her body, slowly rousing need until his kisses and caresses weren't enough and she needed more.

In a flurry of motion, Carlos quickly found protection, but he held back, as if seeking her confirmation to continue.

She cradled his shoulders and urged him over her. Urged him to join with her and as he did, need gave way to satisfaction which gave way to peace.

For the first time in a long time, she felt peace as she lay cradled in his arms, in the aftermath of their loving.

"That was…beautiful," she said, struggling to find the right word to describe their lovemaking.

"It was amazing," he said and dropped a kiss on her forehead as she lay tucked into his side.

But as they lay there, enjoying the peace, there was no doubting the tension slowly building in his body.

She propped an arm on the pillow and looked down at him. "Is something wrong?"

"I want to stay but I have to get back to Lucas. I'm sorry," he said, apology alive in his tone.

She'd be lying if she said she didn't want him to stay the night, to wake with him in the morning, but she understood.

"It's okay, Carlos. I know you have other responsibilities and I know it may still be too soon for more between us," she said, even while hoping that what had happened between them would continue to grow.

Chapter Seventeen

Carlos wanted to stay. He wanted to make love to her again. He wanted to see how her skin looked in the rosy glow of morning and her hazel eyes opening slowly to gaze at him. But he did have responsibilities and as much as he wanted her, it would be too soon to have Lucas think that it was something more permanent with Natalie.

And maybe *he* wasn't sure if it was something more permanent building with Natalie.

And Missy, of course, he thought as the dog wandered in from the other room and stood by the bedside, glancing at them quizzically.

"I'm sorry, Natalie. I want to stay," he said, even as he was gathering up his clothes and dressing.

"I understand," she said but her hazel eyes were dark and like two big bruises in the middle of her face.

He couldn't leave her like that.

He sat back down on the edge of the bed and cradled her jaw. "Why don't you come with me?"

She shook her head vehemently. "We both know that's too soon. Because of Lucas."

Blowing out a rough breath, he dragged a hand through his hair in frustration and nodded. "Will you come over in the morning? I make some mean pancakes."

She nodded and forced a smile. "I love pancakes." Gesturing to the bundle of papers and laptop on the floor, she said, "Hopefully I can finish going over this information and confirm with Trey what our next steps should be."

"I'll be ready," he said, and with a kiss that lingered with promise, he shot to his feet.

Missy followed him to the door, and he patted the Lab's head before leaving.

But even as he walked to his home, his gaze was focused on the RV's bedroom window. Light blared from behind the closed blinds. Light and a shadow as a crack appeared in the blinds as Natalie looked out.

He smiled, waved and took the steps to his house two at a time. The alarm blared its warning beeps as he entered, and he quickly disarmed it before setting it once more.

Inside he hurried to Lucas's room. His son was still soundly and peacefully asleep.

After a quick sweep around the rest of the house, he went to his bedroom, ready to rest. Both sad that Natalie wasn't there and worried that he wanted her to be.

It had only been two years since Daniela had died and so many emotions were still too raw. Still an open wound, especially for his son.

And then there were the poachers and the possibility that Daniela had been murdered. He hadn't said anything to Lucas about that, fearing how he would react.

Dios, he was still having trouble processing the possibility that someone had murdered his sweet, smart Daniela.

All the more reason to keep this thing with Natalie from escalating until his life settled down. But as he slipped beneath the sheets, the scent of her that lingered on his skin, so clean and floral, kept him awake for long hours until exhaustion finally claimed him.

NATALIE HADN'T BEEN able to sleep after Carlos had left so she had turned to work to occupy her mind from going to dangerous places.

After reading the various witness statements about the night that Daniela had died, she was convinced more than ever that they needed to chat with Sandy Cruz. She also had no doubt that the wardens were due for a visit and the sooner the better.

It was well past midnight when she finally gave in to sleep because she had to be sharp in the morning. Trey and the rest of the crew would be calling to firm up the day's plans and she and Missy had to be ready.

She showered in the cramped RV bathroom, missing the spacious one in her apartment. She'd have to ask Carlos if she could borrow his bathroom to bathe Missy again. She really should have done it the night before but there had been too many people and too much activity with the visit from the Gonzalez family.

After she finished dressing, she fed Missy and then took her around for a morning patrol and to relieve herself before heading to Carlos's for the promised pancakes.

He opened the door as she approached. He was smiling, but it was a cautious smile, and his gaze was filled with uncertainty.

She tried not to let it bother her because in truth, she was feeling much the same way.

"Buenos dias," he said and gestured for her to enter.

"Buenos dias," she replied and when she walked in, Lucas came running over, his grin so much like Carlos's it made her heart ache. It would be so easy to love this young boy.

"Good morning," Lucas said. He hugged her hard and then rubbed Missy's head affectionately. "Good morning, Missy," he said, laughter alive in his voice.

"Good morning, Lucas. How are you today?" she asked, his joy stripping away some of her reticence.

"I'm good except that I have a math test today. I'm not very good at math," he said with a twist of his lips and hurried over to the breakfast table where he kept up a nonstop conversation until only the remnants of the blueberry pancakes, sticky syrup and bacon were left on their plates.

"I hope you liked the pancakes," Carlos said, expectant.

"They were delicious, and the company was even better."

"I'm glad," he said and started cleaning up the table, but she laid a hand on his arm to stop him.

"Let me. I'm sure you have to take Lucas to the bus stop."

He nodded. "*Gracias*. Make yourself at home while I'm gone."

Lucas ran over to give her another hug, and Missy another ear rub, before rushing off to get his knapsack.

Carlos came over and laid a hand at her waist. He brushed a kiss across her temple and said, "I won't be long."

After a reassuring squeeze at her waist, he hurried out the door with Lucas. The roar of the pickup engine coming to life warned her she had to get moving as well.

Carlos was a very neat cook who cleaned up after himself, so it didn't take her long to clear off the table and put everything away in the dishwasher.

She had just finished when Trey called.

"*Buenos dias*, Trey."

He responded enthusiastically. "It is a good day. The local PD found the CCTV footage from the night of Dani's death. I'm emailing it to you."

"Great. I was thinking that it's time to talk to Sandy Cruz and the wardens, especially Dale Adams. I want to see if Missy finds a scent on him again."

"I agree. Do you need backup for that?"

Sandy was Daniela's friend and would cooperate. As for the wardens, they would likely not be as helpful, but the SBS resources would be better spent on other things.

"I think we're good but if Sophie and Robbie could take a look at the CCTV footage also, that would be great."

"I'll get them working on that and also, that list of possible poaching suspects Carlos provided," Trey confirmed.

"*Gracias.* I'll keep you posted on anything that happens," she said and ended the call.

The warning beep-beep-beep of the alarm had her spinning around defensively, but it was Carlos returning.

She waved the phone in the air. "Good news. They have the CCTV footage. I just need to get my laptop from the RV."

Jerking a thumb in the RV's direction, he said, "I'll go with you. We can watch it there."

"Sure," she said, and they hurried to the RV where she powered up her laptop and accessed the email with the video footage.

She played the first video which showed part of the bar as well as a few tables, but several tables were only partially visible in the footage.

Carlos squinted at the video. "Is there any way to make it bigger?"

She pointed to the large monitor on the one wall of the RV. "I'll feed it there."

The video was even grainier on the large screen, but easier to see. It was time-stamped at 2:00 a.m., long after Daniela had left the bar with her friends.

She pulled up the second video which was time-stamped hours earlier.

Carlos shot to his feet and circled a table whose occupants were just outside the camera range. "That's Dani and her friends. I recognize Sandy's sneakers. She always gets ones with the craziest colors and designs."

Leaning closer to the monitor, he outlined a smaller area showing a headless woman. "I think this is Dani. I recognize the blouse she was wearing."

"Are you sure?" she asked, since the woman's face wasn't visible.

"Freeze it," Carlos shouted, and she did. As he had before, he pointed out something in the video. This time it was the woman's hands. "These are Dani's wedding and engagement rings. If you want to see them, I have them."

She nodded. She trusted that Carlos could recognize things that had been so important to his wife and him.

Starting up the video again, she watched a man walk up to the bar, his face not visible since he was too close to the camera. But the patch on his sleeve and badge had her pausing the video again.

She rose, walked up to the monitor and peered at the image closely. The circular badge with the six-pointed star in the center was familiar as was the oval patch on the sleeve.

"Is that what I think it is?"

Carlos nodded. "It's what the Florida Fish and Wildlife Conservation Commission wardens wear."

"Whoever it is—"

"It's Dale Adams. I'm sure of it," he said and jammed his hands on his hips.

"We can't be sure just yet," she said and quickly added, "We can have Sophie and Robbie try to clean up the image. See if there's a badge number."

"The badges don't have numbers."

"Okay, but it can't hurt to have them try to clean up this video. Plus now we know one important thing," she said and ran a hand down his arm to try to reassure him.

"What do we know? I can't even see Dani's face," he said, his frustration making him lose focus.

"For starters we know it's Dani and her friends. We know an FWC warden—"

"Dale Adams," he interjected again.

"We know the warden was there at the same time as Dani but not later that night. That places him at the scene," she clarified and returned to her laptop to start up the video again.

The CCTV footage ran for another few minutes when another man came into view and sat next to the FWC warden. They weren't together, or at least it didn't appear that way, but then the man slipped something under a bowl with nuts and walked away.

Long minutes passed before the FWC warden took whatever it was and tucked it into his shirt pocket.

She had been so distracted by that action, that she had missed what was happening at the table where Daniela and her friends had been sitting. Daniela had stood and so had the woman with the sneakers—Sandy Cruz if Carlos was right. As soon as Sandy was up on her feet, the other women also rose.

Natalie paused the video again and looked at the time stamp. It was just shortly before midnight and less than half an hour before Daniela's estimated time of death.

She rewound the video to the exchange and said, "Do you think Sandy saw the warden and this man together? Maybe even saw this interaction?"

Carlos stood by silently as the video played, showing the two men and, several minutes later, Daniela and her friends leaving.

The group disappeared from view but suddenly the FWC warden stood and walked away too.

Carlos muttered a curse. "He knows Dani saw him and what happened."

"Do you recognize the man who slipped him the note or whatever it was?" she asked.

Carlos shook his head. "Hard to say. He's keeping his face down under the brim of the ball cap, as if he knows where the camera is, and the video isn't the best."

"No, it isn't. Let's get Sophie and Robbie working on it. Once they do, maybe they can run one of their facial recognition programs to identify him."

Carlos dragged a hand through his hair. "And in the meantime?"

"In the meantime, we talk to Sandy and see what she has to say. After that, we visit Adams and Garcia."

Shaking his head, Carlos said, "I don't want to think Gemma is involved in this."

"Maybe she isn't, but regardless, we have to question her. Even if she isn't involved, she may know something that will help us find out who killed Dani."

Carlos hesitated, obviously uneasy about speaking to the FWC warden for whom he clearly had some affection. She pushed back the little monster of jealousy that reared up with that thought and said, "We should get going."

At his nod, she went into action, calling the SBS crew to work on the video and packing her laptop into her knapsack. Because Missy had responded to Adams once before, she took a moment to put the tactical vest on her in case she needed better control over her partner.

She met Carlos at the RV door where he had been patiently waiting. "Let's go see Sandy."

Chapter Eighteen

Sandy Cruz walked out of her bedroom holding the sneakers that she'd been wearing in the CCTV footage from the bar.

She handed them to Carlos and said, "You're welcome to keep them."

Carlos raised his eyebrows in surprise. Sandy was usually obsessed about her sneakers.

With a sniffle and tears in her eyes, she said, "That night was the first time I wore them. I could never wear them again."

Natalie stroked a hand across Sandy's shoulders as they rose and dipped in a silent sob. Even Missy reacted to her pain, laying her head on Sandy's thigh.

"*Gracias*, Sandy. These will be important if we can get additional evidence about that night," Natalie said.

"Whatever you need. Dani was my best friend. I'd do anything to help find out what happened to her," Sandy replied.

"You said you'd never been to that bar before," Carlos pressed.

"We hadn't but Carol—the birthday girl—said it would be fun to do a barhop. We went to this bar last and were a little uneasy because the place seemed rough," Sandy said.

"Is that why you left the bar?" Natalie asked.

Sandy glanced between Carlos and Natalie, as if worried about what she might say. "Not really. Carol seemed excited that it wasn't our usual kind of place, so we stayed. We'd been there about an hour when Dani got upset about something."

"Do you know what?" Carlos asked.

Sandy shook her head. "No, I don't know," she said, staying true to her earlier witness statement.

"We looked at the CCTV footage and saw two men sitting at the bar. Did you notice them?" Natalie asked.

Sandy pursed her lips and shook her head. "Not really."

"Do you think Dani saw them and recognized one of them?" Carlos asked, hoping to tie Daniela's upset with the men from the footage.

With a shrug, Sandy said, "I wish I could tell you more, but I can't. All I know is that all of a sudden, Dani wanted to leave and she seemed troubled."

Carlos peered in Natalie's direction, wanting to gauge her reaction. She met his gaze for a brief second and then said, "*Gracias*, Sandy. It may not seem like it, but that's helpful."

"*Sí, gracias*. We're grateful that you took the time to chat with us," Carlos said and rose from the kitchen table where they'd been sitting.

"You know I'd do anything to help. A day doesn't go by that I don't think about Dani. Miss her," Sandy said, and tears slipped from her eyes that she wiped away with shaky hands.

Carlos wrapped his arms around Sandy and hugged her hard. His voice was rough as he said, "I understand. I miss her every day as well."

He met Natalie's gaze as he looked over Sandy's shoulder at her. He had expected to see pain there at his admission, but instead saw only commiseration and understanding.

After a round of good-byes and yet more tears, Carlos and Natalie left Sandy's home.

He paused by his pickup and looked back toward her house. "Do you think she'd remember better if she saw the CCTV footage?"

"It's up to the police to do that through the right channels, otherwise a defense attorney will have a field day with her in court," Natalie said.

While he knew Natalie was right, he was impatient to find out what had really happened the night Daniela had died.

"Let's go talk to Adams and see what he has to say," Carlos said. He rushed to the driver side, and carefully placed Sandy's sneakers onto the backseat.

Natalie slipped into the passenger seat and signaled Missy up into the backseat. Once Missy and she were buckled up, he called the field office to confirm whether Adams was available.

"Good afternoon. I'm trying to reach Warden Adams."

The receptionist quickly explained that he was out of the office.

"He's not at the field office," Carlos said.

"But you have his cell phone number?" Natalie asked.

He nodded and she continued, "If you let me have it, I can have Sophie and Robbie track down where he is—"

"And surprise him?" Carlos said, gaze narrowed as he considered how Adams might respond to their visit.

"We catch him off guard and see what he does. How he reacts," Natalie confirmed with a determined dip of her head and the hint of a sly smile.

"I'll text you the number."

The ding of her phone confirmed she had received it and her fingers flew across the screen as she sent it on to the Gonzalez cousins.

"Will it take long?" he asked.

With a shrug, she explained, "Mobile phones can be tricky since they move around so much, but if GPS is enabled, there are a number of apps available that let you track the phone, and it shouldn't take all that long."

Maybe it wouldn't take long, but it seemed like a long time to him, especially since Natalie was unusually quiet.

"Is everything okay with us?" he said, guessing at the reason for the silence.

A very telling pause came before she said, "It is. It's just that I know you have a lot to deal with. Lucas. The poachers. This investigation. Me. It's complicated, isn't it?"

"It is," he agreed, but clasped her face and tenderly ran a finger across her cheekbone. "But what we shared, what we can have, is worth it, don't you think?"

Unshed tears glimmered in her gaze as she softly said, "Missy and me. It's a lot to deal with."

He realized then, with a clarity he hadn't possessed before, how she saw herself: as something damaged. Maybe even undeserving.

"You're worth it, Natalie."

The tears escaped with his words, slipping down her cheeks, and he wiped them away and then leaned close. "You're worth it and nothing worthwhile is easy," he whispered.

A ghost of a smile slipped onto her lips a second before he kissed her, promising so much with that kiss.

The chirp of the phone shattered the moment and they slowly drifted apart.

Natalie glanced at the phone and said, "We've got his location."

CARLOS LUCKED OUT and found a parking spot in front of the La Carreta restaurant in Little Havana. The eatery with its kitschy wagon wheels and immense rooster wearing a white coat emblazoned with the Cuban flag was a popular eatery on Calle Ocho.

They left the windows on the pickup opened wide so Missy would have air for the short time they expected to be in the restaurant. Or at least Natalie didn't think it would be a long time.

Entering, they walked to the hostess station, but as soon as they entered, she spotted Adams sitting alone at one of the wooden tables in front of the mural of the Malecón in Havana.

A plate with a Cuban steak, ripe plantains, rice and beans sat before him.

She jerked her head in the direction of the table and without waiting for the hostess, they walked over and slipped into the empty chairs at the table for four.

Adams stiffened and glared at them. "I'm at lunch, Ruiz."

Carlos looked at the plate and smiled. "Looks good."

The waitress came over. "Do you need menus?"

Adams didn't glance at her as he said, "They won't be staying."

Sensing the tension, she hurried away, leaving the three of them alone.

"We were hoping you could tell us a little more about those alligator nests that got poached," Natalie said with a sweetness she wasn't feeling.

"What's there to know?" he said. He picked up his knife and fork and cut off a piece of steak with such vehemence that the knife screeched against the plate.

"Any idea how the poachers knew when to go back to empty the nests after you and Gemma restored them?" Carlos asked.

Adams shoved the piece of steak into his mouth and chewed on it noisily. With an almost angry swallow, he said, "Why don't you ask Gemma that?"

"We plan to," Natalie said.

Carlos quickly added, "Have you ever been at Port Glades Brew?"

Adams's hand trembled so much that some of the rice and beans on his fork fell off and back onto the plate.

"Occasionally," he mumbled through the food in his mouth, obviously realizing it would be silly to lie since it would be easy enough to check with one of the bartenders to confirm it.

Natalie's gaze locked with Carlos's, and she forged ahead. "Were you there the night of Dani's crash?"

Adams let his cutlery clatter onto his plate. "How do you

expect me to remember something like that? It's what? Two years since she died?" he challenged.

"Two years, three months and fifteen days, but who's counting?" Carlos parried, rage rousing angry color to his face.

Adams retreated from his condescending attitude, but only slightly. "Sorry, Ruiz. But seriously, how am I supposed to remember?" he said and tossed his hands up in the air. But before they could ask another question, he said, "Do you mind? My lunch is getting cold."

"I wish I could say 'thanks,'" Carlos began, but Adams interrupted him with a muttered vulgar curse.

"That's our cue to go," Natalie said facetiously.

They both rose from the table and left the man to his lunch, although she could feel his gaze digging holes in her back as they walked away.

"What do you think?" Carlos asked as they walked back to the car.

Natalie glanced around the parking lot and spotted the Ford pickup truck with the FWC's distinctive dark green striping and the representations of the badge and patch on the side of the vehicle.

"I think Missy and I will take a short walk so she can relieve herself before we head to Gemma's," she said, and in no time, she had unbuckled the dog from the backseat.

"Please wait here," she said to Carlos, who nodded and waited patiently by the passenger seat.

Not wanting to direct the dog and possibly make a wrong identification, she took Missy from one end of the sidewalk to the other where the Lab took a moment to urinate at the curb. Once Missy was done, she strolled with her to the far end of the parking lot and let Missy sniff all around the tires and trunks of the various vehicles. As they neared the FWC pickup, the Lab began to paw and picked up her pace, tugging Natalie all around the vehicle until she returned to the driver side door, sat and peered up at Natalie, confirming she had found a scent she recognized.

Lips tight, Natalie did a hand command and urged Missy back to Carlos. "She got a hit on Adams's pickup. I'm going to call Trey and see if he can't get Roni and her colleagues to get a warrant for Adams's cell phone records."

"You think that will prove he was at the bar?" he asked as they got back into his vehicle and Natalie secured Missy in the backseat.

"They should tell us if he was in the area at a minimum. That is, if the telephone company still has two-year-old records," she said and immediately phoned Trey.

CARLOS LISTENED AS Natalie put the call on speaker.

"We think it's worth getting Warden Adams's cell phone records to pinpoint his location on the night Dani died," Natalie said.

"We'll need a warrant, but I think with the CCTV footage, the police may have enough. Luckily the phone companies generally hold those records for several years," Trey said.

"Great to hear. We're going to speak to the other warden— Gemma Garcia. If we need anything else once we chat with her, we'll let you know," Natalie said.

When she finished, she asked him, "Do we need Sophie and Robbie to track down Gemma?"

Carlos shook his head. "Gemma is pretty predictable. If the weather is nice, she normally brown-bags and sits at the pier at a local wildlife management area."

"Brown-bags because she's watching her money?" Natalie asked, head tipped at an inquisitive angle.

"Single mom and the warden's pay isn't that great," Carlos explained.

"That could explain why one of them might be looking for a way to make extra money, like getting a cut from the poachers or drug dealers."

He tightened his hands on the wheel, his knuckles tight with pressure as he considered the possibility that Gemma might somehow be involved in such activities, especially as he remembered the shiny new BMW she had been driving the other day. Despite that, he shook his head and said, "I don't think Gemma's dirty."

Circling her index finger around, Natalie said, "Is that because the two of you had a thing?"

A strangled laugh escaped him. "I'm not sure one date constitutes a thing and I think both of us knew it would never turn into a thing," he said and pulled out of the restaurant's parking lot.

From the corner of his eye, he caught Natalie's wry smile.

"I see you don't believe that," he said with a quick look in her direction.

Natalie scoffed, "Men can be so dense. Maybe you're not interested, but Gemma still is."

He let out another rough laugh. "Women's intuition?"

"My job is to observe, remember?" she challenged.

He left it at that, turning the discussion back to their investigation of Daniela's death.

"How long do you think it will take to get Adams's cell phone records?"

"If we can get a judge to issue a warrant, a couple of days—unless we can pull some strings," Natalie said, her attention skipping from him to the landscape passing by out the window.

"I think if anyone can pull strings, Trey and his family can," Carlos said with certainty. The Gonzalez family and their agency were well-known in the Miami community and to law enforcement.

Natalie chimed in with, "I agree and I'm hopeful the PD will have more for us about what they found on that warning note and at the poachers' camp. DNA. Fingerprints. That kind of thing."

He hoped that as well, as he made the trip to the pier that

wasn't all that far from his home and business. He had run across Gemma one day while he had gone to get away and had met her there on occasion to share a quiet lunch before their one and only date.

Gemma had apparently finished her lunch, he thought, as she tossed a brown paper bag in one of the garbage cans and walked toward her FWC pickup.

She stopped short when she noticed him pulling in beside her vehicle but smiled, and he hoped she would remain as happy to see him after their questioning.

He hopped out of the pickup and Natalie did as well. Unlike before, she freed Missy from the backseat and walked with her to where Gemma stood.

"What brings you here?" she asked, that smile still on her face.

NATALIE WAS CERTAIN that Gemma's welcome was more for Carlos than for her, but she'd run with it for now. Beside her, Missy was calm and readily responded to Natalie's command for her to sit.

The warden was wearing sunglasses which made it hard for her to do a complete read of the other woman, but she tried. "We're actually here to talk to you about a few things."

The smile faded a bit and Gemma turned her attention to Carlos. "Like what?"

Carlos avoided her gaze, clearly uncomfortable with what he was about to say. "After you supposedly restored the alligator nests—"

"We did take care of those nests," she said, her tone sharp.

"Do you think it was those same poachers who returned to empty the nests?" Natalie pressed.

"I don't know who else would have done it," Gemma answered without hesitation.

"What about the poachers' camp we located? Had you or Adams ever patrolled that area?" Carlos asked.

Gemma jammed her hands on her hips and looked away, as if searching the air for an answer. When she looked back at them, she said, "As you can tell, Adams and I sometimes split up to do our patrols. To make things easier, we set aside certain areas for our patrols."

"Is this your long way of saying that camp was in Adams's area?" Natalie pushed.

With an abrupt nod, Gemma said, "It is. Those alligator nests were on the border between our two areas."

"Do you think Adams is tied to those poachers?" Carlos asked, his tone more conciliatory. He ran a hand down her arm in a reassuring gesture.

Some of the tension in Gemma's body faded with that touch. "I've had my suspicions over the years."

Natalie picked up on something in the other woman's tone. "Like how many years?" she pushed.

Gemma slipped off her sunglasses and her gaze was almost beseeching as she glanced at Carlos. "A few years. Since before Dani died in the crash."

A shiver worked through Natalie at the connection Gemma had seen between Adams and Dani's death. "You think he had something to do with Dani's crash?"

She wagged her head from side to side and the action sent the thick strands of her almost seal-black shoulder-length hair shifting violently against her face. "I don't know," she almost wailed.

"Gemma, *por favor*. What made you think that?" Carlos asked and took hold of her hands to urge her on.

With a shrug, she said, "The day after the crash, Adams and I had to do a patrol together and he was antsy. Every time the phone rang, and it rang a lot, he almost jumped."

"You think it had something to do with the crash?" Carlos said, his tone sympathetic. Natalie didn't know how he could be so calm, considering what Gemma had just told them.

"I had my suspicions. I just didn't know what to do about them."

"Thank you for that information," Natalie said, and the woman's demeanor grew more relaxed.

"I'm sorry, Carlos. I'm sorry I didn't press or say something to you, but you had so much you were handling," Gemma apologized.

Carlos nodded, but it was almost absentmindedly. "I appreciate you saying something now. We'll let you get back to work," he said and almost raced back to the car, Natalie and Missy chasing after him.

When she was sitting in the passenger seat, she faced Carlos, whose hands were on the steering wheel so tightly that his knuckles were white. His face was mottled red and white with anger.

She laid a hand on his arm. His muscles shook beneath her palm.

"Carlos?" she asked, scared by the force of the emotions filling the vehicle's cab.

"We're going to nail Adams and he better hope the police get to him before I do."

Chapter Nineteen

It was only a short ride from the pier to the road back to his home and business. But as he drove away from Gemma's pickup and onto the road, he caught sight of a mud-splattered four-by-four in his rearview mirror. The four-by-four pulled out of a parking spot and paused at the turn for the road.

The driver was white, middle-aged and scruffy, which raised the hackles down his neck.

Carlos shifted his gaze constantly from the road before him to the four-by-four as it moved onto the road and followed them, keeping several yards back.

"Everything okay?" Natalie asked and turned to see what had his attention. "Do you think he's following us?"

Carlos peered at the rearview mirror again. The four-by-four was keeping its distance.

"I don't know. This is the only road out of the park," he said, but even as he said it, the four-by-four violently accelerated in their direction.

"Hold on," Carlos urged and sped up as well, trying to avoid a collision.

They were moving at a breakneck speed along the windy one-lane road. A wrong turn and they'd end up in the wetlands along the edges—dangerous because of the possible depths of the waters there and the alligators that swam nearby.

Fear gripped him as they neared the turn off for the main road.

He'd have to slow down to make the turn and watch for traffic. Both actions would make him vulnerable to the four-by-four barreling down the road toward them, but he had no choice. A tourist bus from another of the tour group companies was headed straight for a collision with them if he didn't stop.

Slowing, he braced for the impact he was sure would come and swept his arm out to protect Natalie, who gasped as she realized what was about to happen.

The four-by-four crashed into their rear bumper, sending them flying forward from the impact. Metal groaned and plastic cracked as Carlos slammed on his brakes to avoid being propelled onto the main road and into the path of the oncoming tourist bus.

The continued push sent the pickup's rear end forward slightly and twisted the front end of the car until it pointed toward the wetlands. Another shove and the pickup's front wheels lost traction on the softer ground on the edges of the road.

He lost all control as the earth gave way beneath the weight of the pickup.

Fear twisted his gut into a knot as the front end sank into the deadly waters. Grasses and water quickly swallowed up the front end until luck was on their side and the downward movement stopped.

But that luck was short-lived as the driver in the four-by-four opened fire.

The back window exploded in a hail of glass bits and Missy started barking angrily and straining against her harness.

NATALIE WAS DISORIENTED for a second as a shower of glass fell onto the backseat and Missy struggled to be free.

She undid her seat belt, whirled, drew her gun and shot at the four-by-four. Her aim was off as the pickup shifted forward, inching deeper into the waters of the Everglades.

Whoever was driving the four-by-four decided they didn't want to risk getting shot.

With the screech of tires against the pavement, the four-by-four pulled onto the road and sped away.

"Are you okay?" Natalie asked and reached into the backseat to calm Missy, rubbing her ears and back, but the shift of her weight in the seat had the pickup lurching forward and water seeping into the cab.

"Don't move," Carlos warned and glanced all around, trying to figure out what to do.

Suddenly a voice called out, "Carlos, is that you?"

Carlos glanced in the rearview mirror and smiled, obviously recognizing the other man. "It's me, Juan."

"*Mano*, I called 911. Just stay still," Juan shouted back.

The sound of the other man's voice had Missy prancing in the backseat, making the pickup shift again.

"Missy, sit. Sit," Natalie commanded, and luckily the Lab finally responded, sensing her urgency.

The sound of sirens split the air and Carlos turned her way and offered up a weak smile. A thin trickle of blood slipped down the side of his face from a cut along his brow.

She cradled his jaw. "You're hurt."

He winced and said, "That's just a scratch. It's my ribs that feel like someone took a bat to them."

He must have hit the steering wheel hard when the pickup went off the road.

"Carlos. We're going to wrap some chains around the back end and pull you out of there," Gemma called out.

Natalie glanced at the rearview mirror to see the FWC warden and police officers working together. The other woman must have ended her lunch hour and started heading back to work when she ran across them.

Which had Natalie wondering who had called whoever had been in the four-by-four. *Had it been Adams or Garcia? Her money was on Adams, only...*

"Who else knows where Garcia takes her lunch? Adams?"

Carlos nodded. "He knows. Gemma and he have to coordinate when they patrol together."

The rattle of chains came only seconds before metal creaked and grumbled as the pickup moved backward and out of the deadly waters.

The motion had Carlos groaning and grabbing his side.

"We need to get you to a doctor," she said, worried his injuries were worse than just a few sore ribs.

He waved one hand and said, "I'll be fine. Just bruised."

Another lurch of the pickup had him grimacing and moaning again.

She stroked a hand down his arm in commiseration as, with a final tug, the pickup landed on the roadway.

Gemma was immediately at the driver side window while the police officer came over to hers.

"What happened?" Gemma asked, but it was the man called Juan who answered as he came to stand by her.

"Some Jeep rear-ended them and then shot at them," Juan said with broad sweeps of his hands and gesticulations mimicking someone firing a gun.

"Juan is a bus driver with one of the other tours," Carlos explained at Natalie's questioning glance.

"Step back and give your statement to the officers, Juan," Gemma instructed, and the bus driver walked off with the police to give a statement and hopefully get the tourists in the bus to their destination. *Although that might take time since they're all potential witnesses*, Natalie thought.

"Are you two okay?" Gemma asked and peered inside the cab.

"We're okay," Carlos replied and popped open his door while cradling his side.

Natalie exited and opened the door to let Missy out of the pickup. The dog immediately sidled up to her, leaning into her leg for comfort. Missy's body trembled against her leg.

Carlos and Gemma walked around and joined her, heads bent together as if they were discussing something. As it had before, the little green monster rose up again, but she tamed it quickly because Carlos just wasn't a two-timing kind of guy. How she knew that, she didn't know, but she believed it.

The police officer walked over and took their statements about what had happened and when they were done, he examined the pickup.

With a flip of his hand in the direction of the vehicle, he said, "This ain't going anywhere." He held up one finger and continued, "First, I'm not sure it'll drive. Second, it's evidence now."

"We understand, Officer," Natalie said.

"I'll drive you home," Gemma said.

Carlos offered up a grateful, "*Gracias*. We'd appreciate that."

"Are you done here, Officer?" Natalie asked and at the man's nod, they all headed to Gemma's FWC pickup. But before she got in, Carlos grabbed Sandy's sneakers from the backseat and Natalie called Trey to let him know what had happened.

"Were you hurt?" he immediately asked.

Natalie said, "Carlos is a little banged up, but Missy and I are fine."

"Glad to hear. I'll reach out to the police for a copy of the report. Call me as soon as you're settled so we can discuss this further."

"Got it," she said. She ended the call, and at her nod, they all piled into the pickup.

Luckily the ride was smooth until they did the slight dip into Carlos's driveway and a grunt of complaint escaped him.

"You should see a doctor," both she and Gemma said at the same time and the other woman met her gaze in the rearview mirror.

This time it was a laugh that escaped Carlos. "Women," he teased.

"Of course, it's weird to take reasonable steps to make sure you're okay," Natalie said.

"I'm fine," he replied and didn't wait for either of them to say another word before hopping out of the pickup.

Gemma sighed and said, "Ridiculous macho—"

"Men," Natalie finished and the two of them shared a laugh before the gravity of the situation settled in.

"Someone tried to kill you," Gemma said and faced her.

"Maybe the same somebody who killed Dani Ruiz," Natalie said and carefully watched for the warden's reaction.

Gemma's lips tightened into a knife-sharp line. "Dani was a friend. If she was murdered, I want to see her get justice."

"Good to know we can count on you," Natalie said, feeling a sudden sense of camaraderie with her.

"I should get to work, and you—" Gemma pointed at her "—you should make sure he's okay."

"I will," Natalie confirmed, then exited the vehicle with Missy and walked over to where Carlos waited by the front steps of his home, one arm cradling his side.

"Let's get you cleaned up and see to those ribs."

That he didn't argue was a testament to the pain he must have been feeling.

They disarmed the alarm, reset it and headed to his bathroom where she urged him to sit on the toilet seat while she rummaged in his medicine cabinet for some cotton balls, antiseptic and bandages.

Missy sat at the door of the bathroom, watching intently. But as soon as Natalie moved toward Carlos, she hurried over and leaned against her leg—something she did when she was uneasy.

After laying everything out on the edge of the sink, Natalie started by cleaning the dried blood off the side of his face, her strokes determined until she reached the cut at the edge of his brow. She prepped a clean cotton ball with antiseptic and brought it near the wound.

Carlos had been sitting there stoically, but this next step was going to test that restraint. "This is going to sting."

CARLOS BRACED HIMSELF as Natalie gently dabbed his cut with the cotton ball. The antiseptic burned and he sucked in a breath against the pain, but that only made his ribs ache. He groaned and tucked his arm against his side.

"I'm sorry," she said and worried her lower lip with her teeth.

"It's okay," he said and stroked his hand along her arm to offer reassurance.

She nodded. "Let's see to those ribs."

He started to remove his T-shirt but groaned again as pain lanced through his side when he tried to lift his arm.

"I need a little help," he admitted, and she grabbed the hem of his shirt and carefully eased one arm out and then stripped it down the other arm.

The action brought her so close that her warm breath trailed across the side of his face and then the side of his neck. He smelled that floral scent she favored and it roused desire as he remembered how they had made love the night before.

As she finished drawing away the T-shirt, he laid a hand at her waist and tenderly urged her to straddle his legs and sit.

She met his gaze and, in a husky voice, said, "I guess you're not feeling all that bad."

"You make me feel things I shouldn't," he said and lightly stroked his fingers across her face and down until he cradled the fragile line of her neck. "I was so worried you'd be hurt today."

"I'm fine, but you're not," she said and looked down.

He followed her gaze to his ribs, which were already a mottled mess of purple shades.

She danced her fingers along the bruises, probing gently. "Nothing seems broken."

"They're just bruised," he said and cradled her face to urge her gaze to meet his. "I'll be okay."

Missy, who had somehow crammed herself in between the sink and their legs, whined as she sensed the emotion between them.

Natalie did a little half smile and rubbed the Lab's head. "We're good, Missy. Go sleep," she said and did a hand gesture to direct her out of the room. She resisted, obviously still uncomfortable from the crash and attack, but Natalie repeated the command and Missy finally obeyed.

"It's like having a two-year-old sometimes," she said with a wry smile.

"I remember those days," he said with a chuckle.

She stiffened at the reminder that he'd been married and happily at that. He laid his hands on her shoulders and lovingly stroked his thumbs across her collarbones.

"Dani will always be a part of my life, Natalie. But that doesn't mean I can't open my heart to you."

Tears shimmered in her eyes, and she bit her lower lip and looked away. "I know I can't replace her. I don't want to. It's just that...you have this whole life. Lucas. Your business."

When she finally glanced at him again, her voice was a harsh whisper as she said, "I have so little to offer."

He'd sensed that before from her—that she felt she was somehow unworthy. Damaged. Though she was anything but.

"You have everything to offer in here," he said and spread his hand directly over her heart. It skittered almost wildly beneath the palm of his hand.

Laying her hand over his, she stroked it lightly. "You make me feel whole again."

In truth, she made him feel the same way. "I hadn't thought I'd feel that way ever again," he admitted with a sharp shake of his head. "But you changed that, Natalie."

She grasped his hand and urged it over her breast, but as she did so his phone blared a musical chime.

"I'm so sorry, Natalie. I have to go pick up Lucas soon."

Smiling, she said, "I understand. Let me just support those ribs a little."

She hopped off his lap, grabbed some adhesive bandage wrap and expertly taped up his ribs, giving them some bolstering while allowing him to breathe freely.

"That feels good," he said and hurried out to his bedroom to grab a clean T-shirt. As before, she helped him ease the shirt on, and after, they headed out of the house, Missy eagerly chasing after them.

Carlos gestured in the direction of his business. "I'm going to grab one of the company SUVs."

She nodded and motioned toward the RV. "I need to talk to Trey and the team—update them on everything and see where we stand with the investigations. I'll see you back here in a little bit."

Chapter Twenty

Carlos dropped a quick kiss on her cheek and started to walk away, but then stopped and turned. "See you for dinner?"

"Hopefully. It depends on what Trey needs me to do."

He narrowed his gaze, as if worried she was using Trey as an excuse for some space and maybe she was.

"Just let me know," he said and hurried off to pick up Lucas. She almost chased after him, worried about the possibility that their attacker might go after him again, but stopped. The police had a description of their suspect's pickup and he'd be unlikely to be on the street again so soon. If anything, he and his partners would likely be regrouping to decide what to do next.

Much like she and the SBS team. They needed to be ready for whatever their suspects might do.

Missy was still plastered to her leg, and she knelt and rubbed her ears and neck. "It's going to be okay, Missy. Let's take you for a quick walk before we get back to work," she said and strolled with the Lab down to the dock, letting her take her time to sniff and relieve herself. Little by little, Missy lost some of her clinginess and by the time they went back to the RV, her dog seemed almost back to normal.

Once inside, she quickly dialed Trey who had good news to report.

"The judge issued the warrant for the call detail records for Adams's phone. We'll hopefully have the CDRs later tonight."

"That's great. I have no doubt Adams was behind today's attack," she said as she cradled the phone between her ear and shoulder, opened the small fridge and forked out some fresh food for Missy.

"Why do you say that?" Trey asked.

Recalling Adams's behavior at the restaurant, she said, "He clearly wasn't happy to see us and not all that cooperative. He also had enough time to call a partner and have him waiting for us at the pier where we went to speak to Gemma Garcia."

A pause came across the line before Trey hesitantly said, "You've taken Garcia off your suspect list?"

She'd had her qualms about the beautiful FWC warden, but today had cinched it for her that Gemma wasn't involved.

"I have. I suspect the CDRs will show that Adams phoned whoever he's working with right after we left and if he did, that will confirm he's the one we should be following," she said without hesitation.

"Agreed. PD also advised we should have the DNA results later today from the items left on Carlos's door and those located at the poachers' camp. Hopefully that will narrow our list of suspects."

She thought about what Sandy had said and relayed it to Trey. "One of Dani's friends said she was uneasy about something and suddenly wanted to leave the bar. Based on the CCTV footage, it coincides with the arrival of that second man at the bar."

"The one who sat next to the unknown FWC warden?"

"Definitely around the same time. That suspect wasn't there long, but Dani and her friends start moving just after he left. We also noticed the suspect left something behind that the warden took," she said, closing her eyes to visualize what had occurred in the CCTV footage.

"We noticed that too," Trey said and continued, "We're trying to sharpen the image to see what it was and also to see if there are any distinguishing markings on the badge."

"You mean like a scratch or something?" she said and patted Missy's head as the dog came to her side at the small dining table where she sat.

"We think we saw some wear across the blue circle and Florida state seal at the center of the badge and are trying to confirm. If you run across Adams again, be sure to check that out," he said.

"Got it. Carlos went to pick up Lucas and, in the meantime, I'm going to review all those crash reports again and do a patrol around the grounds." Hopefully she'd spot a clue she had missed before.

"Great. The SBS crew will continue to monitor the feeds. I imagine you need to tend to Missy with all that happened today."

The worry in his voice was real and wasn't just reserved for Missy. While she appreciated it, she also didn't want any special treatment. "We're fine. I can take over the monitoring after my last patrol."

A brief pause followed before he quickly said, "I get it, Natalie. You're on-site. Decide how your resources are best used."

"*Gracias*, Trey. I won't disappoint you."

"I never thought you would."

CARLOS STOOD BY the front of the car so Lucas would spot him right away since he wouldn't be looking for one of the company SUVs at the bus stop.

His son came bounding down the steps, smiling and laughing with Gemma's son, but Lucas's smile faded as he noticed that he didn't have his regular pickup and then skipped up to the cut on his brow.

The worry that had filled his son's face over the last two years came back with a vengeance, killing his earlier exuberance.

"What happened?" Lucas asked, his gaze hopping from the cut on Carlos's brow to the business SUV behind him.

"We had a little accident. We're all okay. Well, except for the truck," he said and forced a smile and laugh he wasn't feeling.

"Natalie and Missy too?" Lucas asked, looking into the SUV for any sign of them.

Carlos laid a hand on his son's shoulder and gently squeezed. "They're fine and back at the house. Natalie had some work to do."

Lucas narrowed his gaze, as if he didn't quite believe him, and for a moment his mind flew back to the night of Daniela's death. Lucas had had that same look on his face. That look of disbelief and fear.

"Let's go. Natalie and Missy are coming over for dinner and I'm not sure what to make," he said, trying to restore some sense of normalcy to a day that had been anything but.

In the SUV, Lucas fell silent. While keeping a close eye to see if anyone was following, Carlos did his best to draw out his son, asking him about how school had been that day and what kind of homework he had. He got mostly one-word answers as Lucas retreated into the shell he'd built around himself since his mom's death.

When he pulled into his driveway, Natalie and Missy were down by the dock. They turned and waved, Natalie smiling, and he could swear the dog was smiling as well.

He stopped the car and Lucas threw the door open and ran over to Natalie and Missy. As he approached them, he was relieved to see the smile on Lucas's face and his enthusiastic petting of the dog.

"I'm glad you're okay," he said.

"We are and I bet you have homework to do, right?" Natalie said and ruffled the short strands of Lucas's hair.

Lucas made a moue with his mouth and nodded. "I do. I've got a makeup math quiz tomorrow."

Natalie met his gaze. "I used to hate math too, but now I see how useful it is."

With a disbelieving stare, he said, "Really? Like for what?"

"Writing certain code, like the one Sophie and Robbie used with the drone to find the poachers' camp. I bet your video game programmers use it too," she said and stroked his arm lovingly.

"I guess," he said with a reluctant shrug.

"Go do your homework, *mi'jo*," Carlos said, and his son ran into the house. The beep of the alarm sounded and then quieted as Lucas disarmed it.

Carlos was about to follow his son in when Natalie's phone rang and she answered. She listened and held up a finger to tell him to wait.

"It's Trey," she said and swiped to put it on speaker.

"Are you there, Carlos?" Trey asked.

"I am. What's up, *mano*?"

"The PD got DNA results off the knife left at your business. When they ran them through CODIS, they got a possible hit," Trey said and hesitated before continuing.

"What is it? What's wrong?" Natalie pressed.

"It's bad. The suspect—Luis Hopper—has a long rap sheet. Juvenile record that's sealed. As an adult, small stuff like B&E that escalated to assault and battery and drug dealing. He's also a suspect in the murder of a rival dealer, but there isn't enough evidence to charge him. He's been surprisingly silent lately."

Natalie glanced up and met his worried gaze. "Can you send that info? I'd like to try and find out more about him if you don't mind."

"That would be great. I've got Sophie and Robbie using some facial recognition software to see if Hopper is a match to the man in the bar the night Dani died," Trey said and once again held that disturbing pause.

"PD has brought in DEA because of the drugs. DEA thinks the cocaine originated in Colombia and was trafficked through Venezuela to Honduras for a flight to the US," Trey said, and Carlos now understood his friend's concern.

"Am I wrong to think that we have some serious actors involved in this—like FARC and a cartel of some kind?" Carlos asked.

"You're not wrong. That's why I want Natalie to stand guard in your house and stay glued to your side 24/7," Trey explained.

This time it was Natalie who hesitated before finally saying, "I can do that. What about Lucas? Do we keep him home from school until this is over?"

"I'm not sure that's a good idea. Ever since Dani died, he hasn't been himself, but with school and the routine, he's gotten better," Carlos said with a quick look in her direction.

A heavy sigh came across the line. "I understand. If you send the name of the school and his schedule, I can check out what to do."

"*Gracias*, Trey. I appreciate your understanding," he said.

"I'll send all the latest reports and keep you posted on any developments," Trey said and ended the call.

They stood there for a brief minute, staring at each other as they both seemingly considered the possible complications with Natalie spending the night in his home.

"Are you okay with this?" he asked.

"It's my job. I just need to get a few things from the RV," she said with a flip of her hand in the direction of the vehicle.

He nodded. "I have to make sure Lucas is doing his homework and make dinner."

"I won't be long," she said and hurried off, her stride confident and powerful.

It had been impossible to resist her when they'd been alone in the RV. How hard would it be with her in his home?

Except of course that Lucas would be there, and he would never do anything to hurt his son. Lucas getting his hopes up about Natalie and Missy might bring painful disappointment if it didn't work out.

Only Lucas won't be the only one disappointed, he thought as he walked to his house.

Chapter Twenty-One

Natalie grabbed her laptop, toiletries, a change of clothes and extra ammo and tossed them into her duffel. In the kitchen area, she put Missy's bowls and her food into another bag.

She paused by the door and reached to the small of her back to pull her 9mm from the holster to make sure the magazine was full and the safety was on. As she returned the weapon to the holster, the soreness there and in other parts of her body registered, a result of being jostled so violently in that afternoon's crash.

She grabbed both bags and Missy's leash, then exited the RV, locked it and hurried to Carlos's home.

The alarm beeped as she opened the door, and she was grateful they were being so diligent about it. The security system might not discourage someone like Hopper, but it would give them advance warning and also give the SBS staff a heads-up to send help if it wasn't disarmed in time.

Carlos was in the kitchen, chopping up some onions and bell peppers as Missy and she entered. She laid her bag by the couch in the living room area and walked over, Missy trailing after her.

"Do you need any help?"

"I'm good. Just making a quick *arroz con pollo*," he said.

With a dip of her head, she said, "I'll set the table."

She had seen where most things were kept the day before

and quickly set the table before finding a spot for Missy's bowls. She gave her partner fresh food and water. Missy didn't waste a second before burying her head in the bowl and gobbling down her food.

"Slow down, girl. We're not going anywhere," she said with a laugh and rubbed the dog's head.

After, she went to her bag and took out the various reports she'd brought and placed them and her laptop on the coffee table. Missy came over and lay down beside the sofa.

Powering up her computer, she opened the email with their suspect's rap sheets and downloaded the info. She was about to exit her email when another one from Trey came in and she read it.

Police shared call detail records with us in exchange for SBS processing the data. Sophie and Robbie are working on plotting the locations. I thought I'd send it in advance so you can take a look.

Thanks. We will let you know if we spot anything, she replied and downloaded the report.

Calling out to Carlos, she said, "Do you mind if I use your printer?"

He was slipping something into the oven, but peered her way and said, "Whatever you need."

She printed the information Trey had sent and the whir of the machine and ruffle of paper erupted a second later from Carlos's bedroom.

"The printer is on the desk in my room. Feel free to get anything you need in there," he said. He was busy frying up some plantains, so she rose and walked to his room to retrieve the documents. But she hesitated by the door, as if entering his space without him was way too personal.

It's just work, she told herself, then crossed the threshold and went straight to his desk which was positioned against a far wall. The call detail records were long, forcing her to stand there as the paper kept spewing out of the printer.

She'd been in his room before, after the snake incident, but she hadn't really taken a deep look. Now it was impossible not to take in the details.

The room, like the rest of the house, was neat with an almost Spartan vibe except for the colorful pillows sitting on a comfy looking chair opposite the desk. The chair had a matching ottoman, and she could picture someone sitting there reading.

No, not someone. Daniela. She could picture Daniela sitting there, having a respite from the labors of being a business owner, wife and mother.

That image reminded her that Carlos had a life apart from anything they could share. A life with responsibilities he couldn't ignore.

The silence of the printer dragged her attention to the pile of papers in the output tray.

She gathered them and hurried out of the room.

In the spacious living area, Lucas finished setting out sodas on the kitchen table. He smiled when he saw her and chased after her as she walked to the coffee table.

"What are those?" he asked and pointed to the stack of papers.

"Just some reports your dad and I have to review later," she said, and not wanting to worry the ten-year-old, she laid the suspect's rap sheet at the bottom of the pile.

He plopped down on the sofa beside her and reached down to stroke a hand across Missy's body as she rested there. "Are they important?"

With a hesitant nod, she said, "Possibly." Sensing he wouldn't be satisfied with that answer, she laid the papers on her laptop and ran a finger across the rows of locations and numbers and said, "These are call detail records. CDR for short."

Lucas tracked the movement of her finger and made a face. "Looks like math."

"It is a lot of numbers," she said, and with that, he escaped to the table as Carlos brought over a plate with the fried ripe plantains.

"Maduros!" Lucas shouted happily as he caught sight of them.

"I know they're your favorite," Carlos said with a boyish grin and glanced in her direction.

"Dinner's ready if you are," he said and waited for her answer, almost expectantly.

HE DIDN'T NEED to be a rocket scientist to see that Natalie was uneasy about being in his home 24/7 as Trey had instructed.

He got it. It was almost too intimate even though they'd already made love.

Not that they could do that again with Lucas nearby.

Despite her obvious discomfort, dinner went relatively smoothly until Lucas leaned back, rubbed his belly and said, "That was as good as *Mami*'s."

Natalie perceptibly stiffened, but then said, "It was very good. Your mom must have been a good cook."

"She was," Lucas said, some of his earlier liveliness dimming.

Intuitively, Natalie sensed the reason for it. "My *papi*'s favorite meal was *ropa vieja* but for a long time my *mami* didn't make it after he passed."

"Did you miss it?" Lucas asked, almost timidly.

"I missed it. I missed him. When my *mami* made me *ropa vieja* again, it was even more special and it was because it was like *Papi* was there with us again," she admitted.

Lucas smiled, tears shimmering in his gaze. "That was *Mami*'s favorite too."

Carlos clasped his son's shoulder. "Maybe we can make it together this weekend."

Lucas's grin brightened. "I'd like that. May I be excused?"

With a nod, Carlos said, "You're excused."

Lucas's chair almost tipped over as he raced away from the table.

"He's a good kid. Daniela and you have raised him well," she said wistfully.

"*Gracias.* Did you ever want to have kids?" he asked as he cleared the table.

She stacked some of the dishes and followed him to the sink where she set the plates down.

Since she still hadn't answered, he faced her and leaned his hands on the edge of the counter. "Well? Kids?"

Standing opposite him, she crossed her arms, clearly in defense mode. "Maybe. Someday."

Satisfied that was all he was going to get from her, he said, "I can clean if you want to work."

"*Gracias,*" she said. And much like Lucas had hightailed it from the table earlier, Natalie did the same, racing to the coffee table where she had left her papers and laptop.

It didn't take him long to load everything into the dishwasher and store away any leftovers. As he dried his hands with a kitchen towel, he realized Natalie had shifted to the dining room table and was spreading papers on its surface.

He approached and as he perused the papers, he grinned and repeated Lucas's earlier words, "Looks like math."

Natalie chuckled, some of her earlier discomfort fading. "It does, doesn't it?"

He pointed to a series of numbers identified by the heading *Switch*.

"What does this mean?"

She ran her index finger across the data and explained. "This is the cell site for the outgoing and incoming calls. This is the user's phone number. That's followed by the number dialed." She skipped her finger over a couple of columns and continued, "If it was incoming, this is the number that called you and how long the call lasted."

He jabbed at one entry. "This is Adams's number. I've called it myself to make a report," he said and found his phone number on the CDRs.

"Sophie and Robbie will run programs to sort through all this and map the cell towers, but we can identify things in the meantime," she said and pulled out a pad to take notes.

She flipped through the CDR pages to the date of Daniela's death.

"Adams made calls to the same number, probably a burner phone, until about seven o'clock and then there's a break, but it resumes just after midnight."

"Right around the time of Daniela's crash," Carlos said.

"I'm going to jot down these cell site numbers so we can see where they're located," she said.

"What about after I called them about the alligator nests?" Carlos asked and she shuffled through the papers until they found those entries. Adams had made a series of calls to another number right after Carlos had phoned.

She wrote down the info and said, "I doubt we have today's information, but let's see."

Much as she had assumed, the last data in the report was for yesterday.

"Bummer, but we can work with the other data we have," she said, then grabbed her laptop and opened it so Carlos could watch. While she typed, she explained what she was doing.

"This website lets us check the location of this provider's cell towers. It's not necessarily a hundred percent accurate since it's based on user provided data, but it's a start. We can double-check it using a phone app I have," she said and entered their location to pull up towers in the area.

When the cell tower info appeared on the screen, they saw various cell towers in and around them. One of the tower numbers matched.

"Here's one," she said.

With another click, she displayed the approximate coverage of the tower and what other cell sites it connected to in the area.

"I want to map this," Carlos said and rushed off to his desk.

NATALIE HEARD HIM rummaging around before he returned with a map and colored markers.

Using the information on her laptop as a guide, he carefully matched the locations on his map and used the colored pencils to identify the areas.

When she brought up the information for another tower connected to Adams's calls, Carlos repeated the mapping.

"It's in the same general area." He circled the spots on the map with his index finger.

"They say you shouldn't mess where you eat, but clearly whoever is getting these calls keeps close to home," she said, peering at Carlos's map.

"Could it be because there aren't that many cell towers out here?" he asked, uncertain about the findings.

"Let's see how many towers there are," she said and zoomed out on the program which revealed there were at least half a dozen towers over the many acres in their part of the Everglades.

"Not many, but enough to pinpoint where the callers might have been when they used their phones," she said.

Carlos hesitated for a long moment before he gestured to a spot on the map. "This is that last bar where Dani was the night she died."

It was impossible for her to miss that it was right in the area they had identified.

"Let's see where the towers are for Adams's calls connected to the alligator nests," she said and they repeated their steps of finding and mapping the locations.

This time the area was slightly different, but not far from the earlier spots and surprisingly close to a place she recognized.

"This is where we found the poachers' camp, right?" she said and pointed to Carlos's map.

"It is. There are just too many connections for this to all be coincidence," Carlos said.

Scrutinizing those very basic findings, she had to agree. "Can you mark those spots on the maps so I can snap off a photo and send it to Trey?"

"And once you do?" he asked and did as she had requested.

"I'm sure Sophie and Robbie will find many more points of connection, but even with only these, the police may have enough to bring in Adams for an interview."

"I want to be there when they question him," he said sharply, his body tight with anger.

Chapter Twenty-Two

He wanted to see Adams's face and hear his voice as he tried to explain his connections to Daniela's death and the poachers.

No, not just poachers, he reminded himself. Drug traffickers. Drugs that were killing Americans in record numbers.

Forcing down his anger, he identified key locations on the map: the bar, the poachers' camp and the alligator nests.

Once he finished, he stepped aside so she could get a clear shot.

She took the picture and then also photographed the CDR pages they'd identified for the day of Daniela's death and the poached alligator nests.

Her fingers flew over her phone screen as she sent the information to Trey. Once she had done so, she met his gaze and said, "I should take Missy around for another patrol and so she can do her duty."

"I'll stay here with Lucas if you don't mind," he said and slipped his hands into the pockets of his khaki shorts to keep from touching her.

"Of course. I won't be long." With a soft click of her tongue, she summoned Missy who immediately ran to Natalie's side.

He strolled to the door and disarmed the security system. As she walked out, he laid his hand on her arm and dropped a quick kiss on her lips. "I'll be waiting for you."

NATALIE RUSHED DOWN the steps, Missy bounding beside her as they began their patrol.

She was grateful for the break from Carlos because she had sensed the whirlwind of emotions swirling through him. Anger. Fear. Guilt. Such a powerful combination of feelings was enough to drag someone down into a vortex that would be hard to escape.

The first two emotions were easy to understand. She was angry at Adams as well. Feared what he and his partners might do to Carlos, Lucas, her or her SBS crew. It was the guilt that was throwing her.

Did Carlos feel guilty that he hadn't been with his wife that night? That he hadn't protected her? Or was he feeling guilty about what had happened with her?

It had been so long since she'd been involved with a man. At first it had been because her PTSD issues were not really under control. Later on, it was because she'd been too busy with her new job at SBS.

She hadn't expected the feelings that had so quickly developed for Carlos. She should have resisted them. It was too complicated a situation with everything going on and because he was a client.

That thought sunk its roots deep into her mind as she carefully patrolled the grounds, vigilant for recent activity and signs that someone had been there during their absence. Although if they had, the SBS crew watching the cameras should have notified her.

She finished one last swing around the house, stopping to let Missy relieve herself, and then slowly walked up the steps, girding herself for being with Carlos again. Telling herself to give him some space to deal with the emotions she had sensed earlier.

As she neared the top step, he opened the door, and the light outlined the powerful shape of his body. His broad shoulders nearly filled the doorway and tapered to his slim waist. His legs were spread, thighs and calves thick with muscle.

His face was in shadow, making it impossible to read what he was feeling until he stepped back, and light spilled across his troubled features.

Straightening her spine and pulling her shoulders back, she said, "Nothing to worry about here." Except for her heart, of course.

He nodded abruptly and said, "I made a fresh pot of coffee."

"That would be great." It was going to be a long night while she worked on the information they had gathered earlier that night.

As Carlos walked away, back ramrod straight, she locked up and reset the security system. Unleashing Missy, she let her Lab have free rein to explore her new environment. Missy did a quick loop around the open-concept room and then went into Lucas's bedroom.

He let out an excited, "Missy, come here, girl."

Hurrying to the door of his room, she watched as Missy laid her head on Lucas's lap as he played some kind of race car game. She was hard pressed to end the interaction since both seemed so happy.

Conflicted, she walked back to the table where her laptop and papers were spread next to Carlos's map. It was the map that drew her attention.

She traced the edges of the areas they had identified with a finger. While it wasn't a good thing to make trouble where you lived, criminals often committed crimes in areas with which they were most familiar. Knowledge of the neighborhood made for easier escapes for one. It also made it easier to select areas where it would be simpler to commit the crime, like the distant and well-hidden poachers' camp they had discovered.

Did their suspect live somewhere in the area they had identified?

Pulling out his rap sheet, she read through it again for any clues.

Miami-born, Luis Hopper had grown up in Little Havana. The son of a Hispanic mother and Irish father, he had started acting out at an early age.

She wondered if that had been the result of problems at home. The only way to find out would be to speak to family members and get a sense of what had led Hopper to a life of crime.

Jumping onto the internet, she searched through social media sites for possible relatives but there were more Luis Hoppers than she had expected. Spot checking them for similarly aged men from the Miami area proved useless after half a dozen or more tries.

Logging onto one of the free genealogical sites, she found several Hoppers in the area going back to the early 1800s. Tracing those relationships, she located Hopper's parents and from there, two siblings.

She jotted down their names and birth dates just as Carlos came over with the promised cup of coffee.

He sat beside her. "Did you get something useful?"

"Possibly Hopper's brother and sister. His parents are both deceased."

After a sip of his coffee, he said, "What do you plan to do with that?"

Cradling her mug in her hands and savoring the comforting warmth and aroma of the coffee, she said, "I promised Trey I'd get some background info and I want to know why Hopper is the way he is. Did he have a rough childhood? How did he get on such a wrong path in life?"

"What makes him tick?" Carlos tossed out.

She nodded and took a sip. "Definitely. The more we know about him, the better we can defend against what he might do or even where he might be."

He pointed at the siblings' names. "Do you have a database where you can look up his siblings?"

"SBS has access to a number of databases, but you'd be surprised at the kind of information people share," she said and hopped back onto Facebook to search for the sister.

"Why her first?" Carlos asked, clearly intrigued by her process.

"She's in the right age demographic and women tend to use Facebook more than men." She did a search that revealed about half a dozen women with the same name.

Carlos viewed the screen as she went from one profile to the next and on the fourth one, she found pay dirt.

"Kathy Hopper. She lists Jaime Hopper as her brother. That matches what I got from the genealogy search."

"Here's her workplace, city where she lives and the birth-date matches that you found," Carlos added.

"She's a nurse at University of Miami Hospital. Been there for years," she said and since Kathy had identified her brother, she opened his page.

"Jaime is a partner at a law firm," Carlos said and quickly added, "The apple seems to have fallen far from the tree when it comes to Luis."

"It did." She scrolled through the public information available at both profiles only neither had any reference to their ne'er-do-well brother.

"No mention on either of the pages," Carlos said, obviously picking up on it as well.

"If you were a respectable, law-abiding citizen would you want your friends to know you were related to someone like him?"

No answer was needed to her rhetorical question, so she continued, "If we can track down phone numbers for them, I want to call and see what they have to say about their brother."

She located numbers for their places of employment since their personal numbers seemed to be unlisted. Since it was past typical law office hours, she phoned the hospital first. Luckily Kathy had indicated she was a critical care nurse and she asked for that department and then for Hopper's sister.

"I'm sorry, but Kathy isn't on duty tonight," said the nurse who answered.

"May I ask if she'll be available in the morning?" she asked politely, hoping not to raise suspicion.

The nurse delayed, obviously uncomfortable by the question. Rather than push, Natalie said, "I'm just an old school friend who's in the area. I'll try again tomorrow. Thanks."

"What do we do now?" Carlos asked once she'd hung up.

She gestured to the pad. "I'll send this info to Trey and maybe they can get other numbers."

Once she emailed the information to Trey, she took a bracing sip of the coffee since weariness had started to settle in. That meant it might be a good time to take Missy for a patrol to possibly wake up a bit.

"I'm going to do a last patrol. I won't be long," she said and rose, wincing as she did so.

"Are you sore?" Carlos asked, clearly noticing the expression and slight stiffness of her body.

"I am, but I'm okay. How about you? How are the ribs?"

"Hurting like heck, but I'll be okay too," he said and stood, likewise grimacing with the motion.

"What a pair," she said with a laugh and walked to Lucas's room where Missy had lay down beside his bed.

Lucas was fast asleep in a tangle of sheets.

Missy roused as she came in and walked over, favoring a back leg.

Worried, Natalie checked out her partner once again, but nothing seemed broken. Missy was probably as sore as they were from the impact of the crash.

In a soft voice, she said, "Sit."

Missy immediately obeyed and Natalie shifted to straighten the sheets around Lucas's body and tuck him in.

As she finished, Lucas woke and smiled sleepily. "I like you a lot," he said before closing his eyes again.

A fist constricted around her heart and tears flooded her

eyes. Sniffling, she bent, dropped a kiss on his hair and whispered, "I like you a lot too."

When she turned, Carlos stood there, his features unreadable in the dim illumination of the night-light. But as she approached, the loving glitter in his eyes and tender smile chased away the darkness.

"Do you like me a lot too?"

Chapter Twenty-Three

It was unfair to ask, Carlos knew, and yet the picture of her caring for his son had been so beautiful, so full of love and hope, that it made it impossible for him to hold back.

She offered him a smile that was part teasing and part chastising as she closed the door to Lucas's room.

"Do you mean just *like* or *like like*—"

He silenced her with a kiss, cupping the back of her skull to keep her close as he explored her mouth gently at first until passion roused and he deepened the kiss, greedily exploring the contours of her mouth. Driving her against the wall to press his hardness to all that womanly softness.

But as he did that, Missy growled, misunderstanding his actions for a threat. With a hand gesture, Natalie quieted her partner.

He backed away and dragged his fingers through his hair in both frustration and regret. Hands held out in pleading, he said, "I'm sorry—"

She laid her fingers on his mouth to silence him.

"Don't apologize. *Por favor*. But we need to cool this for now as much as we both might want it."

He did want it. He wanted her and for more than just the physical. With a nod, he whispered against her hand, "I'll be good. I'll wait for you while you patrol."

"I won't be long," she said and hurried out, needing the space from him because despite his promise, he was just too hard to ignore.

She quickly circled the house to make sure everything was in order before detouring toward the dock.

Missy sniffed around the pilings but found nothing new.

As she was heading to the business, Missy stopped dead and started growling as a shadow appeared at the far end of the path. Not a second later, her phone also started chirping, probably the SBS crew warning that they had seen something.

Natalie tightened her hold on the leash, reached to the small of her back, took out her HK P30 and flipped off the safety.

"Hold your ground," she called out to the figure.

The man, she could tell from the height and build, raised his hands as if in surrender. A second later, he said, "It's me. Dale Adams."

"Step forward. Slowly," she said, keeping her attention on him while also keeping her head on a swivel in case he wasn't alone.

Adams did as she asked, slowly advancing until he stepped into the illumination from one of the floodlights they had installed for security.

"What are you doing here?"

He started to lower his hands until she gestured with her pistol muzzle to keep them raised.

"You're treating me like a criminal," he almost whined.

"Maybe because you're acting like one," she said, maintaining her position. Missy sat beside her, her attention riveted to Adams.

"I heard about the accident. I just came to see how you were, but when I was pulling up, I saw someone walking down the driveway for the business. I thought I'd check it out."

The sound of a door opening behind her had her shooting a quick glance over her shoulder. Missy also peered back but remained calm, apparently recognizing Carlos.

He raced out of the house and to her side. "Trey just called to say we had an intruder. He's called the local PD to come out."

"Just one intruder?" she pressed.

Carlos glared at Adams. "Just one."

The sound of an approaching siren shattered the peace of the night. As the cruiser pulled into the driveway, Lucas meandered to the front door, rubbing sleep from his eyes.

"I need to tend to Lucas," he said and hurried back to the house while she kept her gun trained on Adams.

"This is a big mistake," he pleaded.

"You might want to get your story straight for the cops. I'm sure my SBS crew will be providing them surveillance video," she said as the two officers approached.

"We heard you had a trespasser," said the first officer—a young Latina. She eyed Natalie's weapon and Missy.

"I'm licensed to carry. This is my partner," she explained and holstered the 9mm pistol.

Adams jumped in with: "I'm an FWC warden. I was just here to make sure everything is in order."

"You're in civvies," noted the second officer, a handsome mixed-race man, eyes narrowing as he took in Adams's attire.

"I was off duty," Adams replied, but his explanation sounded hollow.

"Is that so? I hope you won't mind coming to the station after we take SBS Agent Rodriguez's statement," said the female officer.

As the male officer took hold of Adams's arm, Adams jerked away, avoiding his grasp. Beside Natalie, Missy rose on her haunches, as if preparing for action, but Natalie controlled her with a quick tug of the leash.

The officer warned, "You don't want to add resisting arrest to trespassing, do you?"

Sensing that he wasn't going to just walk away from this, Adams held his hands up in surrender. "I'll go peacefully," he said, but glared at her fiercely from a face mottled red and white with anger.

"He seems like a charmer," the female officer said as she whipped out her notepad.

"He certainly is," Natalie confirmed and provided the woman with her statement. As she finished, she said, "If you let me have an email address, I'll have my colleagues at SBS send over the CCTV footage."

"We'd appreciate that," the officer said and handed Natalie a card with her contact information.

"*Gracias*, Officer Martinez," she said and gave her business card to the woman.

She walked with Martinez toward the cruiser. Adams sat handcuffed in the backseat with that sullen, angry look still on his face.

"We'll be in touch," Martinez said as she opened the driver side door and her partner sat in the passenger seat. Seconds later, she was pulling out of the driveway to take Adams to the police station.

Natalie watched them go and then headed to the house where Carlos stood at the door waiting. The front porch light bathed his features in a golden glow and there was no mistaking the concern there.

She stopped before him and met his gaze. "Nothing happened."

"But it could have. What was he doing here?" Carlos pressed just as her phone chirped.

She held up a finger to ask him to wait and answered.

"Are you all okay?" Trey asked, worry evident in his voice.

"We are. Whatever Adams planned on doing, he got interrupted," Natalie said and put the phone on speaker.

"Roni and I are headed to the local police station. They've agreed to let Roni sit in on the interview, especially since we have information that might tie Adams to several crimes."

"What kind of info?" Natalie asked, grateful for any progress that might help close the investigation.

"Sophie and Robbie did their magic on the CDRs and then John Wilson added to it by using his probability program to match that data to Dani's crash and other incidents," Trey explained.

She looked up at Carlos after hearing those words. He had gone stock-still and his face was set in unforgiving lines.

"I want to be there when you talk to him. I want to hear what the bastard has to say," Carlos said from behind gritted teeth.

"I'm not sure—"

Carlos cut Trey off. "I want to be there."

Natalie laid a calming hand on his shoulder. "I can stay and watch Lucas. Carlos deserves to know if Adams had anything to do with his wife's death."

Chapter Twenty-Four

Carlos held his breath as he waited for his friend's response, ready to argue with him again. Instead, Trey said, "I'll see what I can do. Roni and I will be there in about half an hour. Local PD is going to let Adams stew in the tank until we arrive."

"Wait for me there," Carlos said.

"Will do," Trey replied and ended the call.

Natalie stroked her hand down his arm. "I know you want to tear him apart—"

"With my bare hands," Carlos said and mimicked ripping something open with his hands.

"Let Trey and Roni handle this. It sounds like they have enough to convince the authorities to hold Adams while they do a more thorough investigation," Natalie said, obviously trying to reassure him.

"Like the investigation they should have done in the first place?" he shot back.

Natalie nodded and pursed her lips. "Like they should have. Maybe there's even evidence we can salvage that will help."

Carlos doubted that. Although insurance had paid to repair the damage to Daniela's car, he'd sold it because seeing it parked by the house had been too painful a reminder of her death.

Shaking his head, he said, "I doubt it. Dani's buried. The car is gone."

"But we have the autopsy results and maybe Adams will turn on his partners," Natalie said, trying to remain optimistic.

He couldn't be as hopeful. "I should go."

"I'll take good care of Lucas," she said and rose on tiptoe to drop a kiss on his cheek.

"I know you will."

He didn't wait for her answer to rush to his company pickup. Once inside, he gunned the engine in his haste to reach the police station. Gripping the wheel hard, he pushed the speed as much as he could without ending up in jail himself. Barely twenty minutes later, he reached the station and as impatient as he was, he waited outside the building until Trey and Roni arrived.

Roni walked up to him and dropped a quick kiss on his cheek. "I talked to the detective who's been assigned to the case. He's willing to let you watch from the viewing room."

Trey clapped him on the back and said, "It's better this way, *mano*."

"So I won't pound the life out of him?" Carlos bit out.

His friend squeezed his shoulder in an effort to calm him. "*Sí*. We need to do this the right way."

He hated that Trey was right. They needed to do things the right way to nail Adams. With a nod, he followed Trey and Roni into the station where the desk sergeant stood upon their entry.

"May I help you?" the female officer asked.

Roni flashed her badge. "Detective Lopez. I spoke to Detective Cunningham earlier about the trespasser who was brought in."

"I'll let him know you're here."

The buzz of the lock at the end of the desk signaled that the gate was open.

Roni pushed through and Trey and he followed into the bull

pen where a tall, redheaded man in a pale beige guayabera stepped out of an office. With a tight smile, he directed them to an interview room down the hall.

Once they were inside, he closed the door and dipped his head in greeting. "Detective. Gonzalez. Mr. Ruiz, I assume?" Detective Cunningham said.

Carlos shook the detective's hand. "Thanks for letting me watch."

"I understand this is difficult, but I promise we will do our best," the detective said.

He bit back his condemnation of their earlier investigation, knowing that wouldn't encourage the officer to assist them.

"I appreciate that, Detective." He sat down at the table as Roni handed a folder to the officer.

"We obtained Adams's CDRs, mapped out the locations of the calls and matched them to possible incidents that have occurred. Are you familiar with the test of John Wilson's probability program?" Roni said.

"I've heard the rumors," Cunningham said and shifted some papers around before jabbing at one entry. "Are you telling me he thinks Adams is involved in all these crimes, including the death of Daniela Ruiz?"

Trey jumped into the discussion. "We do, Detective. Even before all this info, my gut told me something was wrong about Dani's death, but the case had been closed."

The redhead leaned back in his chair and flipped through the pages again before tossing them onto the table and dragging his fingers through his hair. "This department handled that case. Badly, I guess."

It was all Carlos could do to bite back an angry retort. Somehow, he managed to remain calm as he said, "We're hoping you can do better this time."

"I hope so too," Cunningham said with a tired sigh. Shooting to his feet, he said, "Detective Lopez and I will interview

Adams." Pointing at him and Trey, he added, "You two can watch from the viewing room."

Carlos had wanted Adams right in front of him, but he had to settle for this now.

The detective led them to the interrogation area and opened the door to the viewing room. Carlos immediately went to the two-way mirror to watch, and Trey joined him there. A second later, another officer walked in to monitor the video recording equipment.

Barely a minute later, Adams was led in by a uniformed officer who sat him at the table.

Roni and Cunningham sat across from him, and Cunningham took the lead, detailing who was in the room, the date and time and the reason for the interrogation. Then he asked Adams to confirm he had been read his rights and understood them.

"I understand my rights. What I don't understand is why you're treating me like a criminal," Adams said and jerked his handcuffed hands up in question.

Cunningham removed a photo from his folder and slid it in front of Adams.

"I assume you're familiar with Daniela Ruiz's crash," Roni said.

Adams slouched in his chair and did a negligent shrug. "I know she died in a car crash."

"Except we don't think it was an accident and we think you know that too," Roni said.

"I don't know jack about the crash," Adams said, but then Cunningham tossed several more photos in front of their suspect.

Carlos couldn't see what they were and jerked with shock as Roni said, "Autopsy results, but my guess is someone snapped her neck, put her in the car and then faked the crash."

"And you think I had something to do with that?" Adams challenged and jabbed an index finger at his chest.

Roni pulled a CDR report from the folder and placed it over the photos. "You called this number several times, including right around the time that Dani was killed."

She laid another CDR report in front of Adams. "These calls coincide with the poaching at the alligator nests."

Repeating the process with a few other pages, she identified time after time where Adams's actions matched up with criminal activity.

Carlos could tell that Adams was growing more and more nervous with each revelation although he tried to downplay it.

"Pure coincidence," Adams said.

"Seems to me when you have these many coincidences, it's more. It's a conspiracy," Cunningham said and quickly added, "A conspiracy to commit murder. A conspiracy to traffic drugs. A conspiracy to poach endangered species."

Roni didn't waste a second to rush in with, "Do you know the punishment for murder in Florida? Are you going to choose the needle or the chair?"

Adams's face paled to the color of newly fallen snow, and he waved his hands in denial. "I had nothing to do with any of that."

"Facts say otherwise," Cunningham said and jabbed at the pile of papers.

"All circumstantial," Adams shot back but with little confidence.

"You're hoping that's all it is because otherwise you're looking at the death penalty. A murder committed in connection with a felony. I think drug dealing and poaching are both felonies, aren't they, Detective Cunningham?" Roni said.

"Totally right, Detective Lopez," Cunningham replied.

"What will it be, Adams? Needle or chair?" she repeated since she'd obviously gotten a reaction from him the first time.

It was like watching a balloon leak in slow-motion as Adams collapsed into the chair, losing all of his earlier bravado.

Sensing victory, Cunningham pushed him. "If we get your

help, we can talk to the DA and take the death penalty off the table."

Adams hesitated, but then he shot forward and jabbed a finger at the papers on the table. "I want a lawyer. I'm not saying anything else without one."

Chapter Twenty-Five

Natalie dropped a kiss on Lucas's forehead and carefully slipped out of bed.

It had taken her some time to calm the young boy after he had spotted the police car. Lucas had admitted to her that it had made him remember the night the police had come to their door to say his mom was dead.

Her heart had almost broken with his story and the sadness in his eyes.

She'd hugged him close and then taken him to his bedroom where she'd tucked him into bed and read him a book until he'd fallen fast asleep.

Satisfied that Lucas was good for the moment, she walked out into the great room to wait for Carlos. Antsy, she boiled some water for a cup of chamomile tea and was just sitting down to review her papers when the beep of the alarm pulled her attention to the door. Missy lifted her head from where she'd been sleeping at Natalie's feet, ready to spring into action.

Carlos's shoulders had a weary droop as he entered and then reset and locked the alarm. Seeing who it was, Missy settled back down.

Natalie walked over to him and, cradling his jaw, offered comfort with her touch.

"How did it go?"

With a tense quirk of his mouth, Carlos said, "He lawyered up, but not before we got a good read that he's involved."

She nodded and said, "What happens now?"

"The detectives are talking to the DA about a plea deal to try and get more info," Carlos said and drew her into a tight bear hug.

His body trembled with the rage and pain he was holding in, and she stroked her hands down his back, trying to soothe him. "He will get punished."

"Maybe," he said. He loosened his embrace but kept her close to his side as they walked to the kitchen table.

When they reached it, he handed her a folder that she hadn't realized he'd been holding. "This is a copy of the materials that Trey and Roni gave to the detective investigating Adams."

Natalie laid the folder down on the table, opened it and spread out the papers, organizing them into different piles. One pile had a map where Sophie and Robbie had identified several areas and the CDRs that had produced the map. A second pile held a list of crime reports, also selected by the SBS team and John Wilson as possibly connected to Adams. The third and final pile had an SBS expert's fresh examination of Daniela's autopsy and crash results.

She traced a finger over the map. "Pretty much the area we had identified. Maybe slightly larger here."

"That's a lot of ground to cover even with drones," Carlos said with a low whistle.

"It is, but we have to assume he won't return to his old poaching camp. That eliminates some ground."

Carlos grunted his agreement and then picked up the crime report list. After a quick perusal, he said, "Is Wilson's program that accurate?"

"Scarily accurate in deciding the probabilities," she replied, recalling a few other investigations where the program's output had helped identify suspects out of dozens of possible hits.

"If it is accurate, Adams and Hopper are responsible for a number of poaching incidents and drug-related crimes."

Natalie skimmed through the report. With a nod, she said, "Not enough for a judge to issue an arrest warrant unless Adams gives us more."

CARLOS REACHED FOR the SBS report on his wife's murder.

Anger filled him at the thought that the FWC warden would likely never pay the price for Daniela's death.

Natalie stayed his hand as he went to pick up the papers. "You will get justice for what happened to Dani."

He shook his head. "If Adams rolls on Hopper, he'll make a deal to not get the death penalty."

Natalie stroked his face with her hand. "But he'll spend the rest of his life in prison."

Not enough punishment as far as he was concerned, although others might think that a life in confinement might be worse than death.

He twined his fingers with hers. "We should get some rest. The morning is likely to be busy."

"I'd like to talk to Hopper's siblings in the morning."

"Do you think that will help?" Carlos asked and Natalie nodded.

"It may help us get a clue as to how he thinks. What he might do if Adams rolls on him."

With a reluctant shrug, Carlos said, "Whatever you think we should do."

She smiled, rose on tiptoe and brushed a kiss across his cheek. "I should finish that patrol that got interrupted and then I have to take a deep dive into those papers. You should get some rest."

He wasn't about to go to sleep if she was still hard at work. "I'll make you some coffee."

She hesitated, ready to argue with him, but he stopped her

by laying a finger on her lips. "We're a team, Natalie. If you're up, I'm up."

She nodded, kissed the tip of his finger, and with a hand command to Missy, they walked to the door where she clipped on her partner's leash. After working the alarm, she hurried into the night.

He busied himself by making the coffee, changing his clothes and taking Natalie's bag to the guest bedroom. As much as he wanted Natalie, he couldn't risk Lucas walking in and jumping to all the wrong conclusions.

Like that this is more than just a fling? warned the little voice in his head that sounded way too much like Daniela.

It wasn't just a fling, he thought, but it was also a way too complicated time for Lucas.

Just Lucas? challenged the voice.

The front door opened, and Natalie and Missy hurried in.

His heart did a funny little jump in his chest, and he knew then it was a way too complicated time for him as well.

Natalie walked to him, a puzzled look on her face. "Everything all right?"

He lied. "All good. I'll get you that coffee," he said and hurried off to the kitchen counter.

SOMETHING WAS BOTHERING HIM, but she didn't press. He'd share when and if he was ready.

She unclipped the leash and Missy headed straight to her water bowl.

Natalie sat at the table and texted Sophie and Robbie to let them know she was back. Of course, their team would know that from monitoring the camera feeds, but she didn't want to take any chances.

Once she heard back from them, she grabbed the map and the crime reports, familiarizing herself with the locations where Adams and Hopper had been active.

Carlos walked over and placed a coffee mug beside her.

"Gracias," she said, and he sat next to her and laid his arm across the back of her chair.

At her questioning look, he repeated what he'd said earlier. "If you're up, I'm up."

Since it was useless to argue, she reviewed the data with him attentively soaking up her comments. Occasionally he'd jump in with an observant question, forcing her to think about her conclusions.

It was well past midnight when they finished those two reports, and too late to tackle the SBS expert's analysis of Daniela's death.

"I think it's time to turn in. I'm a little tired."

With a dip of his head, he said, "I am too. I'll show you to your room. I put your bag in there earlier."

"Gracias," she said and followed him to the guest bedroom which was tucked between his room and Lucas's.

Missy had followed them but surprised her by taking up a position close to the door to Lucas's room.

"She likes him," she said and tacked on, "I do too. He's a good kid."

"He is. I just wish we could put this all behind us so things can get back to normal."

She didn't want to think about the fact that their normal probably didn't include her. Forcing a smile, she said, "I'll see you in the morning."

She was about to close the door when he laid a gentle hand on it, leaned in and brushed a kiss against her lips. "It might be nice if you were part of our normal."

Inside her chest, her heart leaped with joy at that thought, but she controlled that rush of happiness to say, "It might be nice."

He grinned, dropped another kiss on her lips and walked away with a sexy swagger.

Closing the door to avoid the temptation to join him in his bedroom, she quickly changed into pajamas, did a last look through her texts and emails to confirm no action was needed and climbed into bed.

After a few tosses and turns that reminded her of the achy spots thanks to the crash, sleep slowly claimed her but as it did, memories of the day Missy and she had been injured crept in.

The dry heat and scorching sun were alive again as was the taste of dirt in her mouth as a sirocco swirled dust around them. Missy was sniffing around one man who backed away. She tried to balance her concern that he might have something to hide with the possibility that some Muslims thought of dogs as impure and might not like to be near them.

A loud engine roar snared her attention and she whirled, but instead of a battered Toyota with badly painted camo coming at her, it was a smiling Carlos and Lucas in his pickup.

The fear of that day evaporated like morning fog beneath a rising sun until an anguished shout filtered into her dream. Half-awake and unsure if she'd made that pained sound, a second shout pulled her to wakefulness.

She shot up in bed just as Carlos flew to her door.

"It wasn't me," she said just as a third shout tore through the quiet of the night.

Chapter Twenty-Six

Carlos tore away from the door and Natalie followed, racing to Lucas's room where Missy was already at the young boy's bedside, pacing back and forth across the length of the bed.

Carlos sat on the edge of the bed and gently woke his son from the nightmare.

"It's okay, Lucas. We're here," he said, and Lucas shot off the bed and into his arms.

"It's okay," he crooned again as Natalie stood beside them and signaled a nervous Missy to sit.

Lucas frantically looked from him to Natalie and cried, "I dreamed that you were dead. That you left me just like *Mami* did."

"We're not going anywhere," he said and held his son close, stroking his trembling body.

"You did. You left," Lucas argued, his head buried tight to Carlos's chest.

Natalie sat beside them and tenderly brushed her hand up and down Lucas's back. "Your *papi* isn't going anywhere, Lucas. Everything is going to be okay."

Lucas shook his head back and forth but kept silent as the two of them continued to calm him. Little by little, Lucas quieted, but when Carlos tried to lay him back down in bed, his son clung to him tightly.

He knew he had no choice then but to climb into bed with him. "You should get some sleep. He'll be fine."

Natalie nodded and rose. Lucas roused and glanced at her. "Don't go."

"Lucas. Natalie needs to get some sleep—"

"Please don't go," Lucas whined and fretted again.

She met Carlos's gaze and he reluctantly nodded. It was clearly too late to avoid Lucas becoming too attached to someone who might be gone in days.

Carlos shifted Lucas to the middle of the bed while Natalie swung around to the opposite side to lie down. He moved as close as he could to Lucas to avoid falling off the narrow, full bed.

Seemingly not wanting to be left behind, Missy hopped onto the bed and lay in what little free space there was at their feet.

Across the gap above Lucas's head Carlos met Natalie's gaze and mouthed, "I'm sorry."

The smile she gave him radiated understanding and so much love, and his heart ached at the thought that this might be just a temporary thing despite her earlier assertions that she might like being a part of their life.

He reached across his now sleeping son to rest his hand on her waist.

She laid her arm across his and with that, and Missy's slight snore filling the quiet, he allowed himself to believe in the impossible.

HOPPER'S BROTHER WAS less than happy to hear from them. As soon as he heard his younger brother's name, he hung up. Natalie called back and was told not to call again.

She caught Hopper's sister just as she had arrived at the hospital.

"I don't have much time to talk," Kathy Hopper said. The background noise, an assortment of beeps and people chatting, filtered across the line.

"We hate to bother you, but we're trying to find out more about your brother. Anything you can tell us would really help with our investigation," Natalie said in a friendly tone, hoping not to put the other woman off.

A long pause followed, and Natalie worried that the woman would hang up, but Kathy suddenly said, "Luis was always a problem child. My parents thought they did all they could to try and straighten him out."

Natalie met Carlos's gaze over the phone between them and realized he had picked up on the same thing she had when he said, "What do you mean by 'thought they did all they could'?"

With a sigh, Kathy said, "They paid for private schools and a special summer camp that he really seemed to like. What Luis really needed most was therapy, but you know how some people are afraid to admit there's an issue."

"You think Luis is mentally ill?" Natalie pressed.

"I didn't know it at first, but after his second or third time in juvenile detention, he finally got some help in one of the facilities," she explained.

"Would you mind sharing the diagnosis?" Carlos asked.

"Antisocial personality disorder," Kathy said.

"Did they treat him?" Natalie asked, worried about the diagnosis. People with ASPD could sometimes be impulsive, aggressive and have a reckless disregard for their safety and that of others.

"They did therapy and some drugs for like a hot second, but then Luis was released. My parents didn't continue with his treatment and eventually Luis ended up in jail again," Kathy said.

Natalie paused for a second and then pushed on. "When was the last time you either saw or spoke to your brother?"

A tired sigh escaped the other woman. "Years ago. I don't mean to worry you, but he scared me."

Natalie didn't doubt it. Some people with ASPD could be dangerous if they didn't receive proper treatment.

"We appreciate you taking the time to chat with us," Natalie said, and Carlos chimed in with his thanks.

"I hope I helped and… I hope he doesn't hurt anyone, but please don't hurt him. He's still my brother," she pleaded.

"We understand. Hopefully this can be resolved without anyone getting hurt," Natalie said. Even though she couldn't be sure about keeping that promise.

Once they ended the call, Natalie quickly phoned Trey to fill him in on what they had learned. As she was providing her report, Carlos's phone rang.

THE FAMILIAR NUMBER from Lucas's school flashed on his phone and he immediately answered, worried that last night's nightmare might be having lingering effects on his son.

"Mr. Ruiz, we need you here immediately. Someone grabbed your son from the school yard," the principal said.

His blood ran cold and his gut tightened into a knot. "Grabbed? Someone took Lucas?"

Natalie stopped her report to Trey and looked his way.

"We had put the security guard there because of the SBS request, but a man drove his pickup right to the fence, rushed in and took Lucas before the guard could act," the principal explained, then quickly added, "We've already called the police and they're issuing an Amber Alert."

She had barely finished speaking when a warning sound blared out and the alert came across their phones.

"I'm on my way," Carlos said and ended the call.

"He'll be okay," Natalie said, but her words couldn't hide the fear in her eyes, especially considering what Kathy Hopper had told them barely minutes earlier.

Since Trey was still on the phone, Natalie swiped to turn on the speaker even as they rushed to Carlos's pickup.

"Hopper grabbed Lucas. The Amber Alert is out but we have to do something," Natalie said.

"I'll have Sophie and Robbie looking for any CCTV footage near the school, but hopefully someone will spot the vehicle and call it in," Trey said.

Carlos didn't want to say that hope wasn't a plan, but it was all they had at the moment until they could get more info and get his son back.

Once they were on the way to the school, his mind slipped off autopilot and finally began functioning once again.

"Why would he want to take Lucas?" he said.

Natalie shrugged and after a few heartbeats, she said, "Revenge. To trade him for something valuable?"

"Like the drugs?" he said.

"Like the drugs only... DEA and the cops aren't going to give them up," Natalie said, lips thinned into a tight line.

"No, they aren't, but a person with ASPD isn't going to consider all that, right?"

"Right," she said to his almost rhetorical question.

A gloomy silence descended over the inside of the cab as they drove to the school. When they arrived, a trio of police cars, lights flashing, sat by the school yard and the officers were speaking to the children and security guard, likely taking statements.

He pulled up behind them and noticed that the principal stood by the officers as well. When Natalie and he walked toward the group, one of the officers peeled away to stop them, but the principal said, "That's the father."

"If you don't mind, we'd like to ask you a few questions," the officer said and directed him to a sergeant who had apparently been dispatched to oversee the investigation. After the officer had introduced himself, they quickly provided him with their suspicions on who had kidnapped Lucas.

Based on the description of the suspect that had been provided by the security guard, it seemed Hopper had been the one to take his son, which brought little comfort considering what they had learned about Hopper's mental health issues.

As the sergeant was finishing up, his radio chirped with an

incoming communication. The sergeant stepped away to take the call and when he returned, he said, "Detective Cunningham wants you at headquarters. He's heard from the suspect."

Carlos nodded, as if in agreement, but after Natalie and Missy were seated in his pickup, he turned to her and said, "I'm not going to waste my time driving to the police station. We need to find out where Hopper has gone."

NATALIE UNDERSTOOD HIS frustration and fear. "Let's call Trey and see if they have anything. Once we have that info, we can decide what to do."

At his nod, Natalie dialed Trey who immediately answered. "Sophie and Robbie were able to locate CCTV feeds showing Hopper's vehicle as it sped off. They've picked it up several miles from the school and are using Wilson's program to map out possible routes Hopper might take."

"Detective Cunningham wants us to come to the police station but Carlos would rather try to track down Hopper. If Hopper is as unstable as his sister thinks, we can't wait a second to find him," Natalie said.

"I agree. As soon as we have any guess on where Hopper is headed, I'll send it. In the meantime, I'll call Cunningham and patch you in," Trey said, and the line went silent.

Natalie peered at Carlos who sat stiffly, hands clenched on the steering wheel. She stroked her hand across his shoulder, comforting him with her touch.

"I've got Cunningham on the line," Trey said, and crackling sounded as the detective joined them.

"We've heard from Hopper," Cunningham immediately said.

Locking his gaze on hers, Carlos said, "What does he want?"

"Adams and the cocaine, but we all know he's not getting either," the detective replied with a harsh laugh.

"That's my son he's got," Carlos warned, a low, almost feral growl woven through his voice.

She stroked his shoulder again and squeezed reassuringly as she said, "There must be something we can work out, Detective."

"We don't negotiate, Agent Rodriguez. But he doesn't need to know that. Our negotiator will string him along while we work on locating Hopper and taking him down. In the meantime, we'll keep you posted if we have anything," Cunningham said and ended the call, but Trey remained on the line.

"I called in my brother Ricky to give us some additional info on ASPD and he's here with me now."

"Thank you for helping, Ricky," she said, grateful for anything the young psychologist could add to the conversation.

"I wish I could offer more than just basic clinical notes about ASPD, but I can't without speaking with Hopper," he said.

"We're grateful for any info you can provide," Carlos said.

"Sure. In general, people with untreated ASPD struggle to follow social norms. They can be deceitful, impulsive, aggressive and reckless. They often don't sustain consistent work behaviors because of that. They are also indifferent to the harm they may cause to others," Ricky explained.

"Impulsive being something like asking for Adams and the cocaine," Natalie said.

"Like that. He must know Lucas's abduction is unlikely to get him those things, but he acted anyway, without any real plan if he didn't get what he wanted," Ricky confirmed.

"And he doesn't care what happens to Lucas, either emotionally or physically," Carlos said, clenching and unclenching his hands on the wheel.

Natalie imagined that was what he wanted to be doing to Hopper's neck. "If Hopper doesn't get what he wants right away—"

"He may get violent. We can't delay trying to find him and freeing Lucas," Ricky jumped in.

"We're working on that, *hermanito*," Trey replied.

"Keep us posted," Natalie said and swiped to end the call.

They sat there in uneasy silence, both lost in their thoughts, until Carlos said, "My bet is that he's heading deeper into the Everglades."

She didn't think he was wrong but worried about having to search such a large area. Even with their drones, it might take too long to narrow the search enough so that she, and possibly other SBS K-9 agents, could track down Hopper and Lucas.

"I agree, but maybe he's sticking close to places that are familiar," she said and the earlier conversation with Hopper's sister suddenly came to mind.

"Kathy Hopper mentioned a summer camp and that Luis had liked it there. If it's in the Everglades and he felt comfortable there, it might be where he's been hiding out," she said, then grabbed her cell phone and dialed the other woman.

Kathy instantly answered. "I saw the Amber Alert. Please tell me you've found that little boy."

"Not yet, but I think you could be a big help," Natalie said and turned on the speaker.

"Whatever I can do," Kathy answered.

"You mentioned a summer camp Luis really liked. Was it in the Everglades?" Carlos asked.

"It was so long ago, only... I think it was called Everglades Adventures. Billed itself as a camp to help kids learn about nature while becoming disciplined and self-sufficient at the same time."

"*Gracias*, Kathy. That's a big help," Natalie said.

After she had hung up, she glanced at Carlos. "Have you ever heard of that camp?" she asked, hoping he might be familiar with it only he shook his head.

"If that's the right name, it's well before my time in the area."

She nodded. "I'll get Sophie and Robbie and their crew

searching online to see what they find, but maybe you and I should head back to your house and do the same."

Carlos canted his head in her direction, anger and worry mingling in his gaze. She knew he wanted to be out and searching for his son, but sometimes you had to be patient.

She laid a calming hand on his arm. "I promise you we will find something soon."

Chapter Twenty-Seven

Carlos couldn't be as sure as Natalie, but since he was tired of just sitting near the school yard waiting for anything to happen, it made sense to return home. "We'd be heading in the right direction if he, in fact, made an escape into the Everglades," he said to try and convince himself he was making the right choice.

He sped home while Natalie worked with the SBS crew, briefing them about the camp. After she ended the discussion with her SBS counterparts, she said, "Sophie and Robbie were able to spot a similar car pulling into a Miccosukee Casino parking lot. Police are on their way to check it out."

"He knows people saw his truck so he's probably going to ditch it and steal another car."

"That's what makes sense," Natalie said and buried her head in her smartphone, probably to research until they reached his home. After a few minutes, she said, "There are a few references to the camp, but not much info."

Carlos wracked his brain, trying to recall the names of any old-timers who might have been in the area twenty years earlier. One name came to mind.

"I have a friend who runs a bar not far from Miccosukee. He's lived in this area most of his life. Let's give him a call and see if he remembers the place."

Carlos dialed his friend who sounded half-asleep when he answered.

"Carlos, dude. Do you know what time it is?" the man said with a grumble.

"Sorry, Frank. I know you probably worked late last night but this is important. Someone's kidnapped Lucas and we're hoping you can help," he explained.

"Aw, man, I'm so sorry. Anything you need," Frank said, immediately more alert.

"*Gracias*. Have you ever heard of Camp Everglades Adventures?" he asked.

"Wow, dude. That's a blast from the past," Frank replied with surprise.

"What do you know about it?" Natalie pressed.

"Some New-Age-dude-type started it at least twenty years ago. Lasted for a few years but then it went belly up."

"Do you know where it was located?" Carlos asked.

"Not sure. Definitely in the park. My guess is that it was near the old missile base. There was still some private land there," Frank said, voice filled with apology.

"No worries, *mano*. You've been a big help. *Gracias*," Carlos said, grateful that Frank could provide any information.

"Good luck, dude. I hope the little grom gets home safe," Frank said.

"Grom?" Natalie asked after Frank left the call.

"A young surfer or skateboarder. Frank was a big-time surfer before he came back home and bought the bar," Carlos explained.

"And did he say 'missile base'?" Natalie asked, obviously unsure of what she'd heard.

Carlos dipped his head to confirm it. "Right after the Cuban Missile Crisis, a Nike Missile base was built in order to intercept any missiles fired at us from Cuba."

"And it's still there? In the middle of the Everglades?"

"It closed in the late seventies but much of the base is pretty intact. You can take tours of it in the winter months," he said as he pulled into his driveway.

"Let's see what we can find out about the base," she said, and they hurried inside the house where she grabbed her laptop and searched the internet.

Carlos stood by her as she immediately pulled up various articles, images and videos about the HM69 Nike Missile Base.

"Wow, who knew," she said as she flipped through the information on the site that was now listed on the National Register of Historic Places due to its importance during a critical point in American history.

As they gazed at one image, she said, "It looks like a lot of flat grassland."

"The flat lands around the base used to be part of some kind of farm. Hard to hide there, but not in those islands of trees," Carlos said, and pointed out some areas quite a distance from the base.

She looked up at him, doubt alive in her gaze. "Do we wait for more info, or do we risk going there?"

Carlos would lose it just sitting there and doing nothing. "I say we go."

Smiling, she nodded. "I agree. I'm going to take my laptop just in case and we should go prepared for a fight."

Carlos didn't want to think of his son in the middle of a gunfight, but considering what they knew about Hopper, they couldn't be unarmed.

"We should be ready," he confirmed, and they flew into action—prepping their weapons, vests, binoculars and Missy's tactical vest. For good measure, Natalie also grabbed some dirty clothes from Lucas's hamper since they would be sure to have his scent for Missy and other K-9s to track.

Armed and ready, they secured Missy and their equipment into the backseat and hopped into the pickup.

"I'm going to let the SBS crew know what we're doing," Natalie said.

Carlos was sure Trey wouldn't be in favor of them taking off on their own and he wasn't wrong as Natalie put the phone on speaker.

"It's not a good idea," Trey warned, but Carlos wasn't about to give in.

"If it was your child, would you just sit and wait?" he challenged.

Trey paused, obviously hesitant, and then blurted out, "No. I wouldn't."

"We'll keep you posted every step of the way," Natalie said and at her nod, Carlos pulled out of the driveway.

"I expect regular updates and as soon as Sophie and Robbie have anything else on that camp, we'll send it," Trey said.

"Roger that," Carlos responded.

Natalie ended the call and said, "If he grabbed a new car at Miccosukee, how long would it take for him to get to the missile base?"

"About half an hour or so."

NATALIE GUESSTIMATED THAT Hopper had at least an hour and a half lead on them due to the time that had passed since he'd grabbed Lucas.

It had her wondering if that was enough time for Hopper to reach those islands of trees near the base. That was, if they were even on the right track in thinking Hopper was headed to a place from his past and that it was near the base.

She was almost jumping in her seat as they drove along in silence. Missy picked up on her nervous energy, whining and tossing her head in Natalie's direction.

"It's okay, Missy," she said and reached back to rub her partner's ears to calm her.

"She okay?" Carlos asked and did a quick look back at the Lab.

"She's cool. She'll be ready to track Lucas once we get

there," Natalie reassured him. She had no doubt Missy would do her best.

With another stroke of Missy's head, Natalie turned her attention to the road, eyes open for anything out of the ordinary.

They had been traveling for about fifteen minutes when her phone rang with a call from Sophie.

"We think we have the make and model of the car Hopper stole at the casino—a white Honda Civic," Sophie said.

"There must be hundreds of those," she said dejectedly.

"There are, and we haven't been able to get a license plate off the CCTV footage, but we do have more info on that summer camp. I just emailed you an old brochure we found that has the location and details on the programs they offered," Sophie said.

Natalie opened the email and pulled up the brochure. The location of the camp was in the area they had identified based on their call with Frank.

"This brochure confirms our info—that the camp is near the old missile base. Is there any way you can overlay this map with that for the missile base, so we get an idea of where to search?"

"We can and will send it shortly," she confirmed.

"We'll be at the missile base in…"

Natalie paused and glanced at Carlos who mouthed, "Ten minutes."

"Ten minutes. If we're right, there'll be a Honda Civic sitting there and I can let Missy loose to try and track them."

"If it is, we'll get Matt Perez and his K-9, Butter, out there to assist and also call in the police," Sophie explained.

"Sounds good," Natalie said and sat back, nervous energy pumping through her body. Missy occasionally whined as she sensed the growing tension while they got closer and closer to their location.

When Carlos pulled off the main highway, they drove past the last homes on the edges of the Everglades and into the wide-open spaces in the park. It seemed like forever until they reached the turnoff for one of the trails and followed that one-lane highway through the grasslands, turn after turn leading them to the gate for the missile base.

Carlos proceeded to the gate. A long length of heavy metal chain hung from one side, no longer securing the entrance.

"That shouldn't be open. There are no tours or events normally at this time of year," he said.

He inched up to the gate and Natalie said, "I'll get it."

She hopped out and opened the gate wide and once she was back in the car, they pulled up to a large red, white and blue sign warning that it was a US Army restricted area, and that deadly force was authorized. The sign was a throwback to when the location had been an important deterrent to an attack.

They pushed on past a small building with a hand-painted image of a rocket to a much larger concrete block building with a corrugated metal gable roof.

"This is one of the barns where they kept the Nike Hercules missiles because the ground was too wet to have them underground," Carlos said.

Metal sliding doors closed off the interior of the building and Carlos slowed the pickup, but it seemed as if the lock on the doors was intact.

"Nothing to see here," she said, and they continued down the road, past two more missile barns and to a large area of overgrown grass.

Carlos paused there again. "This used to be the launch area."

As they doubled back past one of the missile barns, she noticed a nearby concrete building. It was substantially smaller, with four windows and a tar paper roof, but what immediately caught her eye was what looked like deep indentations in the soft ground beyond the paved area. They looked like tire tracks that led behind the missile barn.

"Stop," she said and pointed to the tracks.

Carlos pulled the pickup to the edge of the pavement, and they hopped out and inspected the area, following the tire tracks around to a tight space behind the barn and a large earthen berm.

A white Honda Civic sat in that tight space, made invisible by the barn and the height of the berm.

Natalie let Missy smell Lucas's clothes and kept a tight leash on her as they approached. The Lab sniffed around the car and immediately pawed the ground and sat, signaling that she had picked up on a scent.

"We have him," Natalie said.

Chapter Twenty-Eight

The fear that had tied Carlos's gut into knots loosened the barest bit with Natalie's words.

He glanced in the direction of the three islands of trees in the distance, knowing his son was in one of them with a dangerous criminal. But regardless of which one, any approach would be dangerous.

"We're totally exposed in these grasslands," he said and gestured with his hand.

"Unless we can flank him once we know his location," Natalie said, scrutinizing the area as well.

Her phone chirped and when she answered and put it on speaker, Robbie said, "We were able to do an overlay from the brochure to a map of the area. I just emailed it to you."

"I'll take a look in a second. We found the car that Hopper stole, and Missy picked up on Lucas's scent," she said.

"That's great. Send your location and we'll get Matt and Butter out there to help you as well as the police," Robbie said.

"I'll send a pin to where the car is at the missile base. I'll turn on the tracker on my phone so you can see where we're going," she said.

"I'm not sure you should go alone," Robbie said and, in the background, they could hear Sophie echo that warning.

"He's got my son and I'm not going to just sit here and wait. He's too unstable," Carlos said.

"I know you're worried—" Robbie began.

"You're wasting time. We have to get going," Carlos said and with a lift of his chin, asked Natalie to end the call.

"We'll let Trey know," Robbie said.

After the line went dead, Natalie glanced at him. "Let's look at the map they sent. It might give us a clue as to where to head."

She rushed to retrieve her laptop. He followed her and Missy and waited while she pulled up the information the SBS crew had sent.

As Robbie indicated, they had overlaid the old brochure over a satellite image of the area. It was almost eerie to see the past coming alive in the present as elements from the brochure connected to the terrain in the image.

Natalie circled her finger around an area where what looked like cabins sat on one of the tree islands. "This would give him a few places to hide."

He peered at the map and noticed a structure in another of the patches of trees in the grasslands. "This looks like some kind of tower."

"Like a forest ranger might use to oversee the grounds," Natalie said and dragged her finger across the map in line from the tower to the cabins. "He could see most everything from there if it's still intact."

"Including when we approach," Carlos said, his stomach turning and twisting with fear.

"We don't have much choice. If Missy directs us toward the tower, we'll have to decide how to proceed," Natalie said, gripped his hand, and squeezed it hard. "We have to get Lucas."

He nodded. "Let's suit up."

As they had in preparation for their approach to the poachers' camp, they put on their bulletproof vests and got their pistols, rifles and ammo. Once they were outfitted and ready, they put on communications gear and called back to the SBS crew to make sure they were monitoring.

Trey was the first one to come across their earpieces. "This is very risky, Natalie."

"I know. But this guy is unstable. The longer he has Lucas…" She couldn't finish, but then again, she didn't have to.

Trey muttered a curse but reluctantly agreed. "Matt and Butter are on the way. So are the local police. Keep us posted so they can provide support."

"We will," Carlos said and with a quick glance at Natalie, she instructed Missy to track the scent.

The Lab leaped into action, sniffing along the grasses. Leading them away from the missile base toward the tree islands.

It was a slow slog as the ground beneath their feet was soft from a recent rain. As Missy searched through the taller grasses and they moved forward, the grasses closed back up, hiding their passage just as it must have hidden Hopper's.

Carlos kept his head on a swivel, looking for the slightest trace of any disturbance that would confirm Missy was on the right track, but couldn't see anything. But Missy kept pulling them forward and as he calculated their path, he realized they were headed toward the island of trees where the cabins had once been located.

Who knows whether the cabins or tower were still intact after nearly twenty years, he thought.

They were about three hundred yards out and well within the range of an AR-15 when Natalie put her hand up in a stop command.

He leaned close and she whispered, "If we detour to the right of that stand of trees, he'll have a harder line of sight for a shot."

Glancing over her shoulder, he realized she was right. A move to the farthest tip of the trees might let them approach more securely. If Hopper was up in the tower, he might even think that they were on the wrong trail thanks to their detour.

"Good point. Let's go."

NATALIE TOOK THE LEAD, directing Missy away from the trail she had picked up in order to do the detour. Missy looked up at her, as if doubting her command, but she issued the command again, and Missy obeyed, almost trotting through the grasslands in her haste to locate Lucas.

Natalie reined her partner in, keeping her on a tight leash until the moment when she'd truly be needed. Her hands were slick on the reins as fear and the late August day oozed sweat from her body. Her heart pounded hard in her chest—a combination of nerves and the workout from plodding through the thick grasses and unstable, wet ground beneath their feet.

The sun beat down relentlessly as they pressed forward and, to her surprise, they reached the tip of the tree of islands without incident. If she hadn't seen the stolen car behind the missile barn, she might have said they had been wrong about Hopper's location. But the car and Missy picking up on a scent confirmed they were right even if Hopper hadn't taken any action against them yet.

They moved carefully as they slipped through the underbrush at the edges of the trees. Silently they pushed forward and had gone no more than about ten yards when she caught sight of a trio of cabins. They were just as indicated in the brochure.

She raised her hand in a stop command, and they crouched down in the underbrush to survey the area.

Two of the cabins were in rough shape. Some of the walls had caved in and were overgrown with ferns and orchids.

The windows and front door on the third cabin were long gone, but the walls were standing, and someone had erected a lean-to of sorts by tacking camo screening to the far side of the building.

A murmur, like that of someone repeating a mantra, softly reached them beneath the sounds of the frogs, insects and birds.

"Is that Hopper?" Carlos asked as he kneeled beside her.

She raised her binoculars and was able to get a line of sight into the cabin through a side window.

Hopper was pacing back and forth across the narrow width of the cabin, seemingly talking to himself and occasionally beating his head with his palms.

Hopper seemed almost manic, which was not a good thing. "He's in there."

Carlos also inspected the cabin with his binoculars and released a sharp expletive beneath his breath. "I can't see Lucas and this guy seems to have lost it."

She couldn't disagree. "We can't wait for backup."

Using the communications gear, she reached out to the SBS crew and Trey immediately came on the line.

"Do you have eyes on him?"

Natalie shared a look with Carlos and held her breath for a sharp second. "We do and he's not stable. We have to move. Now," she said, waiting for Trey to put the stop on any action.

"I trust you, Natalie. Do what you think is best," he said without hesitation.

"*Gracias.* We'll keep you posted."

Natalie gestured to the side window and then to the door. "I'm going to move toward the front door and get eyes inside if I can. You stay here."

Carlos was about to argue, but then acquiesced with a nod. "I'll wait for your instructions."

Natalie stayed low and moved toward an area directly in line with the front door. She kept Missy tight to her side with the leash and a sharp "Heel" since the Lab sensed her target was near and wanted to act.

As they had before, she reached her destination without any attack, which worried her more than if Hopper had opened fire on them immediately. Especially as Hopper continued his manic pacing and mumbling within the cabin.

But there was something else that chilled her skin and made her heart skip a beat.

Lucas's feet were visible from her view through the entrance to the cabin and he wasn't moving.

Dios, por favor, she prayed, hoping Carlos's son was all right.

"I have eyes on Hopper, and I can see Lucas's feet. Nothing else," she said softly into her mic.

"I have eyes on Hopper as well. He's not stable," Carlos said.

No, he wasn't. She had to act to save Lucas. "I need you to create a distraction and draw him toward the side window. Once his attention is on you, Missy and I will go in."

"Say the word," Carlos replied, giving his trust to her.

"On three."

Chapter Twenty-Nine

Carlos sucked in a breath, bracing himself to act as Natalie counted down.

"One."

He gripped the stock of his gun and brought it to his shoulder, ready to fire.

"Two."

He trained the rifle on Hopper—not that he intended to shoot him. He wanted him alive to face justice.

"Three."

Jumping to his feet, he fired into a high corner of the cabin, away from anyone who could be inside.

Hopper stopped his pacing, reached down for something, rushed to the window and wildly opened fire in his direction.

As bullets slammed into the trees around him, Carlos tucked himself behind a large trunk as bits of bark and wood flew into the air.

GUNFIRE ERUPTED BUT Natalie saw her chance as Carlos distracted Hopper.

She rushed through the front door of the cabin and as Hopper whirled in her direction, she released Missy's leash.

"Gong-gyeog," she said, giving the attack command in Korean.

With one sharp bound, Missy launched herself at Hopper

and latched on to the arm holding the rifle. The force of her attack had Hopper reeling backward and he fell against the back wall with a bone-rattling thud.

In that split second, she realized Lucas was alive, but trussed up like a Thanksgiving turkey and lying across the floor.

Hopper raised the rifle despite Missy's hold on his arm and Natalie didn't flinch as she threw herself in front of Lucas as Hopper fired.

HEARING THE MASSIVE thud and rattle of the cabin walls, Carlos rushed toward the front door.

Entering, his blood ran cold as Natalie placed herself in the line of fire and Hopper pulled the trigger.

Natalie's body recoiled from the force of the blow.

Red filled his vision.

He rushed forward and as Missy thrashed Hopper's arm back and forth, he yanked the rifle from Hopper's weakening grasp and tossed it to the side.

"Noh-ajuda," Natalie said weakly, and Missy released Hopper's arm but remained by his side, ready for another command.

Carlos flipped Hopper onto his stomach, grabbed his arms and slipped on handcuffs. Satisfied he was contained, Carlos turned his attention to his loved ones.

Natalie slowly came to her feet, running a hand across her side, and looked down at where the vest had stopped the bullet. But in the next heartbeat she was at Lucas's side, cutting away the ropes binding him.

He rushed over and as soon as Lucas was free, he launched himself at him.

"Papi," Lucas said and hugged him hard as Natalie stood by, Missy at her side, watching the reunion.

Carlos closed his eyes to savor the feel of his very much alive son in his arms and ignored the pain in his ribs from the tight embrace. *"Mi'jo.* Are you okay? Did he hurt you?"

"I'm okay. He didn't hurt me," Lucas said and then broke away to hug Natalie.

She returned his embrace, although awkwardly, as if her ribs were smarting from the impact of the bullet. Despite that, she forced a smile and ruffled Lucas's hair as he turned his attention to Missy.

"*Gracias*, Missy," the boy said and rubbed the Lab's ears, earning doggy kisses.

"Report," Trey said across the communications gear.

"Suspect is secured. No injuries," Natalie said even though Carlos could see she was hurting.

"That's great news. Matt, Butter and the cops should be there in about twenty minutes," Trey said.

"We'll wait for their arrival," Natalie replied.

Carlos walked to her and peered down at the bullet in her vest. "You could have been killed," he said and cradled her face.

Natalie shot a quick glance down at his son and said, "I had to protect Lucas."

He couldn't love her any more than at that moment. Wrapping an arm around her and Lucas's shoulders, he dragged them close for a group hug. When Missy joined in, jumping up against them, he laughed.

No matter what, this nightmare was over.

A FEW HOURS LATER, Natalie stood by Carlos and Trey in the viewing room as Roni, Detective Cunningham and a district attorney sat across from Adams and his attorney.

"Involuntary manslaughter with ten years max in exchange for testifying against Hopper," the attorney said, seemingly confident that the district attorney would jump at that offer.

Roni and the district attorney huddled together for barely a minute. "Involuntary plus ten on the murder charge in exchange for his testifying against Hopper in relation to Daniela Ruiz's murder."

Now it was Adams and the attorney who leaned their heads together, talking in low murmurs, before breaking apart. "That's a deal."

Beside her, Carlos tensed and said, "Ten years. That's all?"

Trey laid a hand on his shoulder to calm him. "He thinks he's smart, but that's only for the murder charge. We've got him on the drug and poaching as well. It'll be a long time until he's free."

At his attorney's nod, Adams testified. "Hopper was the mastermind for all the drugs and poaching."

"What about Gemma Garcia?" Roni asked.

Adams shook his head. "Just me and Hopper. I think Gemma thought something was off, but I kept her away from our business."

"Until you ran Carlos and Natalie off the road right in front of her eyes," she pressed.

Adams waved his hands in denial. "Not me. Hopper."

Roni shot a quick look at Detective Cunningham who nodded and took up the questioning. "But you had something to do with Daniela Ruiz's death?"

Adams hesitated and glanced at his lawyer who dipped his head to advise him to continue. "Dani saw me and Hopper at the bar. He had passed me a note with a schedule for drug drop-offs. I don't think she knew who he was, but she knew me and that something was wrong."

"What happened then?" Detective Cunningham asked.

"Hopper had already left the bar, but then Dani and her friends walked out, and I followed her to try and straighten things out."

Adams hesitated, glanced at his lawyer and then proceeded, cuffed hands held out in pleading. "I didn't kill Dani. She came up to me after her friends left. She wanted to know about Hopper."

"And did you tell her?" Roni pressed, one dark brow arched in question.

Carlos was leaning forward, waiting for the answer, and she slipped her arm around his waist in support.

"I didn't get a chance. Hopper came out of nowhere and pushed Dani. She fell back and smacked her head against one of the concrete parking blocks. There was this sickening thud and crack…"

Carlos's body flinched at Adams's words but then he became stock-still. Deadly still.

"I went over to help, only… She was dead. She must have snapped her neck."

His words angered her. He was acting as if he'd had nothing to do with Dani's death.

"But you didn't call for help? You just decided to fake a crash?" the district attorney said.

Adams shook his head. "Hopper was too dangerous. He wanted to chop her body up and feed it to the gators, but I couldn't do that. I convinced him to fake the crash instead."

Carlos rushed from the room then and at Trey's nod, she followed him out to where he paced in the hall, anger and frustration pouring from his body.

She stepped into his path and laid a gentling hand on his chest to calm him. "We should go and take care of Lucas. We have all we need to nail both Adams and Hopper."

"He wanted to chop her up. Did you hear that? That scum wanted to feed Dani to the gators!" he shouted, and she stroked a hand down his chest and then wrapped her arms around him.

His body vibrated against her. She stroked her hands up and down his back and said again, "We should go and take care of Lucas."

This time her words registered.

He slipped his arm around her waist and together they walked out of the police station. In no time, they were on the way back to his house and to Lucas and Mia, who had come to take care of him.

As they entered the house, the aroma of yeasty dough and earthy sauce filled the air.

Mia was in the kitchen with Lucas. He was helping her make a salad and looked in their direction as they entered.

He rushed over as did Missy, who had been resting in a dog bed at the side of the great room.

Lucas wrapped his arms around their legs, pulling them into another group hug. "You're home. *Tia* Mia and I made some pizza for dinner."

CARLOS PEERED ACROSS the room to where Mia stood at the counter, cutting lettuce.

"*Gracias*, Mia," he said.

She shrugged her fine-boned shoulders and said, "I thought making pizza would be a good way to keep Lucas busy."

"I'm hungry," Lucas said, seemingly not all that worse for wear after the day's scary events.

"Let's see what *Tia* Mia wants to do," Carlos said and ruffled Lucas's hair affectionately.

Mia was drying her hands on a towel but laid it down and walked over to them. "I should go. Now that this is over, John and I can spend some time together."

"I can't thank you all enough for what you've done," he said and hugged her.

"Anything for family," Mia said and shot a look at Natalie.

"I'm sure you're going to need a few days off to heal and regroup. I'll let Trey know so you can get some rest," Mia said and embraced Natalie.

"*GRACIAS,*" NATALIE SAID, and escorted Mia to the front door where the other woman hugged her again and said, "Watch out for Lucas."

"I will," she said with a nod. If anyone knew what it was like to deal with trauma, she did.

"See you in a few days," Mia said and hurried out the door.

Even though the threat was over, Natalie set the alarm and joined Carlos and Lucas where they had resumed making the salad.

She checked on the pizza. Seeing there was still time until it had to come out, she set the table and went about trying to create a sense of normalcy. Trying to recreate a routine because routine was important.

Once she'd set the table, fed Missy and taken her for a walk with Lucas at her side, they washed up and sat down for the pizza that Mia and Lucas had made.

As she ate with Carlos and Lucas at the table, Missy snoring slightly across the way in her bed, she realized this was what she needed in her life. She needed normal. She needed routine. But most of all, she needed this amazing man and loving boy in her life.

They finished dinner, but Lucas didn't go off to play video games. Instead, he hung close, the first sign that he wasn't necessarily dealing with the situation as well as he had made it seem.

Lucas huddled together between them on the sofa as they watched a rom-com and when it came time to go to bed, he grabbed both their hands and wanted them to come with him.

"How about you come into my bed?" Carlos asked, because his king-size bed would be far roomier than Lucas's full.

"Okay," Lucas said eagerly and raced across the room to change into his pajamas.

Carlos led her away from his room and cradled her cheek. "You don't have to stay. I know you must have a lot to do."

"I do, but nothing is more important than Lucas…and you. How are you doing?" she said and gingerly ran her hand across his bruised ribs.

"Sore—much like you, I imagine," he said with a tender smile.

"A little," she admitted. She hesitated, then plowed on. "I don't have to go. I don't want to go…ever."

He strummed his thumb across her cheek, his dark eyes radiant with joy and humor. "Is that a proposal?"

"If it is, do I have to get down on one knee?" she teased.

He surprised her then by kneeling and taking hold of her hand. "Natalie Rodriguez. I know this is sudden, but I'm sure about this. Will you take me and Lucas to be your family for the rest of your life?"

It was sudden but she had only one answer for him. "I will."

He shot to his feet, wrapped her in a bear hug that made her sore ribs ache, but his love drove away the pain.

As Lucas embraced their legs and Missy came over to jump all over them, she knew that she had her normal. She had her routine, but more than anything, she finally saw a future where love would heal their wounds and hers.

It was time to live and love.

* * * * *

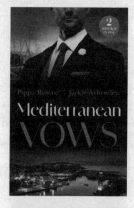

LET'S TALK

Romance

For exclusive extracts, competitions and special offers, find us online:

f MillsandBoon

X @MillsandBoon

◎ @MillsandBoonUK

♪ @MillsandBoonUK

Get in touch on 01413 063 232

COMING SOON!

We really hope you enjoyed reading this book.
If you're looking for more romance
be sure to head to the shops when
new books are available on

Thursday 4th
July

To see which titles are coming soon, please visit
millsandboon.co.uk/nextmonth

MILLS & BOON